8|96
BT

F
TAR

Tarr, Judith.

King and goddess.

DISCARD

$23.95

6/15/17: There is
A Robinson Book-

A 2nd Book
on King TUT
unless stolen by ?

King

and

Goddess

~~~~~~~~~~

Other Historical Novels
by Judith Tarr

LORD OF THE TWO LANDS

THRONE OF ISIS

THE EAGLE'S DAUGHTER

PILLAR OF FIRE

King
and
Goddess

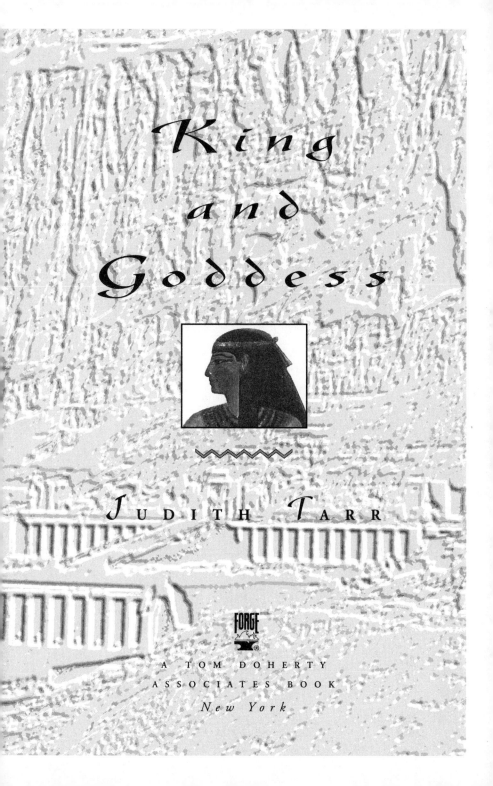

Judith Tarr

FORGE

A TOM DOHERTY
ASSOCIATES BOOK
New York

KING AND GODDESS

Copyright © 1996 by Judith Tarr

This book is printed on acid-free paper.

A FORGE BOOK
Published by Tom Doherty Associates, Inc.
175 Fifth Avenue
New York, N.Y. 10010

Forge® is a registered trademark of Tom Doherty Associates, Inc.

Library of Congress Cataloging-in-Publication Data

Tarr, Judith.
    King and goddess / by Judith Tarr.—1st ed.
      p.   cm.
    "A Tom Doherty Associates book."
    ISBN 0-312-86092-7 (alk. paper)
    1. Hatshepsut, Queen of Egypt—Fiction. 2. Egypt—History—
Eighteenth dynasty, ca. 1570–1320 B.C.—Fiction. 3. Queens—Egypt—
Fiction. I. Title.
PS3570.A655K56   1996
813'.54—dc20   95-48310
                                                    CIP

First Edition: AUGUST 1996
Printed in the United States of America
0 9 8 7 6 5 4 3 2 1

BOOK DESIGN BY DEBORAH KERNER

To the people
who helped to make this book possible:

JOANNE *and* STEVE,
for help with research and development,
and JOHN,
for the means to do it

Great
Royal Wife

〜〜〜〜〜

(Thutmose II,
Years 3–15)

$$1$$

THE BOAT OF THE SUN SAILED SLOWLY over the horizon. All night long it had drifted through the land of the dead, pouring its light upon the dry land. Now it drove the stars away. It ruled all alone in the blue vault of heaven, with no attendance but a lone circling falcon whose eye bent piercing keen upon the land of the living.

Senenmut stirred and groaned and started awake. He was stifling. He could not breathe. He was trapped in the tomb, bound to the body, with no spells or magic to guide him out of the dark and into the Field of Reeds where the blessed dead go.

He gasped. The weight on his face began to purr. The warm solidity that trapped him against the cold wall muttered sleepily till he kicked it; then it yelped. *"Ai!* You're killing me! Mama! Help, Mama!"

He clapped a hand over his brother's mouth. Ahotep's bright black eyes laughed at him. If he lifted it, the brat would shriek till their mother came running, and in no kind mood toward Senenmut. Then Ahotep would laugh and skip off to his breakfast, while Hat-Nufer, who cherished her title of Lady of the House, drowned her eldest in the wine of correction.

Senenmut heaved his brother up, hand still clapped to his mouth, and carried him out into the bustle and clatter of morning in his father's house.

He dropped Ahotep squawking into the tub that they all bathed in, and bathed himself around him. Ahotep splashed in the water while Senenmut dried himself and put on a clean white kilt. Senenmut tossed another at his brother. Ahotep grimaced at it. He was a scant season removed from naked and insouciant childhood; he was not greatly reconciled to the servitude of clothes.

Senenmut left him to find his own way into the kilt. The house had quieted as it did every morning just before sunrise. Everyone—his mother, the aunts, baby Amonhotep with his nurse, the two servants—had gathered in front of the shrine. His father bowed before the image that had resided in the niche for time out of mind, and poured out a drop or two of beer, and offered a bit from the new loaf of barley bread.

Senenmut bowed to the god from force of habit. It was a graceless thing, a grinning, leering dwarf with luck in his stumpy hands and blessing on his head. Bes, dwarf-god, luck-god, presided over the house of Ramose as he did many another middling prosperous house in Thebes.

But in his mind's eyes Senenmut saw another god. A great god, a noble and straight-backed god, a god who was a king: Amon-Re of Thebes, who ruled above such lesser gods as Bes.

At this very moment, in his tall palace set apart in walls from the rest of Thebes, the king offered wine in a golden cup and fruits of the earth on golden platters, as many as all his servants could carry, to the image of Amon in his ancestral shrine. By his offering the sun was persuaded to rise. By the strength of his devotion the Two Lands of Egypt measured their prosperity.

It was a noble thing, to bring the sun back to the sky. Senenmut had never seen the rite, only heard of it. He had seen the king, of course, going by in procession for this reason or that: riding to war, returning in victory, celebrating the festival of a god.

Senenmut was a commoner, a tradesman's son. The king stood as high above him as the moon. But he could dream. Someday he would stand beside the king. Someday he would be a power in the world, a voice in the king's ear, a sharer in his counsels.

"Senenmut!" His mother's voice was sharp, pitched to pierce the veil of fog about her eldest son. "Are you going to break your fast today? We have dates, fresh from the tree."

There was nothing tender about Hat-Nufer. Still she looked after her children well enough, and she knew how Senenmut loved dates. She thrust the bowl at him and said not a word as he gorged himself—at least until Ahotep appeared in a damp and drooping kilt, to lay vociferous claim to the few that were left.

There were more wrapped in a cloth with the bread and cheese and the jar of beer that would sustain him till evening. He grinned and kissed his mother, who slapped him for his presumption, and saluted the aunts, and offered due respect to his father. Ramose, intent on coaxing the baby with a sop of bread in goat's milk, acknowledged him absently.

The memory followed him: the small inelegant room, the noisy inelegant people, even the servants joining in some altercation or other with Hat-Nufer and Ahotep.

"They are so unbearably common," Senenmut said as he shut the door and paused in the street, blinking against the dazzle of sunlight. "Father—gods, father is in trade. How much more common can you be?"

He thrust himself away from the door. He was going to rise in the world. He knew precisely where he was going to begin, if not exactly how. His mother, clear-eyed ungentle creature that she was, had seen to that when he was no older than Ahotep. She had taken the whole profit of a season from Ramose's trading of pots and jars for the brewing and storing and drinking of beer, and delivered it to the temple of Amon, and not the little temple that stood at the head of the street, either, but the great one, the temple in which the king himself had been known to set foot. In return she had demanded schooling for her son, and only the best of that.

The priests had reckoned the payment sufficient, after some discussion with Hat-Nufer. Senenmut even then could have told them what use it was to haggle with his mother. She had never lost a battle.

He had grown from child to man in the temple of Amon. Every morning after sunrise he went there, to the lofty halls and gilded pillars and the murmur of cultivated voices in every tongue that was spoken in the courts of Egypt. Every evening he returned home to his mother's fierce interrogation and his father's vague beneficence, Ahotep's boisterousness and the baby's wailing.

Someday he would be rich. He would live in a high house and dine on a gilded table and never—no, never—share a bed with anyone not of his choosing.

Thebes roared and surged about him. He rode it as a boat rides a cataract, skimming above the eddies, veering in the cross-currents. It was the greatest city in the world, and one of the most ancient, a city of kings beside the river that was the lifeblood of Egypt.

He threaded the narrow ways with the ease of the Theban born, taking no great notice of their squalor, but aware of it nonetheless. Lords and princes never saw the warren of streets hidden behind the temples and the palaces, nor soiled their gilded sandals with the dust of common feet. They rode in chairs on the backs of burly bearers, or in chariots drawn by snorting, dancing horses. And they traveled on the wider roads, the processional ways that ran from end to end of the city, past the splendor of temples and palaces. They did not ever, he was convinced, run barefoot through a clutter of market-stalls, ducking the spray from a hurled chamberpot, making haste to the Temple of Amon before the master of scribes grew impatient with waiting.

■ The temple was enormous, tall as a mountain reaching up to heaven. The air within the shrine was fogged with incense, trembling with awe. The god's wisdom breathed from the walls.

Senenmut had entered that great gate nearly every day since he was seven years old. He had long since learned to pass by the temple proper and slip through a smaller door guarded by one of the priests, into a world of clear and uncompromising daylight. There were no shadowy recesses here, no clouds of incense. In a colonnade off a sunlit courtyard, row on row of boys and young men sat each in the place he had won for himself, clean-shaved head bent, kilt tight-stretched across his knees, papyrus or potsherd resting there while he wrote to his master's dictation.

There was a new gaggle of children in the corner that was warmest at midday, learning to mix the inks and hold the brush and draw painstakingly the first lines of the first glyph that the master was minded to teach them. He had a long rod in his hand, which he whipped out like a serpent's strike, lashing the knuckles of a child who dared to draw a stick-man with an enormous hooked nose instead of the feather of

Maat. The boy sniffled, but he already knew better than to cry in front of old Ranefer.

As Senenmut strode past them, they looked up. Their awe made him swallow a smile. He must have seemed enormously tall to them, enormously haughty, making his way with lordly confidence to the inner wall of the colonnade. There the school gave way to the House of Life, the scribes' hall where those who had passed into the mysteries of the craft sat all day with palette and pen and papyrus, recording the affairs of the Two Lands.

Senenmut was not a scribe yet. But soon. He bowed to the master of masters, Seti-Nakht. Seti-Nakht frowned nearsightedly at him. "You dallied," he said. "Consider yourself properly flogged."

Senenmut bit back a grin. He was never early enough for Seti-Nakht. Even when one day he came in the dark of dawn, before any other student stumbled yawning into the temple, Seti-Nakht had been sitting there already, roll of papyrus on knees, reading by the light of a lamp.

While Seti-Nakht waited in conspicuous patience, Senenmut retrieved his brushes and inks and palette from the chest where he was privileged to keep them, and sought his place up against the wall of the scribes' hall, carefully out of reach of Seti-Nakht's rod. As he crossed his ankles and prepared to sink down, Seti-Nakht said, "Stop. Be still."

Senenmut had obeyed before he thought. He looked down at the plump little shining-pated man who was the most feared of the masters in Amon's temple. Seti-Nakht ran his rod through his fingers. Senenmut did not honestly fear that it would strike him, but his back tightened nonetheless.

Seti-Nakht looked him up and down. "Well," he said. "You're no beauty, if beauty matters. You're arrogant enough for six. Do you think you're good enough yet to take a place in there?" He tilted the end of the rod toward the scribes' hall.

Senenmut's heart leaped. "Are you—am I—"

"Be silent," said Seti-Nakht.

Senenmut bit his tongue.

Seti-Nakht saw it: his brow drifted upward. "Your arrogance," he said, "is a matter of note. Not, mind you, that it's an ill thing for a man to know his own worth. But you reckon yours well above your station."

Senenmut's face was hot. "I am a scribe. My station is whatever my merits make it."

"You are an apprentice in the temple of Amon," said Seti-Nakht, "and not yet of any rank at all. You know, I presume, what your fellows call you when you strut past with that nose of yours in the air. 'His lordship,' they say. 'Mighty in papyrus, beloved of Amon, the great prince Senenmut.' "

The flush crawled out of Senenmut's cheeks and down his neck. "And have I done anything, Master, to earn this reprimand?"

"Was I reprimanding you?" Seti-Nakht tapped his rod lightly against his palm. "I think that you might consider the virtue of reticence, if modesty is beyond you. Pride is an ornament in a prince, but it sits ill on a tradesman's son."

"Even if that tradesman's son is reckoned the most brilliant of the apprentices?"

Seti-Nakht's rod caught Senenmut across the shins. The blow was precisely calculated to sting but to leave no lasting mark. Senenmut's breath hissed between his teeth.

"You are rather extraordinary," Seti-Nakht said mildly, "but the judgment of brilliance is hardly yours to make. It takes more than cleverness to make a great lord. It needs something less common. Intelligence; tact. The art of graciousness toward one's inferiors."

None of which Senenmut had ever noticed in the lords' sons who studied among the scribes, but he was no such fool as to say so. What he understood of this lesson was simple. A lordling who carried himself high was tolerated, because he had been born to do just that. A tradesman's son was expected to conduct himself with greater circumspection. Even—especially—when he knew that he had no equal among the apprentices. No one else was so quick with the pen or so adept in the learning of languages. No one else wrote so clearly and with such elegance.

"Quick wits are a gift of the gods," said Seti-Nakht. "The ability to use them is more seldom bestowed. You are clever. No task is too difficult for you; most are too easy. It would do you little good, I think, to keep you among the apprentices. Boredom, like any other ill, can teach as well as vex the spirit; but you were never of a mind to find lessons in adversity."

And what, Senenmut wondered fiercely, was this? With every word he sank lower, and at the same time grew angrier. "What have I done," he demanded, "but excel in the tasks you set me? Should I have pretended to be less capable?"

"You could," said Seti-Nakht, "have been less careful to let every scribe and master and apprentice know that you excelled in the tasks you were set."

Senenmut threw himself at the master's feet. "I yield! By the gods, I yield! I am unworthy!"

Seti-Nakht's rod did not come whistling down upon his back. It slipped beneath instead, and levered him up, holding him lightly across the throat. He looked into Seti-Nakht's face. The master of scribes stared calmly back. "Until you become a courtier, take this to heart. Never lie to any man who is better armed than you."

"And when I am a courtier?"

"Then make sure that your attendants are most well armed." Seti-Nakht shook his head, and to Senenmut's astonishment he smiled.

Senenmut had never seen him smile before. There was nothing reassuring in it.

Seti-Nakht lowered the rod from Senenmut's throat. "I am not admitting you to the House of Life," he said. "Your talents lie elsewhere."

Senenmut staggered. All of this ordeal, he had thought, was to prepare him for the passage from apprentice to scribe. Not to cast him out. Not the most brilliant of the apprentices, the one who was most often given real scribes' work to do, and not simply endless repetitive copying of old poems.

It came out of him in a cry. "But I was the best of them!"

"You were the most clever," Seti-Nakht said. "The House of Life is no place for the easily bored."

"Then where am I to go? What am I to do? I can't be a seller of pots and jars."

"Why not? Your father is."

Senenmut's fingers clawed. Only a last remnant of prudence kept them from the old man's throat. "I'll die," he said, flat and hurting-hard.

"Contrary to all the tales," said Seti-Nakht, "no one has ever died of frustrated ambition."

This time Senenmut could not stop himself from throttling Seti-Nakht where he sat. Not unless he backed away, whirled, and ran.

The rod caught him as he spun, whirled him back. "Stop that," said Seti-Nakht. "Even more than arrogance, you have a besetting flaw. You listen only as far as it pleases you, and no further. I have decided that you will not enter the House of Life. This I judge best. But," he said as Senenmut came near to erupting yet again, "I find it difficult to imagine you in your father's profession. You have no talent for it. What you do have . . ." He paused. He drew a breath, as if he needed to think; as if it were not thought of thrice and thrice over, since long before Senenmut came to stand before him. He said, "Go to the palace. Tell the chamberlain that Seti-Nakht sends this gift to be used as it may best be used."

Senenmut rocked on his feet; and yet he nearly laughed. No wonder indeed that everyone was terrified of Seti-Nakht. Even his gifts he gave with sting of rod or tongue. He had cast Senenmut into the depths of despair—and then he had set him free. He had sent him to the palace. And in the palace was the king.

"Go," said Seti-Nakht. "Out of my sight. Get!"

Was there a glimmer of something in his eye—sorrow, perhaps? Pride clothed in regret?

Not likely, Senenmut thought. The old horror was glad to be rid of him.

He turned quickly enough, he hoped, that Seti-Nakht could not see the gleam of tears. He had what he wanted, at last, at last. But it was not as effortless as he had dreamed, to depart from the Temple of Amon. Nor was it easy at all to leave Seti-Nakht. The bitter tongue, the merciless rod—gods; what would he do without them?

With the sting of that last blow still clear in his body's memory, Senenmut walked away from the House of Life, toward the palace and the king's service.

2

SENENMUT ENTERED THE PALACE with thudding heart and trembling knees. He would have died before he admitted to either.

He was passed from guard to servant to chamberlain, each time repeating the name of Seti-Nakht, which was his password and his surety. He was too proud—arrogant, his master would have said—to gawp like a yokel, but his eyes darted, taking in splendors. Gold and jewel-colors, painted images, wall after wall limned from vaulted ceiling to stone-tiled floor with prayer or poetry or princely puffery. There were halls as high as the sky, forested with pillars; gardens sweet-scented with rarities, flowers and trees that grew nowhere else in Egypt; even the roar and the pungent reek of a menagerie that seemed filled mostly with enormous cats. And everywhere there were princes, images of elegance drifting or strolling or striding past in clouds of attendants.

None of them took any notice of a weedy young man in a scribe's kilt, clutching palette and ink and brushes as he followed the latest of several guides through a maze of passages. There was no clear order here, no coherence, only the whim of this king or that. One built a wing flying off the palace proper. Another made it greater. A third added a colonnade and closed it in with a garden. And so it went, more like a living thing than the work of any one man's hands.

Senenmut judged that he had gone deep into the palace before he was led to a room and told to wait. It was a small room, nearly bare, with a chair and a table and a woven rug on the floor. There was a bowl on the table, half filled with water, and floating in it a lotus blossom. The walls reflected it, painted with lotuses, simple and somewhat faded, beautiful in their antiquity. A window in one of the walls looked out on yet another colonnade, and a garden of trees.

No one seemed to come here. The crowds of princes were all elsewhere, on the other side of the colonnade and behind a guarded door.
One person trotted past the door of the room in which Senenmut was
left, a woman in a tight linen shift, carrying a tray laden with bottles
and jars.

Senenmut, reflecting on the likelihood of solitude in a crowded
palace, allowed himself to dream. If he had been meant for lesser tasks,
surely he would have been taken to the scribes' hall and set to work.
But he was singled out, led to a room in what surely must be the royal
quarters, and left to his own devices. Was he being tested? Were there
eyes in the painted walls, watching to see what he would do?

He judged it wise, after a circuit or two of the room, to sit in the
best of the light and set out his palette and inks and brushes, and un-
roll the bit of papyrus that he kept for need. For a while he sat still,
empty of inspiration. Then all at once it came to him. He bent to the
papyrus.

■ "What are you doing?"

Senenmut had heard the footsteps, seen the shadows on the floor,
reckoned and counted them. There were only two, one very large and
wide in the shoulders, one much smaller and more slender.

The voice that spoke to him was light, a child's voice or a young
woman's. It had a child's curiosity but a woman's self-possession, with
nothing tentative in it.

He looked up. Yes, a child, but dressed as a woman in a white linen
gown and a wide jeweled collar, with a wig of heavy plaits. A small imperious cat-face regarded him from amid the braids. "Are you writing
a poem," she demanded, "or a hymn to the gods?"

Senenmut quelled the first, impulsive retort. The king might be
watching, judging him by his response to this girlchild, whoever she
was. Royal kin certainly, or royal servant, to carry herself with such sublime self-confidence.

He answered her as sweetly as he knew how. "Why, lady, neither.
I'm writing a letter."

Her painted brows went up. Her eyes tilted upward like a cat's, with no little in them of a cat's expression: fiercely intent, fixing on him as if he were prey. "To whom would you write a letter?"

He bristled at the tone of it. *And who are you,* it said, *to write to anyone at all?*

But he remembered his resolve. The king might be listening. Or the king's chancellor. Or any one of the great lords of the Two Lands. He answered this impudent child as if she were worthy of respect. "I am writing, lady, to my master, Seti-Nakht. He set me lessons, you see, and I am recalling them."

"How dull," said the girlchild. She lifted a hand. Her shadow shifted slightly, coming into the light. Senenmut had thought it a trick of the eyes. No man could be as large as that.

This one was. He was as black as the kohl that lined his lady's eyelids, so tall that he had to stoop to pass the door. And yet he did not move like other giants that Senenmut had seen. He was as light on his feet as a hunting cat, poised as if to spring.

"Nehsi," she said—it was not a name, not properly: it simply meant 'Nubian.' "Fetch wine. And, I think, dates. And bread with cheese baked in."

The Nubian bowed low. His face was still, but his eyes begged her to reconsider. She did not choose to see. He backed away, still bowing.

When his shadow had passed down the colonnade, the girlchild sat in the chair, which happened to be set just in front of the place where Senenmut had chosen to sit. She was pretty rather than beautiful, but she moved with striking grace, as if she had studied to be a dancer.

"Tell me your name," she said abruptly.

Senenmut stiffened. One did not toy with names. There was too much power in them. And to demand a name of a stranger, with such a presumption of obedience— "You are arrogant," he said.

The words escaped before he could call them back. Seti-Nakht would have flayed him with the rod, had he known.

This child seemed taken aback. But not enough, and not for long. "You dare much," she said.

"So do you."

Her lips went tight. "Do you know who I am?"

"Should I?" asked Senenmut.

With late-dawning wisdom, Senenmut began to suspect that she was more than a servant, and perhaps more than a royal cousin. She looked at him as if no one else had ever spoken to her so, with such complete disregard of her station.

When she spoke, she seemed almost amused. "Yes, scribe, you should know who I am. I am called Hatshepsut."

His teeth clicked together. Yes, he should know who that was. Hatshepsut. Daughter of the old king, the king who was dead, and his Great Royal Wife. Wife of the God. The king's wife, Great Royal Wife, queen and goddess.

He could not fling himself on his face. His inks would spatter. He bowed over the palette, cursing the flush that burned his cheeks. "Lady," he said—and cursed himself. He was a scribe. He knew all the proper forms of address, or he had known them once. They were all fled; all forgotten.

The queen had no mercy on him. "Now will you tell me your name?" she demanded.

His eyes flashed up of themselves. Spoiled, he thought. Brat. Queen.

He answered her with as much grace as he could muster. "I am called Senenmut, Ramose's son."

"Senenmut Ramose's son," said the queen, "who sent you here?"

"The Temple of Amon, lady," he answered, "and Seti-Nakht the master of scribes."

"Seti-Nakht." The queen sounded—not pleased. Satisfied, somehow. But when she looked at Senenmut, that satisfaction vanished. "Did he send you to me as a punishment?"

"I am sent—?" But of course he was. This must be the queen's house within the palace. This was certainly the queen: no one else would address him so directly, or with such certainty of her right to do it. He said, "Lady, he simply sent me."

"That would be like him," said Hatshepsut. "He believes that I need reining in. You too, I suppose. You have the look."

Senenmut was blushing again, and cursing his body's folly. "Are you saying, lady, that I should return to him? Shall I tell him that the gift does not suit?"

"Would you do that?" she asked. She sounded honestly curious.

"You are the queen," he said. "I'm bound to obey you."

She did not argue that. "No, don't go back to him. Not yet. He must have had his reasons for sending you. I asked," she said, "for a man of years and wisdom, a scribe well fit to serve a queen."

And Seti-Nakht had sent a boy with few years and no wisdom, who had never learned the meaning of humility.

Hatshepsut was even less familiar with that virtue than Senenmut. He would have thought that only a king could be as haughty as she was.

"Read to me," she said abruptly.

Senenmut's mind emptied of wit. There was nothing to read but the letter in his lap, and he was not minded to regale her with that.

By the gods' good fortune, the Nubian returned just then, bearing the wine and the dates and the bread. He carried other things, too: a case of scrolls and another in the same shape as Senenmut's own, a scribe's satchel, and not a new one, either. This had seen use.

The queen bade him eat, as imperious in that as in everything else. To his surprise, he was hungry. She, it seemed, was not. She watched him, censoriously maybe, or maybe only curious to see how a commoner ate. He took some small pleasure in showing her the manners that he had learned among the scribes.

He could not tell if she was disappointed. When he had had his fill, the Nubian took the rest away—little enough, at that—and left him alone again, for a little while, with the queen.

"Read to me," she said again.

There were indeed scrolls in the case, written in a workmanlike hand, nothing beautiful in them. They were meant to be read and recorded, not to be admired. Why anyone should want to remember them, Senenmut could not imagine. They were only letters from foreign kings to the king of Egypt, begging for gold and offering daughters and whining that they needed his aid in this war or that.

"Surely you can read these," Senenmut said, "lady. There's nothing complicated about them."

Ah: he had stung her, and he had not even been thinking when he did it. She spoke with excessive precision, through tightened lips. "I can read. A little. But not enough."

"What, no one taught you?"

"I was taught," she said, still stiffly. "I was not taught well. My father died, you see. My husband is not a man for, as he puts it, trifles. Scribes read and write. Queens command the scribes."

"You could command a scribe to teach you," Senenmut said.

"I have," said the queen. "Or I thought I had. Seti-Nakht has a nasty sense of humor."

He did indeed, thought Senenmut. "Is that what you want of me, then, lady? To read to you?"

"Read," she commanded him.

In a fit of temper he obeyed her. He read from the scrolls, every word, even to the endless repetitive formulae of greeting and salutation. She sat with hands folded in her lap, listening with all apparent serenity. If the fourth consecutive recounting of the same arguments on behalf of the same king who was, he declared, destitute, did not bore her silly, then she was a stronger spirit than Senenmut.

He could let his eyes glide over the words, and his tongue utter them, and leave his mind to wander as it pleased. It noted that the Nubian came back and established himself on guard at the door. It saw how a strand of the queen's own hair, glossy black and very thick, had escaped beneath her wig. It observed that the sun had shifted toward noon, and that the light in the room was fading slowly, for the window faced east.

She heard the whole of one scroll and most of another. Senenmut's throat was raw, his voice hoarse. As he finished one letter and began another, she said, "Enough."

He lapsed into welcome silence. The Nubian filled the cup that had been empty; he drank. The wine made him dizzy. He had had wine once or twice before, thin sour stuff, nothing like this sweet heady vintage. This must be the wine that kings drank at their feasts.

The queen had drunk nothing. Maybe there was calculation in that. "You read adequately," she said. "I wish to learn. Can you teach me?"

"I am not a schoolmaster," Senenmut said in the heat of the wine. "I do not wish to be one. If I did, would I be here?"

"Probably not," said the queen. "I disappoint you, I see. Had you expected to be taken to the king and appointed Vizier of the Upper Kingdom?"

He was too furious even to blush. He was all cold, white and still.

She went on as if oblivious. "My husband dislikes scribes. He prefers what he calls honest men: soldiers and their kind, men armed with sword and spear instead of brush and palette. He'd be rid of your kind if he could. Scribes and priests, he says, are the bane of a warrior king. They throttle swift action. They diminish the glory of battle in a niggle of numbers."

"I might be different," Senenmut muttered.

She arched a painted brow. "My husband would never have summoned you. I the mere woman, I who am no more than Great Royal Wife—I have a use for you, or someone like you. You may refuse. The palace will be closed to you thereafter, but that surely will be no impediment to a talent as vast as yours."

Senenmut bristled. "And what do I have to gain if I play schoolmaster to your majesty?"

"Why," said the queen, "nothing. Except presence in the palace and the prospect of admittance to my counsels. I do have them, scribe. Yes, even I, who am not a king."

Her irony was honed a shade too keenly. It irked her, then, that someone else must be king. That was a weapon if Senenmut had known how to use it.

He knew the scribe's art. He was learned in the lore of the Two Kingdoms. He had heard of the intrigues of courts, the subtle and deadly games that the high ones played to allay their boredom. Boredom like gold was a luxury; only the wealthy were free to indulge in it.

The queen was bored. Whatever she did with herself, whatever was allowed her as the king's wife, was not enough. She wanted more. This teaching that she asked for was but a means to an end. It would give her something that she needed, further a plan that she had in train. Through it she played the game of princes.

Senenmut meant to be one who ruled the game, not one who was ruled by it: a counter on a board, helpless to move except as his master decreed. Just so would this child-queen use him, take what he had and cast him away.

He rose. He bowed as correctly as he knew how. He said, "I wish my lady well of her ambition."

She had not dismissed him, but neither did she stop him when he turned and left her. Part of him—and rather a large one—was railing at him for a fool. The part that ruled his feet wanted simply to be away from there, away from that imperious, impossible, exasperating girl-child.

〰〰〰〰〰

3

SENEMUT LOOKED BACK ON THE gates of the palace in a kind of bleak exultation. He had talked himself out of his chief ambition. And for what? Because he had taken a dislike to the king's wife.

He was fortunate that she had not had him flogged or worse. Her youth had preserved him: no doubt she had never been spoken to with such rudeness. She had not known how to punish it.

And now he had nowhere to go. The House of Life was closed to him. He had barred himself from the palace. If he went home so early, his mother would not rest until she had discovered the reason. Then she would flay him as royally as the queen had failed to do. And after that . . .

What? Sell jars to the brewers of beer? Write letters for the poor and the feckless? Talk himself into, at best, a lesser temple that stood in need of a scribe?

He stood in the middle of the street, the great processional way that led from the palace into the city, and saw nothing but the magnitude of his folly. "Oh," he said. "Oh, gods."

■ He wandered till evening, not caring where he went. Someone relieved him of his provisions, but even in abstraction he kept a grip on his scribe's satchel. He did not know why he should, when he stopped to think. It was no use to him.

He could, he thought, go back to the queen, grovel at her feet, beg her to let him teach her.

And be schoolmaster to a chit of a girl?

He turned on his heel at that, and looked about him. He knew only vaguely where he was. His feet had carried him down to the river: far down and well away from both the palace and his father's house.

It was running as low as it ever ran, as it did at every turn of the year. When the moon came round again the river would begin to swell; in a remarkably little time it would stretch as vast as a sea, drowning the rich farmlands that now were ripe with the harvest. When after a season it retreated, the black earth that it left behind would grow green again, and burgeon with the wealth of Egypt.

Even so shrunken it was a wide and potent river, thick with barges and with lesser boats: fishermen, ferrymen, a prince in his gilded yacht with musicians following in a smaller vessel, and a second with a cookstove lit and preparing his dinner, and a third laden with the flock of his concubines.

Senenmut leaned perilously far out above the river. He wanted what that man had. Yes, even now, when he was sunk in despair. The prince had a harper on his yacht, a young woman with a piercingly sweet voice. It rang clear over the water, singing of love among the reeds.

"Truer to sing of love betrayed," he said. The singer did not hear him. The little fleet passed away down the river. A barge followed it, heavy laden with cattle; and a fisherman hauling in a net.

As the sun sank low over the red and barren hills beyond the river, Senenmut turned his feet toward his father's house. He would not lie, he had decided. He would simply fail to inform his mother that Seti-Nakht had dismissed him, and that he in turn had dismissed the queen.

The longer he put off the inevitable, the more likely he was to discover a way out of his predicament.

Or it could simply be that he was a coward. He went in as he did every evening. The servants had water for him to wash hands and feet and face. The aunts fluttered. The baby crowed in his nurse's arms. Ahotep demonstrated a new accomplishment: somersaults across the family's gathering room, till he came near to oversetting the table and the dinner that was laid out on it. Their father seemed not to notice. Their mother was abed with the headache.

That much reprieve Senenmut was granted: not to face her stern all-seeing eye. He ate hungrily, which spared him the aunts' worry and fret. He could always eat, even in the depths of adversity.

■ That night, lying in the bed he shared with Ahotep, he dreamed that he had returned to the palace. The queen was there, sitting on a golden throne. Her headdress was shaped and colored like the wings of a falcon. Its head crowned her, its eyes lambent in the dimness of the hall; one blazing gold, one cold unseeing white. Such were the eyes of Horus, falcon-god, protector of kings. His eye that saw clear was the sun. His blind eye was the moon.

He turned his sun-eye on Senenmut, and then his eye that was the moon. He saw; he did not see. In dream it had meaning, but Senenmut was slow in the wits. He did not understand.

He woke still groping for understanding. Ahotep for once was up before him. He felt heavy. His head ached. So: he was ill. He had dreamed it, all of it, even to his meeting with the queen.

A small figure hurtled out of air onto his middle. He grunted. Ahotep bounced with bruising enthusiasm. "Senenmut! Senenmut, do you know who's here? Guess who's here!"

Senenmut growled and heaved the brat off him and shut his eyes tight. But there was no getting rid of Ahotep.

"Mother's up and dressed and acting civil. Father's beside himself. Senenmut, he's asking for *you!*"

"Who in the world—" Senenmut's mind woke more slowly than his tongue. Mother not only awake but dressed and being civil. Father flustered, who never noticed enough to be perturbed by it.

Gods. The queen had done it. She had sent her soldiers to seize him and carry him away, no doubt to a terrible and too richly deserved fate.

It was not courage that brought Senenmut out of the dubious safety of his sleeping-room. He was too practical to imagine that he could escape. If he went over the wall and disappeared into the city, the queen's men would simply assuage her wrath with the blood of his family.

He would happily have seen his brother muzzled and chained in a kennel like the yapping pup he was, but never in the world would Senenmut have wished him dead. Nor Mother, sharp-tongued un-gentle creature that she was, nor Father who was all that his wife was not. The baby, the servants . . .

He took time to bathe first and to make himself properly tidy: head new shaved, kilt his best and cleanest. He brought his satchel, because if he was to die, he wanted to do it as a scribe should: with pen and brush close to hand.

■ Bes must have had his bread and beer early this morning. There was no one near the shrine. They were all in the room the family gathered in to eat. It was no more splendid than Senenmut remembered, but his kinsfolk were on their best behavior. They were almost quiet. No one clamored for attention. Even the baby sucked peacefully at the nurse's breast.

A personage sat in the best chair, where Father usually sat. He had been offered date wine and new bread: both lay on the table beside him. He did not seem to have touched either.

He might be a soldier. Senenmut had not thought to inquire when he was in attendance on the queen. His height and breadth and his ebon darkness were impossibly exotic in that small and common room with its middling bad wall-painting of palm trees and crocodiles. He did not seem discommoded by it, but neither was he at his ease. He simply sat, still as a stone panther, waiting as he must have been ordered to wait.

Senenmut's coming brought him alert. It was a subtle thing: a light in his eyes, expression in his face where had been none before. Senen-

mut did not see death there. Maybe it was only that he could not read
a Nubian face as he might an Egyptian.

Nehsi the queen's servant rose to greet Senenmut. He did not have
to rise quite so high, Senenmut thought nastily, or loom quite so huge.
His head brushed the ceiling. He spoke in good Egyptian, in a voice
as deep as a drum beating. "You are summoned to the queen," he said.

Senenmut bit his tongue. No way in the world could he ask what
he wanted to ask, not here in front of his mother. She was simpering—
she of all people. It shamed him. If she knew what he expected, which
was to be fed to the crocodiles, she would be appalled.

"Imagine," she said with a lilt in her voice such as Senenmut had
never heard. "Our boy is going to be the queen's own teacher and scribe.
Who'd ever have thought it? I would have been content to see him settled in the House of Life."

The Nubian bowed gravely.

"And will he be needing his belongings?" she asked. "Will we be
bidding farewell to the eldest and best of our sons?"

Senenmut opened his mouth, but the Nubian spoke before him.
"Not yet," he said, "lady. The queen requires a master of writing and
reading, but not for every hour of every day. When she has no need of
him, he may do and go as he pleases."

"And," said Hat-Nufer, still much too sweetly but with a return
of her wonted canniness, "will there be any . . . consideration in return?
A man must eat, after all, and buy clothing and ornaments suitable to
his station."

"It will be seen to," said the Nubian.

"Ah, but one does wonder," she said, "how much a queen values
the man who teaches her the arts of the scribe. If we might have some
inkling . . ."

Dear gods, she was haggling, and in that cloying tone, too. For the
first time Senenmut saw an expression in the Nubian's eyes. It must be
amusement. It could not be admiration. "The wages of a royal scribe
are not insignificant," he said. "You may expect that your son will receive the same. Bread and beer for every day, a brace of fat geese on fes-
tivals, clothing as needed and as required by his duties, and a wig of his

choosing; and in addition, if he does well, such ornaments and emoluments as the queen deems appropriate."

"And, I expect, all necessities of his art," said Hat-Nufer with notable lack of shame. "Inks, brushes, pens, a new palette as befits a royal scribe. And papyrus, of course, and such books as he requires for his instruction."

"Of course," said the Nubian blandly. "You may expect that your son will be well rewarded for his service."

Neither clearly had any thought of consulting Senenmut as to whether he wished to be nursemaid to the queen. His mother could only see the rank and the title. She did not know the child, spoiled as she was and imperious, as likely to cast Senenmut off as to demand his service. If he had not refused her, she surely would not have wanted him. But since he had, she had to take vengeance by sending her servitor, guardsman, bedmate, whatever he was, and disarming his mother, and trapping him much too neatly for his comfort.

He had no choice but to follow the Nubian. It never occurred to anyone to feed him. He was too sulky to demand at least a bite of bread. Hungry, seething, he went back to the palace that he had approached with such joy the day before.

4

NEHSI THE NUBIAN DID NOT SEE what his lady saw in the boy from the Temple of Amon. His resistance was naught but puppy-snarling. At heart he was no more high-minded than his mother, and not much less venal, either.

He pondered that as he stood guard over his lady in her lesser garden. She had gone there ostensibly to take the air as a queen might do, actually to be by herself except for the inevitable and inescapable guard.

He, who had been standing about in livery since he grew tall enough to overtop any but the tallest Egyptian, had ample leisure to consider the queen's latest acquisition.

"You are jealous," Hatshepsut said, reading him as easily as she had since she was a small princess and he a callow young guardsman. "You think I might grow too fond of him."

"I think," said Nehsi, "that he is a low and vulgar creature with lofty ambitions."

"And that he's not pretty enough for me?"

Nehsi showed her his teeth. "Pretty is as pretty does. And isn't he a fine one, with that crooked beak of his?"

"And you with yours spread half across your face, you can quibble?" She tossed her head in its wig of many beaded braids. "You're too vain of yourself, that's the trouble with you. Is it going well with the twins? Are they asking you yet to choose which of them you favor more?"

Nehsi had always been glad of skin too dark to show a blush. The queen's two maids, twins and as like as two eggs in the same nest, were each a delicious handful, but together they were another kind of handful entirely. For a fact they were wearing him out; but he would never tell the queen that.

She grinned at him, no heed of dignity here where there was only Nehsi to see. "As bad as that, then? Oh, poor Nehsi! And now you're fretting about the scribe with the crooked nose. I know what he is. He's also quite intelligent when he troubles to be. Seti-Nakht speaks well of him—and Seti-Nakht has never suffered a fool in his life."

"All boys are fools," said Nehsi.

"And when did you stop being a boy yourself?" she demanded. "Years aren't inches, my dear, no matter what people may let you think."

"I'm older than you," he said, "and older than that puppy, too, I'll wager."

"He's not an ill teacher," Hatshepsut mused. She wandered over to the fishpond and sat on its rim, watching the dart of bright bodies from sunlight into shadow. There was a water-lotus blooming just within reach. She craned far out to pluck it, so far that he reached to catch her, but she came back with the blossom before she fell. She buried her nose in it, drinking the sweet scent. "He doesn't like teaching," she said. "That's obvious. But when he forgets how insulted he is, he does it middling well."

"He has no patience," Nehsi said, "and no understanding of those who are slower of wit than he is."

"Oh," she said, "but I'm quick. Very quick. He even admitted it."

"He could hardly deny the truth," Nehsi said.

"Of course not," she said. She darted a glance at him, with one of her sudden shifts of mood. "My husband wants me in his bed tonight. Should I go, do you think? Or should I put him off again?"

Not a shift of mood, then. A shift to the thing that was more truly troubling her.

Nehsi was careful in his reply. "You know you have to do it in the end. Whether now or later."

"That's what he told his messenger to say," she said. "I was to be reminded that I may have been married to him when I was too young a child to do what wives do with husbands, but now I'm a woman. It's time I did my duty as queen."

"He wants a son," Nehsi said.

"Surely," said Hatshepsut with a curl of the lip, "and doesn't every man? Isn't there time enough and more? I've just begun my courses."

Nehsi could find it in himself to pity her, a little. She was very young, yes, and no man had ever touched her or come to her bed.

She saw the pity. It made her angry, as he had expected that it would. "I'm not afraid, Nehsi. Don't you dare think I'm afraid. I just don't—his hands are clammy. And he sweats."

"He is the living god," Nehsi said.

"He is a sweaty, panting lout without the least grain of delicacy." She was shaking, and she seemed unable to stop, but her voice was less difficult to control. "Whenever he tries to kiss me, he slobbers all over my face. All the women he's had, and all the women he's said to have had, and hasn't a one of them ever taught him to do it properly?"

"Some things a man has to learn for himself," said Nehsi.

"Not this one," she said. "He needs a schoolmaster. If a cocky boy can teach me to write, why can't some obliging soul teach my husband how to bed a woman?"

"One doesn't do that with Horus on earth," Nehsi said dryly. "It's not even wise to offer."

"Oh, isn't it?" Her eyes glittered. "I'll send him a teacher. Someone pretty. Someone skilled and willing, but not too clever."

He nearly groaned aloud. She was a clever child—but by no means clever enough. "Lady," he said. "How wise is that? If you send a woman to him, and he falls to her charms as he can't help but do, he might forget you altogether. What then if he gets a son on her while you remain barren? You'd never lose your rank, but you'd lose power and standing. And a concubine's son would be the next king of Egypt."

She heard him. He saw it in her eyes. But she did not hear him clearly enough. "I'll have to trust in the gods. And by the greatest of them, old friend, I do not want to go to my husband's bed for the first time only to be pawed over like a trull in the market."

Nehsi swallowed a sigh. She had a look he knew all too well. She would do what she would do, and no one had any hope of stopping her.

"You," she said, "will hunt down a suitable woman for the king. Let her be young, but not so young as to lack experience in the arts of the bedchamber. Let her be beautiful—that goes without saying. And above all let her be sweet and biddable, and see to it that she is loyal to me."

It was never the habit of queens to set simple tasks for their servants. Nehsi bowed to the ground. He did not pause to see how she responded to that pointed abasement.

■ On his way out of the garden he roused one of the other guards, a good enough man for an Egyptian, and set him on watch over the queen's solitude. He was not entirely sure how to go about his task, but he knew at least where to begin.

The twins were busy with the queen's wardrobe, washing her gowns of state and spreading them in the sun on the roof of her palace.

Most people could not tell them apart. They affected the same waist-long plaited hair and the same blue beads on a string about the hips, and they were identically pretty, with round ripe faces and laughing black eyes. But Nehsi knew that Mutnefer was a very little the taller, and Nutnefer was a very little the more ample of breast. He could aggravate them terribly by knowing which was which when they tried, wickedly, to deceive him.

They greeted him with matched and brilliant smiles. He paid obligatory tribute: a kiss for each, and a quick slap at the hand that strayed under his kilt. "Not now," he said. "I'm on the queen's errand."

"And can't it wait?" Mutnefer abandoned her washbasket with visible relief. Her sister was already pressed to Nehsi's side, stroking him above the kilt since he barred the way below.

"You know the queen can never wait," he said from between them.

"And what does she want?" asked Nutnefer as her fingers walked themselves down to his kilt's fastening. He caught them; she giggled. "Aside from that, of course."

"The queen doesn't know what it is, to want it," Mutnefer said. "Poor thing, she's scared to death. Some idiot told her it hurts the first time; now she doesn't want it at all."

"I don't think she's a coward," said Nutnefer. "Wary, more like. She never rushes into anything."

"Some things one should rush into," Mutnefer said.

Nehsi, listening and fending off determined hands, enjoyed a moment's pleasurable contemplation of a twofold gift to the king. He discarded it with regret. These two were pretty and charming and delightful in bed, and their likeness to one another was a rarity, but the king liked a less substantial armful of woman. A willowy girl would allure him best; and one of exceptional beauty. Which the twins were not. Pretty, that was all, and lively. No more.

"Listen to me," he said over their chatter. "You can help me if you will. I need a woman—"

"And here we are!" they cried, attacking him with delight.

He got a grip on each and set her firmly aside. "Stop that and listen. The queen has taken it into her head to do a thing, and she's harnessed me with the doing of it."

It was slow going, with a great deal of foolery, but in the end he got it all out. The twins were less incredulous than he had been.

"That's like her," Nutnefer said. "Careful. Silly, and no mistake. But it can't be either of us, no."

"Not that we'd mind at all, teaching the king manners," said Mutnefer, "but we've tried already. He'll not take lessoning from us."

They were both almost sober for a moment, with the hint of a frown.

"It's not that he's exactly clumsy," Nutnefer said. "He never commits rape, nothing as bad as that. But she has the right of it. He's awkward. And he sweats."

"Nothing like you," said Mutnefer, but she had stopped trying to drive him wild with wanting her. She was pondering. "Sister, do you think . . ."

"No," said Nutnefer promptly. "But maybe . . ."

"No, not that one, either. And as for . . ."

Nehsi was used to these cryptic conversations. The twins had a magic of sorts: each always seemed to know what the other was thinking. They spoke aloud out of a native courtesy, but broke off in midsentence, since there was so clearly no need to go on. It could drive a listener to distraction.

Nehsi set himself to be patient. Nothing they ever did could match the queen in one of her moods.

As he had expected, after a while they looked at one another and nodded. Then they seemed to remember that he was there, and more to the point, that he had to hear words in order to understand them. Mutnefer said, "There are one or two who might do, and who would be willing. Three, even. Maybe. Four?"

"Enough to choose from," Nutnefer said. "Come, we'll look for them. But you have to promise something."

Nehsi raised a brow.

"You can't have any of them," said Mutnefer. "Even the ones who don't go to the king."

"That's hard," Nehsi said.

"Promise," said Nutnefer.

He heaved a sigh. "I could simply do my own searching."

"Yes, and there are hundreds of women in the palace, and dozens are pretty enough at least to be considered. How long will it take you to examine them all?" Mutnefer demanded.

"He might enjoy it," Nutnefer said, "till the queen ran out of patience and came looking for him."

"Indeed," said Mutnefer. She ran a light hand across his shoulders. "I should so hate to see this beautiful panther-hide ruined with whip-scars."

He shook off her hand. "Enough, enough! I yield. I promise. As long as I enjoy the delights of your companionship, I won't cast my eye on one of the king's women."

They considered that, narrow-eyed. Nutnefer looked ready to argue, but Mutnefer said, "It will do. Come, let's to the hunt."

Nehsi paused. "And this?" He tilted his head toward the baskets and the swaths of drying linen.

"It will wait," Nutnefer said. She tugged at his hand. "Quick! Time's flying."

5

THE QUEEN INSPECTED THE WOMEN whom Nehsi had brought to her. She had taken pains with her appearance: had put on one of her state robes and the tall crown like plumes of gold, and under that an elaborate wig. Her jewels were pure gold, her collar as broad as a breastplate, the wealth of a kingdom weighing down her neck and shoulders. She received her servant and his hoard of living treasure in one of the audience chambers on a throne of faience and gold, with her maids about her and a company of guards standing at rest along the walls.

It was no more state than she was entitled to, but for receiving half a dozen trembling maidservants it was slightly overdone. Nehsi was wiser than to remark on it. For what she intended, which was to terrify his charges into silence, it succeeded admirably. One, ironically enough the most robust-seeming of the lot, looked ready to faint.

She did not disgrace him, however. Nor did the rest. They entered in procession, knelt each as he had instructed, and did obeisance. He observed them out of the corner of his eye. The center of his focus was the queen.

The twins had guided him well. All six whom they had aided him to choose were young—none more than three years past first womanhood—but skilled in the arts of love. They were all beautiful, all lissome and graceful of body. Most could sing well, and one sang remarkably. All played an instrument, none badly. And every one was prepared to offer allegiance to the queen whose whim had raised her fortunes.

Nehsi named each as she came forward, with her age and rank and service and her particular talents. They were all servants, some of the palace, some in lords' houses. Two had been noblemen's concubines, but one lord had died and the other set all his women aside when he married a jealous wife. Four were named Hathor, for the goddess of love and beauty. One was Meritre: Beloved of Re.

The last was named Isis for the mother of Horus. She was the youngest, only a season or two older than the queen, and in Nehsi's estimation the loveliest. She had a face like a flower, and soft ivory skin unkissed by the sun, and masses of blue-black curling hair that she kept fastidiously clean and scented with myrrh. Like the rest she was naked but for a string of beads about the hips, but she had made herself a collar of lotus-blossoms that all but hid her little pink-tipped breasts.

The Hathors stood huddled together like heifers, staring with wide brown eyes at the terrible golden queen. Meritre seemed above such folly: her chin was lifted, her lips tight with scorn. She was the eldest, the one whose lord had died, it was said, in her embrace. She had neither confirmed nor denied the rumor. Nehsi reckoned her too proud to have much sense, but there was passion in her glance as it flicked upon him, a smoldering promise that he knew better than to acknowledge. If she was meant for the king, the least he would lose for trespassing with her would be his two best jewels.

If the king must have a teacher, she would do admirably. The subtleties of courts and kings were beyond her. But in the bedchamber she would have few equals.

Beyond a word or two of greeting and inquiry, the queen ignored her. She was more interested in the Hathors, who had recovered enough to stammer out their names and the places from which they had come: the house of the queen's maids, the household of a lord, one child of a woman who had sold herself on streetcorners but who had found herself a patron of ample means and little concern for his lover's antecedents. The queen's rank and power made them stammer and stumble and cling to one another more tightly than ever.

Isis, like Meritre, preferred to stand erect and a little apart, but not perceptibly for scorn. Like the Hathors she shivered as she darted glances at the queen, but she was not terrified into immobility. She kept her eyes lowered, seeming unaware of how alluring she was with the long lashes on the ivory cheeks.

Hatshepsut left the Hathors in what might have been relief. They had little of intelligence to say. Not, Nehsi thought, that the king would care for witty conversation in the bedchamber, but a woman who would teach him the finer arts would need more than a halting tongue and trembling knees.

"Isis," said Hatshepsut.

The girl stiffened slightly but did not look up. "Lady," she murmured.

"Here, look at me," the queen said with the exasperation of five-times repetition.

Isis lifted her eyes. They were large and dark, less heavily painted with kohl than most women in Egypt preferred. Their expression was at once wary and trusting: wary of the queen's majesty, trusting her to do nothing actively dreadful.

"And what were you before you came to me?" Hatshepsut asked her.

Nehsi had told the queen already, but neither he nor Isis said so. "Lady," Isis said in her soft sweet voice, "before I came to this place I was a servant in your own household, the least of your many children, attendant of an attendant in your majesty's bath."

The queen tilted her head slightly under the weight of the tall crown. "And how, may I ask, did you acquire expertise in the pleasuring of men, if you were a servant of servants in my bath?"

The faintest of delicate flushes stained the ivory cheeks. "Lady, I have only been a servant of servants for a season. Before that I was a maid to Lord Hapi's wife. Lord Hapi was—is—a man who prefers his ladies young. He loves to teach them, lady, and to give them pleasure in such measure as they give him."

Hatshepsut's brows had risen remarkably. So too had Nehsi's when he first heard the child's story. Lord Hapi was a man of late middle years, soft and rolling in fat, with a reputation for subtlety in the poisonous games of the court. His wife was older than he, as wiry thin as he was roundly plump, with all the sweetness and gentility of a hungry crocodile. Astonishing to think of that man, married to that woman, as a beloved preceptor to his wife's young maids.

"He . . . taught you to give men pleasure?" Hatshepsut asked.

"Oh, yes," said Isis. "His own predilections are for maids whose breasts have barely budded; but he takes great pleasure in preparing them for the service of men who prefer their women less youthfully tender. It's a gift he gives, and with great pleasure, too."

"And you," said the queen, "have grown a little old for him."

Isis looked sad. "Yes. Yes, when my breasts grew—it was so sudden, lady; it was distressing—he lost his passion for me. He was very good to me, lady. He saw me placed in your majesty's service. He does that for all his ladies: not here, not before this, lady, but in good service and with fine expectations."

The queen's eyes narrowed. "Yes? And did he say why he chose to send you here?"

"Why," said Isis with all appearance of innocence, "yes, he did. He said that I deserved better than to disappear among some lordling's concubines. I could please the king, he said, but he thought that you, lady, might need me more."

"What need would I have of you?" Hatshepsut demanded.

Isis blinked at her vehemence, but did not flinch. "Lady, a queen needs many things. How may I serve you?"

"You could," said Hatshepsut, "be a trap. Still . . . Lord Hapi? What has he to gain?"

"Your favor, one would suppose," Nehsi answered, though she had not directed the question at him, "and perhaps a useful degree of gratitude."

"No," said Hatshepsut. "It's too subtle. If he had meant to throw her across my path, he would have placed her higher than attendant of an attendant in my bath. He was disposing of her as he best might."

"With maybe some small hope that she would come to your attention," Nehsi said. "Why not? Forcing her on you would dispose you against him. In this he lost nothing and stood the chance of gaining much."

She frowned. "Are you telling me that I should choose this one?"

"I think," said Nehsi carefully, "that you will choose as you are best pleased to do."

"Don't be politic with me," she said sharply. "It makes me feel a fool."

He set his lips together and bowed.

She rose from her throne, moving with slow grace under the crown. The Hathors clung together all the more tightly. Meritre lifted her chin a fraction higher. Isis watched calmly. Was that a gleam of avarice as her eyes rested on the queen's adornments? Or was it only the glitter of gold, dazzling her?

The queen walked down the line of them. She paused before each, searching the face turned up to hers. The Hathors tried to flinch away. She caught each, and held her till she would look up.

She shook her head. "Too shy," she said. "Too much in fear of royalty. Nehsi, was this meant for a mockery?"

"Hardly, lady," he said. "They were bold enough in front of me."

Meritre sniffed loudly. "They didn't think. The palace lured them—it never occurred to them to recall who lives there."

"Did it occur to you?" the queen inquired.

"Immediately," said Meritre. "What do you want of us? You can't have need of our particular skills, surely."

"I admire a sweet singer," Hatshepsut said.

"None of them sings more sweetly than I," said Meritre. "But there are singers among your attendants who put me to shame. What we all have in common, which is the pleasing of men—what is your need of that, great lady and queen? Is it true what they say, that no man has yet touched you? Are you looking for a teacher?"

"You are more clever than I thought," Hatshepsut said. "No, not I. The one I would have you teach . . . he likes his women sweet-spoken and biddable. Or so I'm told."

"Then he must not be overly fond of you," said Meritre.

At least one of the Hathors sucked in her breath. Nehsi held his own.

Hatshepsut smiled. "I, on the other hand, have rather a fondness for insolence in a servant. It's a challenge, you see. To turn insolence into respect; to tame the crocodile." Before any of them could respond, she took Isis by the hand. "Come, my friend. I have a task for you."

Isis had the grace not to look unduly complacent. Meritre shrugged. The Hathors burst into tears.

Hatshepsut shook her head at them. "Find them something to do, Nehsi. I'll be needing more bath attendants, I suppose. But this one"—she indicated Meritre—"may try her hand among the maids of my chamber."

Meritre sniffed again. No gratitude there. Hatshepsut laughed, a startling sound if one was not accustomed to it: it was as free as a boy's, untrammeled by maidenly delicacy. Still leading Isis by the hand, she left Nehsi to contend with the rest.

The Hathors, freed of the constraint of the queen's presence, were not shy at all. They screeched rather alarmingly, in fact. He handed off two to grinning guards, thrust the third into Meritre's unsympathetic grasp, and took the last in his own charge, clapped a hand over her mouth to stop her shrieking and carried her off to the queen's baths.

6

SENENMUT WAS SURPRISED. NOT THAT the queen was a quick study—he had rather thought so—but that the teaching of her was not as unpleasant as he had expected. She showed him no great respect, but she took his instruction without argument, and suffered him to correct her when there was need. There was not, much. She learned swiftly and she learned well. It gave her rather too much pleasure, and she was rather too forthright about it, but that was easy enough to forgive.

As elegantly as she dressed, as beautifully as she was painted and plucked and oiled to seem a lady, she was at heart no lady at all. Someone had failed in the teaching of her. She lacked womanly discretion. Her rich laugh was a boy's, and she had little restraint in indulging it.

Senenmut was too often its target. "You are a brilliant scribe," she said to him once, "and a fair to middling teacher. But the airs you put on—Hathor! How silly you look with your nose in the air. Where did you learn to be so haughty?"

"I begin to think," Senenmut said acidly, "that all the world colludes in taxing me with arrogance. I'll grovel, O living Isis, but only after you're done with this passage from Imhotep."

She grinned at him, unrepentant, and rattled off the passage so quickly that the words ran together. But she read it accurately, as he had expected that she would. Almost in the same breath she said, "I didn't say arrogant. I said haughty. You carry yourself like a prince of princes. Though some of it must be your nose. A falcon would be proud of such a weapon."

He rubbed it, caught himself, scowled. "Not every living creature can be as beautiful as you, lady."

"Oh, I'm not beautiful," she said. "I'm interesting. I much prefer that. Beauty can be crashingly dull."

Was that an apology of sorts? He rather doubted it. Hatshepsut was queen. She did not apologize.

■ Every morning he went to the palace. Every evening he returned to his father's house. He was not with the queen for all or even most of the day. She had duties and pleasures that had no place for him. While she indulged in those, he sat among the queen's scribes in their cramped and antiquated hall, doing whatever the chief of scribes saw fit for him to do.

He was given no preference, offered no favors for that he was the queen's instructor in reading and writing. Nor did her scribes trouble to envy him, that he could discern. They were all men of middle years, and some were elderly. They had been in service in the palace since long before their lady was born. They were rooted in it, bound to it, oblivious to the world beyond their cracked and faded walls.

He regarded them with a kind of horror. Their existence was little different from that of scribes in the House of Life, but it seemed notably worse. It was dull; it led nowhere. Day after day, copying letters, rendering them into the language of this embassy or that, recording accounts of the queen's household, keeping the records in endless and exacting detail.

Senenmut endured it because he did not intend to do it for his life long. He could silence the clatter of his mind and become, as it were, one with the march of words, each glyph drawn swift and sure in his clear firm hand that had won him such praise in the Temple of Amon. There were some, and not all of them ignorant, who said that words were magic, and the glyphs themselves gave it shape.

He had studied little of the hidden arts. They did not engage him. But in those long slow hours while the sun tracked across the worn tiling of the floor, he began to understand the allure of the word without flesh or substance, simply the power of itself.

It was not, nevertheless, enough. One day as he came from the scribes' hall to the queen's lesson-chamber, he found no one there. All her chambers were likewise empty; except for a bored guard or two and a maid desultorily sweeping the floor, they were deserted.

Senenmut stood in the outermost antechamber, at a loss. The sweeper was mute and simple. She had barely looked up as he passed.

This was a child's nightmare, or a courtier's: to find oneself in the palace, but the palace was empty, the king and queen departed, and nothing left but dust and sunlight. There had been no word spoken of the queen's departing for another city or another palace; no rumor of a royal progress. She was simply gone.

After loss came anger. She could at least have informed him that she had no need of him, or told him where else he was to come. He might have nothing better to do than wait about for her, but in merest courtesy she might have left a message.

He was in a fine pitch of temper by the time he approached the guard on the outermost door. The lout had been snoring when he came in, was awake now but barely. He did not seem to understand plain Egyptian. "The queen," Senenmut gritted through clenched teeth. "Your lady, the Great Royal Wife, the living Isis. Where is she?"

"Out," said the guard, yawning and loosing a belch that was purest insolence.

Senenmut's fists clenched on his scribe's satchel. "Out? Out where?"

"On the river," the guard said. "In a boat."

Which could mean a journey of any duration at all, for any purpose. Senenmut was too furious to manage another question. He knew more or less where the royal barges were moored, in the river outside the palace walls. He ran from inner palace to outer palace to river, hardly aware of his speed until he stumbled to a halt on the quay.

A scribe never ran if he could help it. Mostly he sat and wrote, and others ran for him. Senenmut crouched gasping for breath. Only slowly did he become aware that he was watched: there were a number of people about, most with the air of lofty ennui that marked a courtier. Those under parasols, being waited on by servants with fans, were elaborately bored. The lesser luminaries were engrossed in finding what shelter they could from the sun.

They were all waiting as if they had been doing it since time began. Since morning at least, and for much the same reason as Senenmut: they had services to perform, but had met with empty rooms and insolent guards.

One of those who waited was less pretentious than the rest. He was not young, but neither was he old. He wore the robe and the emblems of a priest of Amon and was attended by a gaggle of younger priests, but he squatted in a patch of shade with no more dignity than a laborer in the fields. He even had a jar of beer, which he held out as Senenmut stood staring. "Here, boy," he said. "You look thirsty."

In a calmer mood Senenmut would have declined to do anything so openly vulgar, but at the moment he did not care. He lowered himself beside the priest, tucking up his legs as a scribe learned to do, and took the jar. The beer startled him. "It's good!" he said.

The priest grinned. He was missing a handful of teeth; the rest were decidedly unlovely. Still it was a remarkably appealing grin. "What did you expect? Back-alley cat piss?"

Senenmut choked. The priest pounded him on the back. He gasped and gagged, hiccoughed, swallowed mightily. His eyes were streaming; his nose itched. He glowered at the priest. "You have no dignity," he said.

"None whatsoever," the priest agreed. He reclaimed the jar, downed another draught. His eyes were bright and wicked. "They call me Hapuseneb," he said.

"Senenmut," said Senenmut somewhat grudgingly.

The priest nodded, still grinning. "Ah: I thought so. The young scribe who enjoys the favor of Seti-Nakht. You shouldn't feel too insulted that the queen wants you for a schoolmaster. She's young but she's quick, and she'll not let herself play weak second to the king. Serve her well, and you'll go far."

Senenmut nearly dashed the remnants of the beer in the man's face. Priest or no, he far overstepped his bounds.

He did not seem alarmed by Senenmut's expression. "There now," he said. "Learn a lesson from an old courtier. Bluntness can be the best weapon of all, and truth more dangerous than any deception. People who tell the truth, you see, are difficult. They can't be talked round.

They don't yield to threats, nor will they tell a lie when it would best serve them. The common run of courtiers find them appalling."

"It would seem to me," Senenmut said, "that such people would die early and unpleasantly."

"That's the other half of the lesson," Hapuseneb said. "Always tell the truth, but always tell it from a position of power. Show no fear. Look even the king in the eye, and never think it insolence."

"Dangerous advice," Senenmut said, "for a cocky boy whom you have never seen before."

Hapuseneb laughed and saluted him. "There! You see? You know it. You're not as cocky as you used to be, are you? Waiting on kings can do that. There's no contending with a king for sheer and headlong arrogance."

"What of queens? I'll wager there's one who puts kings to shame."

"She does, at that," Hapuseneb said. He peered under his hand at the river. The sun was descending from noon; in an hour, maybe a little more, it would shine direct into his eyes. "Then again," he said, "it takes a king to drag his entire household off at dawn to hunt river-birds, and never relieve his lesser servants of the obligation to wait on him. So we wait, and he hunts ducks in the reeds."

"Gods may do as they please," Senenmut said.

"So devout," said Hapuseneb. "The gods must love you." He reached under his robe and drew out a packet. "Here, I've dates, and a bit of cheese. Shall we have a feast?"

Why not? thought Senenmut. His anger had lost itself somewhere. This untypical priest was refreshing. Intelligent too, and amusing. Altogether he was excellent company.

If one had to wait about while the queen indulged her husband's whim, there were worse ways than this, sitting on the quay by the palace with courtiers either sneering or looking on incredulous, sharing dates and cheese and beer with a priest of Amon. Senenmut had bread in a napkin, his mother's good baking; it was received with delight. They shared it back and forth, eating till they were replete.

■ The sun rode low when the king came back, riding the current down the river. There had been a wind, but with the approach of evening it had died to a whisper. The last heat of the day lay like a living presence on city and quay: a great slow-breathing animal, heavy with sleep.

Senenmut started out of a drowse. Hapuseneb was still snoring. Others of those who waited had moved away from the riverside, forming in ranks as if they had been in court. The priests and the scribe found themselves set well apart. Since some of the priests out of their season in the temple were courtiers, there was a degree of irony in that.

It was irony also that the priests were farther upriver than the rest, and therefore had a clearer view of the fleet as it approached the quay. Prows and masts were gilded, and the oars likewise, prodigal of wealth as only royalty could be. Strains of music floated over the water, harp and flute and drum, tambour and sistrum, and the high sweet voice of a singer.

Senenmut did not trouble to count the boats in the fleet. Most were full of courtiers or servants. Only one mattered: the great golden barge that rode before the rest, long and broad as a hall in the palace, crowded with oarsmen, musicians, fan-bearers, people trained to fetch this dainty or that. The cooks rode beside and just behind the barge with their oven-fires lit and savory scents wafting on the faint hint of breeze.

As long as it had been since he and Hapuseneb divided the last of the bread, he forgot the growling in his stomach to stare with a wholly different hunger at the man who stood in the prow of the barge. There was a golden canopy amidships, and a pair of golden thrones set under it, and the queen in one with her maids behind her. But the king, it seemed, had grown restless. He had left his throne. He wore the Blue Crown, the crown of a warrior, and a fine white kilt belted with gold, and golden sandals.

He was not a tall man, nor a particularly prepossessing one except for the crown he wore. His face was like his sister-wife's, oval, delicate in features except for a noble jut of nose. His body was lightly but compactly built, his shoulders wide, well-muscled and strong. A woman might find him attractive. Senenmut had no such thoughts, nor would he allow himself to think them.

He was staring at the living god, Horus on earth, lord of the Red Land and the Black Land, Great House of Egypt, Thutmose son of Thutmose of the line of Ahmose. The living god was a man with a stern and rather chilly face and a voice rough-edged as if he had honed it on the battlefield, exchanging some pleasantry with one of the princes privileged to stand behind him. He was a warrior king, a leader of armies: that much everyone knew of him. He looked as if he hated to be still, hated worse to vex himself with the consequentialities of state.

His eyes were quick, as brightly alive as his face was stern. It was a mask, then, a trained thing. What it must do to a man to be king and god, to be constrained to a life of perpetual and unrelenting ceremony . . .

Senenmut had never thought such thoughts before. It came of sitting next to the priest of Amon, full of his beer and wanting badly to piss. But a man could hardly aim a stream into the river, with the king sailing right past him.

The king did not appear to see the people gathered on the quay. The barge had barely touched the bank before he leaped out, striding past rows of men flung suddenly on their faces, with his servants scrambling to follow.

The queen conducted herself with more decorum. Among the servants who followed her from the boat were several with bows and quivers of arrows, and strings of fat geese and ducks and long-legged wading birds. There would be a feast in the palace tonight.

She did not look as if she had quarreled with her husband. Her expression was serene to boredom, her movements languid, unhurried. Bearers waited with a golden chair, to carry her to the palace. She stepped into it without visible reluctance. They carried her away.

One of her servants, a maid whom Senenmut had not seen before, left the company of her fellows and approached the scribe and the priests. She spoke as if the words were grains of barley flung at a flock of geese. "He wants to go hunting again tomorrow. She's to go with him. You'll be here at dawn, ready to embark. Be prepared to be amusing."

Senenmut opened his mouth, but shut it again. Hapuseneb smiled his gaptoothed smile. "We can always be amusing. Are they fighting again?"

"They never fight," the maid said frigidly.

"I'm sure," said Hapuseneb.

The maid turned on her heel. Hapuseneb watched her go with open pleasure.

She was much more pleasant to look at than to listen to. Senenmut caught himself before he sank too deeply into contemplation of her beauty. The way the long plaits of her hair swung as she walked, brushing her hips behind . . .

"Yes," said Hapuseneb. "Oh, yes."

Senenmut thrust himself to his feet. He must have muttered a farewell: Hapuseneb replied to it in kind. He was careful to take another way than the one the maid had taken. Since he was going into the city rather than to the palace, it led him well away from her.

And why he ran away from a maid when he was bold enough to face the queen, he did not know. Maybe because the queen piqued his pride, but the maid aroused a much less lofty portion of his anatomy. Pride he knew. That other thing he had never had much time for, nor indulged it when he had leisure.

She would laugh if she knew. Most women would. He tucked his head down and beat his way through the crowds that thronged the city, escaping to the sanctuary of his father's house.

7

THE KING WAS IN A DANGEROUS MOOD.

"He needs a war," Nehsi said.

The queen's lip curled. "I shall never understand this need of men," she said. "What profit is there in fighting one another?"

"Much," said Nehsi, "if the conquered is rich in gold and captives."

"That is not what I meant," she said. "Why do men fight with spears and swords? Aren't words enough?"

"In most cases, no," Nehsi said. Since, after all, she had asked.

She tossed her head in its heavy plaited wig. She was preparing for the feast. Her maids labored through her temper to make her as beautiful as a queen should be, but she was not making it easy for them.

"He may want a war," she said, "but he won't have one just yet. I'll give him something to think about instead."

Nehsi followed her glance. Isis the maidservant had been given the task of clothing the queen in her court gown of sheerest linen. She had not been given to the king yet. The queen was awaiting her moment.

"Is this the time?" he asked. "With the king so out of sorts, and insisting on hunting when he should be attending to matters of state—"

"When better?" said the queen. "He's bored. He needs distraction. I'll give it to him: set it in his way and let him do with it as he pleases."

"It may work," Nehsi admitted. "But the moment he finds himself a war, he'll forget everything but that."

"Certainly," she said, "but it might delay him for a while. If he learns well and quickly, well enough that he's fit to come to my bed, then I may be with child when he goes away again."

"That is an end devoutly to be desired," said Nehsi. "But, lady—"

She ignored him. She beckoned to Isis. "Here, child. Come here."

Isis came obediently, eyes lowered, and bowed as she had been taught, kneeling with becoming grace and touching her forehead to the floor.

"Tonight," the queen said, "do as I told you to do when the time was ripe. Be prominent among my servants. Let the king see you, and let him desire you. If he lacks the wits to do more, enlighten him. See that he takes you to his bed."

Isis, still bowed to the floor, said softly but clearly, "Yes, lady. I remember."

If she trembled with either fear or excitement, Nehsi did not see it. Sometimes he wondered if it was intelligence she lacked, or simply a normal human portion of wariness. She trusted too well. She was afraid of no one, nor saw the need to be.

The queen found that useful. He wondered, himself, how loyal such a creature could be, without fear to bind her.

Whatever his misgivings, the queen had decided. Isis would seduce

the king tonight, and teach him if she could to be a lover of women
rather than a soldier who took his bedmates, like his enemies, by storm.
Nehsi could hope that once Isis was done, the king would turn willingly to the queen.

■ Feasts in the court of Thutmose, son of Thutmose, began before sunset and ran the night long. This one began late but showed no sign of
ending earlier. They were all gathered in the great hall of feasting,
tables laid among the pillars, and the king on his throne at the head of
the hall. Naked servants ran without rest, bringing in jars of wine and
beer, platters of dainties, all the booty of the day's hunt, and for the
great of appetite a whole ox borne in on a palanquin like a prince, with
flowers wound about its horns, and fruits heaped about it, and bread,
and savory cakes.

Most of the men and all of the ladies wore cones of scented fat atop
their wigs, that melted as the night went on and the heat of their rev-
elry mounted, streaming down over the elaborate edifices of curls and
plaits, dripping in their faces. The mingling of a myriad perfumes
shocked the nose into numbness, caught at the back of the throat and
made thirst a constant and urgent thing.

The king was a great man for wine, and he served only the best,
the royal vintage, sweet and dizzyingly strong. He was eating little,
Nehsi noticed. He had the look of a man who drinks to find oblivion,
an expression of boredom sunk deep and gone sour.

He was not in any mood or condition to notice one naked servant
among a hundred, even if she were nearly beside him, waiting on the
queen. His eyes were fixed on the wine in his cup, or, with blurred intensity, on the shadows that flocked near the roof of the hall, fleeing
the lights and clamor below. Perhaps he was seeing the heat and tumult of a battlefield, tasting the heady wine of terror.

Isis sought to catch his eye each time she filled the queen's cup or
arranged a new delicacy on the queen's plate. It was clear but not bla-
tant: a curve of the body just so, to show the lovely line of hip; an inclination forward to let her breasts swing enticingly; a shift about on
pretext of relieving another servant of a platter of spiced cakes, so that

he could see the sweet rounding of her buttocks. Nehsi, schooled though he was to ignore temptation while he stood guard, felt a stirring that he could not mistake. A stone could not have resisted that most lovely of women when she set herself to drive a man wild.

A stone, or the king in his cups. He was not even aware that she existed. He took each filled cup blindly from the hand of his cupbearer, drank it dry, held out his hand for the next.

The queen was watching. Nehsi saw how her eyes narrowed. She beckoned to Isis, whispered. Isis nodded, bowed deeply. She circled round to the king's chair and leaned toward the cupbearer. That personage was well above taking heed of any mere maidservant, but a maidservant bearing a command from the queen required at least a moment of his attention.

He obeyed ungraciously, but obey he did. Quietly, without a word to the king, he drew deep from the jar of water before he filled the cup lightly with wine. The king, as the queen must have hoped, grimaced but did not appear to notice why the flavor of the vintage had grown so weak.

Then Isis did a thing that the queen could not have asked her to do, because it was impossibly, unthinkably bold. She plucked the next cup from the cupbearer's hand and set it teasingly just out of the king's reach. He groped. She shifted it. He lifted bleared eyes.

They must have been full of her. She stood close, so close that he could have seen nothing else. Her smile was impossibly sweet. She slid into his lap, effrontery beyond effrontery, and linked arms about his neck, and said, "Aren't I sweeter than wine, O beloved of Horus?"

To Nehsi's astonishment, no one seemed to have noticed her audacity. The hall was hazy with wine and sweat and the heat of bodies crowded together. Anyone alert enough to see clearly was watching a display of dancers and acrobats, all of them beautiful, all of them impossibly supple.

The queen, who did see, could hardly contest the execution of her own order. She pretended to be engrossed in a confection of flowers dipped in honey. The maid Meritre served her wine that was mostly water, with which she took issue. "If you must feed me water," she said sharply, "feed it untainted with wine."

Meritre bowed low and did just that.

But they were both, surreptitiously, watching how Isis wound herself about the king. No one could hear what she said—the hall was too hideously noisy, and she said it direct to the king's ear. It was difficult to see what he was thinking. His face was never very expressive; when he was sodden with wine it set into a mask.

Isis nibbled the royal ear. The king shivered perceptibly and tensed, lurching to his feet. Isis clung. Now, Nehsi thought, he would fling her off. His arms tightened about her, lifted her. Nehsi held his breath.

Isis giggled, clear in the lull that will fall on any crowd, even the most boisterous. To Nehsi's lasting astonishment, the king echoed her. He shifted her, but not to cast her off; to settle her more securely. Lightly, quickly, and much more steadily than Nehsi would have thought possible, he bore her out of the hall.

■ The queen was not jealous. She told Nehsi so, repeatedly. She had ordered this. She had planned it from the first, set the bait and sprung the trap.

She paced her chambers in the dark before dawn, when the air was as cool as it ever became in Thebes in the season between Inundations of the Nile. Her robes and wig were laid aside; she had on a kilt like a boy, but she was no boy to look at, even so young. She could stride out in it, and stride she did, stiff-legged, fists clenched at her sides, waiting for Isis to come back. If Isis came back. The king might keep her with him. That would be a triumph.

"But she must come back to me," said Hatshepsut fiercely.

Nehsi swallowed a yawn. A sleepless queen meant a sleepless guard; and when she was in this mood she wanted no other guard but Nehsi. She was not above dragging him out of the bed he had just fallen into, and demanding that he watch while she paced her state bedchamber with its golden bed and its headrest of chalcedony inlaid with gold, regarding none of that, aware only of her own confusion.

"You could," he said, "distract yourself."

She stopped her pacing and whirled. Oh, she was distracted: into a fine hot fury, with him as the target. "Are you saying that I am as scatterbrained as my husband, may he live a thousand years?"

"Your husband," said Nehsi, "may he live a thousand years, is as nothing to the brilliance of your sagacity."

"Are you trying to make me laugh, or are you tempting me to kill you?"

He looked her up and down as she stood there. After a while he said, "You aren't a child any longer, that's clear to see."

"And I'm acting like one," she said. She could do that: see with bitter clarity, and say what she must say, as if there were two halves of her, the one that paced and snarled and hissed with temper, and the other, the quiet one, the one that was never less than calm.

But he shook his head. "No," he said. "It's not a child who says these things, or does the thing that sparked them. This is a woman's trouble. You don't love or greatly like your husband, but you're not as willing as you thought you were, to share him. He is, after all, yours."

"Do you think he would share me?" she demanded. And when he was silent: "I thought not. But it's women who have to share, isn't it? Never men. They take what pleases them, and keep it, and never willingly let it go."

"Like you," said Nehsi, "lady and queen."

Someday, he thought with distant clarity, she would have him flayed for the things he said to her. But not yet. It was her eccentricity, in this her youth, to favor servants who spoke freely to her. Time and queenship would alter that.

Until then, he was suffered to live with a whole skin. She stared at him for a long moment, a dark, deadly level stare. "Yes," she said. "Like me. I'm not like other women, am I? I am the queen. The king will learn to be worthy of me. As for the woman I sent to him . . ." She paused. In the pause she wandered to a chair and sat in it, as close to relaxation as she had come since this night began. "If she fails to return by full morning, find her and bring her to me."

Nehsi bowed. "Lady," he said.

And now maybe she would let him go back to his too brief, too often interrupted rest.

He should have known better. "Stay with me," she said, "till she comes back or you go after her. I've no sleep in me. Where's the board? We'll play at Hounds and Jackals till the sun comes up."

Nehsi swallowed a sigh, and the yawn that went with it. The board was where she had left it the last time she challenged him to a match, on a table in her sitting-room. He fetched it and set it before her, slipping the tall counters from their place inside the golden board: ivory hounds, ebon jackals like images of Anubis who watches over the dead. It was her humor to choose the jackals and leave him the hounds, ebony hand on ivory counters as they pursued one another round the board.

He was direly short on sleep and growing short on temper, which made him a deadly player of Hounds and Jackals. He was not in the least minded to let her win, even if she would have suffered it. And win he did, thrice over, and the fourth time she won by a jackal's whisker. And after that the sun came up, and still no Isis bowing at her lady's feet, telling in her soft sweet voice of her night's lessoning of the king.

■ Nehsi had never been a coward, but the thought of approaching the king's chambers and demanding to see the king's new concubine gave him more than a moment's pause. Still he had his orders, and he was an obedient servant.

The gods favored him, though perhaps they mocked the queen. Just as Nehsi girded himself to venture the king's portion of the inner palace, the queen's doorguard let in Isis herself. Nehsi, whom fortune had placed at the door as she entered it, could see her unguarded face, the face he doubted very much that she would show the queen. It had the look of a cat in cream: sleek and richly sated.

Before the queen she was properly demure, keeping her head down lest her eyes betray her. The queen, still in her kilt but with maids fluttering about, trying to coax her toward the baths and the day's toilet, stood over her like an image of a conquering king. "Well?" she demanded.

"Lady," Isis said, soft and seeming shy, "by your leave I did well. He said that he was pleased. He asked me to come back tonight."

"Yes?"

"Yes, lady. I—I tried to do what you said, lady. I made him take a bath first, and anoint himself, not too heavily. He was angry, lady, but it only made him the more eager. He said that I was insolent. Beauty, he said, excuses much, but I should remember who he is. I told him that I never forget."

Hatshepsut frowned, but she was nodding: reluctant but accepting the girl's skill. If of course she told the truth; but what profit could she see in a lie? The slant of her glance was not honest, but it was not false, either. She was telling less than she might but inventing nothing, in Nehsi's judgment.

"And did you rein him in," the queen asked, "and insist that he learn the virtues of gentleness?"

"I tried, lady," Isis said. "He was clumsy, if I may say it, but not cruel. No one ever told him what to do before. He didn't like it at first, but I taught him to think better of it."

"Did you?" Hatshepsut studied her. She did not look up, continued to fix her eyes on the floor, with glances aside: at Nehsi, at the maids, at the glitter of a golden necklace on the queen's table.

She coveted that, Nehsi thought. The king had not sent her away empty-handed: there was something plaited into the thick masses of her hair, something that let slip a gleam of brightness.

The queen, who could be very quick of eye when she chose, saw the direction of Isis' glance. She beckoned to the chief of her maidservants. "Mayet, my lesser jewel-box, if you please."

When Mayet had brought it, the queen plucked from it a pretty thing, a necklace of blue beads and golden blossoms. Isis received it with open pleasure. "Wear it and prosper," Hatshepsut said, "and remember always why you do this. Now go. The king will want you near him; see that he has his desire."

Isis bowed to the floor, slipped the necklace about her neck and backed away. When she came to her feet past the door, still just within Nehsi's sight, she was stroking the necklace and smiling a sly cat-smile.

8

SENENMUT HAD DREAMED WHEN HE was very young of a royal hunt in all its glory. The king, Senenmut imagined, went out in his golden boat with his court and his princes and all their servants and hangers-on. He sat at ease on his throne with the Two Crowns on his head, arranged in the impossible contortion of his painted images, bending a golden bow and bringing down his quarry with an arrow tipped with gold.

Senenmut's dream was not so very far from the truth. Gold of course was too soft to keep either edge or point, but the shafts of the king's arrows were certainly gilded, and likewise the bow. He did not keep to his throne however; he preferred to stand in the prow, face to the wind, while his beaters sent up clamoring flocks for him to shoot. When he signaled by lowering his bow that he had had enough, the rest of his companions could take what quarry was left: always enough, for the beds of reeds were rich in waterfowl.

Senenmut could not see the city from here, though they were not remarkably far from it. They might have been all alone in a wilderness of reeds and river, bounded by the bleak cliffs of the Red Land, the desert that held the Black Land of Egypt in its hard dry hands.

He had not expected to enjoy himself. And yet he was almost happy, sitting at the queen's feet with a book across his knees, dictating to her while she wrote on a bit of papyrus and her husband engrossed himself in his hunt. A canopy shielded them both from the sun; there was a breeze playing over the water, a breath of coolness. The shouts of men, the cries of birds alarmed or wounded, mingled with the lapping of waves and the rustle of reeds and the sound of his own voice reciting a hymn to Amon. He even heard, faintly, the scritch of her pen on papyrus, and the soft snores of Hapuseneb the priest, who, like Senenmut, had obeyed the queen's command to accompany her on this hunt.

She was not as content as Senenmut was. However dazzled by sun and honor and royal splendor he might be, he could not fail to see the shadows under her eyes. Paint obscured but did not altogether conceal them. Her Nubian was not with her, he noticed. Another guardsman stood closest to her, a silent and expressionless Egyptian.

She was attentive enough to Senenmut's teaching, focused on it perhaps as a refuge against tedium. Hunting clearly did not delight her as it did the king. She hardly glanced up when a whoop marked a particularly shrewd shot; she grimaced slightly as a goose, pierced to the heart, fell broken-winged nearly at her feet.

The king seemed oblivious to his queen's lack of enthusiasm. Nothing could free him entirely from the bonds of his kingship, but here, away from the city and the press of the court, he showed himself a different man. He was lighter of heart, quicker, more eager; he laughed at a sally, and cast one back in kind. None of it was particularly witty. It was soldier's humor, more crude than elegant.

How he must love to ride on campaign, Senenmut thought, watching him as he received the news that a herd of river-horses had been found just ahead. He had come prepared to hunt water-birds, but the larger prey brought a gleam to his eye. He barely hesitated before he leaped into one of the smaller boats. His weapons-bearer scrambled after, and as many of his guards as the boat could carry.

The barge could not follow where he went. The thickets of reeds were too dense, the channels too narrow. It moored where the bank was almost clear of reeds, where might have been a village once but was no longer: a stand of date-palms, a mound or two that might have been the remnants of a mudbrick house. The desert had encroached on it, but nearest the river it was green still.

The queen and her attendants, undismayed to be left behind, settled to their various pursuits: reading, sleeping, playing on the harp or singing to it. She alone seemed restless. She was thinking, Senenmut guessed, of the duties she had left behind by her husband's order, the petitioners gathering in the empty audience-hall, the scribes and clerks waiting to inundate her with papyrus. He knew enough of her by now to know that she felt the dereliction of her duty. What else she felt for it, he could not tell.

Some people were cursed to be perpetually dutiful. Senenmut, who shared the curse, found himself closer to liking the queen than he had been before. She did not know how to dally about, either, nor what to do with herself when she was not engaged in something useful.

Her face mastered itself, maintained its expression of royal blandness, but she could not seem to govern her glances. He watched defiance grow in her eyes. The noise of the hunt had faded up the river; the wind that blew from the north carried the last of it away.

It was remarkably easy to read her. One only needed to watch the eyes, and the slight movements of the hands, clenching and unclenching on the arms of her throne. Yesterday she had done all as his majesty desired. Ignored once she was trapped on the throne beside his, unregarded except as mute companion to his splendor, she had whiled the day in deadly tedium.

Today, with her scribe to instruct her and her musicians to play for her and Hapuseneb the priest for amusement, she was all the less willing to be counted among the furnishings of the king's barge. Hapuseneb rattled on at her, some charming nonsense about a monkey and a baboon and the god Thoth. Senenmut barely listened; neither, he suspected, did she.

He watched her resolve harden. She silenced the priest with a gesture, beckoned to the steersman. "Return us to the city," she said.

The steersman stared at her. The others were mute. Not all were hers. Some were the king's, too, many for the smaller boat, or too languid to contest for a place in it.

She faced the steersman with all the arrogance of her blood and breeding. "Do as I say," she commanded him.

For a moment Senenmut thought that the man would resist. But he was only startled. At length he fumbled a bow. "Yes, lady. Yes—yes, lady. At once, lady."

Someone sucked in a breath, perhaps in outrage. No one spoke. She was, after all, the queen. The king was not there to countermand her. He would perforce return home in lesser state than was strictly fitting, but the queen was in no mood to care for that.

Rowing against the freshening wind, taking what aid the current could offer, the royal barge made surprisingly good speed back to Thebes. Senenmut was a little sorry to see the city's walls ahead. He had conceived a fondness, perhaps even a passion, for the freedom of the river.

Still he was as duty-bound as the queen, and there was work to do: two kingdoms' worth. Someday, he swore to himself, he would be rich enough to have not only a boat for the river but a house beside it, an estate worthy of a prince, where he could take his rest from the vexations of power.

■ The king was as angry as Hatshepsut had expected; as Nehsi had known he would be. He came back late, as the sun was setting, with a king of river-horses dead and flyblown in the boat behind him. There would be no feast tonight, although the cooks took the river-horse to prepare it for the morrow.

The queen had taken her dinner in her garden by the lotus pool, where she liked to dine if she was alone. The king found her there. He came with few attendants, in little state, wearing the lapis-and-gold striped linen of the *nemes*-headdress and the simplicity of a soldier's kilt.

He stood over her as she sat by the pool with the remains of her dinner. He was not tall, none of his line were, but he was taller than she, even if she had stood; and he was using every finger-length of it. "You left me out there," he said.

She looked up slowly, taking her time about it, as if she had no fear in the world. In anyone else it would have been insolence. She said in a sweet soft voice that she never used with anyone she liked or trusted, "You had your hunt and your guards and your fleet. I had duties that called me till I had no choice but to answer. Did you know that there's a cattle plague in the Delta? Or that the fourth and fifth nomes are quarrelling again, and their nomarchs would go to war if they could? Or that the priests of Amon and the priests of Ptah are contesting precedence even into the halls of audience? Are you aware of any of that?"

He might have struck her, but her eyes were too steady. She had never been afraid of anything but the dark. He settled for a slash of the hand that was more petulant than royally disdainful, and a curl of the lip as he said, "I am aware of it. Must I concern myself with it every moment of every day? May not even a god enjoy a respite?"

"Certainly," she said. "But not two days running, and not in such haste that it looks like the whim of a child. You left lords and princes dangling while you indulged yourself. One of us at least had to repair the insult."

"Nothing is an insult if a god wills it," the king said haughtily.

"You," she said, "are such a child. Go play with your wooden soldiers, and leave the rest of us to tend your kingdom."

He drew himself rigidly erect. Whatever words might have flooded out of him, he was able or willing to utter none of them. He turned on his heel and stalked out, precisely like the child she had called him.

■ Nehsi remembered at last to breathe. The queen's eyes were fixed on the place where her husband had stood. If a glance could be a sword, his blood would have poured out on the earth.

It was a long while before she spoke. When she did, it was so quietly, so calmly, that one could almost miss the white heat of passion in it. "Why? Why was it all given to him, and only the dregs to me? What is so splendid, so wonderful, so all-powerful about a man, that even a puling child can be king, but a woman cannot even dream of it?"

There were answers to that. Priests had them in plenty, and kings, and soldiers too. Nehsi kept his tongue between his teeth. If he knew every answer a man could imagine, then his lady knew it, too.

Hatshepsut held up her hands. They were small hands, oval, long-fingered but broad in the palm, more strong than delicate. For all the struggles of her maids to keep them white and soft, they were more like a boy's than a woman's. "These can bend a bow," she said, "hold the reins of a chariot-team, clasp a scepter. What can his do that these cannot? Bend a bigger bow? I can bend a bigger one than my scribe can, I'll wager you that. Master a team of half-broken stallions? I've done that, and done it well. Wield the scepter in the hall of audience? And what else did I do today while my great royal husband, my lord of the Two Lands, my living Horus, amused himself hunting river-horses in the reeds?"

She rose and began to pace. She looked remarkably like the king in one of his own fits of restlessness: a likeness she would not have been pleased to acknowledge. "He is older than I," she said. "But I am the daughter of the royal wife. He is the child of a concubine. He holds kingship only through me. And does he thank me for it? Does he even notice that I exist?" She tossed her head in scorn. "Oh, certainly! When I get in the way of his pleasure—then he remembers me."

Nehsi considered for some time before venturing to speak. She paced, prowling round the garden. She plucked a blossom, drew in its scent, let it fall into the lotus pool.

"Lady," he said, "the gods have made him king. There must be gentler ways to remind him of it."

She rounded upon him. "What? Do you mean that girl, that Isis? As if she could be anything more than a goddess' plaything. Would you have her flatter him into doing his duty?"

"She might beguile his nights sufficiently that he can endure the days of drudgery."

"It is not drudgery. It is the price the gods exact for making him one of them. It's a great thing, a noble thing, a thing of beauty and splendor, to wear the Two Crowns; to be king of Egypt. And he," she said, "has no faintest conception of the honor. Only of the burden— which he far too often evades."

"It's no burden to you, either?" asked Nehsi. He honestly wanted to know.

"Of course it is a burden," she said impatiently. "I won't run away from it for that."

"Do you want to be king?"

She stared at him as if she had never seen him before. He wondered briefly if she ever had. High ones, he had noticed, often treated their servants as they did their animals and their furnishings: took them for granted, and never truly looked at them, nor cared to know what thoughts lay behind the familiar faces. True enough, most servants were content with that. But Nehsi was a fool. Nehsi wanted to be seen for himself.

It was a surprising discomfort to be visible. He worried suddenly that his kilt was crooked, his belt ill fastened, his cheeks too roughly shaven.

He was impeccable as he always strove to be. She could not see the flush on his cheeks, either, nor—he hoped—read his expression.

At much too long last she answered the question he had asked. "What does it matter whether I want to be king? I never can be. The least of the laborers in the fields is more likely than I to wear the Two Crowns. He has only to marry me and to claim the throne, and it is his. I who am a woman—I can never be more than the king's wife."

"That is not so little," Nehsi said.

"But is it enough?" she demanded. "Is it, Nehsi? Is it?"

He could not answer her. She did it for him.

"It must be, mustn't it? Since the gods have ordained that he be king, and I be his queen."

The words hinted at resignation, but her voice was sharp still with rebellion. She went on pacing, silent now, ignoring him. He was invisible again: a chair she had no mind to sit in, an image in ebony of a forgotten king.

It was better than being seen, pierced to the heart by those big dark eyes.

Oh, yes. He was in love with his headstrong young queen. It would never be more than it was now, nor did he wish it to be. She trusted him. She told him things that no one else could know. Even this: that she could have worn the Two Crowns with far more grace than her husband ever had.

The gods would never allow it. Pity; but gods were gods. Once they had fixed upon a thing, there was no changing it.

9

ONE MORNING NOT LONG AFTER THE queen sailed away undismissed from the king's hunt, a messenger found Senenmut among the queen's scribes. It was a woman, one of the royal maids: the one with the perpetual sniff of scorn, as if the world were beneath her notice. "She wants you," she said, inelegant to rude-ness.

Senenmut was tempted to keep her waiting. But he had finished the letter he was given to copy into the archives, and the next was both long and difficult, as well as crashingly dull: an accounting of the revenues of the nomes of Upper Egypt. He left it gratefully.

The maid led him not to the queen's chambers as he had expected, nor to the hall where she held audiences and administered the affairs of the Two Kingdoms. The way was not one he had taken before. It led away from the inner palace and even from the outer one, to the wall that rimmed and warded the palace. Built into and along the wall were stables, barracks, armories: a kingdom of men and war, as alien to the scented quiet of the queen's apartments as Senenmut's family's house to the House of Life.

The queen was in the royal stables. She looked strange, a little, with her artfully painted face, in the scent of hay and horses. But her gown was plain and her ornaments simple, and her wig was the short Nu-bian wig that both men and women wore when they would be practi-cal. She was deep in converse with a tall and imposing personage, a hawk-nosed, bearded foreigner in a striped coat. From the look and the scent of him, he was a master of horse.

The subject of their discussion, a chestnut-colored horse with a white nose, stood patiently beside the foreigner. It was newly come, it seemed, as tribute from a king in Asia. The foreigner spoke Egyptian with a heavy accent, but Senenmut understood him well enough. "No, I think not the whitefoot mare for a chariot-mate to this one. She's too short of stride. This beauty pours herself over the ground like a lioness in the desert. The mare they call Star of Hathor—she has the move-ment, and she has some need of a calming influence."

"Well then," the queen said. "Call her Moon of Isis and try her in the yoke with Hathor's Star."

The foreigner bowed deeply in the Asiatic fashion. "It shall be as your majesty wishes."

Hatshepsut nodded briskly and moved down the line of tethered horses. She could not have failed to see Senenmut, but she was choos-ing not to acknowledge him. Partly at a loss, partly to be contrary, he followed her. The master of horse was just ahead of him, the maid just behind.

Near the end of the line, almost to a wall with a door in it, the queen's Nubian guardsman busied himself about a fine blood bay. The queen nodded to him but kept walking through the door and out into a broad and sandy court. It was full of the thunder of hoofs and the rattle of chariot wheels.

Senenmut had never seen a place like it. The glare of sun through a haze of dust. The snorting of horses, the champing of bits, the snap of a whip and the sharper snap of a charioteer's voice, calling to order a fractious team. The reek of dust and dung and sweat that was Egypt was overlaid here with the pungent-pleasant scent of horses.

He had always loved horses. They were new in the Two Lands, brought in by the kings whom no one named, the foreigners who dared to conquer Egypt. Those were a hundred years gone, driven out and rightly so. Egypt had effaced their names from the earth, willed to forget them; but it had kept their gift of horses. Horses drew chariots; chariots carried princes who not so long ago would have been condemned to march and to fight on their own feet. Now they could ride, and carry their weapons without inconvenience, and strike swift against their enemies.

But Senenmut loved the horses for themselves, for their beauty and fire, their strength and their swiftness and the drumming of their feet on the earth. He had not known before how splendid their eyes were, fiercer than the eyes of cattle, with a keener intelligence. Nor had he suspected that they would welcome him with the rush of warm breath in his palm, lipping it, forbearing to bite.

He ventured to stroke a sleek red-brown neck. It arched under his hand, and the horse snorted, tossing its head. He held his ground. It meant him no harm. He could see that in its eyes.

Servants brought out two of the horses: a pair as like as two pups in a litter, red-golden both, with pale manes. A chariot waited, handsome enough but not nearly as magnificent as the state chariots that Senenmut had seen. This was meant for use.

The horses set themselves in place for the yoke, opened mouths for the bits. They were eager: one pawed lightly as the chariot was hitched behind.

The queen sprang into the chariot and took the reins from the groom. "You," she said, flashing a glance at Senenmut. "Ride with me."

He stood flatfooted. Of course she would be asking for him, since she had had him brought here. But why in the world . . . ?

The horses backed against the traces, dancing with impatience. The queen reined them in. "Come!" she commanded him.

He hardly knew which foot to lift first. The Nubian seized him with effortless strength and tossed him into the chariot behind the queen. He staggered, clutched at the first thing that presented itself: the queen's body.

She most graciously declined to cry sacrilege. He pried his arms from their panic-lock about her middle and found a more permissible thing to cling to: the side of the chariot, with its rim rolled by design or by accident into the most useful shape for gripping hard to keep one's balance.

Once he had recovered from the shock of being thrust into a swift-moving, sharp-turning chariot, Senenmut began to take a keen and still half-terrified pleasure in it. He saw how the queen stood, light, poised, firm yet supple, riding with the lift and sway of the chariot-floor under her feet. She held the reins lightly, not strained back against them as he had seen others do, battling the horses' will to run. She rode with them, coaxing rather than compelling.

She did not, as he had expected, ride among the rest in the court of the chariots. She directed her horses toward the gate and out along the palace wall. A second chariot followed, with the Nubian for charioteer. He had no companion, nor seemed to need any. If there were an attack—as if such a thing could happen in the heart of royal Thebes—Senenmut supposed that he would bind the reins about his waist and fight as kings fought in the histories, strong-armed against thousands.

He still could not imagine what the queen could want of him. He was a scribe. He knew nothing of horses or of chariotry.

As if she had plucked the thought from his mind, she thrust the reins into his hands. They trembled like living things. The right-hand horse tossed its head. Senenmut willed his fingers to unclench. "Lady," he said. "What am I supposed to—"

"Steady," she said. "Light and soft. No, not loose! Feel the horses always."

He fought the rigidity of shock and awe. He—he, Senenmut, whose father was a seller of pots—was a charioteer. A poor and vastly nervous one, as the queen pointed out with acid precision; but he held the reins and the horses obeyed him.

It grew easier, the longer he did it. He declined to commit the error of cockiness; but he felt magnificent, like a prince, driving the queen's chariot round the walls of the palace.

It was glorious. Yet he had to ask. When he was surer of himself, when the horses seemed in hand and the road's curve not too taxing, he spoke the word. "Why?"

The queen could have pretended not to understand. It rather pleased him that she did not. "Because," she said.

He tensed. The horses jibbed. He made himself ease, for their sake. "You thought you could mock me. Didn't you? You expected me to be run away with."

"If I had wanted that," she said mildly, "I would have called for the new mare, and had her yoked with a stranger. These are my best, my queens. No one else has ever driven them, except on occasion my Nubian."

"Then why?" Senenmut demanded.

She shrugged, maddening as a woman can be, and a young one worst of all. "I thought you might like it." She paused. "Do you?"

No. He would not believe it. That she would give him a gift, simply for the sake of giving it. She was a queen. Queens gave nothing of their free will, with no expectation of return.

"What am I supposed to do, to pay for this?" he asked her.

She was angry: he saw the flush on her cheek, that was almost alarmingly close. When the chariot swayed, she swayed against him, inevitably. She did not seem to notice how often their bodies touched.

Nor would he, nor should he, if he had not been a fool. Another woman would have meant to seduce him, if she had done as this one did. But Hatshepsut was hardly aware yet that she was a woman.

"There is a price," he persisted. "There must be."

"Yes," she said. "That you take pleasure in it. That you be as glad of it as I am of the words you teach me."

He felt his brow climbing. "Gratitude? From a queen?"

"Even from a queen," she said.

"But," he said. "Why this?"

That shrug again. "It seemed like nothing you'd tried before. And," she added after a moment, "any number of fine young princes would give their hope of an afterlife to ride where you ride now. Though none of them would suffer me to teach them."

"So that's why," he said. "Because I've never done it. You need to master me."

"I can master any man," said the queen with a lift of the chin. "I saw your face when you looked at the horses. I wanted you to have them. You want them, you see. So many of the rest . . . they don't care. You do."

What, a hint of softness? Senenmut was astonished.

It dawned on him that perhaps she liked him. He did not see why. He was sharp-tongued, waspish for a fact; he had no patience to speak of; and he had never been pretty to look at.

Strange was the mind of a woman.

"You should," she said, "exercise your body as well as your mind and hand. I'll not have you squatting like a toad in the scribes' house whenever you aren't instructing me. You may consider yourself commanded to learn the art of chariotry. The bow, too, I think; and perhaps the spear, for hunting."

"I thought you hated to hunt," Senenmut broke in on her.

"Oh, no," she said. "Why would you think that?"

He opened his mouth, closed it again.

She laughed. "Ah! You saw me in my husband's hunt. But that, O scribe of mine, was folly, time wasted, a kingdom left dangling while its king indulged his whim. The kingdom must come first in the heart of a king. When he's attended to it—then let him hunt, let him race his chariots, let him do whatever he pleases."

Somewhere in their colloquy she had taken back the reins and slowed the horses to a walk. They had nearly circled the palace round. Just as they would have turned and passed through the gate that led to the court of the chariots, she straightened their heads, bidding them circle the palace again.

They rode for a while in silence. Senenmut understood at last: or well enough. It was not a simple thing that she was doing. At its heart it was a message to her husband, a lesson that he should learn.

Senenmut doubted that the king would even notice. He had not seemed an observant man. And with this queen, one must watch every movement, measure every moment. She was headstrong, and she could be reckless, but in her way she was subtle. Too subtle for such a man as the king seemed to be.

He had never thought that he could pity a queen. Poor child: yoked to a man whom she understood no better than he understood her. If they had been a chariot team, the master of horse would have separated them long since.

10

A LL THE QUEEN'S PLOTTING seemed like to shatter on the rock of her own obstinacy. She would not oblige her husband. She would not indulge his escapes from kingship. She was not even slightly grateful to the concubine Isis, who kept him sufficiently distracted that he showed no sign of riding off to war.

Nehsi had learned not to fret himself into a fever when his lady flew in the face of all common sense. That was well; for on an evening when she had not spoken to the king, nor he to her, in three full days, even as they sat side by side at the feast and in the hall of audience, she ordered her maids to prepare her for the king's bedchamber.

She went about it like a king preparing for war. She mustered the weapons of her beauty. She arrayed her troops: a gown as sheer as mist in the desert, a collar of gold and lapis and carnelian, a wig of elaborate plaits and curls, garlanded with golden flowers. She was washed in the scent of musk, cloaked and armored in it.

As she swept her maids behind her in a flurry of light robes and shrill voices, Nehsi did a thing that he had sworn never to do. He caught the queen as she passed him. He demanded, "Why? Why now?"

She slipped free, but she paused. "I have to," she said.

"Now?"

"Now."

"But what if—"

She was gone. He could hasten after; or he could stay where he was, on guard over empty rooms.

His was the coward's choice. Later he would drown his sorrows with the twins, a jar of beer for each. Now he paced a sentry's track through the queen's chambers, startling maids and chamberlains, putting them to flight with a hard flat stare.

He could imagine what went on in the king's chambers. There were not so very many different things that a man could do with a woman. But what they said to one another, how she approached him, he did not know, nor want to know.

He knew only that she came back while the night was still young, gowned and adorned as before, but walking with a difference. He would not call it pain. She was too proud for that. She had done, it was clear, what she had set out to do.

Her maids put her to bed as always, with order and ritual as old as the throne of Egypt. When she was abed, she called for Nehsi as she sometimes did, and sent the maids away.

He said what he always said. "This is not seemly, lady."

Always before she had laughed at him and told him to sit down, and challenged him to a game of Hounds and Jackals, or simply to a battle of wit. Tonight she had no laughter in her. She clasped her knees, sitting up in the splendid bed with its lion-feet and its coverlets of whitest linen. She looked small and bruised and defiant. "It wasn't as bad as I thought it would be," she said.

Nehsi did not want to hear it. No more did she care that he shrank from the telling.

"He had had a little lessoning," she said. "He was polite enough, once he got over his incredulity."

Nehsi raised his brows. "Polite? Then you did no more than talk."

"No," she said. She had no humor: it was a flaw, though she had never known it. "No. Once he'd observed a few amenities, he was very . . . direct. He agreed with me, you see. There must be an heir."

"Were you astonished?"

She frowned at him. "What, that he understood one part of his kingly duty? No, I was not astonished. I was glad that he would oblige me."

"I doubt he had much difficulty," Nehsi muttered.

He rather hoped she had not heard him; but her ears were keen. Humor she had none, but her wits were quick. She flushed. "You are a low, coarse man. Why do I trust you?"

"Perhaps, lady," he answered, "because I tell the truth."

She shook her head. "No. That's the worst of you. You don't think I should have gone to him. Do you?"

"It is not my place to judge the actions of the queen's majesty," Nehsi said in his coldest voice.

She had never been in awe of him, and certainly never feared his temper. "What should I have done, then? Let someone else present him with an heir?"

Since he had argued against that very thing, he could hardly gainsay her now. He shrugged. He supposed he looked sullen. "It was sudden."

"It was years in coming," she said.

"And an hour in the doing," he shot back, "and not a tenth of that devoted to thinking about it. It was poor generalship, if that had been a battle."

"It was a battle," she said. "I won it."

"Did you?"

But she was not to be conquered by the edge of his tongue. She lay down on her bed, turned her back on him, shut him out. She looked like a child, small and bird-boned and fragile.

She did not want his pity. She would sneer at his compassion. He gave her the only thing he could give, which was his silence.

■ She must have wrought well. The next night she did not have to in-trude upon the king's peace. He summoned her with something ap-proaching grace, sending a chamberlain with pretty words and a pret-tier face, to invite her to attend him. The night after that she did not return to her rooms from the court's banquet. The king had taken her by the hand after the wine went round, and led her away.

Among the king's attendants Nehsi happened to notice Isis. Pro-priety kept the royal concubines in their own chambers, away from pry-ing eyes and wagging tongues. But Isis had always made free of the court, a freedom that she turned into an image of self-effacement. Her head was demurely lowered, her posture humble. She ventured noth-ing bold, nothing openly defiant.

When the king departed with the queen, Nehsi watched the con-cubine carefully. She did not move from her place that had been at the king's feet. He could read nothing in her face, as little of it as he could see. Perhaps there was nothing to read. Still it troubled him that she, so innocent, so tenderhearted, shed no tears as she watched her lord and beloved walk away from her, and never a glance back. He was en-grossed in some sally of the queen's.

It well might be that she was loyal to the queen. Nehsi could not convince himself of it. He was a low, coarse man as his lady had said, wary and trusting no one. So must a guardsman be, or fail of his guardianship.

After a month and more of doing her wifely duty to the king, Hat-shepsut woke one morning looking green and ill. Nehsi, who saw her, watched carefully. And the next morning she was ill again, and the morning after that.

Even a man could hardly mistake it; and Nehsi was not as some men were, willfully ignorant. The queen, young as she was, might well have failed to understand, but her maids were wise in the ways of women. "Wait," they bade her, "and count the days. If your courses are late . . ."

"They will be," the queen said. She spoke as one who knows for a certainty, with relief that she did not try overly hard to hide. "I shall bear the king a son, and he shall be king."

"Gods grant," murmured the more pious of the maids.

■ As the count of days stretched, and no sign of her woman's courses, the queen went less often to the king's bed. Then one evening as she took her ease with a book and a flute-player, his messenger came to bid her attend her husband.

"May my royal lord forgive me," said Hatshepsut; and humble though the words were, her tone had never known humility: "but my majesty is indisposed."

The messenger was taken aback. "Lady! You cannot—"

"The queen's majesty," she said, sweetly precise, "is indisposed."

He must leave or be ejected. He bowed and retreated.

"When he comes back," the queen said, "my door is closed."

■ She could not, however, keep out the king. It took him a handful of nights and a dozen summonings through messengers who were not permitted to pass the door. Nehsi would have expected him to drown his sorrows with one of his concubines—Isis might have rejoiced in the victory—but if he had done that, it had not removed the shame of his royal wife's refusal.

The queen received him perforce, in as little state as she might. She lay in her bed, wrapped in a robe, with only her eyes painted, and no wig, only the plait of her own hair. Nehsi thought her quite fetching, like the girlchild she so seldom permitted herself to be.

There was no telling what the king thought. He was in a temper, with a high flush under the bronzing of wind and sun on his cheeks. The scent of wine swept in with him. "Lady!" he said brusquely, not troubling with a greeting. "Are you ill? No one has seen you for a good hand of days."

"I am not ill," she said. "I am indisposed."

"And what of your royal duties?"

Her eyes flashed up at that. He grinned without humor. She smiled back, with an edge of cold mockery. "I have done what must be done," she said, "from these chambers, with the aid of servants and chamberlains."

That rather lowered his crest; but he was in too high a dudgeon to come down all at once. "Well, then. You are ill. That doesn't give you leave to refuse my messengers."

She lay back as if suddenly too weary to face him. "Your messengers are tedious. I thought I told the first two or three that they were not welcome."

"They were *my* messengers," the king said.

"So they were," said the queen without a flicker of guilt.

He glared at her. He was not, Nehsi must remember, an unintelligent man; simply one who used sparingly the wits the gods had given him. He could see perfectly well what his wife was telling him.

She regarded him calmly. "I am carrying your child, who will be your heir. My duty to you is done until that child is born."

He understood her. Nehsi saw how his body stiffened as if at a blow. "Then," he said in a tone that perhaps no one had heard from him before, "all the words you said . . . all the sweetness you showered on me, the promises, the kisses . . . those were only duty."

"Did I not do it well?" she inquired.

He drew a sharp breath. "You did it most well."

She nodded, cool as ever. "Then I am content. I shall appear tomorrow in the hall of audience as befits your queen and consort. You will see no further failing in my public duty, not at least until the child demands it."

"And . . . your private duty?"

"That is done," she said. "I wish you goodnight, my lord. May the gods grant you dreams of honor and prosperity."

He heard the dismissal; he moved slightly as if to indicate that he would go. But not quite yet. "Lady," he said, "you are cold: cold and too perfectly the queen. I could have loved you."

"The gods commanded that we be mated to one another," she said. "Therefore it was done. I give you the heir you require."

"And no more," he said. He straightened. "Well. I should have known how you would be. Your father was the same."

"He was your father also," she said.

"No," said the king. "I was always the lesser, the son of a woman who was not the queen. You were his child in heart and soul."

She did not gainsay that. "Goodnight, my lord," she said.

This time he went as she bade him. Nehsi could not see that she watched him go, or that she cared how she had stung him.

She could have had a lover, a husband who cherished her. Instead she might well have made an enemy.

It was not Nehsi's place, no more than it had ever been, to remind the queen that she was fortunate. She had not been beaten or visibly harmed. Her husband had been entranced with her; had been wounded deeply when she cast him off. She was a fool to have done it, and no matter how awkward he might have been, or how little pleasure he might have given her.

He kept his tongue between his teeth. She slept, to all appearances, with a clear conscience. She woke greensick but triumphant, because it was proof. She had done as she intended, as her duty bade her. She was free of the nightly battle—for so she must think of it.

"When my son is born," she said to the silent and, he hoped, unreadable Nehsi, "he'll forgive me anything. You'll see. He's not half the hardened soldier he pretends to be."

"Then why," Nehsi made bold to ask, "can you not love him?"

She was in the mood for once to answer. "Because I can't," she said. "He grates on me like a sour note on a flute. He ruts like a bull, grunting and straining. He smells like a goat. He could bathe in oil of myrrh and still reek of the byre."

"Many women seem to find him irresistible," Nehsi observed.

"His title is irresistible," said the queen. "I don't like him, Nehsi. I never have. When did the gods ever say that I should fall in love with the man they bound me to?"

"Love," said Nehsi, "is hardly required. But liking, respect, consideration—those might be worth a moment's thought."

She turned her shoulder to him, ostensibly to oblige the maid who was arranging her pectoral. He started to speak again, sighed, held his peace. Not for him would she see sense. Her father might have enforced it on her, but her father was years dead.

A queen, like a king, could do much as she pleased. If that was to drive her king away and teach him to hate her, then no mere servant could deter her.

■ It would have been fair enough if the king had declared war against his wife. He chose however to declare war in Asia. He gathered his armies with fierce and singleminded speed, swept them with him, led them away just as the river began to rise in its yearly flood.

The queen remained behind as was proper, ruled as regent in his place, suffered with exemplary patience the slow days and months until she was brought to bed of the king's heir. Well might she be patient. She had no husband there to vex her. She greeted news of victories with what seemed to be honest joy, and sent felicitations as a queen should, and with them such gold and provisions and reinforcements as he asked for. She was a very perfect queenly queen.

She could afford to be generous. He had not taken Isis with him to the war, though she had begged and schemed and done everything in her power to persuade him. She had even—the little fool—tried to enlist the queen's aid. Hatshepsut declined, smiling as demurely as Isis herself, murmuring, "War is no place for a woman—he himself has said it."

And maybe she took care to remind the king of that. Certainly, when he rode away, Isis stood with the rest of his servants and his concubines, and watched him go. It was ill luck to weep for a man who went off to war; but her great eyes swam with unshed tears.

He could not have seen. He had forgotten even the favorite of his concubines, the greatest solace against the queen's cold heart. All of his mind was focused on the war, and on the road that he must travel before he came to it.

11

*I*N THE DAYS OF THE QUEEN'S GRAVIDITY, Senenmut came to know her perhaps better than he had any right to. She did not settle into the bovine calm that he had heard was the way of bearing women; but she was less sharp-tongued than she had been.

She had more patience for the exactitudes of the priestly script, more willingness to accept correction if there was need.

He admired her for that. It was not an easy pregnancy, nor did it grow easier as it went on. Her doctors hovered. They would have confined her to her bed, but she would have none of that. Shorter public audiences, longer private gatherings in which she could recline on a couch with little sacrifice of dignity: to those she would concede.

She had two kingdoms to rule, and a husband spending the wealth of both in his war in Asia. War was noble; war was the proper pursuit of kings. That, Senenmut had been taught. But he saw war as a queen must see it: lengthy, expensive, taxing her lessened strength.

She had scribes and clerks in dozens and hundreds, but she took to expecting that Senenmut be present while she conferred with embassies and heard the counsels of high lords of the Two Lands. He recorded what was said, which was a scribe's task; but after, she would keep him with her, often with no other attendants but a guardsman and a maid or two. Then she would ask what he thought of the things that had been said.

At first he did not think. He had no time. He was an instrument, a pen and a strip of papyrus, recording without judgment. But she challenged him. She demanded that he listen as well as write. She never cared how difficult it was. She asked it; she expected that he do it.

He had learned in the Temple of Amon that it did no good to hate one's master for demanding the impossible. Either one did it or one suffered. Because he had been well taught, and because he had his pride, he taught himself to drive two horses at once, to both record and think. It was hard; it sent him home night after night with a splitting headache. But he persevered.

And he learned. The queen granted him neither thanks nor admiration; but from asking him on occasion she advanced to asking him every day after audience, what he would have done or thought in her place.

It dawned on him after an embarrassingly long while that she was teaching herself even as she compelled him to learn. He was the youngest of those she trusted, the closest to her in age and experience. Even the trust was a revelation: she trusted almost no one. Her Nubian. A maid or two. Hapuseneb the priest of Amon. Senenmut. Perhaps one or two of the courtiers and counsellors, but with those she was always on guard, saying nothing that was not carefully judged.

There grew by degrees a custom. After the public and private audiences, the queen would withdraw to rest and refresh herself before the tables were laid for the evening banquet. With her she would take a few companions: Senenmut, the priest, the Nubian who was her shadow. Maids would attend her for propriety's sake, but always the same few. There was wine; there were little cakes, and dates for Senenmut, and such other fruits as were in season.

They sat at ease, conversing in comfort that had grown over the days and months. The queen, swelling into immobility with the child, clung fiercely to her mind's acuity.

That one particular day, Senenmut remembered after, she had seen an embassy from Libya, and conversed with the leader of a caravan of traders that had ventured into the fabled country of Punt. He had brought her gifts, most of which had gone to the storehouses; but she had kept a branch from the myrrh-tree, dried and sere but heavy with scent.

She loved the scent of myrrh, would drink it in when no one else could bear the strength of it. If she could, she would bathe in it; but her maids kept her sensible, and urged on her less potent unguents. Senenmut did not mind it terribly, but the other two, he noticed, were holding their breaths.

She was oblivious as she usually was to others' inconvenience. The caravan-master had enchanted her with his tales. "Imagine!" she said. "Whole forests of myrrh, and fields of spices. What a country that must be! And its people—black, like Nubians, but smaller-statured, in robes of leopardskins."

Nehsi, who was rumored to sleep wrapped in the skin of a leopard that he had killed, looked more disdainful than usual. "They are only savages," he said.

Hapuseneb laughed between cups of wine. "So says one who would know! And you, sir: in what den of lions were you born?"

"In Thebes of the kings," he answered with dignity, "among the king's Nubians. I am a civilized man."

It was impossible to chasten Hapuseneb. He grinned. "So may the people of Punt be civilized, by their own lights. I wonder what their wine is like, if they have wine."

"We must call the trader back again," the queen said, "and ask him all our questions."

"Surely!" said Hapuseneb. "And you, sir scribe: have you nothing to ask?"

Senenmut had been sliding into a doze. He was short on sleep, and not for any reason that he could explain to these of all people. His brother's nightlong spate of sickness had kept him awake perforce. Better they should all believe his nights held hostage to a woman.

He roused hastily. "What's to ask? We should send someone to see."

The queen clapped her hands. "Yes!" But then her face fell. It hurt, almost, to see so much animation turned dour. "Yes. Someday. Maybe. When this war is paid for."

"Wars are paid for in the booty the warriors bring back," Nehsi said.

"Not always," she said. "Not even often. I hate wars, I think. They're wasteful."

"Never tell a man that," Hapuseneb said, cheerful as ever.

"Ah," she said, a snort of disgust. "Men." She shifted on her couch, settling her ungainly weight as best she might. Her maids were quick to help, offering cushions, a footrest, the cooling breeze of a fan. She waved them all away. She was irritable suddenly, more than usual.

Senenmut was not so fogged with sleep that he could not see the obvious. The others seemed blind. But maybe they did not have a mother who bore a child a year all through their youth, and had miscarried of the last only this year past. He knew the signs.

When she stiffened and tried to hide it, he was certain. He clapped his hands as imperiously as the queen ever had. "Fetch the physicians!" he commanded the startled maids.

They stared at him as if he had been a dog that suddenly sat up and spoke. He had never played the lord before.

He armed his glare and fixed it on them. One broke and ran, he hoped in the proper direction.

The queen's eyes were closed. Her face was pale. Her voice was thin, a little breathless. "It hurts," she said, "rather more than I was told."

"Women forget," said Hapuseneb. "It's a mercy, Taweret's gift."

He had forsaken his wonted levity. It had taken him some little time, but now he saw what Senenmut had seen: that the baby was coming. Even the Nubian seemed to have comprehended, late and last, why his lady was so abruptly indisposed.

Senenmut was closest and therefore most convenient. She seized his hand. He started, and winced: her grip was bruisingly strong. She did not see his pain for the immensity of her own.

She would not let him go, even when the physicians came, pondered, and ordered that she be brought into her bedchamber. When he tried to work his hand free, she caught it in both of hers and held fast. She dragged him with her perforce, and kept him there.

Childbirth was seldom either easy or quick. A child bearing a child, young and small as she was, needed long hours and great pain. Senenmut, young and male and never a father, had no place there; but she had fixed on him. Gods knew why. Her Nubian, now, or even the priest, would have made more sense. Or even better, some woman who knew what to say and how to say it.

Senenmut knew nothing to say or do but babble at her while the hours stretched. He said whatever came into his head: stories, snatches of song, memories of his mother's descents into Taweret's arms. The goddess was here as she was at every child's birth, a memory and a shadow, grotesque but oddly beautiful, like the woman who labored and suffered on the childbirth-stool. He held her up when she grew weary, cradling her against him, an impropriety that should have sent the maids and chamberlains into hysterics.

But it was the chief of physicians who commanded it, and the shriveled harridan of a midwife who slapped him into place. "Here, you," she snapped, "make yourself useful. Hold her up. No, not like a sack of meal. Like a queen who will be mother to a king."

He had dreamed often enough of holding a woman in his arms. He had never dreamed as high as a queen, nor ever imagined himself as he was now, aiding her to bear another man's child. She was fever-warm, slick with sweat, swollen and shapeless and struggling. There was no beauty left in her, and no dignity.

There were moments of quiet, pauses between battles, when she lay and simply breathed. She seemed grateful then to lean against him, to let her body go slack, to use his strength in place of her own. She never asked his leave.

He dared not laugh, but his belly tightened with it. There was trust—or insult too deep for words. He was a thing, a wall to lean against, nothing more.

But the wall was living flesh, and it knew that it upheld a woman. There was no talking sense to it. Senenmut gritted his teeth and endured. She would never know what it cost him, nor if she knew would she care. He could not even resent her for it. She was the queen. She knew no other way to be.

12

*I*N THE DARK BEFORE DAWN, IN THE hour when the night wind dies and the dead walk, a child was born to the living Horus and to his Great Royal Wife. The midwife raised it in bloodied hands, offering it up to the gods' sight and to the sight of its mother.

Hatshepsut looked once, long enough to be certain, then turned her face away.

"A daughter," said the chief of physicians. "A strong daughter for the Great House."

The queen's voice came too low almost to catch, yet bitterly distinct. "It was supposed to be a son."

None of the flock of attendants had the wits to speak. The midwife, who might have said what needed saying, was engrossed in the child, cutting and tying up the cord, bathing her, crooning to her in an astonishingly sweet voice.

There was only Senenmut, still serving as throne and birthing-chair, to shake her till she stiffened against him, but turned her head at least and glared. He glared back. "This is your child," he said. "Your daughter, lady and queen: a princess royal, just as you were. She proves your fertility. She carries the right to kingship, that is given to no man except through a woman of your line. Why do you turn your face away from her?"

"Because," Hatshepsut cried out, nearly spitting the words, "if it had been a son, I'd not have it all to go through again!"

"Hush," the physicians chided her. "Be still, lady. You'll injure yourself."

"I don't care!" But she subsided, though she was rigid in Senenmut's arms. "It should have been a son."

"This child is exactly what the gods wish her to be," Senenmut said sternly. "She is beautiful. Look at her."

The queen would not. "She is hideous. All babies are."

"She will be beautiful," Senenmut persisted. He was stubborn—not perhaps as stubborn as the queen, but quite enough to go on with.

"I wanted a son," the queen said yet again. But the hard edge had softened. She sounded almost weary, almost sad: a child balked of her desire, rather than a queen in her wrath.

"You'll have a son," Senenmut said. "Next time."

"I wanted him now," she said.

"What you have now," he shot back with a resurgence of temper, "should delight you to no end. She's whole, healthy, and lively enough for any two children. There are women who would sell one of their souls to be so blessed."

She met temper with temper, even in her exhaustion. "You love her so much, you raise her. I'll not trouble myself with her."

"You will," he said, reckless of rank or respect.

"Make me."

She sounded exactly like Ahotep. Senenmut could not clip her ear as he would his brother's: and that was a great pity. He had to settle for the lash of words. "Very well; since your majesty commands it. I'll take the challenge."

"And the baby."

"Oh, no," he said, backing away from the maid who held the child. "I'm no wetnurse."

"She won't be a nurseling forever," the queen said. "I give her to you."

"You can't do that," said Senenmut. "You shouldn't. You're exhausted; your mind is fogged. When you come to yourself—"

"I am perfectly and completely myself," she said with chilly precision. "I have spoken. You have all witnessed it. Now go away and let me be."

"Lady—" Senenmut began.

"Go," she said.

He went—not because she ordered him, but because he was too angry to linger. He paused once, to bid farewell to the newborn princess. And if that convinced her bitch of a mother that he was besotted, then so be it. He had seen her born nearly in his lap. How could he fail to marvel at her?

■ They named the child Neferure, Beauty of Re. Senenmut was given a title: Tutor of the King's Daughter, first servant of Neferure. He found himself lord and master of the entire suite of a princess, from the wetnurse to the girlchild who washed the princess' bedlinens.

He also found himself in a most embarrassing position.

Hat-Nufer was grimly proud of her son. But not too proud to inform him, when he brought home his new title and the bafflement of his new duties, that he was a blathering fool. "Never mind the honor," she said. "What are you supposed to eat and dress and live on while you're dancing attendance on a suckling baby?"

He had begun to outgrow the gawkiness of his youth, but the edge of his mother's tongue flayed away all pretense of maturity. He was a clumsy child again, gifted with the pen but with little else, ducking his head and mumbling a weak defense.

"Nonsense," his mother said. "You are brilliant, talented, and beloved of the gods, but you have no more sense than a new-hatched gosling. Any idiot would know that with new titles comes new recompense."

Somewhere he found his voice. It was a dim and feeble thing, but it was all he had. "I'm sure the queen would—"

"Queens are like anyone else. They'll take what they can, and pay as little as they can manage."

Hat-Nufer sent him to bed as if he had been a child, and would hear no objections, either. He lay in the suffocating warmth of his sleeping-room, free for once from Ahotep's pestering: the brat had been sent to the Temple of Amon to learn the scribe's trade, and would not be back till evening. So far he had shown little aptitude for the arts of the pen. Games, now—games he had mastered, whether a child's game of sticks and pebbles or a headlong tumble after a ball made of sewn oxhide.

Senenmut the eldest and best, favored of the Great Royal Wife, sent to bed without his supper, reflected more wryly than sullenly on the ironies of fate. He had no honor in his own house, no respect from his blood kin.

Of course, he thought, he had a choice. He could leave. He was a man in years, favored servant of a queen. He supposed that he had the wherewithal to manage lodgings, maybe even a servant to bake his bread and wash his kilts.

He supposed. He did not know. His mother kept the accounts. His wages fed and clothed him; he thought that she might be keeping the rest in reserve against fear or famine.

If he was to be free of his mother, then he must learn to reckon his own accounts. He shuddered at the thought. The reckonings of the Two Kingdoms were dull, but he could keep them in his head. Petty frettings over a measure of barley or a length of linen for a kilt or a bed-sheet . . . those bored him to tears. Hat-Nufer could reckon whole tallies in her head, keep them in order and lose not a single grain of barley.

He needed her. He cursed the need, but there was no escaping it. Not unless he took a wife; and that prospect was even less alluring than the constant, niggling presence of his mother.

Sleep dragged at him, too heavy to resist. He had had none since the night before last. His body lingered in a memory: the queen lying limp in his arms, worn down with bearing her daughter. She was warm, sweat-slicked, smelling of nothing but herself: none of the myrrh she so loved, no flowers or unguents.

He dreamed of her, but the dreams vanished at waking. He had spent himself in the night. By rare good fortune, Ahotep was sound asleep and not to be roused for anything his brother did. Senenmut bathed and dressed and recovered what dignity he had.

He could not elude his mother, not unless he went hungry, but she carried on as she always had. She made no mention of Senenmut's failure to be properly concerned for the welfare of his fortune.

He gathered his belongings as he did every morning, endured the rituals of farewell: vague from his father, brusque from his mother, exuberant from his brothers. He went to the palace as always, to the same duties and more, and his hour, mandated by the queen, of driving a team of obedient mares round the court of the chariots.

As he returned from that, flushed and windblown and full of sun and sand and the snorting of horses, he found his lady engaged in a private audience. The petitioner made him gasp and step back, tensed to bolt.

Too late. They had seen him. "Come," the queen said: soft, but a command nonetheless. "Sit with us."

Sit therefore he must, on a stool with legs carved like lotus-flowers, in the queen's lesser hall of audience. It was a small room, made larger by the paintings on the walls: river and reeds, ducks swimming and feeding and sitting on the nest. They were vivid, colored and painted in the semblance of life. Sometimes during very dull audiences Senenmut imagined that he sat in a boat on the river, watching the water slide past, listening to the calling of birds in the reeds.

This audience was interesting. Too interesting. "Lady," said Hat-Nufer, bold as if this were one of her neighbors, and a young and foolish one at that: "I thank you most profoundly for raising my son to his first eminence. But eminence requires more than the simple title. It has a certain state to keep, in the honor of the king and his royal kin."

Hatshepsut betrayed no outrage at the insolence of this commoner. She was as gracious as she could be with the ambassador of a foreign king, listening gravely and responding, "Yes, it is commonly thought that the servant should show himself in a manner fitting to the rank of his master."

"And that," Hat-Nufer said, "is difficult on the wages of a simple scribe and teacher. The princess' tutor and guardian holds, surely, a higher rank?"

"He does," the queen said.

"Then," said Hat-Nufer, "should not his rank perhaps require him to occupy a house of suitable size and location, and a household to maintain it, and the means to maintain them?"

Hatshepsut's brows raised slightly, imperceptible perhaps to one who did not know her well. Senenmut could not be certain, but he thought she might be amused. He could have wished for high indignation and the ejection of his mother from her presence; but she had no such mercy. "You are saying," she said with grave intentness, as if she truly wished to make no mistake, "that I should ennoble my daughter's tutor? Since, after all, a house and servants and all their maintenance are the province of a lord of men."

"I am saying," said Hat-Nufer, unabashed, "that my son has duties and obligations that require more of him than he can manage on a scribe's wages. He comes home at all hours, stumbling with exhaustion; he forgets to eat; he would forget to draw his allotment of barley and wine and beer and kilt-linen, except that his father sees to it that that is done."

Senenmut bit his tongue. Rahotep had never seen to anything in his life. It was Hat-Nufer who saw to it in Rahotep's name.

He could not remember when he had been more humiliated. His mother in front of the queen looked like what she was: a common little woman with neither delicacy nor breeding, and not much beauty, either; he had his face from her. She was in no visible awe of the queen's majesty. And she talked of him as if he were a hapless child.

The queen did not laugh at her, which was a tribute to royal upbringing and queenly restraint. "Granted," she said, "that your son has taken on himself a difficult if not impossible task: does that render him worthy of a noble estate?"

Hat-Nufer snorted. "Oh, come! There are perfectly acceptable houses to be had in decent quarters of the city, that don't need a prince to call them home. Set him up in one of them, with a household appropriate to its size and dignity, and give him a comfortable place to return to when you've worn him out. Not," she said, "that his father's house is precisely uncomfortable, but it's small. He has to share a bed with his brother, who is not the most subdued of children. Don't you think that's a trifle absurd? He is, after all, your daughter's tutor."

"So he is," the queen said. "I had considered the matter of suitable recompense. Since, however, he never asks, nor demands more than he has—"

"Lady," said Hat-Nufer, "you know how boys are. When they're not too proud to use their wits, they don't have any to use."

"Indeed," said the queen blandly. She refrained from glancing at Senenmut, but he saw the glitter of eyes under the lowered lids. Oh, yes, she was laughing. If he could have shrunk to a shadow and vanished, he would joyfully have done it.

The queen beckoned to one of her chamberlains. "Escort the lady to my private dining-hall. See that she has anything she wishes to eat or drink, and that she is provided with a chair and an escort when it pleases her to depart."

Hat-Nufer bridled. She was new to the royal art of dismissal. It was a nasty pleasure to see her escorted deftly out.

He, however, had not been dismissed. He remained where he was, too stiff with indignation to move or speak.

Hatshepsut preserved her image of queenly dignity. By that, Senenmut knew that she was plotting something dire. When she spoke, it was not to him but to her Nubian. "Nehsi. Show him."

The Nubian wore his habitual expression of lofty scorn, but there was a gleam in his eye. Senenmut's anger warmed him, which was well: his heart was cold. His mother had done him a great ill turn. Now he would pay for it.

He did not try to linger. If he had, no doubt the Nubian would have lifted him and carried him out.

Nehsi would not answer any questions. Threats, Senenmut had none. Surely nothing could frighten that great beautiful panther of a man.

He led Senenmut through the queen's palace and out. A chariot was waiting, drawn by a pair of the queen's mares: the Star of Hathor and her yokemate, the Moon of Isis. Nehsi ascended and took the reins. Senenmut refused to hesitate. He stepped up behind the Nubian, got a grip on the chariot-rim, braced as the horses danced forward.

He could not imagine where he was being taken. It could be anywhere. Back in disgrace to the Temple of Amon. Back to his father's house. Even to the mines, or among the builders of tombs across the river in the cliffs of the Red Land.

They turned down the processional way. The horses stepped out boldly, moving well together, matching stride and stride. The sun was strong, its light dazzling his eyes that had grown accustomed to the dimness of the palace.

He was still half blind, eyes running with tears, when the chariot turned and passed under the shadow of a gate. For a moment he wavered in darkness; then the light returned, but lessened, softened by a rustle of greenery.

The chariot stood in a courtyard that was also a garden, bounded with rows of trees in pots. The trees were in flower: their sweet scent drifted round him. A fountain played in the center of the court. Lotus-flowers grew in it; bright fish darted among the broad green leaves.

It was beautiful and quiet, and cool with water and greenery. The tiles underfoot as Senenmut stepped down from the chariot were worn, their bright hard colors faded to browns and greens and blues.

Beyond the court was a house, worn like the courtyard to a soft sheen. It must have been nigh as old as Thebes. An air of antiquity sat on it: a faint scent of dust and age. Yet it was meticulously clean, its furnishings opulent in their simplicity: the carved ebony of a chair, the inlaid ivory of a table, the gilded feet of a couch. The walls were painted with images apt to each room: dancers at a feast in the dining-room, in one of the smaller gathering-rooms a procession of cats and geese, and in the master's bedchamber a man and a woman in a boat, hunting ducks in thickets of reeds.

The house was old and quiet but not altogether empty. There were servants in the kitchen, clustered there as if they had been commanded to wait. They fell on their faces before Senenmut.

The scent of baking bread wound round him, and the rich smell of beer in the brewing. The truth dawned on him with distressing slowness.

"This," he said, trying not to stammer. "This is what she—what my mother asked for."

The Nubian nodded. "This is your house. The queen has given it to you."

Senenmut was shaking. Gods knew why. He was a man grown, the servant of a queen. Why should he not have a house that was his to dwell in?

He had expected the mines, that was all; or the shadow of disgrace. He was caught off guard.

At length he persuaded the servants to stand erect and face him. They did not seem to be castoffs of the queen's palace; none was very young or very old, and they were all sound and hale and clear of eye. Now that it was clear to them that he would not be the sort of lord who demanded groveling respect, they held up their heads willingly enough, named themselves to him, proved that he was not mistaken. "Yes, we are yours," said the whip-thin nervous man who had named himself the cook. "The queen's majesty has commanded it." His eyes narrowed. "You *are* the princess' guardian?"

"I am Senenmut," he said, "who oversees the servants of Neferure."

"Then we belong to you," the cook said. "We're free, mind you. We're not criminals or captives. You pay our wages; you don't own us. You do understand that, I'm sure."

Senenmut did not know whether to laugh or scowl. He settled for a level stare and a sharp nod. "I understand. I treat you well, you serve me well, of your free will."

"You pay us well, we serve you well," the cook said with a spark of humor. "You're young; you've much to learn. Never had servants before, have you?"

"We have a nurse and a maid at home," Senenmut said; then caught himself. Home was no longer his father's house. Home was here, in this noble residence with its garden court and its proliferation of rooms and its blunt-spoken servants. The queen had commanded it; so must it be.

"Never," the cook repeated. "Well; you'll learn. Better a babe in arms than a prince with too high an opinion of himself. Do believe that, sir: princes are miserable masters. Cheap, too. They'll fill their houses with captives, then wonder why nothing works as it should."

"I see you can teach me a great deal," Senenmut said with thinly veiled irony. "Is that the queen's command, too?"

"She'd never need to order us in that," said one of the other servants, the boy with the beautiful eyes, whose voice was just breaking. It cracked abominably as he spoke. He blushed, but he kept his eyes up and steady.

Senenmut could give way to dismay, or he could cast himself on the gods' mercy. He uttered his first command as a master of servants: "Go on with what you were doing. You—Hapi, is that your name? Did you call yourself a master of horse?"

"A very young master," said the man who seemed made of leather and dried sinew, bald by nature and not by the razor's art, with a lean and ageless face. Clearly he did not mean youth of the body.

"But," said Senenmut, "that must mean—"

It was probably unpardonably rude, but he could not help himself. He left the servants—his servants—and ran in the one direction that he had not yet taken. It led out of the kitchen and through a kitchen garden ripe with the scents of a midden, into a perfect miniature of the king's stables.

This could hold perhaps a dozen horses and half a dozen chariots, with all their fodder and accouterments. There was a single chariot in it, and the mares who had brought him here, the Moon and the Star, matched beauties pacing nervously in strange stalls. He comforted them with strokings and a handful each of barley. They ate in snatches, watchful, wary of this new place.

He had not thought that he might be watched, but of course he was. The stablemaster stood near the doorway. The Nubian bulked in it, leaning against the post, arms folded.

Senenmut addressed the latter, a shade too eagerly perhaps, but he was beginning to understand what the queen had done. "She's done it. Hasn't she? She's made me a lord."

"It would hardly be appropriate if she had not," the Nubian said. "Since you are the guardian of the Princess Neferure, and the queen's particular scribe and servant."

"Am I that?" Senenmut sounded like a fool. He knew it; but he could not help it. His mother had the truth of it. He had never thought past his service to the queen, nor reflected on what it could signify.

And he had thought himself a man of ambition. The queen had shown him what an innocent he was.

Why, he thought, she was even a match for his mother.

Maybe.

13

ENENMUT GREW TO LOVE HIS FADED unfashionable house. Other and newer noble houses were larger, more brightly painted, more imposingly adorned. But his house near the palace, with its garden wall that at the height of Inundation was a quay upon the river, seemed to him much warmer in its heart.

He did not live alone there. His mother made a show of insisting that the family stay in his father's house; but he had room and to spare for them all, even the ancient and doddering woman who had been his mother's nurse.

The baby, who was not so small any longer, had a nursery. Ahotep had a room of his own. Senenmut would have given up the master's rooms to his father, but Hat-Nufer would not hear of that. "Don't be an idiot," she said. "You earned it. You keep it. We'll take the rooms over by the river garden. They're bigger than the whole of our old house."

So they were. Rahotep and Hat-Nufer settled into them with the aunts and the maid and a servant or two. Hat-Nufer made herself lady of the house. Rahotep went his vague benevolent way from market to temple to tavern, remembering to come home when his wife sent a boy after him. They were happy, as far as Senenmut could tell.

Hat-Nufer took credit for it all, though it was clear to Senenmut that the queen had set it in train well before his mother came to compel her. It was like Hatshepsut to subject Senenmut to humiliation, and never say a word in his defense.

The queen and the tradesman's wife got on wondrous well. They were the same kind of woman. Hard, Senenmut thought. Ruthless. Stronger-willed than any man he knew. What each wanted, she took, nor asked a man's leave.

He was cursed with such women; surrounded by them. Even tiny Neferure had an imperious way about her, demanding her nurse's breast.

■ The king came back as the Inundation of the Nile shrank and dwindled into the dry season, the green and thriving winter of Egypt. The black earth that the river had left grew tall with emmer wheat and barley, onions and lentils and lettuces, fruits of tree and vine and earth, a rich harvest to feed the people of Egypt.

The king returned victorious at the head of his army. They brought with them the spoils of Asia, gold and captives, a whole great train of them behind the king's chariot.

"It's not enough," the queen said.

She had met her husband at the gate of the city, with her daughter in her arms. Neferure had grown out of early infancy into bright-eyed babyhood, alert to everything that passed, and afraid of nothing. She regarded the glittering figure of her father with utter fascination. He swept her up and carried her in his chariot, small naked child with her necklace of blue beads, crowing as she clasped the false beard that was strapped to his chin.

He evinced no disappointment that this, his first child of the queen's body, was a daughter. He was still holding her in Hatshepsut's chambers, dandling her on his knee, trying to teach her to laugh. She was too young for that; but she could smile, and did, to his manifest delight.

The queen was much less easily distracted. "Your war cost far more than it gained us. Have you given a moment's thought to how we're to manage the rest?"

"We'll raise taxes," he said, and not as if it mattered. He cooed at his daughter, who cooed back obligingly. "Look! She's smitten with me."

"She's smitten with everyone," Hatshepsut said. "Listen to me. You can't raise taxes. The people won't stand for it."

"The people will stand for whatever I tell them to stand for," the king said as if to his daughter. "Yes, little one. I am king and god. They exist to serve me."

"They can't serve you if they're dying of starvation," the queen snapped.

"So," he said. "They can trade their harvest, you said. Let them live on that."

"How can they, if you're taxing it out of existence?"

He hissed in frustration. "I am not taxing them into destitution. The Great House takes much less than a half-share of all that grows and thrives in the Two Lands, as tribute to the king's majesty. The rest is theirs to do with as they please. Even to sell it to the barbarians in Asia—who, my dear lady, are far less haughty than they were before my war swept over them."

"And through your war and the destruction it brought, you compel them to purchase our grain, which feeds our people whom you have taxed in order to pursue your war." Hatshepsut tossed her head as if to clear it. Senenmut, quiet in the shadow of her Nubian shadow, noticed how careful she was, instinctively so, not to disarrange her wig and her tall crown. "My lord, that is very tidy, if somewhat convoluted, but it does not remove the essential fact. Your war was an extravagance."

"Then what would you have me do?" he flared in sudden temper. "A king fights to defend his kingdom. He wins new lands for it, new peoples to pay him tribute. Would you have us retreat to the smallest compass, even to this city and its walls? The wages of conquest built this palace, lady, and won the gold that adorns your neck."

"This is gold of the mine," she said.

"Mined by captives," he shot back. "No, lady. I was always slower of wit than you, but this I know. You would be content if I never left this palace at all—and it would please you best if I never left my throne. If I were bound there, condemned to sit in it day and night without respite, I would go thoroughly mad."

"The gods made you a living god," the queen said. "I would that they had also given you sense."

"And what is sense? To sit here like a spider in her web, with all her husbands neatly wrapped in her larder?" He was on his feet, bulking over her. "Madam, you will remember that I am Horus in the land of the living."

"I never forget it," she said. Sweetly. Fearlessly. Calculated to a nicety, to madden him until surely he must strike her for her presumption.

But she had calculated also that he would not go so far. He turned on his heel and stalked out. Her eyes gleamed as she watched him go.

But when he was well gone, when the baby, howling, had been removed by her nurse, Hatshepsut lowered her head into her hands. "Oh," she said. "Oh, gods. He tempts me so—one day I'll destroy myself."

"I doubt that," the Nubian said dryly. He was free of his tongue when the queen was at ease. He was not a mere guardsman, Senenmut had come to know. He had a house in the city, and a household of imposing size, larger than Senenmut's own. He had titles, offices, occupations that he pursued, it must be, when other men were asleep; for he seemed to spend every waking moment standing guard over the queen. That was his chief duty and evidently his pleasure.

He maintained his position behind his lady, proper in every respect, save in the words he spoke. "I doubt it's ever you who will be destroyed. You're too canny. You got rid of him, which was exactly what you intended."

"But," she said, "he left angry. That was poorly done. I should have sent him away smiling. I have yet to give him a son, you see. Until I do, I have no choice. I must suffer his presence." She looked up at him, her face torn, as if she could not choose whether to laugh or to weep. "But I can't, Nehsi. I can't stand him."

Even he had nothing to say to that. And what must it have cost her, Senenmut thought, to go to her husband's bed night after night,

to speak softly to him, indulge his whims, refrain from quarreling—
and she had gained Neferure, but it was a son she had prayed for. Now
she had it all to do again, and from the look of her, her gorge rose at
the thought.

"I have failed of my duty," she said. "I let myself be ruled by a mere
human dislike. But I don't . . . think . . . I can be reasonable. If he were
an evil man, or terribly ugly, or riddled by some ghastly disease—but
there is nothing wrong with him. I simply can't like him."

"You might," Senenmut ventured to suggest, "go to him as your
duty commands, but dream of another while he does what a man must
do with a woman."

She rounded on him in such flat astonishment that he wondered
if she had forgotten he was there. Then, and that was cruel, she laughed.
"Dream? Dream of whom, scribe? You?"

Her mockery stung him into wit. "Why not, if it passes the time?"

"Then I shall," she said, still laughing. She sobered, however, as
the bent of her thoughts shifted. "But first I have to mend what I've
broken." She closed her eyes as if in pain. "Gods! I do know better. I
do."

■ The king was terribly angry, but the queen exerted herself to the utmost to be pleasing to him. She went to him in her own person, attended only by a pair of maids, dressed with the greatest care, so that
she might seem at once irresistibly beautiful and alluringly humble.
Senenmut heard from the maids a little of what she had said: words
that in another woman would have been groveling abasement, but as
the maid Mayet said, "She makes even abjection seem queenly." The
king turned his face away from her, but she persisted, going so far as
to kneel at his feet and clasp his knees, though she could not manage
a flood of tears.

He would not have been a man if he had continued in his resistance. And the king, living god though he was, was flesh and blood.
He let her beg for a while longer, but the battle was won. The queen
had returned to favor.

The cost to her seemed less high than she had professed. Servants
of the king's bedchamber whispered that he was a rather dull lover,

doing his duty with dispatch and falling asleep directly after. He never wanted to talk, and he was seldom in a mood to listen. Once he was asleep, his queen was free to return to her own chambers, where she would bathe, always, before she went to her bed.

Meritre, the second of the maids whom she favored, observed in Senenmut's hearing that the baths were ritual cleansing. "Pity, too," she said, "that her majesty doesn't have a greater appreciation of the honor his majesty does her. He is the king, after all. Every night she holds the living Horus in her arms."

Senenmut found the irony somewhat over-rich, but Mayet, who was a charming innocent like the kitten she was named for, said seriously, "The living Horus is a bore."

"Exactly," said Meritre.

14

WHEN THE QUEEN CONCEIVED again, her household knew a profound relief. In steeling herself to be pleasant to her husband, she had grown more than a little unreasonable in small things: a razor that cut too close, a jar of unguent that fell from a table and shattered, a gown that had been washed but was not dry at the precise moment when she needed it. Her maids took to keeping their distance. Her guards and attendants, and her scribe, walked soft in her presence.

But once it was certain that she would bear another child, she returned to her older self: haughty, imperious, but sensible enough as royalty went. The king, denied her favors, sought comfort elsewhere. There was no war in the offing, and for once he was not agitating for one.

"He's calmed down," Senenmut observed to Hapuseneb one morning as they waited for the queen to be done with her toilet. It was an unusually elaborate one: there was a grand audience, a gathering of the great lords of the Two Lands, who must offer each his domain's taxes and its tribute, and be recorded in the rolls of the House of Life.

Senenmut was wearing his best kilt and a pectoral that the queen had given him. The collar was heavy, for it was made of gold among the beads of lapis and carnelian and turquoise and faience. He fancied that it weighed as armor did on the shoulders of a prince.

Reflection on princely burdens led him to judge the king's conduct of late, and to find it none so baffling. "Horses are like that," he said, "especially stallions. As they grow older, most of them grow calmer. Maybe the king fought himself out in that last campaign."

"Or maybe," said Hapuseneb, "his calm has a face, and a remarkably pretty one at that."

Senenmut was barely interested. "What, another concubine?"

"Another several," said Hapuseneb with a glint of wickedness, "but one in particular, who exerts herself strenuously to please him—and claims to do it in the queen's name, too."

"Isis?" Senenmut had had to grope for the name. "She was here yesterday. She has friends among the queen's maids."

"That one has friends everywhere," Hapuseneb said. "And hasn't she grown up lovely, too?"

"I hadn't particularly noticed," Senenmut said.

That was not the truth, not exactly, but close enough. Isis had grown from a lovely child into a breathtakingly beautiful woman. But in front of the queen she shrank to insignificance. The queen, whose beauty had more to do with voice and movement and manner than with perfection of feature, had only to stir or to speak, and one forgot that there could be other or greater beauty.

Hapuseneb was grinning at him. "Ah," he said. "You were distracted. Such distraction! Some are calling Isis the most beautiful woman in Egypt."

"Maybe she is," Senenmut said. "I'm not as enthralled with her as everyone else seems to be. She and the king are well matched, I suppose. Neither of them has any conversation."

Hapuseneb laughed so heartily that the queen, coming forth from her inner chambers in a blaze of golden splendor, stopped in amazement. He bowed extravagantly. "But you, O living Isis, unlike certain others who may claim that name, have both beauty and conversation. We salute you, queen and goddess. We worship at your most erudite feet."

She, long accustomed to his absurdities, managed a smile in the mask of her face. She did indeed look like a goddess, but one carved in ivory, too stiffly perfect to be living flesh.

This child was not treating her even as kindly as Neferure had. She was ill daylong; her duties had become an ordeal. But she would not forsake or even curtail them. Nor would she speak of what she must be fearing: that she would again be forced to take to her bed for the child's sake.

She was, it seemed, the kind of woman who conceived easily enough but bore poorly. That was a pity. A queen more than any other woman lived by and for the children she bore to her king. She was the line's hope and its continuance. Through her and through her daughters came the right to the Two Crowns.

Hapuseneb's laughter must have eased the knot of anxiety that Senenmut could sense in her. Its close kin clenched in his middle. He had not feared for her while she was carrying Neferure. He had not known enough then, nor cared. Now he was afraid. When her maids had not worked their magic of brush and paint, she was haggard, her cheeks hollowed, her face pale. A woman in pregnancy should grow round and rich with it. She grew lean as the child waxed within her, as if it sucked the life and blood from her, and gave nothing back.

Her lack of curiosity as to the cause of Hapuseneb's laughter alarmed Senenmut unduly. She should have been demanding an explanation. Instead she only smiled, and that faded as she turned her face toward the door. Her attendants fell into place about and behind her. Was she walking a trifle stiffly?

Of course she would, in those robes. They were of linen starched to rigidity and weighted with gold: golden collar, golden armlets and bracelets, golden girdle above the swell of her middle. Gold crowned her, the tall plumed crown of the queen, that demanded a high head and a taut line of neck. It was to her great credit that she could move with any grace at all.

She walked to the great hall as was her custom, refusing a chair for so little a distance. When the lords and rulers of Egypt were admitted, the king and queen would be seated in royal state, immovable as the images that marched in carven ranks down the hall.

Senenmut could not avoid the tedium of that long audience, even if he had been minded to let the queen out of his sight. He was one of the scribes who recorded the tally of gifts and tribute. They did turn and turn about as the lords and ladies passed in procession. He had time to sit in a shadow where he preferred to be, watching the queen.

She was gracious as always, inclining her head to each of those who bowed at her feet. She remembered names, as her husband did not. He had learned years since to maintain a hieratic silence, and to let her speak where words were required.

She spoke less than was her wont, nor did she indulge those who were minded to linger. That was only good sense, Senenmut told himself. There were twenty-two nomes in Upper Egypt, twenty in Lower Egypt. Forty-two in the Two Lands together, each with its nomarch and his wife and family and his lesser lords and chamberlains and servants. They passed in procession with their trains of gifts and taxes, from the nomarch of the farthest south with his Nubian face and his high Egyptian manners, to the lord of the farthest north whose nome looked upon the sea.

They began in the morning. They ended near sunset. The lords who had passed were suffered to depart if they pleased, until they were called to the feast that would complete their day of homage. The queen and the king must remain unmoving, unresting save for brief intervals, from the first to the last; and then they were given little respite, but must sit in state in the hall of feasting as they had sat in the hall of audience, living images of the gods' presence in the Two Lands.

Ancient custom and long habit compelled the lords to be civil on this of all days, though they would go back in the morning to their endless squabbles. That was well, Senenmut thought. His lady was steady on her throne, but she ate nothing and drank little. She did not snap at the maid who pressed her to take at least a sop of bread in broth from the stewed goose. She ignored her, in what might have been contrariness, or it might have been exhaustion. He feared that it was the latter.

Because the procession had ended so late, the feast began late and went into the deep hours of the night. The queen could have excused herself once the carvers had departed with the remains of the whole ox, but she did not rise, did not take her leave. She had been toying with her untouched cup of wine. She ceased even that, and sat still. The arms of her chair were concealed beneath the table. Only those who stood closest to her could see that her hands were clenched till the knuckles whitened.

Senenmut met Nehsi's glance. He had not intended to stand so prominently, but worry had set him at her left hand as Nehsi stood at her right. The Nubian's brows were drawn together: as much expression as Senenmut had ever seen in him in a public place.

And how, short of lifting her and carrying her, could they persuade her to rest? She would not hear Senenmut's murmur in her ear—perhaps she could not. She seemed enspelled, motionless and voiceless, while the princes of Egypt waxed riotous with wine.

When she sighed and crumpled, both of them were there, the Nubian's strong arms and Senenmut's fierce urgency, bearing her out of the hall. They were quick, and so quiet that no one called after them or pursued them.

While Nehsi bore the queen in his arms, striding long and smooth and swift, Senenmut mustered the scatter of servants. One he sent to fetch the chief physician; another, with a prayer that it might not be necessary, he bade seek out the midwife. He had chosen as carefully as he could; his messengers ran with all speed.

■ It was a fever she had, and great pain in her throat. Her body burned as if with fire. She could eat nothing, nor would she have drunk the physician's potions or even water cooled in earthen jars, had he not persisted until she surrendered. He wrapped her in cloths steeped in water that he had blessed and scented with herbs and made strong with healer's magic. He labored long over her, administering his medicines and chanting his invocations.

The midwife stood aside and scowled. "Fever's bad," she said to Senenmut. "It gets too hot, it burns the baby. Maims it; kills it."

Senenmut prayed that it would not be so. The queen tossed in delirium. Her lips moved. Her eyes wandered. When they fell on him, they burned hotter even than her fever. She stretched out her hands.

He could not refuse her. He took her hands in his, bone-thin and burning hot as they were. With strength that astonished him, she pulled him down till he half sat, half knelt on the bed beside her. She eased her grip just as it became excruciating, but she would not let him go.

He settled as comfortably as he could. That, as it happened, was in the scribe's posture, cross-legged on the bed beside the queen, with her hands in his. Her fever was like a living thing, a creature of fire. It conquered her will and her heart's resistance. It made her see visions.

He saw them reflected in her eyes. The physician's ministrations blurred them, softened their edges, but they were strange still, like dreams of the dead. She walked in the dry land beyond the western horizon, where the sun shone by night and the day was black and beset with demons. Only his hands held her to the world of the living. She clung to them with all her strength.

Such thoughts as he had, dim and scattered, wondered why she came to him. Why not to her Nubian, whom she clearly cherished, and who loved her? It could not be that he had conversation, or that he could write a clear hand. It was certainly not because he had any beauty. Nehsi was the beautiful one. Senenmut with his beaky unlovely face and his narrow shoulders was massively ordinary.

He would never understand this woman. She, beauty and queen, with her army of servants, might have chosen to cling to any or all of them. But when she walked the borders of the dry land, she turned to Senenmut.

Perhaps it was only that he was a scribe; he had the power of words, and through them the spells that guided a soul through the hall of judgment and into the Field of Reeds.

He was not comforted. If anything his fear had grown greater. She could die. He knew it with clarity that seers must know, a deep and rooted certainty. If she died, inevitably he must go on living. And he could not endure the thought of it.

Not because he was her servant, and all that he had was by her favor. He would manage well enough; he could seek employment wherever there was need of a scribe, or if that did not please him, he could go back to the Temple of Amon. He had no great fear for himself. But to live in a world without this woman in it . . .

Dear gods. He did not even like her. She was sharp-tongued, quick-tempered, and mightily arrogant. She vexed him endlessly, demanded the impossible, and when he accomplished it, rarely rewarded him with so much as a smile. Gratitude was beneath her.

And for all of that, as she clung to his hands as to life itself, he knew perfectly calmly and perfectly inevitably that he could not live without her. She was the breath in his lungs. She was the heart in his breast. As much of life as he had to give, he gave her, counting nothing of the cost.

She would never thank him. Nor did he want her gratitude, with all the burdens that rode on it. This was enough: to be the one she sought. To be granted the right to give her what he had.

He almost laughed. Seti-Nakht would have been mightily amused. So much for arrogance, he would say if he ever knew of this. All that pride, all that cockiness, and Senenmut had fallen as headlong as any yokel.

Ah well, he thought. He was mortal flesh. She was queen and goddess. Who was he, then, to resist her?

15

THE QUEEN WALKED LIVING OUT of the dry land. But she left her child behind: a tiny handful that would have been her son, the king who would rule when the king her husband was dead. He was not well grown enough to go to the house of the embalmers, or to be given space in his father's tomb. In the life beyond death as in this world of the living, he had no presence, no name, no souls. He was a might-have-been, no more.

She mourned him as one mourns a might-have-been, in grief that somehow lacked a heart. She had never loved him, never known him. But he would have been king. For that she could honestly weep.

And for herself, too, that she had failed a second time to provide her husband with an heir. "I can't do it again," she said. "Dear gods, I can't."

Senenmut held his tongue while she wept on his shoulder. She had not let him out of her sight since she came to herself and found the child gone, taken away, and her body much weakened with fever. There were others who could comfort her—Hapuseneb and her Nubian not least—but Senenmut seemed to have become her bulwark.

It was nothing improper, he told himself. There were servants about, always, and guards, and priests and physicians. Not her husband; but that was explained away. The king dared not risk her fever. He was much preoccupied, it was said, in ruling the Two Kingdoms alone, without his queen to aid him.

She wanted nothing of her scribe but his strength. He wanted nothing of her that was not proper. She was the queen. He was her servant.

He was let go at last because she reckoned herself fit to put on her state robes and lift up the weight of the crown and appear before the court. She managed it by sheer strength of will. The court received her with what, for courtiers, was joy. The king embraced and kissed her, which was a great concession in the face of royal dignity. Senenmut saw how she gained life and vigor in the light of her people's welcome.

She collapsed after, but it was a sleep of honest exhaustion, with no sickness in it. She dismissed him before it overwhelmed her, sent him home to rest. He was so astonished that he obeyed.

■ He rested indeed, though in that house, with two young children and his mother and a crowd of servants that seemed to swell with every sunrise, he found nothing resembling peace. Exhaustion dulled his ears and shut his mind to the clamor about him. He walked straight through it without a word, fell into his bed and dropped into sleep as into deep water.

When he swam up out of it, the world was much as before. But the center of it had changed. He looked at his wide airy room, at its walls painted with fans of papyrus, and saw that it was lovely, but that it was empty. She was not in it.

He had no doubt that she woke to her great chamber and her army of servants, and missed him little if at all. Fever had driven her to cling to him. Now that it was gone, she would return to herself, queen and goddess, trusting in no man for her heart's ease.

That was as it should be. He could not fault her for it, nor wish it otherwise.

■ The morning was well advanced as he left the bath—having concluded that there were twice as many servants as he remembered; and what, he wondered, was paying for them all? They were quiet, which was in their favor, and they performed their tasks well and quickly. That would be his mother's doing. She had a hard hand with servants, but she was fair; and they seemed to obey her with a good will.

Breakfast waited for him, and a small mincing person who said, "When you have eaten your fill, your lady mother requests the honor of your presence."

"And where," Senenmut asked him, "did she come by such formality?"

The servant blushed and dipped his head and would not answer. Senenmut sighed heavily. He took his time in eating and drinking; he was hungry and thirsty, and the bread was fresh and remarkably fine, the cheese likewise, and the spiced fruit very like a dish he had had in the queen's chambers. He would not have put it past his mother to have bullied the queen's cook till he taught her the way of it.

When he was well ready, he sauntered to the rooms in which his mother held court. There seemed to be more servants about than he ever saw in the palace, even in the king's presence. Most were busy: polishing floors, washing or drying linens, running on errands.

His mother did not favor the royal habit of surrounding oneself with idle attendants. She had one of the aunts with her, Aunt Tanit who was a little simple. They entertained guests: a woman whom Senenmut remembered vaguely from their house in the city, and a younger woman, not much more than a child, with a ripe body and a pretty, petulant face. The older woman was deep in gossip with Hat-

Nufer. The younger one, clearly and elaborately bored, looked about her with hungry eyes.

Senenmut could not at first see why she looked so greedy. It was a pleasant room, with its walls painted with images of a lady at home, performing her toilet, dandling her pet monkey, listening to musicians as she chattered with a handful of ladies. The paintings were not badly done, but they were dreadfully old-fashioned, with the lady decked out in ornaments that had been all the rage a hundred years ago.

Still, to a young woman from the city, they must seem wonderfully grand and lordly. The furnishings were no great wonders of richness or quality, not if one knew the palace, but they were pretty enough, with touches of gilt and a carving or two. The eye could slide past the chair-leg on which Amenhotep had cut his first tooth, and the cushions that Aunt Teti's cat had rather neatly shredded. A girlchild from the city well might covet it all, if she knew nothing better.

Just as she caught sight of him, his mother broke off her spate of gossip. "Senenmut! Come here."

When she sounded as brightly lively as that, all her kin had learned to step softly. The woman—Ramerit, that was her name; wife of a potter with whom Senenmut's father had done business—fairly simpered. The girl stared frankly at him, taking him in and finding him reasonably unprepossessing. Since he found her precisely the same, he returned stare for stare, with an arch of brow that had infuriated a better woman than she.

She blushed and lowered her gaze. Senenmut set himself to forget her. His mother beckoned him to a seat beside her. "Here," she said. "You know Ramerit, of course. And this is her daughter Amonmose."

Senenmut's eyes sharpened. He remembered Amonmose: a gratingly shrill child with a talent for tormenting children younger or smaller than she. She had grown up better than he expected. She was almost pretty, and she looked mildly civilized.

He refrained from saying so. He bowed instead, in lordly fashion, and said, "I give you good morning."

Ramerit clapped her hands. She had always been a silly woman: girlish well beyond the years of her girlhood, and given to cooing nonsense at animals and children as if they were too excessively dimwitted to comprehend plain Egyptian. Her shriek of delight made him wince. "Oh, Hat-Nufer! Isn't he charming? He talks just like a prince."

"Doesn't he?" said Hat-Nufer dryly. "It's gone to his head a bit, I'm afraid. But he does well enough."

"Oh, he does beautifully!" cried Ramerit. "Doesn't he, Amonmose? Isn't he princely, with his golden collar and all. Was that a gift, young prince? Did the queen give it to you?"

Her eyes were avid. Senenmut almost sprang to his feet and took his leave, but his mother's eyes warned him. He would be on his best behavior or she would make certain that he heard of it after.

He answered, therefore, with civility that he had learned in service to a queen. "Yes, lady, that was her majesty's gift. All that you see here is of her bestowing."

"Really?" Gods; the woman could not utter a word without a cloying lilt. "How wonderful. She must value you greatly."

"I serve her as well as I can," he said, still civil, but with a tightness in it that should do well to warn his mother. "She rewards me as it pleases her."

Hat-Nufer caught the warning. Her response was ominously bright. "Oh, he's too modest! The queen relies on him as she does on no one else."

"Imagine," said Ramerit with a blissful sigh. "Amonmose, did you hear? This is the most trusted servant of the queen."

"There are others," Senenmut said, "whom she trusts as well."

"But none whom she trusts more," said Hat-Nufer. "Ramerit; Amonmose. Date wine?"

"Oh!" said Ramerit. "No. No, we thank you. We must go. You know how my husband is when I stay away too long."

Her giggle was meant to evoke a smile of complicity. Senenmut could manage no such thing. Nor, he was somewhat relieved to note, could his mother. She pressed the jar of date wine on them. They did not protest too strongly. Ramerit seemed to think that it was the queen's gift, too; she clutched it greedily, with profuse thanks.

"You should have told her you and the aunts brewed it," Senenmut said when they were gone. A reek of perfume lingered: Ramerit must have bathed in it.

Hat-Nufer shrugged. "She can think what she likes. It's the new brewing—it came out extraordinarily well. And her husband adores date wine."

"So, as I recall, does she," said Senenmut. "Father used to make a tidy profit selling her jars to drink her date wine out of. What was it, three jars a day?"

"Two," said Hat-Nufer, "and you are impudent. What did you think of Amonmose? Hasn't she grown up well?"

"I'm amazed she grew up at all. She was a fanged horror in her youth."

"Ah," Hat-Nufer said. "I'd forgotten. She bit you once for snatching away her doll and tossing it into a cistern."

"Before I snatched the doll," Senenmut reminded her, "she had been beating me about the head with it, laughing when I objected, and calling me Baldhead and Scribe's Monkey. You can still see a scar or two when the light falls just so."

"Ah well," said Hat-Nufer. "Children grow up. They change. Have you reflected that you'll be eighteen years old tomorrow? You've grown into a man."

Senenmut had not reflected on it. The queen's sickness had driven all such trifles out of his head. He shrugged. "So? I've been a man in the world's eyes since I entered the queen's service—and what was I then, all of fifteen?"

"Still," his mother said. "You're growing older. You've got your full height now, I think, such as it is; I notice you've a beard to offer the razor. Don't you think it's time to think about what a man thinks about?"

"What? Earning a living? Aren't I doing it well enough to please you?"

She glowered at him. "Stop pretending you don't know what I'm talking about."

He opened his mouth to deny any pretense. But he was only half an idiot, though he might be all a fool. He knew what it meant when a mother summoned a son for brief converse with a woman of her own age and station, who came accompanied by a nubile daughter. Prince or commoner, it was all the same. When he reached a man's years, his mother set herself to marry him off.

Hat-Nufer spoke in his silence. "I do worry about you, you know. As far as anyone can tell, you have no interest at all in women. Is something wrong? Do you . . . prefer men?"

That was difficult for her to say; but she had never minced words in her life, and she did not choose to begin now.

Senenmut laughed with honest mirth. "Oh, Mother! Of course not. What makes you think that?"

"You have no woman," she answered. Her voice was almost flat. "You take no lover. You haven't even tumbled one of the servants. What am I to think? That you're incapable? Or that you incline toward something else?"

It was almost a relief to see how honestly she worried. He laid his arm about her shoulders and shook her lightly. "There, Mother. There. I'm a perfectly ordinary and capable man. It's just . . . there never seems to be time."

"A young man always has time for women," his mother said.

He shook his head. "No, Mother. Not if he serves in the palace."

"Well then," she said. "Have you ever even wanted it?"

His body flushed so suddenly that it took him by surprise. He had been going to deny it. But the memory of a certain woman in his arms, or clinging to his hand, or commanding him with queenly hauteur . . .

Hat-Nufer let out the breath she must have been holding. "Ah. So you aren't altogether backward. There may be hope for you yet."

"Mother," he said rather desperately, "I am backward. Yes. It comes sometimes with intelligence. The body lags behind the mind. I know I'm not ready to marry."

"No man is ever ready to marry," Hat-Nufer said. "And the younger he is, the less ready he professes to be. Readiness is much simpler than you children will admit. You have eyes. They look at a woman. A certain other part of you rises to salute her. That's as ready as a man ever needs to be."

"I do not," he said through clenched teeth, "salute Amonmose. She has a voice like the scrape of a nail on slate."

"She spoke sweetly enough to me," said Hat-Nufer. "You're remembering her as she used to be. She's a woman now, child. She's ripe for a husband."

"Then let her find one who didn't know her when she was the worst breaker of heads in the potters' quarter."

"I think not," his mother said with terrible calm. "Her father is rather surprisingly wealthy: he's been doing well with his line of cookpots. They have feet, you see, like men or lions or dogs; and the lids are the heads of whatever beast the feet belong to. They're ridiculous, but people can't seem to resist them. He could afford a house at least as handsome as this one, but it suits his whim to live in the potters' quarter as he always has."

"And his wife and daughter have nobler ambitions," Senenmut said. "Why don't they simply set themselves to trap a lordling's youngest son?"

"Because," Hat-Nufer said reasonably, "there's no need. You are precisely what they're looking for. You grew up in the city. You speak as they speak, though you've taken to affecting a noble accent. You serve the queen, who is well pleased with you. You're a catch, child, homely face and all."

Senenmut narrowed his eyes. "Am I? Am I, then? Then these aren't the first who've come sniffing. Are they?"

"We have interviewed a number of prospects," she said, and no shame in her, either, that he could see. "This seems the best of them. She brings with her a substantial settlement. If, gods forbid, you ever fall from the queen's favor, or if the queen—and gods prevent it— should be taken from the world of the living, you'll still be well taken care of."

"That," said Senenmut, "is the most venal nonsense I've ever heard. I will not marry for money. If I can help it, I'll not marry at all. I don't want a wife."

"But I," said Hat-Nufer, "want grandsons."

"You have two other sons," Senenmut said. "Do you forget that?"

Her face had gone hard and cold—but no harder or colder than his heart. "I remember well that I have three sons. Two of whom are children still, and neither has been gifted by the gods as you have been."

"Well then," he said. "Surely one of them will do for a stud-bull." He rose and bowed as he would to a lady of the court. "I have duties in the palace, which I am neglecting. Good day, Mother." And with that, headlong and willfully oblivious to the cost, he left her.

He fully expected her to call him back. But she did not. He escaped from the house altogether and fled to the palace. His duties there were onerous enough, and his fear for the queen had abated only slightly since her fever broke; but they were all outside of himself. They had nothing to do with the reality of a commoner raised to royal favor: the eyes of a greedy child slipping past him to drink in his wealth and his proximity to the queen.

"I will never marry," he said when he could, when there was no one about to listen or to demand explanations. "No, never; not without respect at least, and affection. I'll never take a wife who cares nothing for me, only for the riches I can give her."

The words sounded weak in his own ears, the brave and foolish speech of a child. And where in the world would he find such a woman? Not in the palace, certainly—noble ladies would not look at him, and servants were beneath him. And not in the city, either, where they were all like Amonmose and her mother.

His brothers would marry when their time came. Ahotep was a handsome imp, and Amonhotep too—they favored their father for looks. Even the greediest girlchild might find herself charmed by their smooth profiles and their big dark eyes.

They would do well enough. He would go on as he had begun, unbound to any common woman. He did not need the thing that all the young men did, and the young women, too: sweaty, panting, noisy thing, good for nothing but getting children. And what that did to a woman, he had too clearly seen. He had held Hatshepsut in his arms while she delivered herself of a daughter; he had seen how she almost died in failing to deliver a son.

He would not do that to any woman. He would remain as he was, solitary and content, trusted servant of a queen.

16

*H*AT-NUFER DID NOT SURRENDER easily, nor admit that her cause was hopeless. But Senenmut was at least her equal for stubbornness, and he had an advantage: he could escape into the palace, even remain there in a guest-chamber if he were minded. If he had reason to suspect that his mother had invited another eligible young woman to meet her son, he arranged to be elsewhere until the danger was past.

Days spun into years. The procession of prospective wives seemed to be growing younger. Some looked but little older than Neferure.

She weaned herself with a show of self-will that vividly recalled her mother. Likewise she insisted, at the noble age of four years, that Senenmut—and only Senenmut—teach her to read. "I want to know what the birds and the people mean," she said in her sweet lisping voice. "And the bits of people. Hands and arms and legs and—"

Senenmut reined her in before she galloped away on her spate of words. He had a scrap of worn papyrus for her, and an inkblock and a pen. He sat her down, there in her chamber while her nurse snored in a corner, and set the pen in her fist, and guided it to draw the glyph that he had learned first, before all others. "This is the feather of Maat," he said, "the feather of justice, that balances the heart of the dead man when he goes to judgment."

Neferure knew of death and judgment. She was young but she was well taught, as a princess should be—and most of all one who would be queen. She gripped the pen as he had taught her, striving not to clutch it too tightly, and drew a wobbling image of the glyph. She inspected it, frowned. "Another one!" she said imperiously.

"First learn this one," he said, "and make it perfect. Then I'll give you another."

"This is too slow," she said. "Here, read to me. Show me the words when you read them."

"First," he said sweetly but firmly, "draw me a perfect feather."

She set her tongue between her teeth, held the pen exactly as he had shown her, and carefully, painstakingly, drew a feather that was almost straight, almost perfect.

"Again," he said.

And again; until she had it, or near enough for one so young. Another child might have given up, but she would not. And when she had done it, she said, "Read to me. Show me."

Senenmut bowed. "As your highness wishes."

■ The queen had grown, it seemed, nigh as much as her daughter. She was a woman now, her girlhood left behind, her prettiness transmuted into beauty. She had borne no child after the son whom she had miscarried. The physicians whispered that the fever had burned too deep, and charred the seeds that would have sprouted and bloomed into her children.

They whispered only. It was as much as a man's life was worth to confess his fears that the queen was barren. She would have him killed if her husband did not; and if her husband knew, and despaired of an heir, then she too would suffer, and sorely.

She had not gone to the king's bed in a year and more. Fool that Senenmut was, he kept a reckoning—for his heart's ease, he told himself; for if she conceived again, then surely she would cling to him as she had before. He did not know whether he contemplated it in hope or terror. She offered no intimacy of the body, not even the touch of a hand; she preserved a royal distance.

He dreamed of her. In his dreams she was sweeter by far than she was in life, a willing and tender lover, and in their loving no shame or fear. There was no king to stand in their way, no kingdoms to rock with the scandal. Only the two of them in a river of reeds, rocking gently on a river-swell, borne up in a golden boat. Flocks of water-birds swirled above them. River-horses roared in the thickets. They lay body to body in joyful abandon.

He had come to welcome this dream, to seek his bed willingly, plunging into sleep with a prayer that tonight, again, he would lie with his lady whom he loved. The gods could not fault him, surely, while his waking conduct was beyond reproach. Perhaps they suffered a part of her to come to him, her *ka*-spirit wandering afar in the night, coming to his arms.

Dreams. In the fierce light of day they shrank to the shadows they were. He attended the queen, he stood guardian to the princess; he performed the duties that he had been given—more of those, and more onerous, the longer he dwelt in her service. She was merciless with those whom she trusted, but never more so than she was with herself.

■ She was not always in Thebes. Her husband had turned from war to royal hunts and processionals to lighten the burdens of his office. Hunts and processions were costly, but not, she took care to observe, as costly as war. She was expected to accompany him; she in her turn expected her servants to follow.

Senenmut had been born and raised in Thebes, in the great city of the Upper Kingdom. In those days he saw for the first time the rest of Egypt, from the borders of Nubia to the green and humid marshes of the Delta. They were all dimmed by the light of her presence.

The king had his own household and attendants. Among them as always was the concubine called Isis. Lovely as she had been in her girlhood, now that she had grown to a woman she was breathtaking. Wherever she walked she was trailed by an army of men, all moist eyes and panting tongues like dogs.

None of them ventured to touch her. Few were bold enough to approach her. They simply followed her, helpless as moths in pursuit of a flame.

She still had no conversation. The innocence of her youthful beauty had given way to the splendor of the court lady, a perfection of paint and dress and hair that ladies of the court struggled to imitate. But her mind was no quicker than it had ever been, nor was she any more witty or learned.

■ On a night of moonlit chill during the dry season of Egypt, when the river was shrunk to its winter banks and the fields were green with the harvest, the king had taken it into his head to camp under the stars. On the morrow he would hunt lions in the desert beyond Memphis. Tonight he feasted on the river's bounty, drinking deep of the wine that had been a gift to him from the governor of the Lower Kingdom.

It was a great occasion, a night of rejoicing. Isis his concubine had conceived a child. The king was certain that it was a son.

"And how does he know?" his queen demanded in the privacy of her tent, from beside the welcome warmth of a brazier. She had left the feast early as she always did, though later than usual. She could not possibly let the king see what was so bitterly clear to Senenmut: that the news had struck her to the heart.

"He is not a virile man," she said. "Of all the women who have given him comfort, none had produced a child. Now that this simpering idiot swells below the girdle, he trumpets to the world that she must be carrying his son."

"It's said," said Nehsi, "that he has no children because a certain great lady has taken care to make sure of it."

She fixed him with a black and glittering stare. "How? Poison? Incantations?" She shook her head so fiercely that the beads in her wig clicked together. "If I had done any such thing, you can be certain that this child would never have lived long enough to make its presence known."

"I'm sure," the Nubian said. Voice and face were bland as always.

He was no longer a guardsman except by his free choice. She had made him her chamberlain, the master of her palace. Senenmut might have been jealous, except that he was the chief of her scribes, the tutor and guardian of her daughter, overseer of her affairs. They were great princes, Senenmut and Nehsi, the commoner and the foreigner.

Nehsi was given leave to sit in the queen's presence, if she were private and inclined to indulge him. He draped his long panther-body over a gilded frippery of a chair, balancing with insouciant grace. "So," he said. "Why did you let her get with child?"

"I didn't—" She broke off. "Oh," she said. "Oh! May your manly member be infested with boils! I did not *let* that simpleton do anything.

She did it all of herself. Who's to know that she didn't find an obliging soldier or guardsman to assist her?"

"Why, did you?"

He had driven her beyond anger. Senenmut, watching, struggling
not to be amused, suffered the full force of her glare. "You! Do you
think the same?"

"Of course not," he said in perfect honesty. "I think the king had
a shaft or two in his quiver. She was clever enough to catch it. It's not
entirely her fault, after all. If you had so much as crooked a finger, he
would have been in your bed and glad of it."

"Or at least," said Nehsi, "not too terribly disgruntled at the
prospect." He swung his foot idly, regarding her under lowered lids.
"It could still be arranged. An accident to the little mother. His majesty
seeking solace in your arms."

"But no son," she said. "No child of my body." She met both their
stares. "What, you didn't think I knew? Who could hide it from me?
It's as obvious as a solid year in that man's bed, and nothing to show
for it but the shudder when I think of doing it again. I won't, even to
pretend. The gods have emptied my womb."

"Therefore," Nehsi said, "you allowed them to fill the concubine's."

"The gods do as they will," said the queen.

■ Nehsi went out soon after. He had duties, to assure that the queen
was well guarded and protected against the spirits of the night.

Senenmut should have gone with the Nubian. But he was comfortable in the brazier's warmth, cross-legged on a cushion, and she had
not dismissed him.

He started slightly. They were alone. They had never been so,
never that he could remember. There were always others with them.
Maids. Attendants. Guards.

Now there were only the two of them, and the tent striped in gold
and blue like the *nemes*-headdress that the king might wear, and the
sounds of the camp gone soft and dim as the night came down. The
brazier glowed. A tree of lamps cast light across a richness of carpets.

She sat atop a heap of them, cross-legged as he was, but untrained to it.

She rose and stretched, arching her back, yawning like a cat. Her gown was thin, ill suited to the chill of the outer air, but ample for the tent's warmth. The mantle that she had worn over it was abandoned on the carpets. She took off her wig and shook out the crushed plaits of her hair.

"I always wonder," Senenmut heard himself say, "why custom constrains us to the sweaty weight of a wig. For me it keeps off the sun. But you . . . your hair is beautiful. It's a pity it must be hidden."

She unbound the plaits, running her fingers through them, waking them to the life that was in them. Her hair, freed, fanned on her shoulders. She might have been oblivious to him, but his heart knew better. She knew well that he was there.

Beyond that, he dared not think. Nor dared he think of what she was doing. He had served her with perfect propriety since he was little more than a child. His heart had grown accustomed to the constraints of that propriety. The dreams had come more often as he grew older, and every night of late, but he had never ventured to believe that they were prophecy.

She was not enamored of him. How could she be? He was a commoner, no more divine than the earth underfoot, no beauty of face, no grace of body, nothing to recommend him but the quickness of his wits.

Even that had deserted him. She sank down on the carpets and beckoned. "Come here," she said.

A wise man would have retreated rapidly, babbling an excuse. Senenmut was clever but he had never been wise. He obeyed her.

When he was within her reach, she caught his hands and pulled him down. Kneeling, he was taller than she, awkward and fumbling, blushing like the untried boy he was.

He could have been no more appealing than the king at his worst, but she did not recoil from him. Her eyes searched his face. Beautiful eyes, long and dark. He felt as transparent to them as water, as insubstantial as air.

"I dreamed," she said, "that you—and I—"

"The river? The reeds?" He had not willed to speak, but his tongue was living a life of its own, apart from any wit or wisdom.

"The river," she said, nodding. "The reeds. The golden boat."

His heart had begun to beat hard. "We can't be dreaming—the same—"

"If the gods wish it," she said, "we can."

"But why?" he cried. "What am I, that you should even look at me?"

She blinked. "I don't know," she said, direct as a child. "Ever since I saw you standing in my chamber, furious that you had been sent to serve a mere queen, with a curl in your lip and a glitter in your eye—I've been helpless to resist you. You have no beauty and no sweetness of temper, certainly no grace, and only a hard-won elegance, but you make my body sing."

"The gods are mocking us," he said. "I am as far below you as a beetle in a dungheap."

"And is it not the dung-beetle that rolls the sun across the sky? Ra-Harakhte, my beloved."

He caught his breath. He was no slave to superstition, but she tempted the gods with her irreverence.

She laughed at his expression. He seldom heard such laughter from her, light and free, unconstrained by the bonds of her royalty. "My beloved," she repeated. "You do love me."

"Of course I love you," he snapped. "No man could avoid it. But for you to look at the likes of me . . ."

"Your arrogance is a sham," she said. "Your heart is a shy and modest thing, too tender to show itself bare. You see? I see the whole of you."

"You don't—"

Her hand stopped his mouth. It was warm. It lay lightly on his lips, but it shook him like a blow. He gasped and staggered.

She caught him, held him up. He remembered the shape and feel of her body—oh, vividly; every night he dreamed it. Her breasts were fuller than his memory had made them, her skin softer, her scent sweeter. Her lips tasted of honey and wine.

He stiffened to pull away. "We can't—the king—the gods—"

Her eyes caught him, held him. "I am queen and goddess," she said with the calm of perfect surety.

"But I—"

"The gods have given you to me. You are their gift and their consolation."

"But why *now?*"

He could never take her off guard, never catch her unprepared. She smiled a sweet slow smile. "Why not now?"

"Because," he said, though it burned his throat, "your husband's concubine is with child as you are unable to be, and you fear that she will give him the son who will be king when he is dead. I am your defiance. You cast me in his face."

"Yes," she said, serene as ever. "And I love you, and no danger will ever come to you. That is my vow and my promise. I loved you before I learned to hate him. When he is dead and his concubine's son is king, we will endure. We will walk together even in the Field of Reeds, where no power of his will sunder us. I dream, you see. And what I dream, I dream true."

He should do battle with her relentless, illogical logic. He should break away, flee, escape while he still could.

But he did not move. He did not wish to. She was queen and goddess; but she was woman, too, and beautiful, and warm in his arms. His dreams had taught him how she loved to be embraced: tenderly, without haste, till urgency woke in her.

He was awkward, even with dreams to guide him. If she had laughed he would have shriveled, but she was sweetly intent, gentle as he had never seen her, even with her horses. It was strange to be all new to it, and yet to find it utterly familiar. He could believe then what she had told him: that the gods willed it. Why, to what end, he did not know. It might be his death.

Glorious death, if that were so: wrapped in his lady's arms.

"So be it," he said into the fragrance of her hair. "As the gods will: so let it be."

17

NEHSI KNEW NIGH AS SOON AS they did, that his queen and his queen's scribe had become more than lady and servant. It only surprised him that it had taken them so long. He had seen it when Neferure was born, how she sought that waspish unlovely man as the wild goose seeks its mate. Between them then had stretched a bond like a shining cord, never dimmed, never weakened, however far apart their bodies were.

Others had no such eyes as he had, or willed not to see. The king, by the gods' mercy, was one of them. He had never been a jealous husband, but he had had no need to be. And now he had his concubine, whom he doted on and fussed over as if he had been an old grandmother. One would have thought that he had never sired a brat before.

Isis, sly creature that she was, encouraged him in his fretting. She carried well and easily, unlike the queen, but every ache, every flutter of heart or stomach, threw her into prostration that was only to be relieved by the king's presence. When the child roused and began to move, she kept the king by her by day as well as by night, leashed like a dog, and no will in him to protest.

The queen bore perforce the burden of the Two Kingdoms. That of course was nothing new. "I like to rule by myself," she said. "No fool of a man interfering with my decisions. No royal whim to disrupt the course of my judgments."

Her heart might be given to a scribe, but her friendship remained securely in Nehsi's hands. He continued to play the guardsman, though less often than before: for the comfort of it, the pleasure of a task so familiar that it seemed bred in the bone. When she took an hour's grace in her garden, he still stood watch over her solitude. No duty could prevent him, no task interfere.

"Sometimes," she said on that particular day, not long before Isis came to her time, "I wonder what it would be like to yield to no man—to be what the king is."

The earth did not shake at the enormity of the thought, nor did the Horus-falcon stoop out of the sun to rend her. Nehsi, born in Thebes but a foreigner by blood and breeding, paused to consider what an Egyptian would think of a woman who said such a thing. Senenmut, perhaps—

No. Senenmut worshipped her as queen and goddess, loved her as a woman, spoke as freely to her as Nehsi ever had, and quarreled with her, too. He must know what was in her heart. If he did not, he was a blinder man than Nehsi had given him credit for.

She lay on the rim of the fountain, letting the light wind blow its spray across her body. Her hair was free, her gown a shimmer of gauze. He regarded her dispassionately and was glad of the woman who would warm his bed tonight. The twins, in the way of women, had turned their affections elsewhere in the Nubian Guard, finding greater sport in a man for each, to share and share alike. He had dallied for a while with the queen's sharp-tongued maid, Meritre, but she was a strong dose for a weary man.

Of late he had found a kind of contentment with a lady of the queen's wardrobe, half a Nubian, warm and soft-bodied and quiet. Memory of her soothed him now: her rich brown skin, her densely curling hair, her heavy breasts with their great nipples full of milk for the girlchild that she had borne to one of the king's bodyguard. The child was nigh weaned, and toddled about while its mother lay with Nehsi: a quiet child, almost unnaturally so, but very like gentle Kamut.

Half-dreaming though he was, he heard his queen clearly. "I never wish to be a man, but to have what a man has—to claim the power that he claims by the simple fact of his sex—for that I would give much."

"Most men," he said, "would be overjoyed to answer to one man, and one man only."

Her glance was sharp, meant to wound. He raised armor of imperturbability. That piqued her. She said, "I would answer to none. The gods shaped and fashioned me to rule, in all things but one. By accident or oversight, they made me a woman."

"Woman and queen," he said. "No woman stands higher; and only one man."

"One shallow fool," she said. "One man who would have done better to be born a petty lordling of a small domain, with nothing to do but fight and hunt and sire sons."

"I've heard the priests say," said Nehsi, "that the gods set each man where they will, for their own purpose."

The sound she made was pure disgust, vulgar enough for a guardsman. He snorted at it. She closed her eyes, affronted, and would not speak to him again while she lingered in the garden.

He did not trouble himself over her ill humor. Real, true and deep wrath was rare in her. These fits of temper were of no more moment than a fine mare's flattened ears and snapping teeth at the touch of a stranger's hand. They warned a man to move with care, but they set him in no danger.

And perhaps, he thought, her sharpness with him would preserve decorum when she faced the king. She must not offend him, nor give him reason to curtail her power. Courtiers muttered that it was too great already; that she governed too much by her own will, nor consulted the king in whose name she ruled.

Courtiers were always muttering. A wise chamberlain listened and kept his own counsel. Amid the dross, sometimes, one found gold; or poison.

■ Senenmut was a wealthy man. It had crept up on him: a gift here, a reward there, a bribe that he would have refused, but the queen laughed and bade him take it. It amused her to let him enrich himself with the treasure of fools. He might do as he was bribed to do; or not. She left him to choose for himself.

Since that was mostly to present a case to the queen, more often than not he did it, in no expectation that she would favor the petitioner. Sometimes she did; sometimes she refused. He never tried to coax her; and for that she professed to find him refreshing. "Which of course is why I love you," she said. "You never lie to me, nor soften the truth."

He was a dreadful liar. He had learned with difficulty to be silent when he could not be truthful. Even at that, his face too often betrayed him.

But petitioners seeking the queen's favor did not want lies, only a voice on their behalf. He never promised to gain them what they asked. They persevered in spite of it.

And he had become amazingly rich. Rich enough to refurbish his beloved, faded house; to pay his brother Ahotep's way into a company of the king's guard, and to equip his youngest brother Amonhotep with a tutor worthy of a prince. There was no need any longer for his father to peddle pots in the market. Rahotep, whom age had only made the more vague, seemed to feel no lack. He continued to spend his days in the tavern where he had amused himself with friends since he was a young man. The same men downed the same jars of beer as they always had, told the same weary jests, sang the same songs. As far as Senenmut could see, they were happy; and his father was content.

His mother took a fierce delight in the office of lady of his household. She never ceased her efforts to see him married off, though that would set a wife in her place. "Mothers are not logical," she said. "I want grandchildren. It's your duty to give them to me."

It was not likely he ever would. The queen was barren. He had no more doubt of it than he did of her love for him—however unworthy he was. It was grief, but it was relief, too; that she would bear no embarrassment to her baseborn lover.

Though if she had, or could . . .

No. No son of Senenmut would sit the throne of the Two Lands. It was enough for the gods' humor that he lay with the woman whose body belonged to the king alone; who had been born to suffer the embrace of no lesser man.

She was discreet. She called him to her only when there was no fear of discovery: deep in the night, or when she had taken a holiday in her barge upon the river, or when they rode in chariots from Black Land into Red Land, and found secret places where no hunt could find them.

When the king was away she slept alone and decorous. Then a spy might look to see who warmed her bed; but she was wiser than that.

She gave her lover great gifts, heaped him with titles, weighted him with duties. He was not loved in the court, commoner that he was, with no inheritance but cleverness: and so clearly one of the queen's great favorites, one of the few whom she kept closest. But he remained alive and unpoisoned through a simple expedient. He groveled to no courtier, but neither did he play the prince. He was a scribe who had proved himself in the queen's service. Wealthy though he was, he claimed lordship of no domain, nor ruled anywhere but in the queen's palace.

For that, barely, they suffered him. He suffered them in turn, idiots that most of them were. Lordly scions with any grain of intelligence sought the priesthoods, particularly that of Amon, or went for scribes in the House of Life; or, if they were bloody-minded, sought the king's army and rose to high places in it. Those who loitered about the court were the idlers, the witlessly fashionable, the players at intrigue.

But they were lords of the Two Kingdoms. The queen depended on their goodwill for the execution of her commands. The army was the king's. The lords and courtiers, the nomarchs and their servants, could choose to ignore her, to heed only such commands as the king himself chose to utter.

"Even a king," she said once, "rules by his people's sufferance. He commands; they must choose to obey—even if that choice is laid on them by force. Though rule by force is the resort of a weakling. A strong king rules by the will and the love of his subjects. My father taught me that. He was a strong king, was my father; and a great warrior, too. His son, my half-brother, my husband, is but a shadow of him."

Whereas she, thought Senenmut, was the image of her father's strength. Except in war. She had no love for it, and no inclination— no talent, either, perhaps. The battles she chose were all fought in the hall of audience or in the courts of the kingdoms' justice.

■ Senenmut was a wealthy man; but of leisure he had little. Such of it as he was granted, he took grudgingly. He had not known how weary he was, or how short his temper, until what he had thought a civil reply to some question of the queen's made her lips tighten and her eyes glitter. She dismissed him out of hand, bade him go away and not come back until he had taken a full day's holiday.

"But," he protested, "the princess—the palace—the court—"

"Go!" she commanded him, with a glance at her guards. They closed in with purpose that he could not mistake. He would go on his own feet or in their hands.

He left with such dignity as he could muster. He was too shocked to be angry; and too startled by the leap of his heart. Free. Unwillingly, cast out of duties that would multiply tenfold before he came back to them—but free.

He had not known such liberty since he was a boy, when a festival freed the scribes' pupils to do as they pleased. He had wandered at loose ends till he found himself a corner to sit in and practice his letters. Idleness had never been an art that he could master.

And now he was left to his own devices. If he went home, his mother would reckon that he was ill, or that he had fallen out of favor; she would try to cure him with yet another marriageable female. He had no one whom he could call friend; no confidant, no drinking companion. All his heart and his wit were given to the queen.

He was not lonely. He needed no friend. But someone to bear him company, to teach him how to be idle, would have been welcome.

He wandered without purpose, as courtiers constantly seemed to do. He lacked their languid ease, their propensity for gossiping in corners. His heart inclined toward none of their diversions. Wine did not allure him, and of women he desired only one; and he had never seen the sense in poisoning his enemies. If he could call them enemies. He would have had to poison the whole court, and the king too.

There were always the horses. But the Star of Hathor was lame, and the Moon of Isis would not run without her. He had no others; had never had time for them.

Still, he thought, the queen's stablemen knew him. He could command a team and a chariot. It would pass the time, certainly; and if he tarried long enough, he might find his way into the training-court, where the young horses were gentled to the yoke.

His heart was light as he sought the stable, his reluctance diminished to a niggle on the edge of his mind. Such adventure: to go out alone in a chariot, to drive where he pleased and to pause when it suited him, and no one to call him back.

The queen's own master of horse met him at the stable door. "She sent word," he said. And there were her own beauties, her red-golden mares whom she suffered no other to touch, save the master of horse. It was a gift, subtle and splendid. He accepted it with the joy that it deserved.

18

WHEN SENENMUT RETURNED TO the stable near sunset, having run the queen's mares well and far, he found the master of horse in the foaling-stall. The mare who stood there, so huge with foal that she could only brace her feet and endure, was the queen's own darling. She had been foaled herself in this stall, of a mare whom the old king had given his daughter: a queen for a queen, he had said, or so Hatshepsut remembered, and had told Senenmut.

It was a beautiful mare, even so swollen with pregnancy. She was a red horse as the queen preferred, a deeper red than some, the color of dark carnelian. She had no marking, nor any scar or flaw. She was surpassingly light and swift of foot; few could match her, and for this year and more she had had no companion in the traces. She had been put to the swiftest of the stallions, the king's moon-white Eye of Horus.

She had yet a while before the foal came. A mare almost never foaled in daylight. It was horse-magic, moon-magic; the sun enfeebled it.

The master of horse was called Kamose. His true name was something incomprehensible in one of the tongues of Asia; but Kamose did well enough, and he answered to it. He stood in his striped robe, bent from his great height to press his ear to the mare's flank. His hands ran over her belly and slipped beneath. He nodded. "Tonight," he said.

The mare sighed and lipped at a wisp of cut fodder. Kamose stroked her neck and withers. "Ah, beautiful one," he said in sympathy. "It's over soon, and well over."

She knew. She had foaled before. But as all mares will when they are within hours of their time, she chose not to believe him.

Senenmut stayed to comfort her. Kamose welcomed the assistance. As much as he loved this one mare, he had a stableful to look after, and a horde of stablehands who must be driven with a tight rein and watchful eye. Senenmut, sitting on a heap of straw just outside the foaling stall, was out of the way and acceptably quiet.

He even slept, dozing with his back to the wall, but it was a light, uneasy sleep, marked by the movements of the queen's red mare. He was aware, if distantly, of the evening round of the stable: bringing in those horses that had been turned out to run in one of the courts, feeding them all, bedding them down, snuffing the lamps one by one in procession toward the doors. A lamp remained burning on a shelf over his head, casting a glimmer of light into the mare's stall.

She was quiet, but it was a restless quiet. She had picked at her evening's fodder, scattering more than she ate. She went back to it at intervals, but she was beginning to feel the pangs of the foal's coming: stamping, snapping at her sides.

When she went down, Kamose was there as if some god had called him; and another behind, a slight figure in a kilt with its hair in a braid. But for the eyepaint that no Egyptian would be seen without, the queen was bare of adornment, stripped for whatever action the night would bring.

They had foaled mares before, she and Kamose; and Senenmut was no novice, either, though never such a master as the others were. They moved in concert as they had more than once before. The mare knew her duty and did it well and quickly, without fuss. She left them little enough to do until the foal lay wet and glistening on the straw. Then she suffered them near her, inspecting the red filly-foal, uttering words of guard and guidance upon it, awaiting and then examining the afterbirth and finding it all as it should be.

That was great power, great magic, to bring a creature whole and perfect into the world. And such a creature: red like her mother, it seemed she would be, and on her forehead a marking like a crescent moon. It was Senenmut who held her soft and still damp in his arms, welcoming her to the world of the living, finding in her eyes the secret of her name. He whispered it in her ear, and she heard him: the ear twitched; she butted her head against his hand.

She was seeking her mother's teat. He let her go. She wobbled in her soft new feet, tangling them in one another, questing with blind intensity for the thing she must have above all others. The mare, the worst of her task done, nuzzled its outcome and urged it gently toward her flank.

Senenmut was grinning like an idiot. So was Hatshepsut; and Kamose had so far forsaken his dignity as to allow a smile through the thicket of his beard. "She is beautiful," said Senenmut, "like the young moon in the planting time."

"She will be as lovely as her mother," Kamose agreed, "and as noble as her father. See how she stands already, straight for one so young, and strong. She'll be as swift as a wind in the desert."

"Then let her be the Dawn Wind," the queen said. Her eye caught Senenmut's. "And let her belong to my scribe, the tutor of my daughter."

Senenmut caught his breath. "Lady! You can't mean—"

"Do I ever say aught but what I mean?"

He flinched slightly at the edge in her tone, but he was not cowed by it. "Lady, she was to be her mother's heir, the queen of your stable when her time comes. You can't give her to me."

"I can," Hatshepsut said inflexibly, "and I have. Are you fool enough to refuse her?"

"No," he said. "But you are a fool to give her away."

"Sometimes," said the queen, "it pleases me to be a fool."

He shook his head. The filly, just then, chose to wander away from her mother, pressing up against him, unbalancing him till he must embrace her or fall. He could feel the sleep in her, the sated hunger, the drowsy wonder at all this strange new world. As he sank down, she went with him, laid her head in his lap and sighed and went to sleep.

"You see," the queen said. "Even if I hadn't given the gift, she would have given herself."

If anyone else had been standing where Senenmut had stood, that one would have received the gift instead. He did not say so. The gods were playing with him again. It had been a hard lesson; but he had learned not to quarrel with them when they were determined to give him whatever he had dreamed of.

He bowed therefore, as formally as if he had been in court, though somewhat impeded by the weight of the foal in his lap. "I thank my lady," he said, "with all my heart."

■ The king's concubine bore her child on the same night that Senenmut's filly was born. It was a son, as its father had prayed and its mother had serenely expected. He was named Thutmose, like his father and his grandfather before him. That in Senenmut's mind was great presumption.

The queen was astonishingly calm. "It's fitting enough. His father was a concubine's son, too. Now if he had been mine . . . I would have named him something different. Something powerful, something worthy of a queen's son."

■ She went in the morning to call on the king and on the king's concubine. She had dressed with care, as queen and goddess; but not so splendid that she mocked the concubine's rank and station.

The guards at the gate of the king's palace stood firm in front of her and would not let her pass. Nehsi, who spoke as her herald, chose calm reason over wrath. She did not gainsay him, which spoke well for her wisdom. "Send word to his majesty," he said, "that her majesty waits without."

"His majesty is in seclusion," said the captain of the guard, as calm as Nehsi, and as reasonable. "I am certain that when he emerges he will be delighted to receive her majesty."

"Her majesty recognizes the king's desire for quiet," Nehsi said, "but she wishes to speak with him now."

"Alas," said the captain of the guard, "his majesty will see no one."

"He will see her majesty," Nehsi said, suffering a hint of iron to enter the blandness of his voice.

The captain of the guard neither moved nor yielded. Nehsi set himself to thrust past, but the queen's voice halted him. "No. Allow him this indulgence. For the moment."

She did not retreat. She withdrew as if the choice had been hers, with the air of a queen who humors her husband's whim.

■ Not until much later, when she had held the day's audience and judged in the tribunal and entertained a gaggle of court ladies at a feast in honor of one who was to marry the nomarch of Abydos, could she retreat to her chambers. Then she unleashed her temper. It was short, but it was fiery. Her maids fled the blast. Her guards took refuge in the corridor—all but Nehsi, who retreated to the door but did not escape through it.

Senenmut alone was bold enough or fool enough to remain where he was. He had come to read to her from a new book, a collection of poems that he had found thrust inexplicably into a heap of archives from the time of Queen Nefertari. He clutched the scroll-case to his chest, standing in the middle of her sitting-room while the storm broke about his head.

She could swear like a trooper, but when she was truly, bone-searingly angry, she uttered each innocuous word with the mincing precision of a court dandy. Likewise, when she was merely furious, she hurled whatever came to hand, with deadly accuracy. True rage found her motionless, erect and still, hands clenched into fists at her sides.

But ah, such things as she said, such devastating commentary on the king, on his proclivities, on his fondness for leaving her to do all his duties that he found excessively dull. She spoke rapidly, in a tone so flat it might have seemed calm, except for the crisp and crackle of fire on a listener's skin. It was that calm which had struck terror in the

hearts of her servants. Hatshepsut in a rage was dangerous. Hatshepsut in the calm beyond rage was deadly.

Senenmut did not honestly fear for his life, nor overmuch for his
hide. But that he risked exile or return to the rank of his birth, simply
for showing his face in front of her when she was clearly ready to kill
something, he did not doubt for a moment.

"He does not trust me," the queen said to the air just in front of
her. "He dares to tell me, as clearly as if he had written it on papyrus,
that he will not permit me to visit his concubine or to look on her son.
Fool! Does he think that I would strangle the brat in his cradle?"

Senenmut bit his tongue. She wanted no answer, and certainly no
comfort. He had to hope that his presence would calm her, soothe her
rage, turn her mind away from the magnitude of the insult. Vain
hope—arrogant, too. But he could not help it.

"That child," she said, "will be king, the husband of my daughter,
the lord of these two kingdoms. I am their lady and queen. It is my
right that I should see him; that I should know what he is."

"At that age," Nehsi dared to say from the safety of distance,
"there's no telling what a baby will turn into. They all look like shriveled monkeys."

Her eyes blazed. Her chin rose even higher. "I would know. A
queen knows a king. Even when I was small and my so-noble husband
was a handful of years older than I—even then I knew that he was no
match for my father."

"And can't you wait?" Nehsi asked her. "Patience is a queen's best
virtue. If he's healthy he'll live; if not, he'll be out of your way. And
when he's old enough that the kingdoms may see him, and he them,
then you can reckon his worth."

She laughed, a whipcrack of sound with no joy in it. "This is not
about patience. This is about my right as queen to know who—and
what—will be king when my husband is dead. My husband denies it.
Were I a man, O my servant, I would go to war for it."

"You still could," Nehsi observed.

"Yes. Indeed I could. And I could put on wings, too, and leap from
the highest tower of this palace, and command the gods to let me fly."

She dropped down abruptly, heedless of her robes' stiffness, sitting on her heels on the floor. Her fists struck the tiles once, twice: a child's fierce eruption of temper, as swiftly ended as it had begun. "May a jackal devour his liver! I had no love for him ever, but I was never his enemy. Never till now."

"That, I think, may be what Isis is hoping for," Senenmut said.

Both the queen and the Nubian started. He had been standing between them, buffeted by the force of their contention, but they had seen through him as through air and shadows. His return to solidity took them aback.

"I don't think," he said, "that this comes from the king. He's not a subtle man, and he's not afraid of you, either. He didn't try to keep you out while his concubine was carrying the child, when he might well have feared some poison or some curse that would cause her to miscarry. This shutting of his door now that the baby's born—that's another mind at work. Isis is feeling her triumph, I think. She's trying to play the queen."

"Then she can play it properly," Hatshepsut snapped, "and instruct the guards to speak in her name and not in my husband's. That's weakness, if the little idiot only knew it. *I* can demand a guard's obedience, and get it."

Senenmut allowed himself the relief of a sigh. She was still in a fury, but she was thinking. She was arguing sensibly, as far as this whole affair had any sense in it.

He was glad to see her returned to herself again; but he was mildly wary still. She had fallen silent, chin propped on fist, frowning at the air. She was plotting something. But what it was, she was not about to confess.

She rose abruptly. "Nehsi. Fetch my maids. I'll bathe, I think, and rest. Senenmut: read to me while I bathe."

Both men bowed. They did not exchange glances. Nehsi, thought Senenmut, was as watchful as he was, and as mistrustful of her sudden change of mood. It would hardly be like her to send an assassin to the little prince's chamber; but when she was at this pitch of temper, there was no telling what she would do.

19

W HAT THE QUEEN DID, AS FAR as anyone could
tell, was nothing. She went about her duties as before. She
did not approach the king or his chambers, nor ask to look
on his son. She had sunk into a kind of quiet that alarmed Nehsi the
more, the longer it lasted.

When the king's son was presented to the people, given his name
and lifted up to the sun that was the eye of Horus and the protector of
kings, the queen could not be prevented from attending. Nor was she.
She came no nearer to the child however than a spear's length, the half-
width of the circle of guards that stood about her. There was no open
insult in that: the queen was often so guarded, and the king too, a guard
of honor to her majesty. But she was a prisoner, however subtle the
prison. And she knew it.

Nehsi, who had taken command of the guards rather than suffer
the king to set a man of his own over them, saw how the king favored
his concubine. She need not walk in procession to Amon's temple; she
was given a chair like a great lady, and set in it in the gown and ornaments of a queen, though never—and that was well indeed, thought
Nehsi—a queen's crown. Her elaborate plaited wig and her golden cir-
clet were such as any lady of rank might claim.

And rank she had now, by virtue of the bundle in her arms. The
child had a nurse; one could hardly expect her to ruin her beautiful
round breasts with giving suck to her son. But this she would surrender to no other woman: the great joy and honor of standing up before
the Two Lands with the king's son in her arms.

She looked, as ever, like a cat in cream. She was careful not to stare
boldly at the queen. She would not gloat openly; she was no such fool.
But the glances she slid at Hatshepsut were wickedly bright. *See how I*

triumph, they said: *I, the serving-girl, the morsel you sent to be the lion's dinner.*

Hatshepsut's face was still and her eyes quiet, betraying no outrage, offering no insult. Isis was disconcerted, perhaps. Her glances were more frequent as the day went on, procession and rite in the temple, presentation before the people, feast in the court from which the child, sound asleep with his nurse's teat in his mouth, was taken softly away. She had to eat what was set in front of her; a taster was not suitable and would have been a cry to war, but she was careful to touch nothing that the queen had not also eaten.

"Idiot," the queen said when it was over, safe in the sanctuary of her own chambers, with her trusted people about her. "I'd never have poisoned her; only the baby. And seen to it that she conceived no more."

Since that was manifestly true, no one took issue with it. Isis, who might have done so, was locked within the walls of the king's palace, well away from the queen's influence, guarded so scrupulously that she could hardly visit the privy-pot without its being watched and recorded. The queen was a freer woman than she: free of the sky if she chose, and of the palace certainly, all but the rooms in which the king's son grew from a plump quiet infant into a plump quiet boychild.

■ Thutmose, son of Thutmose, son of Thutmose, was hardly a guardsman's son as people sometimes whispered. Even as a young child he had the unmistakable stamp of the king's family: the short compact body, the small square hands, the nose that in the king was a jut like a ship's prow, and in the queen a haughty arch. His half-sister Neferure had it, too, but like her mother she was fortunate; hers was elegant rather than imposing.

She was a lively child. She spoke her first word early, and followed it quickly with a myriad more. She read, wrote, sang and played harp and lute, mastered the arts of a lady as well as the arts of a queen—even to the bow and the chariot—while her brother was still dreaming at his nurse's breast.

He was much quieter than she, by all accounts. Contrary to the wisdom of nurses and tutors, that boys are invariably more boisterous than girls, he never cried, never misbehaved. He was so quiet that people whispered. He was mute, they said, or simple. Or, murmured a few bold spirits, afflicted with a curse.

■ In point of fact, as Senenmut undertook to discover, the boy had a voice and seemed to have a fair sampling of wits. He simply preferred to keep his own counsel. He was a remarkably self-contained baby, content to lie for hours in his cradle, watching the play of sun and shadow on the wall; or to play by himself in the walled garden that adjoined his mother's chambers. His first plaything, so Senenmut was told, was a wooden horse with a wooden chariot. He would gallop the horse through the garden, and cause the rider in the chariot to do battle with enemies made of reeds and woven grass.

When he had passed his third year, he went from his mother's care to that of a tutor. Isis did not give him up easily, but although the king was still besotted with her, willing to yield to her every whim, in this he was adamant. His son would be raised as befit a man and a king.

Therefore the prince came out from among the women and into rooms of his own, with his own servants, his own guardsmen, his own tutor and preceptor.

That was a man whom Senenmut happened to know, if not well. Nebsen as he was called—his proper name and titles were much longer and more dignified—had been a handful of years ahead of Senenmut in the Temple of Amon. He had won a name for easy camaraderie and willingness to please. His skills with the pen were less remarkable, but as Seti-Nakht had been heard to observe, a man did not need to be a great scribe to attract and keep a king's notice.

Nebsen had completed his studies and entered the king's service, assisted by noble connections and a remote claim to kinship with the royal line. His affable ways must have endeared him to the king; as for how he had won the prize, the care of the king's son, he would tilt his head and smile and say as coyly as a woman, "Let us keep our secrets, shall we?"

He did not seem to share Isis' fear of the queen, nor did he trouble to shun the princess' tutor. They shared a jar of beer on occasion, exchanging tales of royal offspring. And in short order Senenmut won what he had been hoping for: an invitation to visit Nebsen in the little prince's chambers. A wiser or less trusting man would have been careful to avoid just that, letting the queen's favorite so close to the king's son. But Nebsen had never seen any harm in Senenmut, nor in much of anyone else, either.

Senenmut came to the prince's chambers as a guest, and carefully not as a spy for the queen. He had been engaged in teaching his own charge the intricacies of poetic metre; he brought with him a gift for the prince, a scrap of papyrus rolled and tied with a ribbon. On it was a poem that Neferure had written, charmingly artless but by no means clumsy, addressed to her brother and admonishing him to be both beautiful and wise. She had insisted that Senenmut bring it, and that he present it to the prince with her greetings.

She had never met her brother, no more than her mother had. When Senenmut was younger he would have sighed with envy, particularly after a night of sharing a bed with a fractious Ahotep. Now that he was older and had a bed to himself, he knew a moment's pity for a sister who was denied all the pleasures and pains of a younger brother.

And why, he thought, should it go on so? These were more than brother and sister. They would be king and queen in their time, wedded as their father and her mother were. Senenmut could hope that they got on better than the two before them.

He would know when he saw Thutmose. If anything could be done to bring these children together, he would do it.

■ The prince's chambers were guarded as all royal chambers were, by men whose service and whose loyalty were to the prince. They offered no objection as Senenmut approached, nor stood in his way. He was known to belong to the queen, but it seemed he was reckoned harmless.

Isis might not agree. But Isis was not in these rooms, nor likely to appear there: she had gone with the king on a several days' hunt, leaving the prince behind under heavy and, she seemed to think, sufficient guard. That was precisely as Senenmut wished it. He entered with a

firm step, turning where the guard directed, through an antechamber
and into a wide airy room.

Its walls were painted with images of war. The king loomed in his
chariot, wearing the Two Crowns, wielding a bow while his horses
trampled a horde of enemies. His soldiers marched behind him, rank
on rank around the room: footsoldiers in their companies, lords and
princes in their chariots.

Senenmut had seen such images in his few brief forays into the
king's chamber. These were new, the paint fresh and vivid. They overwhelmed the two who sat in the room's center.

Nebsen rose with a glad cry. "Senenmut! Welcome!"

Senenmut murmured a greeting, but eyes and mind were fixed on
the other, the small compact figure sitting on a cushion. The prince
was naked as all young children were, his head shaved but for the
plaited lock of a child and a royal heir, which he would wear even into
manhood if his father lived long. He was much as Senenmut remembered from more distant views of him: small for his age but sturdy and
strong, with a gift that was vastly rare in a child so young: to sit still.

He was not feeble of wit. His eyes were quiet, but there was intelligence in them: a calm intelligence, as of one who knows well how to
wait; but Senenmut sensed a fierce intensity beneath.

Senenmut bowed before him and greeted him as a servant should
greet a prince. He inclined his head but said nothing.

"He talks," Nebsen said, perhaps a little quickly. "Just not often.
But when he does, he does it extraordinarily well."

The prince seemed accustomed to being spoken of as if he had not
been there. He regarded Senenmut with that enormous and change-
less calm, as if he measured this stranger and pondered his judgment.

"It was quite strange," Nebsen went on—rattling, it might seem,
but Nebsen's chatter usually had a point concealed somewhere within
it. "He never spoke a word till this past Inundation. Not one; hardly
even baby-babble. Then one day shortly after he was given into my care,
he said to me, 'Nebsen, take me down to the river. I want to watch Father's soldiers practice their marching.' " Nebsen laughed and shook
his head. "Oh, he took me fair aback, he did. Spoke as clear as you or

I, not a lisp or a stammer; and such words as you would hardly expect a baby to know."

Either of Senenmut's brothers at Thutmose's age would have maintained loudly and continually that he was not a baby. The prince did not trouble himself. Having received the guest as was polite, he returned to what he must have been doing before Senenmut came there: playing on the floor with a wooden army.

Senenmut, watching him, observed a little wryly, "I see he is his father's son."

"Oh, no doubt of it," said Nebsen. "Day and night, indoors and out, that's all he thinks about: soldiers and chariots, horses and weapons. He insists that I read to him from accounts of old wars, such as you would think would put him to sleep, but he listens to every word. If I didn't keep him close as his mother commands me, he'd be among the soldiers from dawn till dark."

"And what does his mother think of that?" Senenmut inquired.

Nebsen rolled his eyes. "Ah, his mother! So beautiful a lady, so charming, so perfectly obliging to her husband. Still, she is a woman. Women, Senenmut, are incalculable. Why, my wife . . ."

While Nebsen rambled through a long and crashingly dull tale, Senenmut watched the prince. Thutmose had lined up his troops in orderly rows, foot in front, chariots behind. The enemy were less precise, a scatter of foot and chariots, each appearing to be a lord and his retinue or a barbarian chief and his warband; though that would be very sophisticated for a child as young as he was.

Nebsen ended his story with a sigh and a flourish. Senenmut looked appropriately sympathetic. "Ah well," said Nebsen. "You've never married. Wise of you, to keep yourself free of that bondage."

Senenmut shrugged, mustered a smile. It was probably crooked. He could not help that.

Nebsen did not take offense. "So you see, her gracious highness would prefer that her son be less warlike in his inclinations. To which his majesty the king replies that one might as easily command the lion to eat grass with the ox. His majesty is delighted with my young lord."

"I can imagine," Senenmut said. He bent toward the prince. "Is that a particular battle, my lord?"

The prince looked up. His glance was quick, startling in that placid face. "Yes," he said. "That is the battle in which Ahmose defeated the foreign kings. He could have fought it so many ways, you see. I want to know which one was best."

Indeed, thought Senenmut, he could speak as clearly as a much older child. Senenmut regarded him with respect, but no shock or awe. He too had been precocious; he had had his fill then of astonished exclamations. "Do you always think of battles?" Senenmut asked.

"I like battles," said the prince. "And soldiers, and marching in ranks. A king should always be so, Father says. He has a world to conquer, so that he may rule as the gods meant."

Senenmut raised a brow. "And do you care for nothing else?"

"I like horses," Thutmose said.

"Ah," said Senenmut. "Do you? I came to them much later than you, but I love them dearly. I have a filly—we're training her to the yoke. She has to wait to be a team, for her sister who is a year younger than she, because no one else is swift enough to match her. She was born on the day that you were born, and her sister was born the next year to the day. We call them our two queens."

"I like stallions better," Thutmose said.

"But," said Senenmut, "mares are faster. And quieter. And more sensible in battle."

"Have you ever been in a battle?" asked that astonishing child.

"Oh, not I," Senenmut said. "I'm a scribe, not a soldier. But I can drive a chariot and train a horse." He paused. "If your highness wishes and your guardians allow, you may make the acquaintance of my two queens."

For the first time Thutmose smiled. It was a sweet smile, with a touch of wickedness—like, Senenmut thought, Hatshepsut's.

This could—indeed should—have been her son. He looked like her, talked like her. To be sure, he loved war as much as she hated it; but he was a manchild. Menchildren could be terribly bloody-minded.

Suddenly and quite unexpectedly, Senenmut burned with anger. Such pure white rage in him was rare. Temper he had, and no little share of it. But genuine anger almost never beset him.

He was angry now. Hatshepsut should have known this child.

Should have held him in her arms; should have shared in the teaching of him, in the pleasure of his wits that were so much like her own. But while Isis ruled in the king's bedchamber, Hatshepsut would not be suffered to approach Isis' son.

Senenmut struggled to keep his anger out of his face. Thutmose smiled, so like his father's Great Wife, and said, "It would please me greatly to meet your horses. Even," he added, "if they are only mares."

"Then you shall meet them," Senenmut said. "And you will learn that no mare—or woman either—is *only* a mare."

"I'll always like stallions better," said Thutmose. "But I will be very respectful toward your mares."

"That will do," Senenmut conceded, "until you meet them."

20

ONCE SENENMUT HAD WON THE prince's consent, he made haste before the king and, more to the point, his concubine should return from their several days' hunt. On the morning after he made the prince's acquaintance, he had his fillies, his Dawn Wind and his Storm-in-the-Desert, brought to the palace. They were as like as two birds from the same nest, red-golden beauties marked on the brow with a crescent moon. The Dawn Wind bore no other marking. Storm-in-the-Desert had a ring of white above her right hind hoof.

They had not been in the palace before. He had bought a country house for them outside of the city, that when the river was low, looked down on broad green fields to the water. When the river was high, as it was now, the house stood on an island at the end of a causeway, and his horses dwelt in his stable in the city. They were restive with confinement after their long season of freedom, dancing on their leads, snorting and flagging their tails and calling to the stallions.

"I thought you said mares were quiet," Thutmose said. He had been waiting in the stable court, Senenmut suspected, for much longer than his guards had liked. Nebsen, easygoing soul that he was, had settled in the shade of the colonnade with a cushion and a jar of beer. He had drunk it well down, as Senenmut could see.

Thutmose stood in front of the younger filly, Storm-in-the-Desert. She eyed him with a wicked glint, and reared up over his head, striking playfully with her forefeet.

Senenmut had never moved as fast as he moved then; or stopped so neck-snappingly short. Thutmose had somehow, in the flurry of hoofs, caught the filly's neck and whirled with her, and ended on her back.

She had never carried a rider. She had not even drawn a chariot. It would be a year and more before she began.

And yet she stood still under the weight of the child, nostrils flared and ears flicking nervously back. He stroked her neck and smiled. No one dared move lest the filly erupt. Senenmut was not even breathing. If the king's son died under the hoofs of one of Senenmut's horses, not only Senenmut would suffer for it. Senenmut was the queen's servant, one of her favorites. No one would ever doubt that she had had a part in it.

Easily, smoothly, and completely fearlessly, Thutmose slid from the filly's back and stood beside her, still with his hand on her neck. "Do be calm," he said. "I'll never hurt you."

She snorted in disbelief, but then she lowered her head and sniffed lightly at his palm. When she found no sweetmeat in it, she nipped the air above it and nudged him with her nose. He laughed and wrapped arms about her neck, but gods be thanked, he did not swing himself astride again.

"That was very foolish," said a voice from the colonnade, "but very brave."

Even Nebsen started. The person who had spoken came past him into the light. Senenmut's back both eased and tightened: eased, because he had expected Neferure before this, and tightened because this thing that he had wrought might be more dangerous even than Storm-in-the-Desert's hoofs striking above Thutmose's head.

Thutmose regarded his sister with interest. He did not seem to mind that she had called him a fool. "You look like Father," he said. "And like *her.*"

There was no doubt of whom he meant. Senenmut had heard that precise tone from Isis when she spoke of the queen. Half fear; half resentment.

"Yes, I look like my mother," said Neferure. "So do you. It's all in the family, you know."

"My mother says that you can't be trusted," Thutmose said. "I think she's afraid. You look trustworthy to me."

"Oh, do I?" said Neferure from the grand pinnacle of her nine years—almost ten, as she would insist. "I suppose she tells you not to trust your eyes, either."

"My mother is afraid," Thutmose said, as if that explained everything. And perhaps it did.

Neferure took the Dawn Wind's lead from the stablehand. The older filly was Senenmut's heart's darling as he was hers; but she adored Neferure. The princess always had a sweetmeat for her, a bit of cake or a date or a handful of barley. It was a honeycake today, and a second one for Storm-in-the-Desert—"Not," said Neferure severely, "that you honestly deserve it."

Storm-in-the-Desert devoured her cake and pawed for more. The stablehand, belatedly possessed of sense, pulled her away and set her to running round him on a long line, far out in the court where she could trample no one.

Her sister, having coaxed another cake out of Neferure, turned from the princess to thrust her nose into Senenmut's hand. When he declined to give tribute, she nipped him sharply in reprimand and laid her head on his shoulder. He smoothed the mane on her neck. It was slightly paler than her coat, more gold than red, thick and long. The neck on which it lay was beautiful; she was all beautiful even in her awkward youth, with her delicate strength and the lightness of her stride. She reminded him piercingly of the queen who had given her to him.

For that, and because she was herself, he loved her. He rested for a while in the calm of her presence.

But the world went on about him, nor waited for him to take notice of it. Nebsen had drained his jar of beer and fallen asleep. His snores rasped beneath the thud of Storm-in-the-Desert's hoofs on sand, the Dawn Wind's soft whicker in his ear, the voices of the two children as they withdrew to a patch of shade.

They crouched on their haunches like peasants in the market, even haughty Neferure, and watched the filly dance and curvet at the end of her line. Shoulder to shoulder, companionable, comfortable in each other's presence, they conversed as if they had known one another for far more than these few moments.

It was not so much what they said—questions about one another; commentary on the horses; idle ramblings such as children could wander into—as that they said it at all, and with such ease. Senenmut doubted that their father and Neferure's mother had ever conversed so. They would always quarrel, no matter how innocuous its beginning. They rasped on one another like mismatched halves of a door, meeting only to thrust one another apart.

Neferure was wise for her years. Some found her frightening; Senenmut was only glad that he need not suffer the frustration of contending with ordinary childish stupidity. Her brother, for all his extreme youth, was as quick-witted as she. He understood a great deal; and when he did not understand, he was never too proud to say so.

"I think you must be our grandfather all over again," Neferure said. "He was clever, too, and wise, and he loved to play the soldier. You aren't anything like your mother; and you're much brighter than your father ever was."

"You shouldn't say that," Thutmose said. "They'll hate you if they find out."

Neferure was unperturbed. "Do you?" she asked.

He shook his head. "Oh, no. They don't think very fast. They worry too much; they're afraid all the time."

"That's because my mother makes them afraid," Neferure said. "She never intends to, but she does. You must, too. You think so much faster than they do."

"I pretend," said Thutmose. "I make believe I'm still a baby." He lightened his voice to a shrill child-whine, and mustered a remarkably convincing lisp. "Oh, mama, I'm hungwy, mama. Give me a honey-cake, mama."

Neferure roared with laughter. He gaped at her. Senenmut almost laughed himself, though he knew that laugh of hers, astonishingly deep and infectious to come from so delicate-seeming a girlchild. "O my brother!" she said, still laughing. "Oh, how they must simper over you."

He grimaced. "Just the ladies, and Mama. Father tells me to stand up straight and talk like a man. But I can't do that. He'd be afraid." He paused. "I'll be glad when I'm big enough to stop pretending."

"Then you'll have to start pretending something else," Neferure said, somber of a sudden, and pensive. She nibbled on her finger as she did when she thought hard on a thing that did not please her. "I scare people, too. But not Mother, and not Senenmut. I tried to pretend to be ordinary once: giggling over nothing, shrieking at the boys, worrying about my hair and my eyepaint and my dress. Mother told me to stop the foolishness, and Senenmut set me a lesson so hard I had to do it perfectly or die of shame."

"They scared people when they were little," Thutmose said. "I know. Father said, about *her*—about your mother. She was terrifying. Unnat—unnatural."

"So are we," said Neferure.

He looked at her, long and level, as serious as only a small child can be. "I'm afraid," he said. "If I stopped pretending, Mama would hate me. She hates your mother, she hates you. She'll hate me, too."

"That's not why she hates us," Neferure said. Her tone was not particularly soothing, but he seemed to take comfort from it. "She hates us because my mother gave her to your father, and in a way gave you to them both; and she's going to have to pay for it someday. She thinks the price will be your life. So she protects you, and wraps you in worry, tight as a mummy in a tomb; and she tells you stories about my mother, to make you hate her, too."

"Mama says," said Thutmose, "that *she* will kill me because she wants her own son to be the prince."

"My mother doesn't have a son," Neferure said, "and she won't. She means you no harm at all. She doesn't even hate your mother, though you must think that's impossible. She feels sorry for her."

"I do, too," Thutmose said. "I'm still afraid of your mother. Father says she wants to be king."

"Well, she can't be," Neferure said briskly. "So there's nothing to be afraid of. You'll be king when our father dies and becomes Osiris, and I'll be queen because that's how it's done."

His eyes widened. "You will? *You'll* be queen?"

"What, nobody told you?"

He shook his head.

Neferure tossed her own in disgust. "What idiots! Telling you wild stories about my terrible mother, but never letting you know the important thing. It's not she who will be queen when our father is dead—if she lives that long. I will. You can't be king without me."

He drew himself up, affronted. "I *will* be king! I'm Father's son."

"No man is king," Neferure said, "unless he marries the woman who carries the king-right. That's the daughter of a ruling queen, brother; a descendant of Queen Nefertari."

"That's you," Thutmose said. His eyes were wide still. "They didn't tell me. Tell me why they didn't tell me."

"I think you know," Neferure said; but she did not tease him with it. "Because they didn't want you to know. They don't want you to know me, either, or talk to me. Maybe they're planning to get rid of me somehow, or to convince the priests to change the law. Then they can marry you to someone they choose, who has nothing to do with me or with my mother."

That was perhaps too complicated for him; but perhaps not. He said, "I don't mind if I marry you. You won't make me pretend. And you aren't afraid of me."

"But if you marry me," Neferure pointed out, "you'll have to know my mother."

"I won't be afraid of her if I see her," he said. "I'm afraid of things in the dark. Things that hide. Not things I can see."

She tilted her head, puzzling out the logic, maybe, or simply studying her brother. "Mother always stands in the bright sun. It's you who've been kept in the shadows."

"Mama is afraid," Thutmose said with the hint of a sigh. Storm-in-the-Desert had come to a snorting, foaming halt, still full of herself, but a little more willing to greet him calmly as he came to her. He seemed to take comfort from the lowering of her nose into his cupped palms, the warm hot horse-smell of her, the brightness of her red-golden coat in the sunlight.

Neferure sighed, too, and said to the air, or perhaps to Senenmut, "I wish people wouldn't quarrel. Wouldn't it be so much better if everybody just admitted that the gods made me to be queen and him to be king, and let us grow up decently together?"

She was not asking for an answer. She went to drown her own sorrows with the Dawn Wind, sent her out to run on the line as Storm-in-the-Desert had done just now. The task absorbed her, perhaps completely; perhaps not. Senenmut forbore to ask. So young, and so much a woman already—and so very like her mother.

21

DECEPTION, SENENMUT HAD discovered long ago, was the meat and drink of courts. No one told the truth if he could help it; and no one ever walked a straight path. A web of lies bound the royal court together, so intricate that even the most skillful courtier could not distinguish the truth beneath the weaving.

Senenmut was no more innocent of deception than any other courtier. From the time he first shared the queen's bed, he came to it in subtle and devious ways. If he happened to be attending her toward evening, he departed as a proper servant should, but later he came back. There were passages where no one walked, even servants; chambers that no one saw, and doors concealed in cleverly carved or painted walls. The last of them opened behind the queen's bed, disguised subtly as itself: a door framed in papyrus pillars.

It was proof, if he ever needed it, that his queen was not the first of her line to seek the arms of a man other than the king. "It's inevitable, I suppose," he said to her, "when even the muddiest fieldhand can marry to suit himself, but the queen is given no choice in the matter. She's bound to the man who will be king when her father is dead, who as often as not is her cousin or her uncle or her brother—since the kingship should properly stay in the family. And if she detests him—if she can't abide the sight of him—what grace is she given but to suffer in silence?"

"Or to take a lover," she said. They lay together in her great bed under its canopy of netting, he tangled in her hair, she in his arms. No maid spied on them. The guards were all without.

It was known that the queen preferred to sleep in solitude. Every night a priest set wards of magic and of incense about her bed, and the guards retreated, and the maids went to their own beds, more often in company than not. Nothing and no one could come near the queen, living or dead or spirit of ill.

Nothing and no one but Senenmut, who knew the secret of the hidden door. He was all the guard and ward she professed to need. He came in the quiet hours of the night, and left in the dark before dawn. Sleep was nothing he needed a great deal of, and that was fortunate; or he would have succumbed to exhaustion long ago.

Tonight he was in a reflective mood, and she was pensive. They were as comfortable as years could make them. Their bodies were grown familiar, woven together like two strands in a carpet. He knew the exact curve of her shoulder, the precise softness of her breast. She knew exactly how his head sat on his neck, and how his little fingers were crooked, and that he preferred slow and gentle loving to swift and fierce.

The fear of discovery had sunk to a murmur. No one had ever caught them. "The gods guard us, I suppose," Senenmut said.

"One god," said Hatshepsut. "There's one who guards me above all. I feel him all about me, burning but never consuming."

He stared at her. She was never one to invoke the gods with every breath she took. She mentioned them seldom except in their place: in rites in the temples, in invocations in the court.

On this night like so many other nights, no more or less magical than any that had gone before, she seemed to have fallen into a strange half-dream. Her voice was soft, slurred a little as if with sleep.

"Amon," she said, or sighed. "Father Amon. He loves me. He protects me. He even suffers you. You love me, you see. You honor me. You would never betray me."

"And the king's right to you? His honor and his reputation?"

She arched her back, curving away from him. Her hair streamed down on either side of his face. He saw hers above him, white and fierce. "What honor is there in lying like a fish while he pumps me full of his seed? What joy is there in listening to him boast of all the heads that he has broken, the booty he has won in battle? He hears nothing that I tell him; cares nothing for me, except that he wears the Two Crowns through his marriage to me."

He had seldom heard her so bitter, or with so little apparent cause. The king was back from his long hunt, somewhat indisposed with a fever that he had caught in the marshes. She had had to hold audience alone today, and fend off those fools who would speak only to the king. That should have troubled her not at all. She was most content when she could rule alone, unfettered by her husband's presence.

She should be all sweetness, all warm and smiling, delighted to have had a day free of the king. Senenmut coaxed her down, smoothed her tangled hair, kissed her till she stopped frowning quite so terribly.

She stilled in his grasp, looking hard at him. "Stop trying so hard not to ask. No, there's nothing troubling me. I don't know why my mood is so black tonight."

"Not black," Senenmut said. "God-ridden. It's that, isn't it?"

Warm as the night was, she shivered. Her fists clenched and unclenched. She said in a voice that might have seemed light if one had not known her, "When I was small, I saw gods everywhere. I saw Amon in the sun; Hathor in every cow with horns like the young moon; Sobek in the crocodile that sunned itself on the riverbank. I dreamed that the gods hovered about me as I slept. I heard their voices; I knew what was to be.

"But I grew older," she said, "and the dreams faded. The sun was only the sun, a fire in the sky. An ox was an ox, a crocodile a simple beast, all belly and teeth. I forgot what they had been before."

"And now you remember," Senenmut said.

She peered narrow-eyed into the dark beyond the nightlamp's glimmer. "I don't know why it came back. Nothing is different. There have been no signs, no portents. The world is quiet."

"My mother has always said," Senenmut said, half somber, half wry, "that when the house is quiet, then she's most certain one of her sons is about to afflict her with a scandal."

"You will not," said the queen with a return of her royal manner, "tell your mother where you spend your nights."

His lips twitched. So did his body at the thought of Hat-Nufer's merciless eye on this of all improprieties. "The gods witness it," he said: "if she ever learns, it will not be from me."

"See that she never learns at all."

"I can try," he said, "your majesty."

She did hate it when he laughed at her; but the darkness was in her again, blinding her to his mockery. She faced it wordlessly, cold and still beside him, unwarmed by his warmth. Even when he wrapped himself about her, she was chill, unmoving. The gods had claimed her, he thought a little wildly. They left nothing for any mortal man.

In the morning the queen was utterly herself. He, heavy-eyed and woolly-minded, was hard put to make sense of anything. He performed his duties somehow, handed Neferure into the care of a lute-master and then of a master of the bow, slid past her babble about her brother. She had the sense not to burst out with it until she was alone with her tutor; but he had nearly forgotten the whole of the day before, lost it in the queen's night fancies. He baffled Neferure, he could see, but he had no comfort to offer.

It was as if the dark had slipped from the queen with the coming of dawn, and hidden inside of Senenmut. In her it had unfolded itself in dreams and visions. In him who was neither king nor god, was only darkness.

The king was still indisposed. Marsh-fevers could be tenacious; and the king was nursed by the chief of his concubines, whose fretting could turn a touch of fever into deadly sickness. None but she would have fetched priests and physicians together and set them to curing the king of what needed but time and rest and a cool bath or two.

Rumors of the to-do in the king's chambers made their way even as far as the queen's ears. Senenmut, his mind still fogged, reckoned the tale nonsense. He wondered dimly if Isis was sliding into a madness of her own. She seemed to see fear everywhere, threats to her son or her husband, terrible things that to other eyes were no more than shadows.

He left earlier than was his wont, declined to eat, sought his bed in his own house for, he thought, a few moments' rest. Then he would go back to the palace through the secret ways. Perhaps not the same as he had been using. Perhaps another that he had found. And perhaps he was as mad as Isis, seeing threats in empty air.

■ He woke with a start. It was black dark and very still. For a moment he did not know where he was. Not with the queen; the air's scent was wrong, the bed under him harder, the linens less princely fine.

He was at home in the bed he so seldom slept in nightlong. If a lamp had been burning, it had long since emptied of oil, guttered and gone out.

Slowly his eyes discerned shapes in the dark. Bed; chests; a chair. Walls, and the dark shape of a door. A window through which glimmered a wan ray of moonlight.

Something chittered in the roof. It could have been a bat, or a bird, or a spirit: dead soul or wandering magician, lingering in his rafters. Except for that he was alone. He, like the queen, was known to cherish solitude in the nights. None who noted the likeness seemed to see what it signified.

And maybe a god did protect the queen, and therefore her lover. Senenmut was sure of nothing, here in the dark; not even that he was truly alive. He might be dead, and this might all be nightmare, a taste of torment before his soul went to the hall of judgment.

He was breathing hard. His skin prickled with apprehension. What he was afraid of, he did not know. The dark itself, maybe. Maybe something worse.

He rose, stumbling, catching himself against the bedframe. The silence was immense. He heard no voice in the house, no sound of snoring, not even Amonhotep's pet monkey chittering in its cage.

He had to go to the palace. It struck him with a snap of urgency that had nothing to do with reason. He must go—he must be there. He knew no more than that.

■ Senenmut was not the only fool stumbling about in the dark, warding off night-demons with a bit of torch and a borrowed cat. Aunt Teti's cat shrieked at the loom of shadow out of shadow near the palace gate, raked Senenmut's shoulder, and bolted into the night.

He stood with stinging, bleeding shoulder, glaring half-blind at the figure that bobbed under a torch of its own. The light gleamed on a shaven skull and a pair of bright black eyes. "Why, good morning," said Hapuseneb.

Senenmut's nose twitched. Yes, he could smell the morning coming, though the night seemed as black as ever. Soon enough it would be dawn, and then the sun would rise, and all his night fancies would vanish with the demons that had spawned them.

"Oh, I don't think so," Hapuseneb said, though Senenmut had no memory of speaking aloud. "We've all had dreams and sendings. The temple is like an anthill stirred with a stick."

"But," said Senenmut, "it's quiet. There's nothing to make us think—"

"Dreams aren't enough?" Hapuseneb grasped his arm and pulled him toward the gate. The guard was surly and sleepy, but for the priest of Amon and the queen's scribe he agreed grudgingly to open the gate.

Senenmut had nothing to do with it. Hapuseneb was a priest; gods must vex him endlessly, clamoring for his notice. He was as cheerful as ever, and as difficult to resist. He even coaxed the guard into a twist of the lip that might have been a snarl, or might have been a smile.

Whether in exasperation or in respect for the queen's servants, the guard let them into the palace. They found all quiet, as it should be at this ungodly hour. The first bread of the day's baking sent forth its fragrance from the ovens near the king's palace. Apart from the bakers, no one else seemed yet awake.

But as Hapuseneb dragged Senenmut past the queen's palace and into that which could only belong to the king, a murmur rose, as it seemed, out of the stones of wall and paving. Someone deep within was shouting or weeping or praying. The guards on the door had a pale, haunted look. Like dead men in a dream, Senenmut thought.

He dreamed this, perhaps. The dark that seemed a living thing, lying even on this palace, breathing vast and slow beyond the flicker of lamps or torches. The distant cries, sounds like women keening, wailing for the dead. What it signified—that was nightmare. It could not be—

"The king is dying," Hapuseneb said, "or dead."

Senenmut's hand slashed the air in a sign against evil. "Avert! If he hears of this, if he believes you have ill-wished him—"

"I've done nothing," said Hapuseneb. "A little fever, an imp of the marshes, a few days' inconvenience, has conquered our lord and king. Who'd have thought it?"

"Who," muttered Senenmut, "except the Lady Isis?" He paused. "Do you think—?"

"No," Hapuseneb said. He smiled sweetly at the king's door-guard. "You will let us in," he said.

The guard opened his mouth, then shut it again. Maybe Hapuseneb laid a small magic on him. Maybe not. Senenmut was no priest, to know the truth of it.

■ The king lay in his bed which was much grander and higher than the queen's, in a room full of the images of his kingship: Thutmose in the Two Crowns, Thutmose administering justice, hunting lions, conquering enemies in their hundreds and thousands. Senenmut's eye, wandering, took in a scrap of inscription: "Mighty am I, unconquerable, living Horus, god and ruler, Great House of Egypt."

The mighty, the unconquerable, the living Horus, Thutmose son of Thutmose of the line of Ahmose, had fallen not to the sword of an enemy but to the indignity of a fever. He seemed to have felt the shame of it before it stripped the life and souls from him. His face was set in lines of petulance, small niggling irritation that he must die so soon, and for so little.

The one who had shrieked and wailed over him was gone, carried away on a wide black shoulder. Nehsi the Nubian came back as Senenmut stood like a witling in the door. "Her women will tend her," he said in his voice like a lion's purr.

Hatshepsut nodded briefly. Of all the crowd of priests and physicians, guards and servants, not one dared interfere as she stood over the body of her husband. How she must have come in where for so long she had been forbidden, Senenmut could well guess. She had done it as simply as he had. She had walked up to the door and informed the guard that she would enter.

Her eyes were clear, untormented by visions. Her face was calm. She could hardly mourn this man whom she had liked so little. But he had been king, and her husband. She must know at least some small stabbing of regret.

There was none that he could see. "How like you," she said to the king, heedless of any who heard, "to go galloping off into the Field of Reeds without a thought for the turmoil you leave behind. Your son is three years old. My daughter, whom he must marry, has hardly begun her tenth year. You leave the Two Kingdoms in the care of children."

He had nothing to say. His eyes were open, blind as the eyes of the dead must always be. If any of his souls lingered, fluttering in the dark, it offered no response.

She loosed a sound that was half a sigh, half a snort of disgust. Her voice rose. "You! Yes, you, sniveling there. Fetch the embalmers."

The sniveler was a great prince, a darling of the court, but under her cold eye he could do no other than obey. She sent others on errands of like import: summoning the king's counselors, passing word to the court, informing the temples that the living Horus was become the dead Osiris. None protested. None dared disobey her. She was terrible in her calm, goddess and queen; and no king now to stand against her will.

22

"YOU DID IT!" ISIS SHRIEKED. "YOU poisoned him! You ill-wished him! I know it! I smell it in you!"

"Please," said the queen in silence that rang after the shrilling of Isis' voice. "Sit down. Will you have wine? It might calm you."

Isis gasped and sucked in breath like a great, whooping sob. Nehsi braced to leap if she succumbed yet again to hysterics.

But she seemed to have mastered herself. She could even weep beautifully, he noticed: a glistening trail of tears down those ivory cheeks, and a pathetic charm to that mouth all twisted with grief. In the hour and more since he had carried her into her chamber and entrusted her to her servants, she had managed to bathe, refresh the paint of cheeks and eyes, and put on a mourning robe. He contemplated that without great surprise. No one else had been prepared for this; but Isis in her fear and her foolishness, Isis had expected that the king would die.

He admired her no more for that. Nor even for her sudden, lightly trembling calm, her big eyes fixed on Hatshepsut's face. "I do not need wine," she said in a small, contained voice. "You do not need to treat me like an idiot child."

"I treat you as your conduct deserves," the queen said. She stood while Isis sat, in Isis' chambers deep in the king's palace, but it was she who ruled here and Isis who remained by her sufferance.

"You were my servant," said Hatshepsut, "before I gave you to my husband. Now that my husband is dead, you hold a certain rank as the mother of his heir. You continue in that rank; no one will or can deprive you of it. But you will remember, O concubine whom men call Isis: I am Great Royal Wife. I am the daughter of daughters of Queen

Nefertari. If I am given the smallest reason to suspect that you aided my husband on his passage to the realm of Osiris, then you will join him on the journey."

Isis had gone even whiter than paint and artifice could make her. "You cannot blame me for his death. He died of a fever."

"Certainly," Hatshepsut said. "And whose yearning to hunt in the marshes caused him to fall ill? He could have remained here, horrendously bored but safely alive."

Nehsi thought that Isis would burst into tears again, but she seemed to have wept herself dry. Burning dry; or perhaps that was hate. "He never loved you," she said with sudden venom. "He detested you."

"And I detested him," said Hatshepsut. "He was still the king, and I was his wife. You may cherish illusions of ruling as regent in your son's minority. Dispose of them. I am the daughter and wife of kings. You were born into servitude, of a line of servants. You have risen higher than any before you. But you will rise no higher."

"I have friends," Isis said. "Those who were the king's loyal servants, who have no love for you, nor ever will—"

"They may not love me," said Hatshepsut, "but they know whose daughter I am. What will you do to contest it? Seduce them singly or all together?"

"You are reckoned beautiful," Isis said, "but I am more beautiful than you. And the prince—the king—is my son."

"You mew like a cat," Hatshepsut said to her. "Have you claws, then? Will you wage war with me? Or have you just enough sense to understand how tedious it is to rule two kingdoms? Dispose of me, destroy me with treachery, and it all falls to you. All of it, little kitten. Forty-two nomes, forty-two nomarchs, a hundred scribes for each one, each reckoning up a hundred accounts for his lord and master. How many baskets of grain, how many cattle, how many fat geese and how many jars of beer are in each name, and who receives them, and how, and for what services—"

Isis clapped her hands to her ears. "Oh, stop that! He told me what it was like. He hated it. He said you love it—live for it."

"I loathe it," said Hatshepsut. "But it is necessary; and I have a gift for it. Before you dream of seizing power, of making yourself regent while I languish in exile or worse, consider that without me you have no one to bear the tedium."

"A queen can command anyone she pleases," Isis said with what perhaps she fancied was queenly hauteur.

Hatshepsut, who was queen in truth, lifted her chin a fraction. "A queen may. A regent who was a concubine, who has no gift or talent for ruling kingdoms . . ." She shrugged. "Perhaps I should leave you to it. It would be pleasant to be free; to call my time my own, to do and go as I please."

"You would go into exile," Isis said.

Hatshepsut laughed, light and free. "Oh, how hard you try to roar like a lion, and still you mew like a kitten. Of course I would not be exiled. You might demand it, but the lords of Egypt would decline to obey you. No man will touch or harm the living Isis."

"*I* am—" Isis stopped. Nehsi doubted that it was wisdom that constrained her. She was afraid of Hatshepsut—deathly afraid; and hating her for it.

The hatred of a child was a frail and changeable thing. Hatshepsut seemed undismayed by it. Nehsi was more wary. A child could harm where it hated; could kill, if it came upon a weapon. It lacked the sense that would stay a wiser hand.

"The kingdoms will look to us for strength in this time of trouble," Hatshepsut said: "a king dead before his time, his heir hardly more than an infant. We must present to them the face of amity, and give them a strong regency, that they may have no fear of the kingdoms' fall."

"The Two Lands can never—"

Almost Nehsi thought that Hatshepsut would strike the little fool. But she struck the arm of her chair instead. "A hundred years ago, the king in Thebes was subject to a foreign king. Yes, the Two Lands can fall. They can topple in a night, if the gods will it. You who do not know this, whose faith is as blind as it is inviolate: would you presume to demand a share in this regency?"

"I must." Isis' voice was light and sweet; it could not be otherwise. Yet it was astonishingly firm. "My son is not safe with you."

"Which?" demanded Hatshepsut. "His life or his adoration of you? Are you afraid that once he knows me, he may learn to despise you?"

"You would teach him to hate me," said Isis. She was perhaps close to tears, but too stubborn to give way to them.

"And therefore you teach him to hate me," Hatshepsut said: "as if one hatred could fill him up, and leave no room for more."

Isis twisted her hands in her lap. She was grievously overmatched, and she must know it. "I am his mother," she said. "To you he is nothing but a head on which to set the Two Crowns, since you can't wear them yourself."

"And whose fault is that? Who has kept me rigorously apart from him, and never allowed me to come within a spearlength? He must marry my daughter. What will she have of him who is her brother, whom she has never spoken to, whom she has never known?"

Nehsi drew breath to speak, but said nothing. What the tutors had done was common knowledge among the servants: that they had brought sister and brother together, and the two had begun to be friends.

The high ones knew nothing of it. He was not sure why he kept silence. Out of circumspection, he hoped; to forestall a war. It was not loyal, but it seemed to him that it was wise.

"She will know him now," Isis said, "since they will marry. But until he's old enough to do what a husband does, it were best if—"

"My husband and I were kept apart," said Hatshepsut. "No one was afraid, and no one feared that my mother would corrupt my husband until he turned against his mother. It was simply the way of things. I am a woman, he was a man. Our worlds seldom met."

Isis brightened visibly. "Then they can—"

"No," said Hatshepsut. "That way lies division, and eventually hatred. The king and his queen are the twinned souls of Egypt. When they are at odds, the kingdoms suffer. These children who will be king and queen—for them I would wish a better fortune."

Isis did not understand. Nehsi did not think that she ever would. She lacked both subtlety and wit. Nor was she one who changed her mind once she had made it up. She had decided that Hatshepsut was a threat to her son. She would not alter that decision, nor yield to reason.

Yet fear could sway her; and Hatshepsut wielded it as a king should wield a sword. "We will preserve all semblance of amity," Hatshepsut said. "Our children will be wedded and crowned as soon as may be: when the seventy days of the king's embalming are over and he is laid in his tomb, and the kingdoms turn again to the world of the living. Now and hereafter, I am queen regent of the Two Lands. You may continue in this place, or in another if you so wish. One properly distant and appropriately secluded."

"I will stay here," said Isis, shaking but standing fast. "Someone must protect my son."

"The whole of Egypt will protect him," Hatshepsut said, not troubling to conceal her exasperation. "Very well. Stay and fret. It matters nothing."

■ "You could have handled that better," Nehsi observed in the quiet of the queen's inner chamber.

Hatshepsut paused in readying herself for sleep. The maid Mayet, deft and circumspect, continued to brush out her mistress' hair. Hatshepsut took no notice of her except to refrain from turning to glare at Nehsi. "And how should I have handled it? The woman is an idiot."

"She was a perfect match for your late and too little lamented husband." Nehsi leaned back in the chair that he preferred: the tall one nearest the door. "It's the gods' jest, you know: to give you the gift of winning hearts—all but those of your husband and the mother of his heir. Nothing that they say or do can please you."

"It's always calculated to the finest degree, to drive me into screaming fits." The queen sighed. "Oh, gods, Nehsi, I have no self-control around either of them. If anything she's worse than he was. He had a glimmer of intelligence, hidden deep. She has none at all."

"Maybe not," said Nehsi, "but she has a certain level of cunning. She knows what will vex you past the edge of reason."

"So does that blasted monkey Neferure used to keep," Hatshepsut snapped. "It had the grace to die before someone throttled it."

"One can always hope," Nehsi said with careful lack of expression.

Her brows rose; then lowered and drew together. "No. Don't think of it. Don't say it. Such things solve nothing. Her only crime is that she provokes me into fits."

"And she teaches her son to hate and fear you."

She barely paused. "I shall put an end to that. Watch and see how I teach him to love me."

23

WHEN THE DAYS OF THE embalming were over, the king was laid in his tomb far away in the bleak hills of the west, out of sight or scent of the Black Land. Then those who mourned him came back to the green and living places, to Thebes that had turned from grief to gladness. So it had been since the world was young, and so it would be for thousands and thousands of years. One king died. A new king was raised in his place: took the crowns and the crook and the flail, the throne and the titles, the name and power of a god.

Menkheperre Thutmose was raised up in the Temple of Amon, and then before the people, on a day that was a rarity. Many reckoned it a portent. It rained, a storm out of a turbulent heaven, lashing the people who thronged the processional way. It drenched those who marched in the procession, draggled the feathers of the great fans that should have cooled and shaded the king; it buffeted the little king riding high in the great state chair, and threatened the balance of his bearers, who were hard put not to slip and stumble on paving stones gone suddenly treacherous.

He seemed unafraid. The tall crowns, White within Red, had been cut to his measure and bound securely to his head. The false beard, which looked truly absurd on that soft young chin, had gone somewhat limp, but he did not try to remove it. That was a relief: Senenmut had labored long with the boy's own tutor to persuade him that he must wear it.

Senenmut should have been trudging in the king's following, cradling a dripping feather of honor as did the rest of the notables nearest to the new young majesty; but he had escaped when the rain began, and slipped and wriggled along the crowd's edge till he could see the procession as one apart from it.

It was an antic impulse, a child of the storm. He did not often yield to such things. It was the rain: it was all out of nature. It pummeled his head even through the wig, deafened his ears and fuddled his wits— or perhaps cleared them as they had not been since the last king died.

The crowd's roar drowned all sound, but he could see how the king bent his head back to catch the rain in his mouth, and laughed. He seemed oblivious to the throngs about him, or the weight of his crowns, or the burden that would fall on him when he set foot again in the palace.

Neferure rode in a chair beside his. He was her husband now. They had stood together in the temple, and would stand again in the palace, to swear the vows and affirm the contract between husband and wife, between the king and his queen. He had spoken the words as he was taught, though how much he understood, Senenmut could not be certain. Neferure had understood them all. Her voice had trembled ever so slightly, but she had not refused; she had not turned coward and fled.

Brave child. She had years to wait before she must fulfill the whole of vow and contract. She would be a woman grown and well ready, when at last Thutmose was old enough to do what a man does with a woman.

She admitted to no regret that she was bound to a child so much younger than she. "At least I like him," she had said to Senenmut before she went out to her wedding. "Not as a woman likes a man, I don't think—but I can talk to him. I'm not grieved that he must be my husband."

"Do you wish he were older?" Senenmut had asked.

She thought about it for rather a long while before she answered. "No," she said. "No, I don't. I'm not old enough yet, either. We'll both wait. And when we're ready . . ."

A dozen years, thought Senenmut, or precious little less, before Thutmose was of age to be a proper husband to his bride. She might not find the waiting so easy when she was a young woman and he was still a child.

But it was done. There was no undoing it. They rocked and swayed through the rain, gleaming in gold, a small erect boychild and a girl-child who was not so far from being a woman. King and queen of Egypt, Great House and Great Royal Wife, bound and sealed before the face of Amon.

And Amon had hidden that face, veiled it in rain. Water from the sky: a blessing, one might suppose, a promise of prosperity for the Two Lands.

The procession made its slow way past Senenmut's vantage. His place was open, just: a gap in the ranks of higher functionaries, behind the nomarchs and the princes and the lords of lesser rank. He slid back into it. He was hemmed in again, surrounded by men in their best finery, able to see no more before or behind than bewigged and befeathered personages.

■ On this of all days, the queen regent effaced herself with great and exacting care. The king must be seen to be king, and his queen beside him.

"Time enough later," Hatshepsut said, "to remind the Two Lands that there is still a firm hand on the steering-oar."

Senenmut had come to her tonight, against his better judgment—if they were caught now, no matter that her husband was dead and she was nominally free to choose her bedmate; that choice was narrow, and did not encompass a tradesman's son. But she had looked so worn at the king's first high court, so thin and drawn, that he could not leave her to face sleep alone.

Nor had she cast him out when he slipped through the hidden door into her bed. She wrapped arms and legs about him and clung, face buried in his breast. It was a long while before she eased enough to do more than lie against him; longer yet before she could speak.

He had thought she would not say anything at all: would love him into exhaustion, and then sleep. But the heat of body and body seemed to warm her spirit. She lay cradled in his arms, tracing twisting patterns on his chest, murmuring more to herself than to him. "The world needs the appearance of order. Order is a male fundament upon the throne, no matter how young or how incapable it may be."

"I wouldn't call him incapable," Senenmut said. "Only very young."

"Is there a difference?" She laid her hand on his lips. "No, don't answer that. When I consider his parentage, I wonder what the gods were thinking. If he were a stud colt, I'd pray he took after his grand-sire."

"I think he did," said Senenmut, kissing her fingers as she drew them away.

"It will be years before we can know for certain," she said. "Sometimes a young one fails of his promise. He grows up as his father did. As a fool."

Senenmut had not known the elder Thutmose before he was king. But that his son was more than he had been—Senenmut was certain of it. Such children as the younger Thutmose were rare; and they did not grow into fools.

He held his tongue. She sighed against him. Her body softened slowly. Her breathing eased and deepened.

She slept in his arms, while he lay awake, counting the slow passage of hours toward the dawn.

Very near to first light, when he should rise and slip away or be betrayed, she stirred. Her eyes opened. They were dark with sleep, but a brightness hid in the heart of them. She looked into his face as if she had not seen it before: not a hostile stare, nor fearful. Simply intent.

Then she smiled. It was a slow smile, almost unbearably sweet. He yearned to kiss her, but he dared not.

"I dreamed," she said drowsily. "Such a dream . . . oh, my friend! Such a dream as I dreamed—you would never guess—"

He bit his tongue. She never saw. She laughed against him and clasped him tight. And yet, he thought, there was a tension in her, a tautness that mingled strangely with her laughter.

Out of that tension she said, "No, don't guess. Don't think. Forget."

That, he could not. But he could keep silence. He could even conceal the resentment, the irrational stab of jealousy. Jealous of a dream— and how did he know she had been dreaming of a lover? He was all she had, that he had ever known. He had thought he was all she wanted.

He berated himself for a fool. Whatever she had dreamed, it was nothing merely mortal. Some god had walked in her. He saw the marks: the brightness, the brittle mirth, the arms that bound him and would not let him go.

He had to put them aside, and rise though his heart protested. "I'll come back," he said, "through the front door, with proper servility. Wait for me."

Once he had freed himself, she did not try to recapture him. She lay as he had left her, eyes drifting past him to peer into the dark. He saw how her mind drifted with them.

Fear made him pause. But morning was coming: a greater fear, and a far worse scandal than if she woke strange-eyed from a god's visitation. A god would have been reckoned a worthy lover for a queen. A scribe, never.

He must trust in her guards and in her own good sense, and hope that morning came quickly once he was gone. He kissed her brow. It was chill, like smooth-carved stone. She did not stir under his touch. "Father," she said, half as if she called to him, half as if she prayed. "Father Amon."

The god did not answer. He was gone. Senenmut followed him by much more earthly ways, in much more earthly wise.

Queen
Regent

〰〰〰

(Thutmose III,
Years 5-7)

24

INENI THE ARCHITECT AND HAPUSENEB the priest of
Amon and Senenmut, whose titles had multiplied until he could
hardly keep count of them all, crouched together in one of the
courts of Senenmut's house. They must have seemed like aged boys bent
over some game of surpassing interest: a fortress made of sand, or a war
of pebble soldiers. The thing that absorbed them had no such clarity
of form: scraps of wood and papyrus, a table of sand smoothed and
smoothed again as they argued the shape and substance of a dream of
the queen's. She would build a temple, she had told him, sacred to
Hathor of Thebes, the beautiful goddess, watcher over the dead in the
desert west of the city.

Ineni had built the greatest temple in the world, the temple of
Amon at Karnak. Hapuseneb was a priest therein, when he was not
waiting on the queen or building her tomb deep in the bleak valley of
the tombs of queens. Senenmut was a simple fool with a peculiarity of
eye that let him see a shape in stone where others saw only air.

He had always been able to look at a house or a temple or a palace
and see it both in its parts and in the whole. People baffled him who
could attach a stable or a garden or a harem to a house, and not consider
the purity of its line or the harmony of its proportions. It was so simple,
so very obvious, where everything should go. There was nothing more
or less to it than to ordering glyphs properly on a page, each in the place
that the gods and the mind of the maker had ordained for it.

The others understood, in their fashion. He could not admit his
disappointment. They should see as clearly as he did, not in clouded
images, blurred markings in the dampened sand, a structure of twigs
and papyrus that bore no resemblance to the vision of his mind.

"No," he said with barely bridled impatience. "No, and no, and no! Here is the land as the gods made it: not so level now, maybe, but strong backs and clever hands will take care of that. And here is the rise of the cliff, as sheer as makes no matter, sharp-edged against the vault of heaven. Look behind your eyes and *see.*"

"We do try," Hapuseneb said mildly. "Maybe if we went out there, saw the land itself, felt it underfoot . . ."

Ineni was less conciliatory. He was a proud man, haughty for a fact, lord mayor of Thebes and builder of the great temple and the tombs of kings. He did not sneer at the queen's parvenu, her scribe whom she persisted in elevating to a ridiculous number of offices, but he did not suffer Senenmut's impatience, either. "Even if a mere queen were worthy to raise such a monument—and not even a Great Royal Wife, either, but regent for a king who is fast coming to man's years—what possesses you to imagine that you can build it?"

"She ordered me to try," Senenmut replied, reining in the snap that was his first impulse. He needed Ineni: he needed the skill that the man had, the builders he knew and could command, and the long years' mastery of an art that Senenmut had only dabbled in. He had doubled the compass of his house outside the city, made it beautiful as he thought, and it was celebrated in the court for its size and splendor; and he had overseen the building of his own tomb, as every nobleman should do. But he had never ventured anything as great as this.

It might never grow beyond this set of scratchings in the sand. It was not the monument of a queen, who should efface herself in the name of the king through whom she ruled. She had bidden him conceive a temple such as had never been seen before, a monument to her name that would stand for everlasting.

And why she had asked it of him and not of Ineni, or even of Hapuseneb, was a matter of no little resentment, at least on Ineni's part. "You have the eye," she had said when they were alone together. "You see what no one else can see. Do you remember how you looked at the old court in my palace, and saw that it could be beautiful? It was a barren place, unblessed by any god. You set a fountain in it, taught the water to fall so that it catches the light of sun or moon, planted trees about it and raised a colonnade round the rim, and now it seems made not of stone but of light."

"Light," he said now in his own courtyard, to the man who was his friend and the man who was too proud for friendship. "And shadow. What is a rank of pillars but an image of the sun's rays? What are the spaces between them but images of the shade that grants respite from the sun?"

"Pillars hold up the roof," Ineni said as if to a child. "One makes them as vast as one can, to overawe the man who dares approach them. One shapes them as one can, like the trunk of a palm-tree or a bundle of papyrus. But all they do is keep the roof from falling down."

Senenmut opened his mouth, but closed it again. He would make a bitter enemy if he voiced his thought. How in all the world had a mind so pedestrian conceived of a temple as monstrously imposing as that of Amon?

Perhaps he had had help. There were priests in Amon's temple whose eyes saw past the simple matter of separating a roof from a floor, and who knew more of beauty than the correct angulation of a tomb-shaft. As for the size of the temple, what did that signify but itself? It was huge. It was not graceful. It did not celebrate the sun, or the shadow that defined the sun's splendor.

Senenmut had been dreaming the queen's dream. That stretch of Red Land on the west bank of the river, up against the cliff that was too stark for beauty, cried out for the touch of man's hand—or woman's. Beauty should shine forth there as it did from the queen's palace and her throne.

A queen did not build herself a temple, that she be remembered when she was dead. That was the province of a king.

But she could dream, and her servants could dream with her. It did no harm, except to his patience. How could these others fail to see what he saw?

"It is so simple," he said. "In the Black Land, lines are soft; the light falls through greenery, and the stark face of the earth is blurred, made gentle. In the Red Land the earth stands bare. Sun beats down on it. Shadows are sharp-edged as if cut with a blade. If one were to build a temple, one should build it of shadow and light. Stark lines, like the lines of the land about it; but clean, with the harmony of notes on a lute, each flowing from the one before. See, one builds with pillars, because pillars hold up the roof—but one shapes and angles them so that they seem made of light."

"Dreamers dream," Ineni muttered. "Builders build. You dream, scribe; but of building you know nothing."

"But you," said Senenmut, "know all that I do not."

Ineni sniffed audibly. "Do you imagine that I would give you any part of the knowledge that I labored so long and so hard to acquire?"

"Certainly not," Senenmut said. "Not to me. To the queen."

"A queen regent has no authority to command such a monument in her name. In the name of the king, perhaps. But—"

"It's only a dream," Hapuseneb said. "She honors us by asking us to dream it with her."

Ineni forbore to sneer. He loved the queen as they all did, because she was beautiful, and because she had a way of knowing what would touch the heart of every man who served her. It should be less difficult, Senenmut thought, for Ineni to resist this fancy of hers.

"I will dream," Ineni said, "in my own bed, without assistance from her royal highness. This"—he flicked a hand at the sand-table and its poor attempt at a drawing—"is a waste of effort. The site might not do badly for a temple, but not in the name of a queen: even such a queen as ours. If the king takes it into his mind to set a structure there . . ."

"The only structure the king will set is a siege-engine outside of some Asiatic city." Senenmut did not mean to sound bitter, let alone contemptuous. He feared that he did both. "Besides, he's too young. He's only eight years old. It will be years before he takes thought for his tomb and temple."

"No man is too young to remember that he is mortal," Ineni said grimly. "Nor is any woman so old that she can claim a temple worthy of a king. People might think that she has ambitions in that direction."

"And if she did," asked Hapuseneb, "what could she do about it?"

"Order her servants to imagine what they would build if it were possible," Senenmut answered promptly. "I would create beauty in the king's name, if my queen asked it of me. Probably she will. She's sensible enough when she's not dreaming dreams."

"Does she ever stop dreaming?" Hapuseneb met Senenmut's stare. "Don't tell me you believe what you're saying. Whatever she does for our master, the living Horus, the Lord of the Two Lands, it will not be to set his name above hers in any monument that she bids us build. She'll build it for herself. I do love her, my friend, but I'm not blind. I can see how she revels in the exercise of power."

"She does what she has to do," Senenmut said tightly. This was an argument he had had before, but not with Hapuseneb. The priest, he had thought, had more sense.

"Necessity may drive her," said Hapuseneb, "but what it drives her to is rather more than might be proper. I see how she forgets to mention that she rules in the king's name. She issues decrees and establishes laws as she pleases, without consulting him."

"The king is eight years old," Senenmut said. "He's a child. His judgment is still unformed; his sense of justice lacks complexity. He's consulted where he's needed, in matters that he can understand. In the rest, she acts for him. She stands well within the compass of her powers as regent."

Hapuseneb tilted his head toward the sand-table. "That's not a regent's dream, old friend. That's the dream of one who will rule."

Senenmut narrowed his eyes. He had too much intelligence, sometimes. He saw so much that he failed to see what dangled from the end of his nose. "What are you saying?" he asked the priest. "Is this something that comes from Amon's temple? Or are you carrying tales from the court?"

"Neither," said Hapuseneb, "though temple and court aren't blind. They see what's clear to see. We have a queen regent who would prefer to rule as king."

"And if she would?" Senenmut demanded. "What difference does it make? She's a woman. You said so yourself. She's risen as high as she can. When the king is old enough, she'll step down. She'll be given no choice in the matter."

"She might try," Hapuseneb said.

Senenmut shook his head. Not because he disbelieved. Because his heart knew that none of them should say such things. It was a great pity that Hatshepsut had been born a woman. She ruled as well as any king—better in fact than most. But she must rule through a man, even if that man were no more than a boy, a solemn-faced compact child who never said more than he must.

The gods had made the world so. Even she, as strong and self-willed as she was, could do nothing to change it. She could only dream, and envision a temple like an edifice of light.

Truth was a stark thing. A queen regent who would step aside when her king was a man. A royal lady who would lie in a tomb among the rest of the royal ladies, apart from the kings, with great treasure, but not as great as the treasure of a king.

So must it be. He sighed, thinking of it. Ineni who had never dreamed a dream in his life, Hapuseneb who saw too clearly for sense, went away hardly aware they had been got rid of. He lingered, staring at the sand-table but seeing no such poor thing as was laid out in it. His mind's eye saw beauty; saw splendor. Saw her glory in stone, raised to endure till the earth grew old.

25

ALL GLORY PASSED. THAT WAS THE truth which all men living knew, or should know. Life was brief; death, once begun, knew no ending. For most it was oblivion: their names forgotten, their bodies lost in the dust of ages.

For kings and for the children of kings, and in these later years for any who amassed wealth to any notable degree, death could be as life. It required mighty effort, the labor of years to build a tomb, equip it, ward it with spells of guard and guidance. When the tomb was built, if the gods were kind its master might live for years in the surety of his life-after-death; so that when he died, and the seventy days of embalming were over and he was laid in the tomb, he was prepared for the journey. He had his servants, his banquets, his house in the other-world; his kin if he loved them, his animals, his children. All that had been his in life would be his in death, so that he might have joy there as in the land of the living.

Senenmut had been granted a rare and precious privilege: a tomb near the tombs of kings and near the place that his queen had chosen, if only in her heart, for her marvelous temple. He had dug it deep and hidden it well lest the robbers have too easy a time of it, and adorned it himself, through such hours as he had amid his many duties.

It was not his tomb alone. A lord expected his family to share the life-after-death. Those whom he loved would dwell with him as in life, no doubt in the same prickly amity.

In the fourth year of the reign of Menkheperre Thutmose, Senenmut's father had wandered vaguely into death as he had wandered through life. One morning he had simply failed to wake. He had died in his sleep, peacefully, of no sickness that anyone could see. The gods had taken him, and shown him mercy: for all anyone knew, he never even realized that he was dead.

He lay now in the tomb that his son had built, in the awful calm of death. For companion he had his wife's old nurse who had died not long after the tomb was finished. In time the rest would join them—long time, they could hope.

That was the year of grief, but also the year of joy: the year Ahotep took a wife.

Ahotep had grown well from unpromising beginnings. He was prettier than Senenmut, handsome indeed in the livery of the king's guard. His wife was a captain's daughter, sweet-faced if not remarkably sweet-tempered, with a talent for keeping her husband in hand. Since he remained irrepressible even in manhood, that was a welcome gift.

They lived in Senenmut's house. It seemed absurd for them to live anywhere else. When Ahotep journeyed with the king on royal progresses from city to city of the Two Lands, Iuty contested with Hat-Nufer for mastery of the house. Their battles drove Senenmut into retreat more often than not, to palace or temple or his own chambers, but he never quite mustered the bravado to put a stop to them. He was lazy, he supposed, and certainly a fool.

Still there was a little wisdom in it. After a mighty war that had gone on for days, for what cause Senenmut never understood, when at last the women had declared a barbed and muttering truce, he said to his mother, "Now do you see why I never brought home a wife?"

Hat-Nufer sniffed audibly. *"Your* wife would have had the sense not to argue with me. What is a daughter-in-law if not a woman's loyal servant? She'll be lady and mistress of the house when I am dead. The least she can do is submit to me while I'm alive."

Iuty's sniff was just as loud and just as indignant when she trapped Senenmut in the sanctuary of his reading-room, in the long light of evening. "I'll be as good a daughter-in-law as I can be," she said, "but before the gods, brother, she can be impossible."

Senenmut could hardly deny that, nor could he deny his mother's contention that Iuty lacked somewhat of submission. "You are," he ventured to Iuty, "remarkably alike."

He had known better than to say such a thing to his mother. His brother's wife bridled. "I am not impossible!"

"Well," Senenmut admitted, "not yet."

If a look could flay, he would have been stripped to the bone. She spun on her heel and departed in high dudgeon.

He was not a wise man. He laughed long and well. His younger brother caught him at it: young Amonhotep who had some time since discovered the beauties of women, but refrained yet from asking any of them to wife. He dropped his lanky elegance into Senenmut's own favorite chair, propped his feet on the winetable, and said, "Don't tell me. The ladies are at it again."

"What, you haven't been here for the past hand of days?" Senenmut tipped him out of the chair and settled himself in it. "It's been open war."

Amonhotep picked himself up without resentment and found another chair, over which he draped himself, the image of languid ease. Except for his eyes: those were wickedly bright. "I've been off hunting waterfowl at Ptahmose's villa. Hadn't you noticed I was gone?"

"Not really," Senenmut said. "Waterfowl, yes? The kind with feathers, or the kind with a soft skin and sweet lips and willing arms?"

Amonhotep grinned. "Why, both! You should have come. You'd have had a little peace of mind."

"It wasn't so terrible," said Senenmut. "I managed to escape all day; then during the worst of it I borrowed a room in the palace."

"You work too hard," Amonhotep said with sudden seriousness. "Don't you ever rest?"

"Often," said Senenmut. "I have a villa, too, you know. And the horses."

"Certainly. A villa you visit maybe once in a season, and horses who are as much work as anything else you do. Do you know what they say of you? That you'd play the stablehand if you could."

"Why not? It's a cleaner task than some." Senenmut laughed at his brother's expression. "Look at you! Anyone would think you were born in a palace."

Amonhotep sat up, stung to the quick. "If you refuse to conduct yourself with proper decorum, then someone surely must. Why not I? I have no rank or wealth except by your bestowing. I claim nothing that is my own; no office, no duty, no service. What is there for me to do but try to be worthy of you?"

There was deep injury there, but not deep enough. "Oh, stop that," Senenmut said. "You didn't want to join the guard as Ahotep did. You've no aptitude for the House of Life. What else shall I find for you to do? I thought it bored you immeasurably to look after my estate."

"It did bore me," Amonhotep said. "But that was years ago. I need something to do, brother, besides hunt waterfowl on other men's estates."

"Well then," Senenmut said. "What do you want to do?"

Amonhotep shrugged. Senenmut could remember being seventeen years old. It was not so very long ago. Had he been so bored, so perfectly without focus?

He rather doubted it. He had by then been some years in the queen's service. He stood guardian already to the princess Neferure, and held a handful of offices besides. Idleness had never vexed him; as for boredom, he barely knew the meaning of the word.

And here was the youngest of Hat-Nufer's sons, a man in years but never in responsibility. He lacked the petulance of most petty lordlings, but he certainly had the air of ennui.

"Suppose," Senenmut said, "that I make you steward of my estate. Would that be too dull a duty?"

Amonhotep did not leap up in eagerness, but neither did he recoil as if in insult. "I could learn to like it," he said. "May I have hunting parties?"

"Not too often," Senenmut said, "and not too extravagant. You'll have an allowance, paid at each new moon. If you exceed it, I'll give you no more till the next new moon. If you fall into debt, I'll not lift you out."

"You won't need to," said Amonhotep with the confidence of the young. "I can cipher—I was good at that, though you'll not likely remember. I'll keep a good reckoning of your accounts."

"I do remember," Senenmut said, "though the shock of your expulsion from the Temple of Amon rather obscured the pleasure of it."

Amonhotep neither blushed nor avoided Senenmut's stare. "Ah. Well. I couldn't sit still. It was so dull—except for the numbers."

"Setting fire to the store of papyrus was hardly a proper means of alleviating boredom," Senenmut observed dryly.

"It was only the scrap-heap," Amonhotep said, "as you know very well. And they put it out directly. It never threatened the best stock, nor would I have let it."

"Which," said Senenmut, "is why you were merely expelled and not whipped till you bled." He sighed. "Ah well. That's years past, and you say you've grown wiser. I'll trust you to keep a good accounting of my estate."

Amonhotep regarded him narrowly. "You will send a man or two along to assist me. Won't you? To make sure."

"Would you respect me if I didn't?"

"No," Amonhotep said. He bounded to his feet. "When do I begin?"

"In the morning," Senenmut said. The gods knew this for certain: he had never been as lively as that, even when he was young. His brother grinned, saluted him, and trod lightly out into the evening, no doubt to while it away in wine and song and a woman or two.

Senenmut had a slight leaning toward wine. Song he loved, but not tonight. Women . . .

He sighed again, deeper this time, with more of resignation than of regret. The queen had indicated that she would rest tonight. Tomorrow was a festival day, with rites in the temples, processions, feasts and high audiences, all of which she must adorn with her presence. It was not that she could not sleep in his arms; it was what else she would want to do, that could run far into the night.

No doubt of it, he thought as he poured wine into his best silver cup, the one that had come from far away in Asia, with a herd of horses running one by one around the rim. They were no longer as young as they had been, he and she. Not old, no, not yet; but he was past thirty, and she was near it.

He sipped the strong sweet wine, resting for a moment in the memory of her face. How swiftly time flew, yet how slowly it could pass, bearing them all to the sanctuary of their tombs.

His mood was strange tonight, not dark, but not light, either. He had no inclination toward his bed. When he sought his garden, the last light was fading from the sky. It was the season that in Asia they called winter, cold to his thin southern blood. He wrapped a lionskin about him, his brother Ahotep's gift, that that bold soldier had caught and killed on some campaign or other. It was warm, and smelled still, a little, of lion.

One of the servants set a lamp in the niche by the door. He sat on the edge of its light, watching the stars come out. It was astonishingly quiet. The bustle and hum of his house under the sun had died to a murmur. Now that the women's war was ended, no one rent the night with contention. Amonhotep had gone out; Ahotep was on night-duty in the palace—as he had arranged to do every night since the war began.

Senenmut was as nearly alone as he could ever be. He thought briefly of going to the stable to visit the Dawn Wind and perhaps to offer her a sweet; but he was too lazy to move.

Perhaps Amonhotep had the right of it. Perhaps he did rest too seldom. But there was so much to do. All that he did, the queen did and more; how could he retreat, when she knew even less peace than he?

"There's rest enough in the tomb," he said, "if I want it even then."

The night breathed about him. The stars stared coldly down. The moon, the blind eye of Horus, rose slowly over the roof of his house. It was waxing but not yet full. He paid it reverence as a wise man should.

He should go in. Nightwalkers and demons of the dark could walk even within walls, with the moon to guide them. Still he lingered. If he had been unwise to trust Amonhotep with the management of his estate, and hence of his horses, he would learn it quickly, and perhaps to his grief. But he could hardly call back the gift, now that it was given.

He shook his head at himself. The moon invited him to rest in its quiet, but he could not stop the yapping and circling of his mind. Best go in, pour another cup of wine, sleep if he could. The morning came early, and the festival in which he had a notable part. He had a new office: Steward of Amon. He managed the estates of the god much as he had given Amonhotep leave to manage Senenmut's own.

In the court they called him Mighty of Offices, not seeming to know that he heard, or to care. He had chosen to take the title as a compliment. The envy in it could not diminish him. Only in the night, under the moon, did he stop to wonder when the weight of all his offices would bow him down.

"Not yet," he said abruptly, briskly, rising and gathering his lionskin about him. "By the gods' mercy, not ever. They made me to serve my queen. No one serves her better."

Which no doubt made him a braggart; but it was no less true for that. Grinning at himself, clutching his lionskin, he went in to the light and the warmth and the sweet headiness of the wine.

26

SOMEHOW, WHILE NO ONE WAS LOOKING, the child Neferure had become a woman. She was if anything more beautiful than her mother, and willful with it, without her mother's firm good sense.

In that she reminded Senenmut of Amonhotep. Like him she had no such burden of duties as had weighed down her mother. She was queen, and must rule to some degree, but under her mother's regency she had little to do but be beautiful, tyrannize her servants, and try to evade Senenmut's quelling hand.

She was, like Amonhotep, enormously and dangerously bored. The duties of a queen did not greatly interest her. She lacked her mother's tolerance for tedium; nor did she seem to love the Two Lands as Hatshepsut did.

"You take too much for granted," Senenmut was driven to snap at her, one day when she was particularly obstreperous. She had agreed to attend an audience with an embassy from Lagash, but had sat through it speechless and sullen while her mother exerted herself to be charming. She would have left before it properly ended, had not Senenmut all but sat on her.

When at last he did allow her to leave, it was to herd her into her workroom and stand over her while she sulked through an hour of reading and ciphering.

"Truly," he said at last in pure exasperation, "you know neither gratitude nor sense. You are Great Royal Wife in the Great House of Egypt. You have duties and obligations. You were born for them. The gods made you a goddess, but no such gift is without price."

She sneered at him. "Oh, please! I've heard it a thousand times before. Can't you think of something else to beat me about the head with? If I'm the queen, then where is the king? Why does he get to play with his little wooden soldiers while I have to sit through days of crashing boredom?"

"The king," Senenmut said through gritted teeth, "is learning the arts of a man."

"It isn't manly to sit in audience while bearded foreigners babble on and on about nothing?"

"When you were eight years old," Senenmut said, "you enjoyed a child's freedom, too. You are a woman now. You should learn to think and act as one."

"Oh, don't I?" She arched her back and tilted her chin and sleeked at him like a cat, as women did in the market when they would drive the young men wild. "Am I a woman, really? Do I look like one? Am I beautiful? Do you love me?"

Senenmut dared not laugh. Pride was so fragile when one was young; and this was a queen, than whom nothing could be prouder. "Of course you are a woman," he said, "and of course I love you. I've known you since you were born."

She hissed and flounced and abandoned her wanton posing—and not before time, either. "Oh, you are so dull! Everyone is dull. The king is dullest of all. He's such a child. Will he never be a man?"

Ah, thought Senenmut. He could remind her that she had known since she married a child barely weaned, that she must wait long years until he could love her as a man loves a woman. But young womanhood did not want to hear what it had agreed to while it was still a child. The blood was hot; boredom was fierce, made worse by resentment that she must be queen while her king indulged himself in the pleasures of youth.

Best cut that off before it grew and flowered into hatred. "Here," said Senenmut. "Since you clearly have no mind for anything useful, shall we do something outrageous?"

She brightened at once, though she was wary still. She knew him too well to expect that such pleasure could come without a price. "What? The chariot again?"

"Actually," he said, "no. I was thinking of something truly different. Have you ever seen a house that was not a palace?"

"I went to Lord Hapu's villa once," she said.

"That's nearly as big as the White Hall in Memphis," Senenmut said, "and somewhat more imposing. No: I mean a real house. Mine."

There. He had caught her. She looked herself again, the Neferure whom he had loved so long, bright-eyed and laughing, clapping her hands. "*Your* house? Oh, can we? We never have." She darkened abruptly. "There will be a reason why I can't go. Someone will stop me."

"I don't think so," Senenmut said.

"Then why did you never invite me before?" she asked with devastating logic.

He looked her in the eye and told her the truth. "I never thought

of it. You have this palace, the palace in Memphis, the palace in Abydos, the hunting lodge in—"

"They are all so *dull*," she said: her old refrain, begun anew.

"So," he said. "My house is dull, too, but it's a different kind of
dull. For one thing, my mother is in it."

That made her smile again. "I do like your mother. She's never flustered when she talks to me."

"Nothing flusters my mother," Senenmut said. "Here, will you
come? We'll take one maid—Tuyu, I think. She can hold her tongue
when she's told to."

"And my monkey," said Neferure. "He'll come, too. Tuyu can hold
him."

Senenmut drew breath to refuse, but thought better of it. One dog-
nosed monkey and one discreet little maid would not encumber them
unduly. They were fetched quickly enough, the monkey clinging to
Tuyu's neck and chittering nervously at Senenmut. "There," he said
to it, "stop that. You're going exploring."

The monkey grimaced at him, baring formidable fangs. Senenmut
grinned back. Senenmut had excellent teeth for his age: not too badly
blunted, nor too yellow, and missing only one or two. The monkey subsided, startled, muttering to itself.

■ They were careful as they went abroad, to attract no notice. Neferure was only a little more elegantly clad than her maid; her ornaments
were almost plain, and her wig was such as any wellborn woman might
wear. She advanced with an air of grand adventure, taking the way that
Senenmut walked every day. Her presence transformed it from daily
ordinariness to a kind of well-worn splendor.

Neferure had forgotten her sulks and her ennui. She would have
pressed ahead if Senenmut had not stretched his stride. The monkey
had left the maid's shoulder to cling to its mistress' neck, peering
through the plaits of her wig and chittering at people who passed.

It was remarkable how few people spared them a glance. Senenmut was noticed: he was expected; it was known that he passed every
day on foot from his house to the palace, commanding a chair only

when he was ill or indisposed. His companions were nigh invisible in the company of his escort, his guards and the servants whose number and quality proclaimed the loftiness of his estate. That they hung about idle while he labored in his queen's service was an irony that he could, in wry moments, appreciate.

The whole gaudy procession amused Neferure to no end. She was accustomed to far greater, but she had never walked among the servants, nor been jostled when she lagged, and hissed at for a sluggard. The maid Tuyu bristled, but Neferure's glare restrained her when she would have spoken.

Senenmut might not have seen, had he not been inclined to wander a bit himself, leaving the servants to maintain the dignity of his rank. Tall portly Ptahotep with his air of mighty consequence and his complete lack of measurable wits made a fine semblance of a personage; he hardly needed to be persuaded to stride just behind the four toplofty guardsmen, nose in the air, condescending to notice nothing and no one.

Neferure had this much of a queen's training: she did not burst out laughing in the middle of the processional way. She had no parasol, either, to protect her soft ivory skin; but Tuyu was far more alarmed by that than she.

In peculiar state, behind a servant who carried himself like a prince, they made their way to Senenmut's house.

It was the same that he had had since he became Neferure's tutor. He could have demanded one higher and prouder and newer, but that he chose not to do. It was an eccentricity; a simple and unadorned preference for that small, faded, undistinguished house in sight of the palace. It had been the queen's first gift to him, and cherished the more for that.

He had brightened it a little, to be sure. There was a new garden, a stable much enlarged, the women's quarters built all anew since Ahotep took a wife. But the outer wall was the same, and his own chambers, and the court into which he led his young queen.

She looked about with interest and no perceptible disappointment. This after all was hardly a laborer's hut. It had been a noble mansion in its day. But it was no palace nor had ever been; and its chattering flock of servants kept no dignity even in their lord's presence. They judged it enough to do so everywhere else; here they fell into an ease that would have appalled the masters of servants in the palace.

It was, like the refusal of chair or chariot, an eccentricity in which Senenmut took a peculiar pleasure. He was the queen's commoner, the nobleman whom she had made from a tradesman's son. He could command servants as sternly as any king; and so he did in all his ranks and offices. But in this house that was his refuge, he chose to be indulgent.

He could afford the luxury. As lenient as he allowed himself to be, when Hat-Nufer appeared in the courtyard, every one of that unruly throng snapped to attention. Idle they might be daylong, but in this house they worked for their bread and barley beer. She drove them as a general drives his troops, with rough justice and no mercy.

Nor did she spare her son, though he hung well back in the ranks. "You! Hiding with the fan-bearers again. What use is rank if you don't flaunt it?"

"But, Mother," he said sweetly, "everybody is so vulgar about it. Don't you think Ptahotep makes a wonderful personage?"

"That idiot," said Hat-Nufer. "If you had any self-respect—"

Neferure had labored nobly to conceal her laughter; but at that she whooped. It was completely unexpected, and completely without restraint. Hat-Nufer rounded on her, glaring formidably.

She had a keen eye. She knew that face, though no crown adorned it. She did not flinch, not by the slightest fraction. "Great Mother Isis! You, too?"

Neferure could not be said to creep from behind the shelter of her maid. She was proud and she was queen. But she lowered her head a very little, and said in something close to meekness, "I was bored."

"Bored?" Hat-Nufer fairly spat the word. "No one is bored who has anything useful to do."

"But I don't," said Neferure.

Hat-Nufer shook her head. "Oh, you children. Fools, all of you. Stop gawping and come here."

Neferure had not been gawping, not that Senenmut could see, but she did as she was told. No one but Hat-Nufer had ever been able to address her so, nor would anyone else have dared. She must have found it refreshing.

Senenmut was enjoying himself. The small cold knot in the center of his stomach had begun to unravel. This was not entirely wise, nor was it as carefully judged as it might have been. He had acted on impulse. He might well learn to regret it.

At the moment he did not care. He had been bored, too, perhaps. So many duties, so many responsibilities. So much that was a burden, so little that gave him honest pleasure.

Hat-Nufer bore her royal guest away, sweeping Senenmut in their wake. She had words in plenty for both of them. Neferure listened no more assiduously than Senenmut did: he saw the sidewise slant of her smile, the wandering of her glance as she took in the halls and courts through which she was half-led, half-dragged.

It was worth his mother's disgust and the possibility of uproar in the palace to see Neferure returned to herself again. He had rather hoped the women would go off for women-talk and leave him to rest in peace, but Hat-Nufer had no intention of sparing him. He found himself in the room he seldom used, which was meant for the lord of the house when he entertained noble guests. The chairs were stiff with disuse, but the room was clean and the wine was good—as it ought to be: it was the royal vintage.

His young queen had never dined in comfort with a few friends. Either she feasted in court or she ate alone under the eyes of maids and guards. She did not sneer at the mere six courses or the lack of a wine for each—there was only the one vintage, and date wine for Iuty, who could not stomach the nobler grape.

Iuty had appeared in some indignation, prepared to inveigh loudly against this change in the nightly ritual. Senenmut seldom dined at home; when he did, he dined alone. Hat-Nufer and her sons and her second son's wife gathered in the women's hall, never in Senenmut's; and how much more comfortable that hall was than this, Iuty spared no effort to make clear.

"And my husband and his brother unaccountably late," she said, "and now it seems you've brought in another child-bride for Senenmut to refuse to look at—mother-in-law, such lack of consideration is quite beyond endurance."

Before anyone else could cure Iuty of her misperception, Neferure said with demure expression and glinting eyes, "Oh, no, I'm not one of your noble brother's brides. I am already married."

"Are you, then?" Iuty demanded. "Then have you come to offer him a sister? A cousin? A mother?"

"My mother likes him very well," said Neferure—wicked, wicked child. "But I don't think he'll marry if he can help it. He's wise, maybe. Don't you think?"

"I think that you have a terribly affected accent," Iuty said. "Have you been listening to ladies chatter in the court?"

Senenmut could only watch and listen in shocked fascination. Hat-Nufer wore an expression of unholy glee. Neferure was enjoying herself much too much. "They do run on, don't they? At such length—and with such monstrous dullness."

"It's not as if they had anything better to do," said Iuty. She glowered. "Where *are* those boys?"

Neferure's delight must be complete. Ahotep strode in just exactly then, and Amonhotep behind, the former gleaming in the livery of the king's guard, the latter managing to look enormously languid and elegant in nothing more elaborate than a linen kilt. Ahotep stopped short, so abrupt that his brother collided with him. Equally abruptly he dropped down in front of Neferure. "Majesty! How in the world—"

"I was bored," Neferure said to him as she had to Hat-Nufer. "This is wonderful. Here, get up. I'm not wearing my crown tonight."

He got up with alacrity and no little dismay. "Lady, you can't—"

"I decide what the queen's majesty may and may not do," Senenmut said mildly, "when she does not choose to decide it for herself. She was, as she says, bored. I brought her where she might safely be entertained."

"At *my* expense!" Iuty was whitely furious. Too furious, Senenmut noted, to throw herself at the queen's feet as her husband had—if she could ever have done such a thing. "You were making sport of me."

"I am sorry for that," Neferure said quickly, with honesty that

Senenmut had always loved in her. Perhaps it was his fault. Queens had to be circumspect; but Neferure had never entirely mastered the art. "It was only . . . you see, no one ever talks to me like that. I'm always the queen's majesty. I'm never the guest who comes unlooked for, and who must have designs on the lord of the house. It's rather delightful."

It was difficult to resist Neferure at her most charmingly apologetic. Iuty was proof against much, but even she warmed a little.

Ahotep was appalled. Manhood had transformed him from a lively child into a sternly dutiful soldier in the king's guard. Whenever Senenmut had in mind to marvel at the gods' whims, he remembered the child who had been and the man who was now. All that was left of that boisterous infant was a certain inclination toward levity when he was not vexed with royal follies.

Before Iuty could say anything to provoke the queen further, Ahotep said, "Lady, you are safe here. But surely—"

"Oh, do let her stay," Amonhotep said in a tone he must have studied long: it was half a drawl and half a yawn. "If the palace has sent out its hounds, we'll head them off soon enough."

"No one has followed me," said Neferure, "or will." She lifted her chin as she said it, tilting eyes at him. "Have we been introduced?"

"I doubt it," Amonhotep said, "majesty. My name is Amonhotep. These tedious old men are my brothers."

"All men are tedious," Neferure said with an air that invited him to contradict her.

Amonhotep smiled lazily. "Yes, aren't they? Life is so dull."

"No one knows that better than I." She sighed deeply. "But still, there are moments . . . have you ever driven a chariot as fast as the horses will gallop, straight through the city and out into the Red Land?"

"I have never driven a chariot," he said. "I leave that to my brothers."

"Oh, then you must learn," she said. "Senenmut, give him horses. Teach him. He'll die of boredom else."

"I have horses," he said before Senenmut could speak. "I look after my brother's estate. We've bred one or two that will carry a man."

"What, on their backs?" Neferure was intrigued. "I've heard of such a thing, but nobody does it."

"I do," said Amonhotep.

"But don't you fall off?"

"One learns not to," he said.

"Still," she said. "What possible use is it?"

"Why, think," he said. "A chariot is a noble thing, but it requires two horses and a harness and rather a lot of time to get it ready. A horse that's to be ridden, now: bridle it, spring onto its back, and off you can go. And you can go where a chariot can't. I've ridden up the crags of the Red Land, faster than a man can go, and sat my horse on top of the world."

Well, Senenmut thought. That was the first he had heard of that. His little brother had secrets. Wonderful ones, from Neferure's expression. She seemed to have forgotten that there was anyone else in the room.

Women loved Amonhotep. He was not as handsome as Ahotep, but his face was pretty enough, and he had a beguiling way about him. He certainly knew how to capture the young queen's interest. She had left the chair she had been sitting in, to take the one nearest him. The others were invisible, inaudible, forgotten.

Ahotep caught Senenmut's eye. He was frowning. Senenmut raised his brows and shrugged. "It seems," he said, "that boredom loves company."

The prisoners of ennui did not hear. They had bent their heads together, deep in converse. Horses at first, but any number of things as they went on. Senenmut had not known that Amonhotep could be so very interesting—or so interested in so many faces of the world. He had always seemed immensely and hopelessly bored.

Senenmut had to pry his charge loose. Even then he might not have succeeded, but Ahotep the guardsman took her deftly in hand. He used no lure but common sense. "It's getting dark," he said. "Best you be in your proper place when they close the gates for the night."

If Senenmut had said it, she would not have yielded. But Ahotep had no expectation that she would disregard him. She frowned, dallied, sulked a little, but in the end she went away with him.

Amonhotep included himself in the party. He did not ask; he simply followed. Perhaps she would have changed her mind, but his presence persuaded her to be sensible. Or at least, thought Senenmut, it allowed her to pretend to sense.

〰〰〰

27

*I*N AMONHOTEP, NEFERURE HAD found a friend. They met in shared ennui and continued in conjoined fascination. Senenmut had never known that his brother had such wit or such an abundance of skills. He had always been the baby, the youngest son, the one who had no talent for anything in particular.

Perhaps he was no great master of anything, but he was a fair journeyman in a remarkable number of things.

"It does astonish me," Senenmut said to Ahotep one evening when they happened to be in the house together, "that I could know a man from birth, and never know him at all."

"Yes," Ahotep said. "You who have a name for keen perception—you never have seen very clearly where your kin are concerned."

Senenmut had been speaking lightly, sipping a new vintage of wine and expecting nothing but companionship. Ahotep's severity took him by surprise. "What, do you have secrets, too?"

"All men have secrets," his brother said.

Senenmut's eyes narrowed. His light mood had gone abruptly dark. "What are you telling me?"

Ahotep did not answer at once. He sipped his wine slowly—he was not as fond of the thinner, drier vintages as Senenmut was—and appeared to be engrossed in the pattern of lotus-flowers painted on the wall.

Senenmut did not choose to press him. After a while that stretched long, he said, "I don't know that I'm telling you anything. People are talking about the young queen's new favorite. The king likes him, too."

"The king finds him nearly as refreshing as she does," said Senen-mut. "They do grow weary of the same faces over and over. Courtly faces, faces that never look directly at them, but bow and turn aside. Our brother knows how to accord a king proper respect, but without ever seeming obsequious."

"He learned that from you." Ahotep set down his cup half-finished, stretched and sighed and slid down in his chair, for once like the child he had been. No one could be more exuberantly tired than Ahotep. "You haven't heard what people are saying, have you?"

"People are always saying things," Senenmut said. "They say the king is insisting that the kingdom go to war, so that he can see whether real soldiers fight as well as his wooden ones. They say also that the queen regent objects firmly to any such notion, and that the young queen cares little what either of them does."

"You would know the truth of that," Ahotep said. "You sit in all their councils. But do you listen to rumors? Most of them are nonsense. The one for example that makes you rather more than the queen's friend and counsellor."

Senenmut went very still. He hoped that his expression did not alter. "Oh, is that still lurking in corners? It's inevitable, I suppose. The queen is still young enough to attract such whispers; and all her coun-sellors are men. Does anyone say why I must be the one who comforts her in more ways than the usual?"

"Maybe," said Ahotep, "because you do."

Senenmut found that his mouth was open. He shut it.

His brother regarded him levelly, sternly, till he began to bristle. Then, startlingly, Ahotep laughed. "Gods, brother! You look so guilty."

"I am not—"

"Don't," said Ahotep with a return of his sternness. "Don't lie to me. I've known for years. I followed you once or twice, long ago. You never knew. I saw where you went. I could guess what you did there. There's not much else a man will do in a queen's chamber in the hours between midnight and dawn."

Senenmut sat back, suddenly limp. He felt as if the air had been driven out of his lungs. And yet he knew an enormous, almost giddy relief. "You never said a word," he said.

Ahotep shrugged, looking faintly embarrassed. "By the time I'd turned into a dutiful soldier of the king, it had been going on for years, and the king her husband was dead. What was betrayal had become a kind of comfort. She can't marry again, not without complicating the regency. You've always been discreet: I've heard barely a word of what you are to each other. The little I have heard is simply the spite of courts. They say she's taken the priest Hapuseneb to her bed, too, and her Nubian—that's the heaviest wager—and even some of her less likely counsellors. Ahmose Pen-Nekhbet, Ahmose the General, has a surprisingly large faction."

"Old Ahmose? Gods! I didn't know he still had a shaft to raise. He's absolutely ancient. He even fought against the Hyksos, when he was just old enough to carry a spear."

"So he says," Ahotep said. His voice rose to an old man's quaver. "Yes, yes, I served under King Ahmose himself. Now that was a king, that was!"

Senenmut laughed too loud, perhaps, and too long, but he needed the release. "Oh, yes! That's Ahmose Pen-Nekhbet to the life." He sobered. "And do you despise me, brother?"

"For what?" Ahotep asked. "Keeping the queen so content with you that she's never looked at another man?"

"No," Senenmut said. "Keeping the secret from you."

"That was only sensible," said Ahotep. "I admit, I was angry at first. You could have told me. But when I grew a little older I reflected on what I was then, how I never could keep quiet. You were wise to keep your counsel."

"I'm glad," said Senenmut. He meant it. Ahotep the child had been an endless nuisance. Ahotep the man was friend as well as brother. As much a friend, he acknowledged to himself, as Hapuseneb; as much even as the queen.

They did not embrace one another. It would have been false somehow; as if they protested too much.

They drank wine for a while in companionable silence. As Senenmut poured a second cup for each, Ahotep said, "People are saying that our brother and the queen are sharing more than confidences in those long hours they've begun to spend together."

Senenmut had been hoping, foolishly enough, that Ahotep would not say what he had been leading up to since he invited Senenmut to share a new jar of wine. It was not that Senenmut preferred to avoid the truth. He had not seen it; had refused to see it. But Ahotep had forced him to open his eyes.

"It may be," said Senenmut, "that the rumor is as false as the queen regent's laison with her Nubian."

"Do you think that?" Ahotep asked.

Senenmut had to meet that steady stare. It was not easy. Too many things were coming clear. The sudden vanishing of Neferure's boredom. The way she sang to herself when she thought no one was listening. The sheen on her, the beauty grown notably greater, and not because she had changed her wigs or her eyepaint or her jewels. She had the look of a woman with a lover.

Or a friend. He clung to that, as feeble as it was. "It is so difficult," he said, "to be a queen. To have a friend—a person who wants nothing of her but her company, who loves her for herself—is well-nigh impossible. She's enough like her mother that she takes little pleasure in women's company. Why shouldn't she have chosen a man for a friend?"

"When a woman is as young as that," said Ahotep, "and has as little to do, it's not only friendship she looks for in a handsome and charming young man. Our brother is both."

Senenmut shook his head. "I don't want to believe it."

"Neither do I," Ahotep said, "but someone must. When you became more than the queen's friend, you knew as well as she that there would be no more children. This queen's husband is a child. If her belly swells as is the way of things, the world will know that the king had nothing to do with it."

"Thutmose might prove precocious," Senenmut said. But he stopped himself before Ahotep could begin. "No, don't say it. He's much more intelligent than he looks, but his body is a child's still. He was late to walk, late to talk. He'll likely be late to manhood, too."

Ahotep nodded. "So. Which of us corners Amonhotep and convinces him to see sense?"

"You don't think the queen will?"

"I think we can wield a stronger flail against our erring brother than against the Great Royal Wife."

Senenmut closed his eyes. He was weary suddenly, weary to the bone. "Sweet Hathor. And it's I who brought her here where she could meet the boy. I never imagined—"

"One never does," Ahotep said. "I wonder. Has anyone ever said it of you and the queen regent?"

"Seti-Nakht has never regretted a thing in his life," said Senenmut. "For all I know he intended it."

"Seti-Nakht is a wiser man than either of us." Ahotep drained his cup and rose. "I say we do it now. Soonest done, soonest over."

Senenmut swallowed his protests. He had never felt less decisive than he did now. But Ahotep the soldier more than made up for it. That came of training in combat, Senenmut thought. A man learned to face his fear and kill it quickly. Courtiers were more inclined to run away from it.

Senenmut was a courtier. He had never liked to think of himself as such. He was the queen's servant, the commoner whom she had made a prince. Courtiers were idlers, cat-sleek creatures born to rank that they had never earned. The queen's true servants, the men and women who labored long in her service, must be something other; something more honorable.

But courtiers they were, and courtiers they would always be.

He sighed. "Well then," he said. "Let's do it."

■ Amonhotep was not in his rooms. The lone drowsy manservant knew nothing. "He went to the villa," he said yawning. "Or maybe to dinner."

Ahotep would have whipped the truth out of the fool, but Senenmut stopped him. "Don't waste time. You know where he is."

Ahotep nodded heavily. "We'll wait till morning, I suppose. He'll creep back in the night."

So had Senenmut done for nights out of count. So would he be doing tonight if Ahotep had not delayed him. He set his lips together and withdrew from the empty rooms. He did not seriously consider confronting the lovers in the queen's own chamber. It was not a scan-

dal he wanted. A quiet meeting among the brothers, a measure of per-
suasion—a thump or two if the boy needed it. That would do. It would
have to.

~~~~~~~

28

AMONHOTEP DID NOT RETURN home in the morn-
ing. He had, Senenmut discovered, gone to the villa. It was
the season for the stallions to be put to the mares—apt
enough, if one stopped to think.

Senenmut could not ride in pursuit. He had too many duties, too
many obligations in Thebes; and the queen regent was considering another royal progress into Lower Egypt. Senenmut would be expected
to assist in preparations, and to accompany her.

The queen and the young king would go. It was their progress, their
faces whom the people should see. Which, Senenmut, thought, might
resolve the dilemma of Neferure and Amonhotep. Amonhotep was
bound to his brother's estate till breeding season was done. If he had
hoped to slip back at intervals, creep into the palace by night and leave
before morning, then he would be disappointed.

It was well, thought Senenmut. He allowed himself to cease fretting.
Except for the doubled guard on Neferure's chambers, with instructions
to admit no one through any door or passage, secret or otherwise, he did
nothing, nor confronted his brother among the herds of horses.

He continued to visit Hatshepsut: an irony that he could well appreciate. He had said nothing to her of her daughter's indiscretion. She
did not need to know it, nor would it serve any of them if she did.

■ As royal progresses went, this one was brief: down to Memphis in
barges on the river, then up again to Thebes. Hatshepsut wished to secure the people's loyalty by showing them their king and his beautiful

young queen. The king accepted his duty as he did all else: quietly, meekly as befit a child-ruler under his regent's guidance.

His mother accompanied him as she always did. She was constrained to silence, to say or do nothing that would persuade the queen regent to dispose of her. She had settled into it with a kind of contentment: like a hound accustomed to its chain, or a bird to its cage.

It was all very quiet, very calm, very civilized. The tension beneath was barely perceptible. Often Senenmut wondered if it was there at all—if he deceived himself with night fears and useless frettings. The king accepted his lot. He would rule in the end; there could be no doubt of it. In this his minority, while he was still so young as to require a regent, he demanded no more power than Hatshepsut would give him, nor seemed to feel any lack.

In front of her he was utterly still, as if quenched. The brightness that Senenmut had seen in him so often when he was in others' company was sunk to an ember. It was as if the fire that burned in her had turned his own all cold.

"He has hardly a word to say for himself," Hatshepsut said as she lay with Senenmut in the palace of Memphis. The secret ways there were many and intricate, more than enough to be lost in, if he had not had a gods-given memory for any place that he had seen more than once.

They had to be circumspect here. The servants of this palace knew little of the queen regent and less of her scribe and servant. There was a certain slither to them, a remembrance of ancient rivalries. Memphis had shrunk since it was the chief city of the Two Lands; since it was taken captive by foreign kings, and freed by kings out of Thebes.

Sometimes Senenmut thought that he could smell the foreign kings still: a hint of incense, a ghost of outland unguents. They had brought horses into Egypt, their one great gift and their downfall, because Egypt embraced the new creatures and with them a new art of war.

Their spirits watched and whispered while the queen regent lay with her common-born lover, embracing him with urgency that had faded but little since they were young together. In the quiet after, she shook her head over the king in whose name she ruled. "For all that I see of him, he could be a simpleton," she said. "He hardly says a word. He sits the throne, wears the crown and grips the crook and flail as if he were a carven king. Does he have a thought in his head, do you think?"

"I know he has many," Senenmut said. "He's afraid of you. You are so strong, and you rule so well; and he's so young."

"And with such a mother as he has . . ." She hissed a little as she always did when she spoke of Isis, in exasperation. "It's a wonder he can walk without her hand to hold him up."

"You could be rid of her," Senenmut pointed out.

She shook her head. "No. Too many people love her. They'd cause me far more trouble than they prevented."

"And maybe you need her," he said. "To prove that you were chosen wisely; that no one else is as well fit to hold the office of regent."

"Certainly no other woman," Hatshepsut said, "and what man would dare?"

She was beautiful in her arrogance. He could not help himself: he kissed her. She responded with passion enough, but it was all of the body. Her mind was elsewhere. "I do worry. What if the king is as great a fool as he seems? You say he has intelligence. But what is that worth, if he's too weak-willed to use it?"

"He's very young," said Senenmut.

"And some children never grow up. He was a slow child, you know that. Slow to walk, slow to talk, slow to show himself apart from his mother. We may find ourselves afflicted with an idiot king."

Senenmut set his lips together. Thutmose was anything but an idiot. It was Hatshepsut who made of him a useless thing, a mute and passive creature who could only go where he was led. Sometimes Senenmut thought the child must be in love; or so deep in hate and fear that he could not see for the force of it.

Hatshepsut did not need to hear any of that. "We've years yet," he said, "before you'll need to fear."

She pulled free of his grasp. "You think I want that. You think I'll be glad to hold a regency my life long."

"I think you'll do ill in retirement," he said: "forbidden the heights of rule, forced to see your daughter and her husband in the place of power, and you outside of it."

She shivered. It was not anything she willed: he saw how she glowered, and shook herself with a sharp, fierce movement. "As you say. It will be years before I need to fear that. Love me now. Help me drive away the dark."

"Always," he said, "my lady and queen."

They returned to Thebes in a kind of triumph, with the Two Lands well secured behind them, and the king's face known as well as could be expected. To most he would be no more than a glitter in the distance, the height of the Two Crowns and the weapons of his guards. The people loved a king who was young; if he was too young to rule, if others ruled for him, they doted on him as on a favored child.

Hatshepsut professed herself content. Her night fears faded with the sunlight. In Thebes she was altogether herself. If anything she was stronger than she had been before she began that brief and successful progress.

■ Neferure was not strengthened by her journey through the Two Lands. She pined for her lover, Senenmut thought. He had taken steps to assure that when she returned to Thebes, Amonhotep would have gone up to Abydos, administering Senenmut's affairs there. They had not passed on the way. Amonhotep traveled by land, Neferure on the river. If either suspected the ruse, Senenmut did not know of it.

In any event, Neferure was unwell. She had caught a bit of fever in the marshes of the Delta. It passed, but her malaise lingered. She withdrew to her chambers, curtailed her duties, hid herself behind a wall of maids and guards.

"The queen is indisposed," one of those guards said to Senenmut as he approached the door.

"I am aware of that," Senenmut said with studied calm. "I'll not keep the queen's majesty any longer than I must."

The guard frowned, but he, like all his fellows, knew better than to gainsay the queen's tutor. She was grown and a woman now, and had no need of his presence every day; but Senenmut had been remiss in failing to attend her since she returned from her journey. How remiss, he had just now discovered. Rumor had it that Neferure was not merely indisposed; that she was honestly ill, but would suffer no physician to examine her, nor permit a priest to invoke the gods in her name.

He found her just come from the bath, wrapped in soft cloths like a mantle, with her hair spread wet on her shoulders and a maid combing sweet unguent into it. She did not look ill. She looked in the splendid peak of health.

"Senenmut!" she said in surprise and, he hoped, honest welcome. "I hadn't expected you. Is something wrong?"

He took his time in replying. He sat in the chair that he often favored, accepted a cup of what proved to be wine cooled in an earthen jar and made sweet with spices, sipped till his head had cleared and his heart stopped thudding. Nothing that he saw eased his fears. She sat opposite him and did not touch her own cup, wrapped about in her mantle despite the day's warmth. Her eyes were vivid and clear—too much so, perhaps. He saw in them a challenge, though she would never voice it.

At length he said, "I am pleased that, rumors to the contrary, you are anything but deathly ill."

She smiled a bright, brittle smile. "Oh, I am well. Quite well. Just a little indisposed."

"Ah," he said. He paused. "A temporary indisposition, I trust?"

"Oh, yes," she said. "Temporary."

"Of about, perhaps, nine months' duration?" he inquired.

She started. She caught herself, but not before he saw. Her cheeks flushed, and then paled. She looked truly indisposed then, nigh as white as her linen wrappings.

He spoke carefully, as one often did with queens. "Lady, did you think you could hide it for as long as it's wont to take? You have, what, five months left? Four?"

"Four," she said. It was like her not to deny it once there was no purpose in it. He saw how she braced, expecting the next and inevitable question.

Which he had no need to ask. "Such a secret is near impossible to keep. Servants talk. Rumors fly. And a queen must appear at least in-

termittently, and her garments conceal very little. You must envy the
queens of Asia, who live forever in seclusion, and clothe themselves in
great wraps and swathings, and never show more of their bodies than
they must."

He had caught her off balance, but she recovered quickly. "I envy
no one. I have no shame, either."

"I'm sure," Senenmut said mildly.

She leaned forward. He could, if he peered, see the gentle rounding of her middle, the betrayal that would be unmistakable in only a
little while. "You understand," she said. "I was so afraid you wouldn't.
But Am—he said—he said you—"

Senenmut shook his head once, sharply, and frowned: a signal
that they had devised long ago, which she did not now mistake. Her
eyes flicked to the maids who stood about, the servants who came and
went on errands of the bath.

Her hands smote together like a whipcrack. "Out!" she cried. "All
of you, out! Out or feel my rod on your backs!"

They scurried to obey. She raised her voice seldom, nor threatened
aught but what she meant to do.

When they were well gone, Senenmut walked the edges of the
room, prodding at the hangings, opening doors swiftly and setting a
firm kick in the backside of the maid he found crouching behind one.
Only when all the doors were clear, with no one on the other side, and
all the walls and crannies empty, would he return to his seat.

Neferure waited like a student facing the master's rod, too proud
to droop or beg. Her shoulders were set as if against a blow.

"Child," Senenmut said with all the love in his heart, and all the
grief, and no little exasperation, either. "Oh, child, what are we going
to do?"

Her hand sought her middle. Her chin lifted. "I won't kill the baby.
Tuyu says I should, and says she knows how. But I won't."

"Nor is it safe now," he said. "Though if you had agreed to it when
you first knew . . ."

"I wouldn't," she said. "I won't. I love this baby. It lives, Senenmut. It moves; it kicks me." She grimaced. "Sometimes it hurts."

"Indeed," said Senenmut. "Alas for you that your king is still a child. You could have played out the deception else, brought him to your bed and borne him an eight-months' child. It's too late for that, and too early for him. The world will know that you warmed your bed with a man who was not the king."

Neferure shook her head. Her hair, drying into curls, swirled in her face. "I've been thinking, truly I have. I'll be ill, ill in spirit—so ill I need the gods' help. I'll go on a pilgrimage. I'll seek out temples. I'll pray to every god who is powerful in Egypt. I'll make it a new progress, but only for myself, and in the gods' name. I can travel the length of the river, and do it slowly. If I'm wise and the gods love me, I'll deliver the baby somewhere round about the City of the Sun, all the way to the Delta."

"Clever," Senenmut said. "But have you thought that a woman with child is rather obvious about it, and many people will see you— the whole of the Two Lands will know?"

"No, they won't," she said with sublime assurance. "I'll travel in my litter, hidden from the eyes of men, because my soul-sickness wishes it and the gods command it. My women will speak for me to the priests and people. I'll do my devotions in the inner shrines, pray to each god before his living face. I'm granted that, because I'm queen."

"And so you will conceal a commoner's child from the knowledge of Egypt." Senenmut sighed. "And when it's born? What then? Will you drown it in the Nile? Feed it to a crocodile?"

She stiffened, furious. "I will not! I will send it away. Some kind soul will foster it."

"And if it is female, it may, all unknowing, carry the right to the throne of Egypt."

"It won't know," said Neferure. "I won't kill it, Senenmut. If you so much as lay a hand on it, I'll kill *you.*"

She was fiercer than he had ever seen her, dangerous as a lioness protecting her cubs. He trod softly, spoke gently. "I will threaten no child of yours. But, my dear, your plan is so elaborate; it trusts in so much, and walks so close to the edge of betrayal."

"What else can I do?" she demanded. "I can't wish it away. I tried that. All it gave me was a headache."

"Does the father know?"

That at last was a question she had expected: unexpected now, and sudden. She drew a sharp breath. "No. No, I haven't told him."

"That's probably well," said Senenmut.

"I think so," she said, if somewhat uncertainly. "You know who it is."

He nodded.

"Then you do understand. You won't kill him."

"No," he said, "though I might break every bone in his body."

"Oh, don't!" she cried. "It was my fault. He would have been too shy, if I hadn't pressed him. I had to press hard. Even then he almost refused me."

"I almost believe you," Senenmut said. "And now you pay as every woman pays, unless the gods have either blessed or cursed her. A pilgrimage won't save you, infant."

"Then what will? I can't stay here, with all the servants whispering, and the court catching wind of it."

"No," said Senenmut. His thoughts rattled in his mind, somewhere aft of his liver. None of them served any useful purpose. He had never been so utterly at a loss before; so perfectly without the solace of wit.

Her mother would have to know. That would not be a pleasant meeting. His brother, her daughter: well they might argue that they did nothing that Senenmut and Hatshepsut had not done before them. But Hatshepsut had given her king a daughter and lost a son, and with him her hope of bearing another, before she sought comfort in a commoner's arms.

And yet she must know, and soon. Her wrath would be terrible; and worse, the later she discovered the truth.

There were no easy choices; no simple evasions. And no resolution that he could see, not anywhere.

Neferure flung up her hands. "You see? You have no arguments, and no recourse, either. I'll have my pilgrimage. The Two Lands will lose me for a while, and my weak spirit with me. Then I'll come back all strong and sure."

"And succumb again to temptation, because your husband is too young to give you pleasure?"

"No," she said, not even in anger. "No, I won't—I can't—"

"Oh, you won't," Senenmut said grimly, "and if you do, I'll make sure it's not with that particular comforter of lorn wives."

29

THE QUEEN REGENT WAS NOT merely angry. She was in a fair rage. And she could indulge the barest fraction of it.

"This will be kept quiet," she said through clenched teeth. "And you, O my scribe, will stand surety for it."

Senenmut bowed low. There was nothing of the lover in her now, and no remembrance of their nights together. She was queen wholly, and queen in wrath.

What she said to Neferure he did not know. They spoke alone together in a chamber bare of listening places, with Nehsi on guard at the door. They spoke long; and when Neferure came out she was white and shaken, too shocked for tears.

There would be no pilgrimage. But this far Hatshepsut granted the wisdom of Neferure's stratagem: she allowed the queen to announce that, in sickness of the spirit, she would retreat for a time to the temple of Isis in Abydos. It was far enough from Thebes to be out of the court's sphere, high and holy enough to suit a queen, and well enough guarded that Neferure's secret might be safe there. There was no surety; but of this both Hatshepsut and Senenmut were certain. If Neferure remained in the palace at Thebes, there would be a magnificent scandal.

Neferure prepared with care. She began to summon priests and soothsayers, prophets and sorcerers, wisewomen and physicians. All of them found her lying languid in her bed, well and discreetly covered, professing no interest in rising to face the sun. They performed their rites and sacrifices, raised their reeks, even danced round her bed while she lay limp, arm flung over her eyes to conceal the helpless laughter.

"I grant you," she said to Senenmut, some three handfuls of days after she had begun her deception, "they do mean well. But oh, Senenmut! The potion of oxtongue and crocodile egg and the dung of a maiden heifer born on the night of the new moon—it was all I could do not to shove it down that idiot doctor's throat."

"It's well you didn't," Senenmut said. They were granted a rare few moments' privacy: it was late, the horde of healers and priests had been dismissed, the maids were preparing their lady's bath. He kept his voice low, even so; one never knew who might be listening. "That idiot doctor was kind enough to offer a highly satisfactory diagnosis. You are, he says, haunted by nightwalkers. They're draining your blood and souls. You need greater help than mortal man can give."

"Yes," she said, "and Mother Isis is a great healer and protector of women. They'll prescribe a pilgrimage, of course. Gods know they've been long enough about it. I thought no one would ever get to it."

"That is your punishment for falsehood," he said severely. She was laughing at him. He frowned as blackly as he could. "This is no matter for levity, child."

"If I don't laugh," she said as soberly as he could have wished, "I'll break and run screaming. I can't hide . . . this . . . much longer." Nor could she: the swell of the baby under her hand was distinct, the shape impossible to mistake. Her maids were all bound to silence. Those whom she did not trust had been sent days since to attend the lesser wives of the Governor of Nubia, far in the south of Upper Egypt. If they chattered overmuch there, it would be a sufficient while before word of it came back to Thebes.

"You will of course depart with all dispatch, once your physicians prescribe the pilgrimage," Senenmut said. "And pray Mother Isis you come safely to Abydos."

"I shall," she said. "Mother is sending Nehsi to lead my escort. No one ever argues with Nehsi, or does anything he objects to."

Since that was eminently true, Senenmut could not protest that the task should have been his. He was the queen's tutor. But he was not a great ebon giant of a Nubian with a voice like a drumbeat and a face that struck terror in the hearts of his enemies.

Neferure raised herself from her couch, stretched luxuriously, strode across the room and back again. She dropped back on the couch and struck her hands together. "Oh, I shall be so glad when this is over! I'm dying to get out and run."

"You must be hungry, too," Senenmut said, not too sympathetically.

"No," she said. "The maids have all been eating a great deal of late, while the world knows that I refuse to touch more than a bite of bread and a small cup of watered wine. But they can't do my walking for me, or drive my chariot."

"Bear in mind," he said, "that all this began because you were bored."

"This isn't boredom. This is a fierce imp of restlessness. Can you even imagine what it's like to lie here day after day, feigning a half-swoon, while the sun shines outside and my horses languish for lack of exercise?"

"You will not," Senenmut said firmly, "ride your chariot to Abydos. It's the covered barge for you, and the litter when you come to land. Maybe the priests will encourage you to strengthen yourself with exertion, preferably under the sun."

"Yes," she said. "Oh, yes. Nightwalkers wither under the sun, everybody knows that. If I'm out all day, from dawn to sunset, and doing something strenuous to drive the demons away . . ."

"Not outside the temple walls," Senenmut warned her. "Still, there are great courts within, and sunlit gardens, and maybe enough to do until you grow unwieldy. Then you'll be glad of a soft bed to lie on, and no need to do anything more strenuous than watch the clouds pass overhead."

"Not I," said Neferure. She embraced him, so sudden that he started. "I did want you to come with me. But Mother said it should be Nehsi."

"Your mother had the right of it," Senenmut said, however unwilling he might be. "You need a better guardian than I."

"You've protected me as well as any man can," she said. "I did as my heart bade. If that was folly, it is my folly. You were never at fault.

No, not even for making that one known to me. If it had not been he, it would have been someone else, some guardsman maybe, with less wisdom and more inclination to boast."

"You are much too wise," Senenmut said.

She shook her head. "That's not wisdom. That's days of lying here with nothing better to do than reflect on my transgressions."

"What else do you think wisdom is?" The maids were returning: the sound of quick feet, rustle of gowns, muffled laughter. Senenmut bent and kissed Neferure's brow. "May the gods protect you. I'll come again in the morning. Maybe we can work a little magic of our own on one of your sorcerers, so that he insists that no goddess but Isis will heal you, and no temple of hers but the one in Abydos."

She nodded. She was drooping again for her maids' benefit, languishing on her couch while they flocked shrilly about her. Senenmut slipped away unnoticed.

■ He had not gone to the queen regent's bed since this uproar began. Tonight however as he sought his own bed, one of the shadows by the wall opened dark cold eyes.

Senenmut jumped like a cat. He came down hunting wildly for a weapon; but he kept none in this room, not even a knife for cutting bread.

Nehsi the Nubian waited with unruffled patience until Senenmut recovered some fraction of his wits. In a dark kilt, with his dark skin, he was all but invisible in the dim light of the lamp. Yet his presence was a fire-bright thing, now that Senenmut knew of it.

"What in the gods' name—" Senenmut began.

"She summons you," Nehsi said. Ever the man of few words, was Nehsi.

"Now?" Senenmut's heart was still beating hard, struggling to leap out of his breast. "It's ungodly late."

Nehsi said nothing.

"Someday," Senenmut said, "she will stop using you for her errand-boy. Then what will you do?"

"Go on being her chancellor," Nehsi replied coolly. "Enjoy the leisure of my evenings. She was mildly urgent tonight; and that was hours past."

"I was reviewing accounts with a scribe from the House of Life," Senenmut said. His mouth snapped shut. And why he should justify himself to this man, he did not know. It was that perfect lack of expression, that massive quiet. It made a man babble to fill the void.

He snatched his mantle against the night chill and the sting of insects, and turned toward the door. Nehsi followed, seeming at leisure, but he walked at the bodyguard's distance. Habit, Senenmut supposed. It was ingrained in him from youth; he would never lose it, however high he rose or how lordly he became.

So guarded, like a prince or a prisoner, Senenmut answered his lady's summons.

■ Hatshepsut was in her bedchamber, her face stripped of paint, her hair combed and braided for sleep. The light linen robe that she wore was meant to come off when she slept. She did not mean to be alluring, save that she could not help it. She was always beautiful; she could no more make herself ugly than Senenmut could transform himself into a handsome man.

He called his thoughts to order. It was never wise to let them wander while he suffered the queen's judgment. She loved him; he never doubted it. But she was queen first and always. She knew no other way to be.

She did not greet him with a smile, nor offer him wine, nor even invite him to sit. He had to stand alone and growing cold, while she pondered whatever it was that had moved her to summon him so late.

While he stood there, Nehsi retreated beyond the door. The sound of its closing was soft and distinct. Senenmut had never been greatly fond of the Nubian; the man did not invite friendship. And yet now, in his absence, Senenmut felt oddly bereft. Nehsi forbore to judge. That was his strength and his defense. Hatshepsut could not do otherwise than judge, and judge harshly.

At length she started as if out of a waking dream, and seemed for the first time to notice that he was there. "What are you standing about for?" she demanded. "Sit down, for the gods' sake."

As irritable as she was, Senenmut was comforted. Better irritation than royal anger.

He did as she bade, but he did not quite, yet, venture to speak. She seemed to have slid back into her reverie. Her chin lowered to her hand; she frowned slightly, gazing into the dark beyond the lamp's light.

When she spoke, her voice was almost too soft to hear. She might have been talking to herself, except that she addressed him by name. "Ah, Senenmut. Do you wonder sometimes if these children of ours are truly so feckless, or if we're simply growing old?"

"You will never be old," he said, "my lady and my queen. Your beauty will endure forever."

Her frown darkened. "I didn't ask for flattery. Were we ever as young as that?"

"I don't think so," Senenmut said.

"Ah." She sighed, frowning still. "I should have foreseen it. For me it was difficult, but easier than this. He was older, and had to wait for me. And a man may beguile his waiting as he pleases. Whereas a woman . . ."

"You know why that must be," said Senenmut. "It's happened here. Until the gods permit women to choose when they will conceive and when they will not, no woman can be as free of herself as a man."

"Truly," Hatshepsut said with an edge that he had not looked for. "Unless of course she is barren and a queen. Then she may do as she pleases. But never as a man may, in the light of the sun. She must creep about in the dark, and hide, and pretend to be as every woman is."

"Do you wish you were a man?" he asked her.

"I wish . . ." She looked as if she would rise, but she chose to remain where she was, fists clenched in her lap. "I wish that I could be as I was meant to be. I wish—I would rule. I would command, and ask no man's leave."

"And be a man?"

"No," she said. "Oh, no. Have you noticed? Men have to struggle to think clearly, particularly when they are young. The sight of a woman robs them of all intelligence."

Senenmut felt himself flushing. She had not meant it, perhaps, but she had drawn him to the life.

"I can think," she said, "even when my body is on fire. My heart can see clear. Or not. It chooses. And yet I must bow my head to a halfwit child, simply because he is male. *I*, Senenmut. I who was born to rule."

He was silent. He had heard much of this before, but never so clear, never so bitter. Never so strong a resentment.

"I have dreamed," she said. "In the nights when I have worn my body to a rag with ruling in that child's name; in the days when the tedium of royal ritual has lulled my mind to sleep. I have dreamed . . . such dreams, Senenmut. Such dreams as woman never knew."

"Nor man either?"

"No one," she said. "No one but me. Listen, beloved. Hear what I dreamed."

His heart leaped at the endearment. He was not forgiven—no, nothing as easy as that—but she had gone beyond the simplicity of anger. Perhaps for a while she had even forgotten her daughter's scandal.

"I dreamed," she said, "that Amon came to me—yes, Amon-Re the mighty, whose face is the sun. He came as a man, though the radiance of his face came near to blinding me. 'Daughter,' he said. 'O my daughter, whom I love. Be strong; be patient. Only a little while, and your suffering is ended.' "

As swiftly as it had leaped, Senenmut's heart went still. "He was not—you are not—if you die, I'll die, too."

She stared at him. "What? You foresee my death?"

"No," he said. "The god. The god said—"

"The god said," said Hatshepsut, "that I am his daughter, his beloved. He said nothing of freeing me from this world."

Senenmut could breathe again, though his breath came hard. "Is that how it seems to you? Freedom?"

"To a god it is," Hatshepsut said. "Flesh is heavy; it drags at the souls. It's their greatest joy to fly free."

"But if the god said—"

"The god showed me a thing," she said. "A wonderful thing. A marvel. All queens in Thebes are children of Amon. Queen Nefertari is their foremother: she who lay with the god and conceived her daughter, and her sons, too, so that Egypt's king might be the god's own son. And the god was content, and favored his children.

"But the world grows old, and the line of Nefertari stretches long from its source. The god bethought himself of the line's continuance, and in so thinking, looked on her who then was queen, and loved her in his heart. She was beautiful, but all queens are beautiful. She was proud, as all queens are. But he loved most her swift wit, her intelligence that yielded to no man's. He came to her in the night, wearing the guise of the king her husband. He loved her as a man loves a woman, but his seed in her was living fire." She paused. Her breath came quickly, caught as she went on, living the dream as if it had just now waked in her.

"She knew him then—she knew, and clung to him as if she would never let him go. She loved him with all her heart. She called him by name, there in the heat of it, and with his name she bound him.

"And she conceived," Hatshepsut said, "and bore a child. And that child—that child was I. She was my mother, Senenmut. The god came to her, and he made me. Me, not my brother, not my brother's son. I am Amon's child. I know it. I feel it in my blood."

Senenmut could think of nothing to say. He should be awed; he should bow down. But she had always been queen and goddess. Whether the god's blood was near or far, in her mother or in her foremother—it did not matter. To him she was the same.

Yet it mattered greatly to her. She was exalted with it. Her eyes were shining—glittering, he would almost have said.

"Do you know what this means?" she asked him. "Do you understand?"

He shook his head. "Should I understand? Should I see anything but that you are the same—you are still my lady, my queen and my beloved?"

"But I'm not the same!" she cried. *"Think,* Senenmut. The god has told me himself. I am his child, the fruit of his begetting. He intended more for me than that I rule in a king's name."

Oh, she was mad, or obsessed. He should have known; he should have foreseen. All her resentment, her envy of her brother-husband and now of her brother's son, had curdled and soured until she escaped into dreams of the god.

She read the doubt in his face. Her own grew the fiercer for it. "You! I thought you loved me. Are you no better than the rest of them? Will you never be more than a smug and lackwitted man?"

"Lady," he said, "I can't help what I am. But this—"

"It is a true dream," she said. "The god is my witness. I am not a creature of whims and fancies. I never dream but to the purpose."

"What purpose is that?" he dared to ask her.

But she was too angry, or had grown belatedly wise. She would not answer.

30

ON THE DAY THAT QUEEN NEFERURE was to begin her pilgrimage to Abydos, Senenmut went to say goodbye to her. He found her still abed though the barge was nearly ready to sail. Her face was white and etched with pain.

This was no feigned indisposition, no too-clever avoidance of a journey that she had no desire to make. Her maids were nearly as white as she, and nearly as scared. Senenmut shook the truth out of the one who seemed most coherent. "The baby is coming," she said. "Oh, sweet Taweret, it's too early!"

Senenmut slapped her just as she began to wail, and thrust her at another of her fellows. "Where are your wits?" he demanded. "Fetch the queen's physician. Now."

The one nearest the door nodded, a jerk of the head, and bolted. And why she had not done it the moment she knew her lady could not rise, the gods alone knew. It was as if they were all possessed; as if they had forgotten everything that could have been useful. Maybe there truly was a nightwalker haunting these chambers.

Certainly the flock of them would know the kiss of the lash when this was over.

Senenmut composed his face before he bent over Neferure. She had doubled up with pain, but as he approached she unfolded slowly. Her expression was half tearful, half terrified. When she spoke her voice was determinedly light. "Well, old friend. I don't suppose you'll be weeping over this. It's convenient, isn't it?"

"Child," Senenmut said with such vehemence that he startled himself, "never say that I would fail to mourn any child of yours. But you haven't lost it yet. Some women know such false pangs; they have to rest well and take great care, but their children are born alive."

She shook her head. Her hair had slipped from its plait, tangling on her shoulders. He reached to smooth it. She was fiery hot under his hand, yet she shivered as with cold. "No. No, it's dead. I felt it die. Deep in the night, when the heart's river runs lowest, and the shadows whisper, and one sees eyes where no eyes should be . . . I felt its life slip out of me."

"Oh, my child," Senenmut said. "And you never called anyone? You never summoned a priest or a sorcerer, or at the very least a physician?"

"How could I?" she demanded with a flare of sudden heat. "This is my scandal, my secret."

"You could have called for me," he said.

Her eyes on him were steady, burning. "What, and betray you, too?"

"I was not—" But that would have been a lie. He bent his head. "My poor child. However well this may resolve your dilemma, it grieves me still."

Her eyes closed. A spasm racked her. He reached as he had with her mother on the day that Neferure was born, and took her hands in his, and held them as he had her mother's. It was anguish to remember that other face, so like this one.

He had never been one to run away from heart's pain. He held her until the physician came, a dour man with a thin slot of a mouth and gentle hands. He took in what there was to see; frowned—perhaps at the gravity of the case, perhaps at his own failure before this to comprehend the nature of his queen's indisposition—and set to work.

It was midwife's work, but the midwife was too well known in the palace. Her coming would be noted, and her going; and people would know the queen's secret. Neferure must live though her child did not, and rule, and be a wife to the king when he was old enough. She could not be tainted with the rumor of this.

With the physician's assent, Senenmut let one or two of the maids run abroad with news of the queen's sudden, fierce fever. If they whispered of ill-doing, he did not choose to prevent them. No more did he know for certain that this had come about at the gods' hands. Men—or a woman—might have taken part in it.

That was not a thought he cared to think, but it niggled at him till he could not help but think it. Hatshepsut was the beloved of his heart. She was also queen and goddess. She might well have judged it necessary to be rid of this child; to be certain that it would not live to challenge any trueborn daughter of her daughter.

If she had done that, then she had not considered the cost to Neferure—and that, he thought, was unlike her. He took what comfort he could in it.

That was little enough. It did not go well. Neferure was young, she was strong, she was built to carry a child. She should have suffered less, even miscarrying, than she so clearly did. She had not cried much even as an infant, nor did she now, but when her eyes squeezed shut, the tears ran out of them, tracking down her cheeks into her sweat-sodden hair. The physician gave her a stick of wood to bite on, to focus the pain. She bit it through.

It went ill, and it went on too long. Senenmut did not remember so much blood when she was born, nor even when Hatshepsut lost the second child, the son who closed the gates of her womb behind him. It was a river of blood, a river in spate.

The physician muttered to himself. The maids had all fled. Senenmut could not follow, to make certain that none of them chattered untimely. He could only hope, and trust in their loyalty.

There were only the two men, and the woman straining between them. And in time a fourth, a pair of strong hands bracing Senenmut's, and clear eyes over them, too stark for grief.

Those were not the eyes of a woman who had moved to slay a child, or to cause its mother so much pain. Senenmut had not known how taut his back was, until the tension had gone and he nearly fell.

Hatshepsut held him up. Neferure tossed in her bed. The sheets were scarlet. Senenmut and the physician had changed them twice; must do it again, and see them all burned, for the secret's sake.

Yes, even if she was dying. Her name's honor must continue, nor be besmirched.

He saw death creep over her face. Nothing that he did, no rite or magic of the physician, not even her mother's will could stop or even slow it. This child conceived untimely, this unwanted burden, slipped out of her with her life's blood.

When the last of the stillbirth was ended, she drew a breath, hardly more than a sigh. No more came after.

Neferure was dead. She had been the anchor of Senenmut's life since she was born, as her mother was its center. Without her he drifted astray, too shocked to weep.

It was only evening. It had been a long day of suffering, and yet too devastatingly brief. The sun's rays slanted through the high windows. Their light poured like blood upon the floor.

"May Amon-Re protect her," Hatshepsut said, soft and steady, "and guide her on the dark ways. May Anubis speak for her in the Hall of Judgment; may the feather of Maat be as light as a breath in the balance, and her heart as heavy as worlds. May she walk in the Field of Reeds, and know contentment everlasting."

■ The king did not weep at the death of his sister-wife. He mourned, Senenmut thought and his tutor insisted, but Thutmose had grown from a silent and self-contained infant into a silent and secretive boy. He spoke as seldom as ever, and then mostly of war and warriors.

He had, perhaps, loved his wife, as a brother loves his sister or a friend loves a friend. She had been able to coax him out of his silence, to trick him into laughter. Without her there was no one possessed of such power.

It was Hatshepsut who told him that Neferure was dead. She went herself, which was a great concession, with an escort of trusted servants:

Senenmut, Nehsi, the priest Hapuseneb, and her two most favored maids.

Thutmose had been, as usual, in the courts of the soldiers, learning the arts of sword and spear, bow and chariot. Now that it was evening and nearly full dark, he had come in to be bathed and fed and put to bed. He was still enough of a child that his nurse hovered, fretting over him, but he was enough of a man to be embarrassed. He dismissed her summarily, rather too much so perhaps. He had not yet learned the precise balance of discipline between master and servant.

And perhaps he had learned it very well, but nervousness caused him to forget it. He was always so around Hatshepsut: more awkward than usual, clumsy, seeming younger than he was. If he could drop a scepter or stumble over a footstool, he would do it in front of his queen regent.

Tonight he failed of courtesy: he did not offer her wine or refreshment. He received her in his bedchamber, since she had refused to wait until he could compose himself in a more dignified place. A hastily fetched chair served as a throne; another, offered to Hatshepsut, was refused.

Hatshepsut had been very quiet since she left Neferure's body to the wailing crowds of maids. The embalmers would have come and gone before she returned. She wanted that, perhaps. Senenmut remembered from his father's death, how they came with their hard dry hands and their sharp reek of natron; how they lifted the corpse with little ceremony, and carried it off as if it had been a sack of barley.

The royal embalmers would be more respectful, perhaps. Perhaps not. Dead was dead, as Senenmut had heard one of them observe. They lived with death. It had not lost its terror; not in the least. To mask their fear they learned to laugh in its face, and to deal casually with its leavings.

And so Hatshepsut was her own messenger to the king, and Neferure was taken away in her absence. She was cold and still in front of him, her face locked shut. She must have been terrifying to one who did not know her.

The king never spoke to her if he could avoid it. When he did, he stammered. Therefore he was silent now, and waited for her to speak.

She did so without adornment and without preliminary. "Your queen is dead," she said.

Thutmose regarded her as if he could not understand the words. He still did not say anything.

"Neferure has died," said Hatshepsut when it was clear that the king was not going to speak. She was impatient as she always and only was with him, intolerant of his hesitations. "She had a fever. It seized her and consumed her."

Thutmose shook his head very slowly. Disbelieving, denying, there was no telling. He seemed to have gone mute.

"The embalmers by now have taken her," the queen said, brisk and seeming cold. His silence did that to her, Senenmut was sure. "You will mourn her as is proper. My chancellor here will instruct you."

"I know how to mourn," Thutmose muttered, so low that Senenmut barely heard him.

The queen's ears were keen. She heard: she frowned. "You will inform your mother. She will be so kind as to join in the mourning. This after all was the queen."

Thutmose's jaw set. Perhaps Hatshepsut did not see: his head was lowered, his *nemes*-headdress slipping forward, hiding most of his face. But Senenmut saw. Thutmose bowed low, lower than a king should.

"Well," said Hatshepsut. His silence offered nothing, asked nothing. It was a dead thing, as dead as Neferure in her bloodied sheets.

Which the physician would have had the wits to change before the embalmers came. Senenmut's mind was chipping and scattering. He had never been so, not for anything that had befallen him. Even tears were more than he could muster.

His eyes were independent of his faltering mind, his ears recording what the queen said to the king.

"Well," she said. "See that you do as you're told. Nehsi will instruct you."

Thutmose nodded, head still bowed. He was a brave child, but Nehsi terrified him almost as much as Hatshepsut herself did. It was the man's size, Senenmut supposed, and his quiet that put even Thutmose's to shame. Nothing dismayed Nehsi, nor did he fear anything.

To a child whose fears were many, he must have seemed as incalculable as one of the gods.

It was not well that the king should so fear his regent and her servant. Senenmut could not see what to do about it, not now. Neferure was dead. He had offices, rank, honors enough; but without her they meant nothing.

He had never believed that a man could die of heartbreak. Nor had he known how much Neferure mattered, how much of his heart she filled, until she was gone. He was as much a fool as ever. And unlike Thutmose, he was not sure that he knew how to mourn.

31

OURNING WAS AN ART. ONE could study it for years, decades, all of one's life; but in the end one simply did it. It was a greyness of the soul, an emptiness in the heart. Wailing and beating of thighs made it a little less, perhaps, but never enough.

Senenmut mourned. He cried aloud; he beat fists on thighs till bruises heaped on bruises. None of it brought her back.

He knew then, in the deeps of a night as empty of sleep as his heart was of the one who had died, that if Hatshepsut died before him, he would not be able to bear it. He prayed aloud in his chamber, invoking the god who walked so often in her dreams: "Amon-Re, great god, beloved of my lady, listen to me. Let me die first. Let me never know the absence of her as I know that of her daughter."

The god gave no sign. Yet he heard. Senemut's heart felt it. Whether the god would grant the prayer, there was no telling. But he had heard it.

■ They mourned for the full seventy days of Neferure's embalming. Then they laid her in her tomb among the queens of the Two Lands, far to the west in the valley of the dead, dug well and deep to thwart the thieves that flocked as thick as vultures round the tombs. It was not the king who performed the great magic, the rite that would open her senses to the world of the dead: the opening of the mouth as it was called. Hatshepsut did it. She spoke the words and performed the gestures, calling the gods to witness that her daughter went whole and blessed upon her journey.

In this she slighted the king, but he ventured no objection. He had been friend and brother to his wife, but never husband, never in truth. No more did he know why she had died. She had fallen to fever. That, everyone believed, and Senenmut repeated until he almost believed it himself. Better a demon of sickness than the truth: the sheets taken and burned; the red and bloodied scrap that had killed her, the son who had never waked to look on the world, disposed of in secret. Nehsi had done that. He had laid magics on it too, perhaps, lest its fragment of a spirit rouse and walk, hunting the self that had never had time to grow.

Whether the Nubian had taken such precautions or no, Senenmut never felt the child's presence. Neferure he sensed often, a flutter of winged spirit, a whisper of longing in the breeze that played through her chambers. Once her body was buried and her spirit-self set upon its journey, her presence shrank to memory. He still fancied that he could see her, hear her voice calling him, feel her hand on his when he worked among the queen's scribes. But she was gone; he had only remembrance.

■ As difficult as Senenmut's mourning was, it was a feeble thing beside Hatshepsut's. Perhaps she too had not known how much she loved her daughter, nor wished to acknowledge it, for love so great could be a weakness.

She continued as she always had, being queen regent, ruling the Two Kingdoms, ignoring the king. He preserved his silence, played with his soldiers, refrained from attracting her notice. It was all as it had been since Thutmose took the throne.

But her heart had conceived a thing, a great thing, a thing of which she would speak to no one, not even Senenmut. He knew only because she took him often to her bed just then, loved him with an urgency that was rare in her, and when he fell asleep was still awake; and when he woke to return to his own house, her eyes were open and staring into the dark.

He did not ask. With Hatshepsut, one did not. She spoke as she chose, and not as any man would compel her.

It was long days, weeks, months before she spoke, except once. "I dream," she said then. "Every night, I dream."

■ One day not long after the queen spoke, if briefly, of her dream, Senenmut visited Hapuseneb in the house that he had acquired recently near the temple of Amon. It was a noble house, the house of a man who had won both wealth and high standing in the service of god and queen. Hapuseneb met his guest in a grand reception hall, with a wry fillip of the hand at its many gauds and flummeries. "The prince who lived here before me had rather elaborate taste in decor," he said. "There never seems to be time to get rid of it all."

Senenmut nodded. "One wonders whether to gape or to gag." He inspected a particularly ornate piece of carving on what was, for lack of a better description, a chair. "This looks like Asiatic work."

"Indeed," said Hapuseneb. "Mitanni, I suppose. Or somewhere farther afield. I speak the language, but I never did understand their predilection for adding insult to injury."

"You've seen how they dress," Senenmut pointed out.

Hapuseneb sighed and shook his head. "Here, come with me. This is doing neither of us any good."

The room to which he led Senenmut was simpler in its furnishings, nearly bare in fact, with new plaster laid over the walls, but nothing as yet painted on them. The artist had begun in a corner: a red-limned sketch of a fan of papyrus.

The scent of new-laid plaster was remarkably pleasant. Hapuseneb sat in a chair that was rather the worse for wear, and gestured Senenmut to another. A small servant, with ears like jar-handles on either side of a round shaven skull, brought bread and cheese and barley beer.

"After your predecessor," Senenmut said, "you must be a profound shock to the servants."

Hapuseneb grinned, as wicked as ever though he had lost most of his teeth. He was aging well except for that, neither gaining nor losing flesh, simply continuing as he always had. His fondness for beer had not gone to the belly as it too often did, nor did it weaken his will. "I am going to shake the servants up," he said. "And while I'm at it, and with the high priest's blessing—or at least his lack of interference—I'm going to show the temple a thing or two, too. Amon's grown so powerful that he's gone soft. He's lost the edge that a man gets, or a god, when he has to struggle for what is his. It's time he tightened his belt again, and remembered where he left his sword."

"You talk like the king," Senenmut said. "All war and weapons."

"Do I?" Hapuseneb sounded surprised, but Senenmut was not deceived. "Dear me. It must be catching." He sighed. The mockery faded. "That is a charming child, old friend. When he chooses to be."

"He often doesn't," said Senenmut. "And never before the queen regent."

"So I noticed," Hapuseneb said. "It's as if there's a curse on them. She can abide no one who is called Thutmose, except for the first of that name, with whom she never ceases to compare the others. This youngest of the line is terrified of her, and knows it. He hates her for it. Hatred makes him stammer; stammering makes him seem a fool. And when he goes silent, he simply proves to her that he has precious little store of wit. Whereas she—"

"Whereas she," said Senenmut, "who has all the patience in the world with recalcitrant princes and truculent embassies, has no patience left for a half-stammering, half-mute fool of a boy."

"He's not a fool," said Hapuseneb. "Not even at his worst. Not ever."

"I know that," Senenmut said almost impatiently. "Gods! It hurts to watch them. She loses all good sense in his presence. She sees nothing but the mooncalf boy, the stumble-tongued half-idiot. If he could bring himself to be as he is everywhere else—but it's too late for that, isn't it? It's been too late since she began her regency."

"It was too late the moment Isis conceived him." Hapuseneb met

Senenmut's stare. "Don't gawp at me like that. You know who's to blame. She's taught him all her own fears and hatreds, and greatest of them all is her fear and hatred of Hatshepsut."

"But Hatshepsut will not dispose of her."

"That's her stubborn pride," said Hapuseneb. "She will not be defeated by a servant whom she herself sent to be concubine to a king."

"And killing her would be defeat." Senenmut sighed. "Yes, I understand. Often I wish I didn't. I can see ill things coming of this, a king who hates his regent, a regent who despises her king."

"If you knew what to do about it, you'd do it," said Hapuseneb. "So would I."

"So too I think would our lady," Senenmut said, more in hope than in expectation that it was the truth.

32

*I*T WAS HATSHEPSUT WHO DECIDED to do something about it. She made a conscious and publicly acknowledged effort to befriend the king. She visited him wherever he happened to be: on the training fields, in his chambers, in court among the princes. She labored to show him patience. She strove to gentle him as one would a frightened small animal, moving slowly, speaking soft.

Senenmut admired her for the effort, but in his estimation it harmed rather than helped her cause. The boy was no fool. He could see beneath the smiles, the gentleness, the inquiries as to his welfare. Her attempts to be interested in the arts of war were particularly unsuccessful. Thutmose did not often show emotion, but Senenmut saw impatience then, as sharp almost as anger, and wariness that was always in the king when he stood before Hatshepsut.

More than once he considered speaking to the king himself, but some god, or simply prudence, restrained him.

He did venture to speak to the king's tutor. Nebsen was if anything lazier than ever. Years and good living had thickened his body and slowed his mind. Senenmut often wondered how the king endured him, as little like a soldier as he was. He was easy to listen to, that was true, and amiable in company. How much he taught his pupil, it was difficult to guess. Rumor had it that other scribes had taken to instructing the king under Nebsen's supervision—meaning that Nebsen snored in a corner with his jar of beer, and the scribes did as they pleased.

Still he was the king's tutor, privy to his counsels; and he had been, if not a friend, then not an enemy, either. Senenmut approached him of a morning, a day like any other in the courts of Thebes. The palace servants were hard at work scouring floors, washing garments, preparing a feast. Today they were celebrating the king's excellence with the bow; he had defeated a flock of rivals in a contest, some of them older than he, almost men. It was like Thutmose not to strut the victory. He was holding audience in proper form and formality, but his companions had insisted on a celebration.

Nebsen never attended audiences if he could help it. That he left to the king's advisors and the queen regent. When Senenmut avoided royal functions, it was to pursue some duty that could not wait. With Nebsen that duty was simply and always a jar of beer.

Senenmut found him in the king's chambers, well into the jar but not yet prostrate. That would do well enough. Nebsen greeted him with apparent gladness, groped about for a cup despite his objections, filled it sloppily and thrust it toward him across a table meant to bear fine jars of wine, not simple earthen jugs of barley beer.

It was a while before Senenmut could come to the point. Nebsen chattered as always, heedless of attempts to get a word in. "And wasn't he just splendid with his bow? So strong an archer for one so young; so gifted in everything that a king must be."

"Indeed," said Senenmut, finding a gap at last in the thicket of words. "But isn't it a pity that he can't get along with the queen regent?"

"Oh," said Nebsen with a wave of the hand. "That's nothing to fret about. She's intimidating, you know. Odd. Such a little woman—

they're all little, these children of Ahmose—and so pretty, but so terrifying when she looks at you."

"Well then, and so is the king. He's of the same blood. He's remarkably like her, if either of them could see it."

"Ah, so," said Nebsen. "You know how that is. Like to like, bull
to bull in the field of the herds. They'll never see how they should love
one another."

"Listen to me," Senenmut said, as impatient suddenly as Hatshepsut had ever been with the king. "I don't need you to be wise. I
need you to help. The king isn't just afraid of my lady. He hates her.
I worry about that, Nebsen. He's only a child now, but he's not so very
far from becoming a man. What then? What becomes of my lady? He'll
drive her out if he can. He might even kill her."

Nebsen shrugged and drank deep from his cup of beer. "Why do
you fret so much? He's barely nine years old. It will be years before he's
old enough to challenge her."

"And what then?" Senenmut demanded. "What then, Nebsen?"

"Why, I don't know. Maybe we'll be lucky. Maybe we'll all be
dead."

Senenmut came near to spitting in disgust. No great delicacy prevented him, but rather a kind of greater repugnance. This cheerful sot
was never worth the trouble.

Nebsen did not seem to care that Senenmut walked out without a
farewell. The last Senenmut saw of him, he had gone for the cup that
he had filled for Senenmut, and proceeded to gulp it down.

They said that men who drowned themselves in beer were troubled in the heart. Senenmut could not see what Nebsen's trouble was,
aside from bone-deep laziness. Great wallowing useless man; small
wonder the king dealt so ill with the queen regent, if he had so poor a
teacher.

Well; and there was something Senenmut could do to remedy
that. He spoke a word here and a word there, and let this be known
and that be mentioned. And within the month, Nebsen was gone, and
in his place an eager young man from the Temple of Amon.

Perhaps Senenmut had outsmarted himself. This man was young, hardly more than a boy, and as wild for soldiers as the king was. He was no friend to Senenmut, nor was he likely to be: he came of a line of princes, and looked far down his elegantly arched nose at any mere commoner, however high the rank he might have risen to.

Communications between the queen regent's household and the king's had grown as mannered and distant as those between foreign kings. Messengers and ambassadors went back and forth. Even when they sat side by side in audience or in the courts of justice or in receiving embassies, they did not speak to one another. Their servants spoke for them.

■ "And he," said Hatshepsut at last, "that infant who wears the crowns and clings so tightly to crook and flail—he has not one word to say for himself. These kingdoms are not well served, Nehsi. Their king is a fool, as slow of wit as of speech. Like his father before him, he cares nothing for the tedium of rule. He lives for war, dreams of it, yearns after it."

Nehsi did not see that he should answer her. Often of late she had come in a temper from this function or that, in which she must speak in the king's name, yield humbly to his rank and authority, and bow before his face. It galled her.

"Why in the world he does not simply ape his father," she said, "and refuse to come at all, I will never know. That's his mother, I suppose. She hides herself well, makes excellent pretense of retirement, but no one doubts whose counsel he listens to."

"It seems to me," Nehsi said after a pause, "that he does very little except sit in state while you do as it best pleases you. Has he ever resisted you? Has he ever advised you to do anything against your will?"

"Of course not," said Hatshepsut. "He's too much an idiot. I doubt there's a thought in his head, except what's been put there by one of his soldiers, or by his mother's nagging."

"Maybe he's wise," said Nehsi, "and maybe he's more intelligent than you give him credit for."

"Not likely," she said with a toss of her head that nearly sent her wig flying. "Don't you think I've hoped, hunted, prayed for any sign of wit in the child? He's the king. When he's a man he will rule. Do you remember how I used to ask him to judge in this matter or that? He stumbled and stammered. 'I don't know,' was all he could ever say. "He knows nothing, Nehsi. He's a fool and a lackwit. And don't tell me he only seems so to me! If he were born to be a king, he would at least be able to answer sensibly when I ask him a question."

Nehsi did not suppose he could deny that. Pity, rather. The boy would make a good soldier. He might even make a general: he had a grasp of strategy that caused the old soldier Ahmose to speak well of him. Ahmose spoke well of no one; his best estimate of a man was to growl that he could follow orders if he had a whip to his backside. Yet of the king he said, "He can keep two things in his head at a time. He might even amount to something."

Hatshepsut knew none of that.

"Some men," Nehsi ventured, "are hopelessly shy with women. I'll wager the king is one. And you, great lady, are terrifying."

She snorted. "Senenmut says the same thing. You're both fools. Are you so in awe of the Two Crowns that you can't honestly see the one who wears them?"

"Are you so convinced of the king's incapacity that you can't honestly see any evidence to the contrary?"

Nehsi held his breath. He walked very close to the edge; dared what might be too much. But it seemed necessary.

She did not burst out in rage. That in its way was more alarming than if she had, but he held his ground. Softly, calmly, she said, "Fetch my counsellors. Yes, even Ahmose the General, who is so enamored of the king. Fetch them all, and bid them attend me in my hall of audience."

Nehsi had ceased some time since to run errands for any man, or woman either. But for Hatshepsut he did this. He set aside his rank and position, forgot everything that he had become, and was her guardsman again, her messenger and her defender. She would never know how great a gift he gave her, nor would he ever tell her.

He fetched them as she commanded: Ahmose from the training field, Senenmut from among the scribes, Hapuseneb from the temple; haughty Ineni the builder of tombs and temples, Thuty the Treasurer from his strongrooms and his bushels of gold; and the others with them, the handful of men whom the queen trusted. She had not summoned them so before, not all together and out of season, bidding them come at once. They were proud men and they had risen high, but for her they left what they were doing and came at her command.

She received them in deliberate lack of state, sitting in her audience-chamber, dressed in a simple gown with few jewels, and a plain wig, and no mark of rank. Her chair was no higher than theirs, her manner quiet, but beneath it she was drawn as taut as a bowstring.

If she paused for preliminaries, none of them after remembered. She favored each with a long look, both those whom she had raised to this eminence and those who had been great lords and princes while she was still a small princess in her father's house. Nehsi noticed that none shrank from her stare, nor tried to defy it. No cowards here, nor fools either. She had chosen them well.

But then, he thought, she did most things well. It was the gods' gift to her, one of many, and far from the least.

After what seemed a very long while she spoke. Her voice was quiet, as she herself was, and without pretension. She said it simply. "I have dreamed," she said. "Hear the dream that I have had."

Nehsi had heard it before, and so, from their expressions, had Senenmut and Hapuseneb. To the others it was a new thing; they heard her in silence, as they must.

"I dreamed," she said, "that great Amon came to my mother, and put on the face of her lord the king, and lay with her. But she knew him; she felt the fire of him within her, and knew that this was no mortal man. She called him by name, and he answered her. He loved her, and for all that night she lay with a god, and when morning came, she knew that she had conceived a child.

"She expected that it would be a son. She was astonished when the child was born, and it was a daughter. But it was the child of Amon. She saw the light of him in those eyes, and knew from whom it came. She named the child First Chosen of the Palace—Hatshepsut. It was a princess' name, fitting for a queen. But she knew what else it signified.

"So I dreamed, my friends. I dreamed, and the god came to me and called me his own. 'Beloved,' he said. 'Daughter. Chosen of my heart.' "

There was a silence. None of them moved, none spoke. Hapuseneb, ever garrulous, stirred as if he would venture a word or six, but for once he chose to remain mute.

It was Ahmose Pen-Nekhbet who spoke at last, and not to the queen regent; to Hapuseneb. "Well, priest. You belong to Amon. What dreams has he sent you?"

"Why, none," Hapuseneb answered him.

"Is she telling the truth?"

Hapuseneb glanced at the queen regent. She sat still, expressionless. "Well," he said, "that's difficult to say. She's royal born, daughter of a king and a queen. They're all descended from Amon. Who's to say that he didn't decide to visit his descendants, and take one look at Queen Ahmose, and fall head over heels? He wouldn't have been the first, man or god, to do that. She was a beautiful woman."

"So you don't know," the old general said. He had no fear of royal wrath, having weathered storms of it since the foreign invaders were driven out. "Imagine that. A priest of Amon admitting to ignorance. Will the world end now?"

"I hope not," Hapuseneb said. He grinned at Ahmose, who grinned toothlessly back. In the old days, Nehsi had heard, Ahmose had had handsome white teeth and a face that won many a lady's heart—and the rest of her, too, if even half the stories were true.

His rakehell days were ended, but his wits were as keen as ever. He said, and this time he spoke to the queen regent, "You didn't bring us here at the run and with our whole day's duties half done, to tell us bawdy stories. That's not like you. What are you getting at?"

Hatshepsut did not forgive impertinence, but from Ahmose she could endure much. "I am telling you," she said, "that I dreamed, and I dreamed true. This dream has been with me since I was young. It's come again and again since my royal husband died. Now it comes on me every night. Every night Amon comes to me, shows me the night of my conception, says to me, 'Daughter. Beloved. I chose you; why do you close your eyes to me?' "

"I'd say he wanted you to do something," Ahmose observed. "If it's he who comes, and not a lie or a wish made flesh."

"It is he," Hatshepsut said with bone-deep certainty. "He burns like fire. Last night he laid his hand on me." She lifted her arm that she had kept close to her side, wrapped in her mantle for the day was rather cool.

More than one man caught his breath. There were the marks of fingers above her elbow, red as if branded. One could think, Nehsi reflected rather sourly, that she had had an altercation with her lover, and he had bruised her; but Senenmut seemed as taken aback as the others.

She lowered her arm, covered it again with her mantle. "This he gave me as proof, and not only to you. I too have wondered if my dreams were false. But they are not. Amon comes to me; he calls me his daughter. He bids me do somewhat that I am to discover for myself." She drew a long breath, lifting her head as if she gathered strength. "I've been slow to understand, my friends. Criminally slow perhaps, but what he intends for me . . . I tell you true, it makes me afraid."

They were silent again, even Ahmose. The tension stretched so taut that it thrummed.

She snapped it with a word. "I've thought long. I've prayed. I've invoked other gods than Amon. And every day it's come clearer, that I must do what Amon bids me do. When my daughter died"—her voice caught on that, but steadied—"I knew surely; but I could not bring myself to face it. Now I cannot escape. I must do as I am bid. I must be Amon's chosen one. I must be king."

33

AHMOSE SPOKE FOR ALL OF THEM. "You are mad." She met his eyes. "That, I may well be. But I have dreamed as I have dreamed, and I have prayed, and pondered every side of it. The god's will is clear. I am to be king."

"A woman cannot be king," said Ineni the builder.

"That too I know," she said, and without impatience, which was remarkable. "I said as much to the god. He said to me, 'I have chosen you. You will be as you were meant to be.' "

"Did he admit that he'd made a mistake?" Hapuseneb grinned at all the shocked expressions. "Oh, yes, and I a priest of Amon, too. How irreverent of me. Still, lady, do think. If he had meant you to be king, surely he would not have omitted one small detail."

"And what," she demanded with sudden ferocity, "does a man's rod do for him but pass water and get sons? Am I so much the less for lacking one?"

"It is traditional that the king have one," Senenmut said dryly. "If you go ahead with this, the scribes will be in fits. There is no word for a king who is a woman; no place in the language for one. There is the Great House, the ruler of the Two Lands; there is the Great Royal Wife, the woman who stands beside him and assists him in his rule. There is no way to conceive of a woman who wears on her head the Two Crowns."

"I am not the first," she said. "Perhaps not the second, either, or the third."

"And why is that?" Senenmut asked sharply; then answered himself. "Because, O my lady, neither gods nor men find it fitting that a woman's head should uphold the Two Crowns."

"Amon finds it fitting," she said very softly, almost gently. "Now tell me, my servant whom I had thought loyal to me: in what way am I less than the child who wears the crowns? Do I lack his strength of will? Do I waver in diplomacy? Have I no such gift of speech as he has shown us all?"

Senenmut cut through her mockery with a slash of the hand. "Please, lady. You know well that no matter how little he pleases you, he pleased the gods and the people sufficiently that they allowed him to be crowned king of Egypt."

"I will not strip him of his crowns," she said. "I will simply do as I would have done had I been a man and not a woman: I will rule beside him, as his equal. So should I have done from the first. This regency is a travesty. Even the river-bargemen know whose hand in truth has steadied the steering-oar these past six years and more."

"But," said Senenmut, "they want to see that hand resting lightly atop the hand of a manchild. It's always been the way, lady, that a man rules."

"Not all ancient ways are good," she said. "What of the very old ones? Shall we go back to sanctifying every tomb and temple with a man's blood? Or shall we command that every king devote the wealth and power of his reign to raising a great vaunt of a tomb like those at Giza? Shall we do that, Senenmut?"

"Don't be ridiculous," he said.

"Then open your mind," she shot back, "and think of what the god has willed for me. I fought it, too. I argued exactly as you have. He never wavered. 'You are my chosen one,' he said."

"Did he happen to tell you," Hapuseneb inquired, "why he took it into his head to choose you?"

"It was time," she said, "and I was fit. Am fit. I rule now in all but name. He bids me take the name as well, so that my rule is blessed by truth, untainted by falsehood."

"So you claim to do it in the name of truth." Nehsi had let them forget he was there; now, to the shock of some, he reminded them. "Is that how you will present it? A regency in its way is a lie, a pretense of lesser power than the king himself possesses. You will strip yourself of deception and rule undisguised."

"Yes," she said. "Yes. That is the way of it."

"In the kilt?" Senenmut asked. "With crook and flail across your naked breasts? With the false beard strapped to your chin?"

A faint flush stained her cheeks, but that might have been anger. "If need be, yes."

"I don't think we need to go that far," Hapuseneb said as if to soothe them both. It was a lovers' quarrel; a blind man could have seen it. "There are variations on the royal robe that would be more suited to a woman's body than a kilt. As for the beard . . ." He sighed. "Well. Maybe we're doomed to that. It is so much a part of the regalia, and so very ancient."

"So is a man's body," Senenmut said nastily. "Will she find a way to put that on, too?"

"If I could," she snapped, "I would."

"Then why don't you?"

"Now," said Hapuseneb. "There now. Stop it. You," he said to Senenmut, "sit down. You, lady, if you will, listen to me. What you propose may be the god's will, but the Two Kingdoms will never accept it. They live by tradition. Tradition commands that a man be king."

"I will change it," she said inflexibly. "Haven't you heard me? I've considered every argument. The god has countered every one. It will be as it must be."

"It can't," Senenmut said, though Hapuseneb moved to hush him.

"I say it can," she said. "Remember who I am. Is there anyone who can deny me?"

"Certainly," he said. "The king. And the king's mother."

She laughed aloud. "They, you say? The king, who cannot put together a coherent sentence in front of me? The king's mother, who hasn't shown her face outside her apartments since the gods know when? What friends have they? What allies can they claim? Have you ever seen the court follow them as it follows me?"

"The court has followed you," said Nehsi, again speaking unlooked for, "because you uphold the kingship. If you claim the title yourself, you may discover that your allies have fled."

"I think not," she said. She was growing more determined rather than less, the more they resisted her. "My friends, I lay you a wager. I'll win the Two Lands into my hand, even if I call myself king."

"A wager?" Hapuseneb could not seem to help himself: his eyes gleamed at the prospect. "And what are the stakes, my lady?"

Senenmut hissed at him, but she took no notice. "All our lives, I would say, but since we are practical people . . . shall we wager something more tangible? When I'm crowned as king, you shall provide the wine for my coronation feast."

He blanched. He was a wealthy man, and Amon the wealthiest god in Egypt, but a king's coronation feast required the wealth of a kingdom to do it justice.

Still he loved a gamble, and he could not be thinking that he would lose. "When I win," he said to Hatshepsut, "you shall grant me whatever I ask."

"Oh, no," she said, as hot for this wager as he. "You must tell me what you expect me to pay. Although of course," she said, "I'll never need to pay it."

"It will be nothing too terribly unreasonable," he said. "Something within your power to grant, even as queen regent."

"Not the regency," she said quickly.

He grinned. "Oh, I should ask for that! But no; I'm not a fool. Make me chief prophet of Amon—the great god's high priest. That should be stakes enough to match a king's wealth of wine."

"Oh," she said. "Indeed. To persuade the temple; to win over the king . . . yes. That will be difficult enough to be worth the hazard."

"Then it's done," said Hapuseneb.

"Not," Senenmut interceded, "until the rest of this madness is played out. Lady, will you insist on it?"

"Not I," she said. "The god."

He pressed his lips together and conspicuously refused to say another word.

Nehsi said it for him. "You grieve for the Lady Neferure; your anger is strong, and your sense of betrayal. Will you challenge the gods now? Is that why you do this?"

"No!" she cried in a fever of impatience. "Have you heard no word I've said? The god challenges *me*—and with me the whole of Egypt. Maybe he does it to punish me; to make me suffer as my daughter suffered, because I gave her too little to do."

"You could tell him," said Senenmut, "that saving his grace, what he asks of you is impossible."

"One does not say such things to a god." Her voice was chill. Oh, the lovers were quarrelling, and no mistake.

"*You* would say such things," said Senenmut, "and escape unharmed. Even from a god. But you will not. You want it, O lady who would be king. You want it with all your heart."

"Maybe I do," she said. "Maybe I'm glad. Maybe I'll shock you all, and not only take the Two Crowns but hold them, and be such a king as these kingdoms have not seen in many a year."

"Now that," said Senenmut acidly, "is true enough."

34

*I*N ALL THEIR YEARS OF PRICKLY friendship, Senenmut had never quarreled so with Hatshepsut. Lovers they had been, but they had never been excessively tender in it, nor inclined to spare one another.

Still this went far beyond plain speaking or hard words. That she could rule as well as any king, Senenmut did not for a moment doubt. But that she should be king . . .

No. He could not accept it. A woman in those crowns, claiming that title, made mockery of all that they were.

And if he could not accept it, who loved her, how would the rest of Egypt be? He feared for her. He dreaded what this world of theirs would do to a woman who insisted that she would be king.

She would not speak to him. When he applied for admittance to her chambers, the guards were apologetic, but they would not yield. "She said," they said, all but shuffling their feet. "She won't see you."

The door that he had used for so long, the secret way, was locked and barred. He came near to beating on it in frustration; but that would have betrayed them both. He did not care greatly for his own skin, but her he loved, even as he quarrelled bitterly with her.

Desperation drove him to come to her in public audience, when she would refuse no one, from the least to the greatest. He had no petition to offer. He simply wished her to see his face—and himself to see hers. What good it could do, he did not know. She was not sane then, not in any way that he could name.

Perhaps after all it was a god who drove her. She was set on it; immovable, implacable.

She had sworn her counsellors to silence. When the time had

ripened, she would speak to the rest of Egypt. All of it, lords and commons both. On that she was determined.

She prepared them. Senenmut had been too blind to notice before, how little by little the king shrank from public scrutiny. He appeared less and less in hall of audience or court of justice. He was indisposed, it was said; or occupied among his soldiers; or engrossed in prayer to the gods. He had become very devout.

For all Senenmut knew, that was the truth. Children had odd enthusiasms, and this child was odder than most. He might well have turned to the gods in defense against the terror of his regent.

She continued to act in his name. She was careful of that, meticulous in her reverence. "The king's majesty is sacred," she said—and if those who heard only knew, how well they would understand why she so guarded the rights and privileges of the king.

She could charm a crocodile away from its dinner, as people said. A smile, a tilt of the head, a word exactly chosen to make her victim preen, and she had an ally, a man whom she had flattered into taking her part in whatever it was she intended.

She never lied. She might stretch the truth, but never to breaking. That was her boast and her pride.

It was pain to see her winning Egypt to her cause, and Egypt never knew what it was. Senenmut saw one day how she entertained a gaggle of princelings from the nomes of Upper Egypt, vain and purse-proud men who reckoned it only their due that the queen regent should regale them with a gazelle-hunt in the desert beyond the city, and then a feast in the palace, with such pleasures laid on as those provincial princes had hardly dared to dream of. A pretty maid for each, well trained in the arts of pleasing a man, and devoted each to her allotted princeling.

Senenmut had been spared the task of finding and preparing the women, but he happened on the room where they all waited, a round two dozen naked and begauded beauties, gossiping among themselves until they should be summoned to the hall. He had only been passing by on his way somewhere onerous. The sound of their voices and the scent of their perfumes in a room that heretofore had always been deserted, brought him to a halt in the doorway.

They saw him, but forbore to shriek or scatter. He did admire a woman who kept her composure in the face of the unexpected. They reminded him rather forcibly of Hatshepsut. And indeed, while he stood there gaping like a bee in a field of flowers, she herself appeared in the inner door. She who had come in from the hunt windblown and sheened with dust, had bathed and dressed and adorned herself as befit a queen.

Her chosen ladies bowed low before her. She raised them with a word, looked them over as a general inspects his armies, nodded crisply and said, "You'll do. Remember what I told you. This is war—as fierce as any battle, and rather more dangerous to the unwary. See that your man is well pleased, his every need met, his whims indulged."

"And if he gets unreasonable?" one of them wanted to know.

"Yes," said someone else. "Sometimes they want things they shouldn't have: things with whips, or games of pain."

"No whips," Hatshepsut said. "No pain. My word on that. This is simple seduction: wine, perfume, flowers. If your lord takes a particular liking to you, be aware that you'll be given to him as a gift."

They all exchanged glances. One said, "No one ever thought to tell us this before."

"That's foolish," Hatshepsut said. "Doesn't everyone serve better if she understands the stakes?"

"But no one *asks,*" the maidservant said. She paused, as if in thought. Then she said, "I hope I like the lord you've allotted me. If I do, may I have him?"

Hatshepsut laughed. "Why, certainly. Win his heart, or his body at least, and persuade him to ask for you. Then he's yours, and my word on it."

She was a warmer presence here than she ever was among princes, a woman among women, teaching these servants of hers to love her. When only a little while thereafter she had entered the hall of feasting with pomp and fanfare, and received the lords' homage as a queen should, she was never the woman who had spoken face to face with servants; she was all royal, haughty and subtly terrible.

And these men loved her for that. So should royalty be, remote and set apart, but watchful as a god, intent upon their welfare. The hunt, the feast, the pleasures promised by each smiling, scented maidservant, said all that she need say, without the vulgarity of words.

Then when they were done, drowned deep in wine and in their servants' arms, she slipped away to receive an embassy from somewhere far in Asia. They never knew she was gone; would swear, come morning, that she had been with them till nightfall, when the last of them dropped insensible to the floor.

Hatshepsut seduced them as adeptly as her servants. She made herself more beautiful than they, and more alluring: far too high for any of them, thus he must content himself with a lesser woman; but he could dream of her, and perhaps he did, while he lay with the woman whom she had given him.

Senenmut, relegated to the shadows, denied her touch or her glance, watched and knew how it was to be a spirit of the dead, all eyes, strengthless and powerless. If he told them why she did this, they would turn, not on her, but on him. She had laid a spell on them, the same spell that she meant to lay on the whole of Egypt.

■ Egypt, ancient and weary and wise, succumbed to her as had the lords of its nomes, blind to the truth till she spoke it where every one must hear. She chose a great festival for it, the day the river rose to its highest. There was a measuring-stick in every town and city, marker of the flood and proof of its strength or weakness; but the great marker, the measure of all the rest, was in Memphis at the gate of the Delta.

She went down to the city in advance of the crest, sailing on the swollen river over inundated fields. The Black Land was at its narrowest, all its people crowded up against the Red Land, but in joy and in celebration, for there had not been such a flood in living memory. It was the highest since the foreign kings were driven out; what it signified was splendid, a broader spread of rich black earth, and from it a greater harvest, sufficient not only for the year ahead but for a year and more beyond. Even if the flood failed utterly in its next rising, there would be no famine. Egypt's prosperity was safe.

It was given to the king to sanctify the festival. But the king was left behind in Thebes, where he nursed a sniffle and played with his soldiers. The sniffle was his regent's excuse. Small sickness could become greater, too deadly swift to turn aside. For his protection therefore, she said, he would remain in his gods-guarded palace, closely watched by his physicians, while his regent performed the rite for him in the heart of royal Memphis.

Thutmose might have no choice but to be left behind, but Senenmut was made of sterner stuff. He simply assumed that he was going. He had his own boat; in Memphis he had a house, a pretty place that he had bought on a whim, when it seemed that one of his brothers might wish to seek his fortune in Lower Egypt. As it happened, Ahotep and Amonhotep were content to dwell in Thebes, but he kept the house. It was most useful now, when he would not rely upon the queen regent's charity.

Their quarrel was stretching longer than either of them could have expected. She would not yield, of course not. She was Hatshepsut.

No more would Senenmut give way to this madness of hers. Queen and regent he would serve till his last breath. Queen become king was a freak of nature, a thing that should never be. A woman belonged in a woman's place, beside a man, equal to him in most things, superior even, if she were royal born and he a commoner. But the king was a man. He could not be a woman.

She called it utter unreason. He called it tradition. If women had been meant to be kings, the gods would have made them so.

He loved her no less because she was both mad and obsessed. He went to Memphis therefore, following in his boat with his own flock of servants, and settled in his house that stood within sight of the White Palace.

They arrived some days in advance of the day that the priests had foretold would see the flood to its height. Already it had risen as high as it ever had. And still it rose. Those whose houses stood close to the river at its widest heretofore, found themselves with water lapping at their doorsteps. Senenmut's own estate near Thebes had shrunk to a few manlengths of ground before the villa's walls. The servants there had been instructed to move everything of value to the roof and cover it well, lest the river break down the gate.

It was glorious, but it was terrifying. The river was the life of Egypt. Its flood wrought the Black Land—but when it flooded as mightily as now, it could be deadly.

In Memphis people kept festival, singing praises to Hapi who was god of the river, but beseeching him too. He might well have chosen, this year of all years, to cover the whole of Egypt, to conquer all of the Black Land that had ever been, even to the palaces of the kings.

The coming of the queen regent comforted them in no small degree. "It would have been better," Senenmut heard a man opine in the street, "if we had a king here, but she's royal. She'll do."

"Isn't she Amon's child?" his companion reminded him. "Aren't they all, who are descended from Queen Nefertari?"

"Well," said the first man, "that's true enough. But what does a sun-god have to do with the river flooding?"

"Sun dries water," his friend said. "Makes the barley grow, ripens it in the ear."

"So you think she can rule the river, do you?"

"Why not? She's a goddess born. She can do anything."

And that, thought Senenmut, for most who were of common blood and kind, was that. Royalty was divine—yes, even a queen.

He had stopped being a commoner a long while since. It had crept up on him: first familiarity with palaces, then comfort therein, and at length an inability to be altogether content anywhere else. He could not have gone back to the house in which he was born. It would have shrunk about him, dragged him down with its smallness.

■ Every day the city drifted toward the tall post of the river-measure. Every day the priests gathered there, invoking Ptah of Memphis and Hapi of the river and all the gods of Egypt. Once the queen regent was in Memphis, she too went with the rest, borne in her golden chair, wearing a tall plumed crown and carrying a scepter.

Senenmut's heart came near to breaking at the sight of her. She was more beautiful than anything he knew, and more intransigent. He, unregarded in the crowds about her, saw how she sat, how perfectly, royally still. When she moved, it was with a dancer's grace, performing the rite each day as had been prescribed from the dawn of the world. She invoked the gods as the priests had, made obeisance to each quarter of the horizon, bowed last and low to the river that swelled and surged nearly at her feet.

It was as wide as the sea that Senenmut had never seen, but he had heard of it, how it stretched from edge to edge of the world, as if there were no end to it. So it was with the river.

When its waters lapped nigh to the top of the measure, the priests began to be afraid. But the next day it was a little lower. Then they sighed with relief, and their prayers of thanksgiving were heartfelt.

Hatshepsut prayed after them as she had each day since she came to Memphis. She had come this day as every other, in no greater state and in no less, except that she had brought more guards and servants than heretofore. They surrounded the platform on which she stood with the priests, bobbed in boats beyond, and spread along the water's edge. Everyone near her, Senenmut could not fail to notice, was loyal to her, except the priests themselves.

They were few enough, unarmed, apparently unwary. Only those who had come from Thebes, perhaps, knew that the queen intended something other than a simple celebration of the river's rise and descent.

Hapuseneb was nearest her, familiar shaven-headed shape. Senenmut, far back in the flock of her attendants, strained and craned to see if they spoke together. They did not seem to. But when she had finished her prayers, when she should have bowed to the gods and returned to her chair, to be carried back to the palace, instead she paused and stood straighter.

She beckoned to her herald. He came forward. Senenmut's heart twisted. Even that fool of a man with his splendid voice—even he had known. And Senenmut who had been her lover, Senenmut whom she had loved, had been kept in ignorance like the least of the crowds who flocked along the river.

Through the pain of anger and jealousy and plain fear, he heard clearly enough the words that she spoke and the herald echoed. "O my people! Dwellers in Memphis, that next to Thebes is greatest in Egypt. This day the river has begun the descent from its fullest flood. Such an inundation no one has ever seen. The gods have blessed us beyond measure, have granted us such wealth of Black Land as these two kingdoms have never yet known.

"This is an omen, my people. It blesses us. It promises us a glorious harvest. All the world shall come to us, bow low before us, beg us to bless it with the fruits of our rich black earth."

People near Senenmut settled in to listen. Speeches they knew, though kings seldom made them, and queens almost never. This was a novelty, a rare entertainment.

She gave them much more than they could have been looking for. "I too have been blessed," she said, "I who am descended from Queen Nefertari, who was the daughter of a god. Great Amon came to me, my people, while I slept; came walking in my dream."

And she told them what she had told Senenmut, and what she had recounted to her counsellors, the dream of Amon and Queen Ahmose. It was a splendid story. The queen in her beauty, the god smitten till he must love her or know no peace. She told it as well as any spinner of tales in the marketplace. She spun it out, made it grand and glorious, swept them up to the inevitable conclusion.

"And when I woke," she said, "I knew what the god my father had ordained for me. It was a grand thing, a terrible thing, a thing most worthy of a god. He wrought me, my people; begot me of his own seed and set me in the womb of a queen, so that I might rise above all men who were before me. He told me what I must do; what I must be.

"This rising of the river is the omen, O my people. Egypt prospers by the will of Amon. Hapi consents to broaden the Black Land, to make it rich beyond conceiving. This they do, my people, for the honor of my name, and through me for the glory of Amon my father.

"Amon has spoken, O my people," she said. "He has laid his hand upon me. He has willed that I take the Two Crowns, that I lift up the crook and the flail. Amon has willed that I should rise to the Great House. He has made me king, lord in truth of the Two Lands."

35

THE PEOPLE OF EGYPT, TO SENENMUT'S astonishment, were far more accommodating than the lords and princes. Faced with a queen who informed them that she would be king, they stood for an endless moment in shocked silence. Then, raggedly at first but with waxing fervor, they raised up their voices. It sounded like the roar of a lion—but there was no mistaking it. They were crying her name. Cheering her on. Calling her lord, king, Great House of Egypt.

■ "She paid them," Senenmut said to Hapuseneb, late in the evening when they should both have been abed; but there was no sleeping while Egypt woke to knowledge of Hatshepsut's insanity.

"She paid them," he said again. "She showered them with bread and beer in return for their show of adulation."

"Probably she did sow a seed or two," Hapuseneb admitted. "But it would never have grown so ripe so fast unless it fell on fertile ground. The people are wild for her."

"The people have lost their wits." Senenmut stalked the edges of the small reception-room in his house. The walls closed in on him, but he could not bring himself to escape. Just so was it with Hatshepsut: he could not come near her, but neither could he stay away. His heart was bound to her whether he would or no.

"I do think the god wills it," Hapuseneb said. Senenmut had never heard him so nearly somber. "Else why did she escape not only unharmed but with the people cheering her on? Preposterous as it seems, they love the thought of a woman who is king."

"They'll turn on her in a moment," said Senenmut, "when the god's fire leaves them."

"Then we'll have to trust the god, won't we, to protect her while she lives."

Senenmut nearly struck him. No man should be as wearily wise as that—or so reckless with a woman's life and soul.

A woman who was insisting that she was king.

Hapuseneb met his bitter stare with one both wry and calm. "You're angry," he said, "because she won't do what you want her to do. She goes her own way. She always has."

"But if that way is to her death—"

"I think not," Hapuseneb said. "She *is* Amon's child, old friend. The people know it; they love her for it."

"And when they tire of her, they'll kill her."

"Not while Amon protects her."

Senenmut set his lips tight. Hapuseneb was lost, too, besotted; god-maddened, and no doubt of it. "And when she first spoke of what she would do," Senenmut said, "you were as much against her as I. What of your wager, priest? Have you lost all will to win it?"

"I am Amon's servant," Hapuseneb said. He shrugged, sighed. "I am also a practical man. She won't be stopped, my friend. That's as clear to me as the sun at noon. She is the god's child. If that loses me a wager . . . ai, I'll be a poor man, but I'll be alive and in her service."

"You are a weak man," Senenmut said, "a leaf in every wind that blows."

Hapuseneb did not rise up in anger, but neither did he come back to Senenmut's way of thinking. He left as amiably as always, oblivious as it seemed to Senenmut's taut and furious silence.

■ The whole of Egypt had gone mad. Sunstruck, conquered by the will of a god, till it bowed to the will of a woman.

She, indomitable, took ship from Memphis as the river's flood began its slow ebb. Its extent was her proof and her omen. In the year that she made herself king, the Black Land stretched farther than it ever had. Its harvest was not the richest that had been recorded—there were a few that had been richer—but it was splendid enough for the purpose.

The court was in shock. There had been rumor of something new, something enormous, but none of them could have been prepared for the truth. That shock preserved her against assault. She moved swiftly in it, sweeping up from Memphis into Thebes. The roar of the people followed her.

She had not yet taken the Two Crowns. That she would do in Thebes, before the face of Amon her father. But in Memphis she was given the crook of a shepherd and the flail of a master of servants, and those she laid beside her as she sailed southward. They glittered on the cushion, eager, it seemed, for her hands to take them up.

So she would do when she came to Thebes. She sailed as swiftly as she might, but not so swiftly that the people failed to acclaim her from the river's banks, gathering in every village and town and running far in pursuit of her, crying her name.

She seemed to grow greater in the heat of their worship, gleaming like the sun upon her golden barge. Thebes itself received her with a roar that shattered the sky. Amon was this city's own god, father and king. He possessed its people. He struck them blind to aught but the glory of his daughter.

There was no stopping her. Amon's own priesthood met her at the quay, bowed low before her, crowned her with the Two Crowns in a coronation that was like nothing that had been before, just as she herself was.

■ That first fierce heat of passion faded as it inevitably must. But she had foreseen it. Once she was settled in her own city, she commanded that she be crowned in full and proper form, as kings had been crowned in Thebes since before there were Two Lands of Egypt.

She was no fool, was Hatshepsut. There were not a few who noticed that the chief priest of Amon, the god's First Prophet, had not been among those who met her by the river. He had expired quietly of a fever while she was in Memphis. It was convenient; as convenient as the people's blind worship and the lesser priests' acceptance of her lunacy. Some was the god's doing. Some was clearly that of the god's servants.

The new First Prophet of Amon was Hatshepsut's old friend and ally, that supple-minded man, Hapuseneb. He ruled the priesthood and its vast possessions in the kind of comfort that Senenmut, whose ease in the balancing of so many offices was a matter of great care and concentration, could have envied had he been less bleakly angry.

No; he was not angry, not any longer. Merely bleak. He had not been deprived of his offices. They were still his, all the burdens as well as the blessings.

He should be glad that Egypt accepted her; that Amon's temple stood behind her; that the court lacked the courage to resist her. One lone woman had bowed the whole of the Two Lands to her will, had done it simply and completely. She said that it would be, and so it was.

Only Senenmut seemed to stand apart from the crowds that flocked about her. There were others, there must be: men too stubborn or too set in tradition to accept her. But he saw and heard none of them.

The king himself was brought out like an image of a god, decked in gold and crowned with the crowns that were his by right of birth and sex. He was not to be deposed. They were to be kings together, he and she, but she, as the elder, child of two who were the children of a king, was to be the great king. He, who was a child still, son of a concubine, was the lesser, the king-heir, set beside but slightly behind her in the order of rank and precedence.

For that she was greatly praised. A usurper—for that she was; she could be nothing else—could well have disposed of the rightful king and raised up another, more malleable heir.

But she not only suffered Thutmose to live, she permitted him to continue as king. He had no power worth the name, but then he never had. His allies were few, their influence negligible. His mother could do nothing.

She had been wise enough at the time to choose seclusion over an open and public wielding of her power as mother to the king. But now that Hatshepsut was king over the younger king, Isis found herself a prisoner, confined to her chambers and to a narrow round of courts and gardens. She was not prevented from seeing or speaking to her son. She could entertain guests, even appear in court. But she could do nothing that the new king was not aware of, nor act but by the king's will.

■ Hatshepsut held Egypt in her strong small hand. On the day that she was crowned as befit a king in Thebes, the river ran still high though it was late in the season of inundation.

She was by then proclaiming that not only was she the god's daughter; her own putative father, the first Thutmose, had named her his heir upon his deathbed, and foretold that she would rule as he ruled, as king and god. And perhaps he had called her his little king, his god-begotten; who was to say that he had not? Fathers of strong-willed daughters were known to do such things.

Amon's daughter, heir of the last great king: of course she would be king. And if any denied her, that one found himself sent far away to serve on an embassy in Asia, or became lord of a field or two and a pair of oxen on the borders of Nubia.

When she came to her crowning, she came as any king did, with the people's blessing. There was none who dared protest. Not even Senenmut.

She came in splendor, clothed all in gold. Her wits or the cleverness of her maids had found her a royal garment that flattered her woman's body. It was a linen robe of many pleats, gathered at the middle, with a mantle over it, embroidered with gold. A great golden collar glittered on her breast. Her girdle was of gold, and her armlets, and her sandals. She had had them wrought for this her coronation in the image of divine Re, the scarab-beetle that rolled the sun across the sky, enfolded in the falcon-wings of Horus. Her brow was crowned with the Two Ladies, the vulture-goddess of the south, the rearing serpent of the north. Her wig was plaited with gold and precious stones, the colors of sun and sky.

She came in procession, attended by all the priesthoods, by the royal guard, by the soldiery of the Two Kingdoms, and by the whole massed rank of the court, lords and ladies, their children, their servants, all who attended upon them. The song of trumpets preceded them, and priests chanting the names and titles of the king. She had named herself Maatkare, the Truth of Re—an irony, thought Senenmut, if one ever doubted the rightness of what she did. Therefore she was Maatkare Hatshepsut.

As many as marched in that procession, one would have thought there would be no one to line the processional way from the palace to the temple of Min where every king went to perform sacrifice and to receive the crowns; but all of Egypt seemed to have gathered in Thebes to see this woman crowned king.

It was Min who sanctified her, and not Amon her father, because Min blessed every king with life and fertility, and through him the land of Egypt. Min's priests met her, bearing the image of the god and leading his great white bull; and behind the god came the crowns and the crook and the flail, all that would be given to her in token of her office. A place was made for them between palace and temple, a high dais to which they all went up, priests and king and the king's closest attendants.

Of whom Senenmut was not one. He stood below with the rest of the court, unregarded and surely forgotten. She rose above him, a small figure but very erect, and seeming somehow to tower over them all. The god was in her. Even he could see it. Her face was as splendid as the sun. She was beautiful beyond bearing.

She bowed before the god as even a king must do. When she stood straight again, one of the priests let fly four geese to the four corners of heaven, bearing word to all men and gods that a king ruled in the Two Lands. And as they flew, Min's own high priest blessed and consecrated the crowns.

Her servant, the dark man, Nehsi the Nubian, slipped off the wig that she wore. Senenmut's breath escaped in a sigh. She had shorn all her beautiful hair, the better to wear the crowns. She looked no less purely a woman for it.

The crowns, White nested within Red, came down slowly in the priest's hands. He was one of those priests who performed every act as a matter of mighty moment; who had never known the meaning of haste, nor seen the virtue in sparing suspense. It seemed an endless while before the crowns touched her brow. She held her head high, steady, though she must have been trembling within.

Or perhaps she was not. She was no mortal man, to live in fear of gods or men. The god was in her, possessing her. Her eyes were full of him.

The crowns came to rest in supernatural stillness. No one spoke; not one man moved. The only sound was the murmur of wind in the canopy over her head, and the honking of the geese that flew still to west and north and east and south, and the vast soft sigh that was the breath of thousands of people, released at once as she stood up under the two tall crowns.

She took the crook and the flail then, with the priest speaking words that no one heard: for a roar had gone up, sudden and immense, rocking the earth underfoot and thundering to the sky.

36

MY SWEET DAUGHTER, MY CHOSEN one, *King of Upper and Lower Egypt, Maatkare Hatshepsut.*
That was carved in every stone of the Two Lands in the circle that was the king's own, the cartouche as it was called, bearer and emblem of his name—or hers. It was as Senenmut had predicted: the scribes were beside themselves, and the artists and limners too, fitting the needs and uses of their art to the prodigy of a king who was a woman.

Some carved or painted her as a woman, but wearing the false beard and the Two Crowns. Others surrendered to tradition and gave her a man's body but her own face. And in the annals and accountings of the House of Life, she was the lord, she who rules in the Two Lands, her majesty the king.

■ The feast of her coronation went on for seven days without ceasing in the palace and in the city and throughout the Two Kingdoms. Hapuseneb did not after all go bankrupt providing wine for it: she considered it sufficient that he should endow the court with the finest vintage for the banquet on her coronation day. He forbore to object.

She was wealthier far than he: the whole treasure of Egypt was hers, to do with as she would.

Senenmut attended as few of the festivities as he could properly do. He had duties, some of which did not vanish simply because a king had been crowned and set upon the throne. He escaped into them.

On the night of the seventh day, when he had retreated to his house and barred the door, and contemplated departure to his villa in the morning—and no matter that its lands were still no more than a few sodden fields and a vast expanse of muddy river—he sat late awake while the lamp burned down. Sleep held no allure, nor had for nights out of count. Sometimes he succumbed to it; he was mortal, he could not help it. But most nights he sat till dawn, reading if he could, or simply watching the shadows dance upon the wall.

He was doing precisely that, taking a kind of dim pleasure in it, when someone scratched at the door. He thought at first that it was one of the aunts' cats. The creatures made free of the house, and objected strenuously if anyone barred a door to them.

But this was too large to be a cat, and scratching too high. Man-high. He ignored it for a while, but it persisted. At length, with a sigh that was half a groan, he unfolded himself stiffly from his chair and went to unbar the door.

The snap of rebuke died before it passed his tongue. His mind did not want to know this person at all, but his eyes saw too clearly, even in the dim lamplight.

"You should not be here," he heard himself say—stupidly enough, even in the circumstances.

Hatshepsut slipped past him in a fragrance of myrrh. She was gowned in simple linen, with a mantle over it against the night, and a plain wig. No guardian shadow followed her. She seemed to be utterly alone.

She had never been in this house before, and yet she moved as if she knew it, taking the chair opposite the one he favored, propping her sandaled feet on a footstool, regarding him bright-eyed as he stood gaping in his own doorway.

"Well?" she said. "Aren't you going to offer me wine?"

He did not move. "You should never have come here. Are you really alone? How did you escape? What do you think you are—"

"Hush," she said. And he obeyed her, as all of Egypt did, because she quite simply did not expect him to do otherwise. "Not," she went on, "that I'm precisely thirsty for wine. I've been swimming in it for a solid week, till I'm near dying for a jar of plain barley beer. Or even water."

Water he had. He fetched it for her in a plain and ordinary cup. No gold or chalcedony here, where he could be most purely himself. She drank gratefully and accepted a second cupful, at which she sipped, watching him the while. He stood flatfooted, his wits at a standstill, as empty of coherent thought as the water-jar in his hand.

"So," she said after a while, as if he had spoken. "You don't hate me after all."

"I never hated you," he said.

"I'd hardly have known it," she said, "for all the love I've had from you since the river rose in flood."

"Since you named yourself king," he said, yet without bitterness. It was the simple truth.

"You won't forgive me for that, will you?"

"Do you think I should?"

"I think," she said, "that my coming here is worth a moment's respect."

"You have it," he said. "Now go back where you came from, before the scandal overwhelms us both."

"A king," she said, "may love where she pleases."

He opened his mouth, closed it again. When he spoke, it was with the same reckless insouciance that had possessed him since she entered this chamber. "If it is true that you may take any lover who suits your fancy, then why have you come here? I'm nothing to look at. I'm not particularly young. I'm not even willing to accept that you are king."

"Did I say that a king can be reasonable in whom she loves?"

"You should be," he said.

"I do not choose to be." She rose, set aside her cup, and came into his arms. They were not there to receive her, but she made do. She was warm and supple, familiar, beloved.

He stood stiff. She laid her head on his rigid breast. "Why do you resist me? Why you alone in all of Egypt?"

"I'm not the only one," he said through set teeth. "When the rest of the people come to their senses, they'll rise up and destroy you."

"Not while I live," she said with perfect confidence. "The god has promised me."

"But how long will you live?" Senenmut demanded. "How long before someone succeeds in killing you?"

"No one will kill me," she said. Her head moved on his breast. Her lips were soft, circling his heart with kisses. "Beloved," she said. "Oh, how I've missed you!"

Not more than he had missed her. His arms rose to complete the embrace. He still could not speak.

She spoke for him. "We should never have quarreled. It was so cold in the night, so lonely. No one else is as warm in my arms as you. No one else—"

"Has there been anyone else?"

He had thought he spoke calmly, but she drew back, tilting her head till she could look into his face. "I am not required to answer that," she said.

He twisted out of her grasp, thrust past her. She caught at him. She was strong, stronger than he had expected; and he had thought he knew her strength. She held him fast. "No," she said. "No, there has been no one. You know that. You know me."

"Do I?"

She shook him. "Look at me! Am I any different? Have I changed at all?"

"Your hair," he said. "Shorn for the wearing of the crowns. Your name, that you have altered. Your rank and power in the Two Kingdoms."

"I am still myself," she said, shaping each word as if in bronze. "I am still the one whom you love."

"No," he said.

She slapped him. He reeled, more startled than hurt. She had never struck him. Their quarrels were always wars of words, not of blow and furious blow.

While he gaped and staggered, she hissed at him. "Stubborn. Mule-headed. Obstinate. *Man.*" But having slapped him, she kissed him where her hand had struck, caressing him, nearly weeping. "This is nothing but jealousy. You think I'll have no time for you. You think I'll choose someone younger, prettier, more charmingly stupid."

"I think that I will lose you," he said. "That you will die for this intolerable presumption."

"Not before you," she said. "I promise you."

"How will you do that? Poison me first when you feel the dagger sinking into your back?"

"Stop that," she said. She pulled him with her through the chamber and into the one beyond. And how had she known his bed was there, unless a god guided her?

Where else would it be? There was only the outer door and the one that led to this room.

She thrust him down upon the bed and sat on him. Her weight was not inconsiderable. Nor was the force of her temper. "I honor your honesty," she said, "but I weary of your stubbornness. Stop struggling so, and love me."

"How can a mere mortal love a king?"

"As he always has," she said. "As he always will."

There was no fighting her. The harder he struggled, the more determined she was. She was as blind obstinate in that as in taking the Two Crowns, and as perfectly convinced that she was entitled to it.

While she was queen and queen regent, he had been worthy of her. Now that she was king . . .

"You only pursue me because I fight," he said, twisting in vain against the weight of her on his chest. "If I stop, you'll grow bored. You'll wander away. You'll find yourself someone who worships you without restraint."

"I only ever wanted you," she said. "Even when you weren't fighting."

That was manifestly true, but he did not want to hear it. "I'll go on resisting you. I can't help myself. I'm too blind to the god, too deaf to his words. I only see that you do a thing no woman should do, and that you'll die for it."

"All men die," she said. "You love me too much. That's the heart of your resistance. Let me live as I may. Only love me. Let the gods fret over the rest."

"I can't," he said in a strangled voice. "I've always done my own fretting. I'll go on doing it."

"Then I order you to stop."

"How like a king," he said.

"Do you hate me for it?"

"No," he said. "No, never. Only . . ."

"Only?"

"I wish you hadn't done it."

"I could do no other," she said.

"Even the lie? The story about your father, how he named you king after him?"

"It is no lie," she said. "He did say it. He called me king and goddess."

"But his son, your husband, wore the crowns. And you allowed it."

"Because I was afraid. Because I was a child, even as that other king is now. I couldn't be what he wanted me to be. I had to grow to a woman; I had to gather courage. Years, it took, until the god himself forced me to open my eyes to it."

Senenmut shook his head. Even pinned beneath her weight, captive to her will, he could not accept what she had said. It was a kind of pride. And fear, yes. Fear for her; for what she might grow into, and that she might die in the doing of it, for this enormity that she committed upon the face of Egypt.

It was true. He loved her too much. He wanted her to be as she had been, regent to the king, safe in the place that her sex allotted her; not raised to this terrible eminence.

Such eminence, dropping beside him on his own bed, in his own house, where it was never safe for her to be. She kissed him till he gasped, attacked him with such passion that he had no will left to resist.

She had always had more ardor than he. Tonight she burned so hot that he caught fire himself, flared up like a torch, forgot everything, even fear, in the white heat of her.

When he had cooled again, when they lay together, wound in one another, he hugged her to him so tightly that she gasped. "I could never lose you," he said. "Never, not though I die for it."

"You never will," she said.

"Why?"

The question, asked bare, made her lift her head to stare at him.

He asked it again. "Why? Why did you choose me?"

"Because," she said, "you were always arguing with me. And making sense."

"Other people argue with you. Nehsi, Hapuseneb, Ahmose the General—"

"Not as you do, as you always have. Because you love me, but you will never be blind to my failings."

"It's never stopped you."

"No," she said, "but it makes me think."

"You should have thought before you did what you've done."

"I did," she said. "Long and long."

"And then you did it."

"Because I had to."

There was a silence.

Senenmut filled it, in the end, because he had to. "I love you beyond measure. You are more beautiful than anything that is. I believe that the god is in you, that he begot you. But—"

"But?" she asked when he did not go on.

"But I don't want to lose you."

"You won't."

"Promise."

"On my name as king."

"Maatkare," he said. "Hatshepsut. Chosen of Amon, beloved, king and goddess."

"Just so," said the king.

King of
Upper and
Lower Egypt

〰〰〰〰

(Thutmose III, 9-22:
Hatshepsut 3-14)

37

NEHSI THE NUBIAN WAS MORE amused than not to watch Egypt contend with the spectacle of a king who was a woman. And not only Egypt, either. Most of the embassies that came soon after her coronation did not know where to look or whom to approach. Sent, many of them, to address a queen regent on behalf of a child king, they found themselves facing a king enthroned.

They were in no more comfort than her scribes, struggling to address her by the titles that were proper, but most were only made to fit a man. None went so far as to refuse to address her. Curiosity drove them, or a kind of sickened fascination. But they all went away in awe of her.

If she had been a man, Nehsi thought, there would never have been any of this nonsense. People would agree that she was as strong a king as her father was, as firm of will, as intent on the prosperity of the Two Lands.

And they did prosper. After the inundation that had been so wonderfully great, there was a harvest so rich that it fed the whole of the Two Kingdoms for that year and much of the next. And when the floods came round again, they were not so high, but still glorious, still a wonder to the priests and the people. They proved it, people said. The gods blessed the king's accession, and sanctified her reign.

She had taught them to love her. She did what kings seldom thought to do: she spoke to them, admitted them to her audiences, sent them forth in awe of her, loving her, calling her beautiful. It was marvelous how she did it. She never sacrificed her dignity, never forgot that she was king and goddess; and yet she looked on them with unfeigned warmth.

Courtiers muttered that she had always been overfond of commoners. With them she was much less amiable. She was their king. They would obey her or pay such penalty as she deemed just. It was tribute to the strength of her will that she put none to death, nor had the need to do such a thing. The god spoke in her. Even they, proud fools that they were, could see that.

She had a great heart, and strength beyond the lot of mortal woman. Nehsi, who had known her since she was a small imperious princess, delight of her father's eye, knew no great surprise that she wore so well the crowns of the Two Lands. Her late and feckless husband had never done so well, nor did the young Thutmose seem likely to exceed his father. Certainly he seemed inclined to bow to the will of the elder king, nor did he dare oppose her.

Not that anyone had ever succeeded in thwarting Hatshepsut. What she wanted, she got. Now that she had the greatest prize of all, she wielded it with both grace and competence. Nehsi was proud of her.

She had made him her chancellor, which meant in essence that whatever she needed done, he did it. Unlike Senenmut who heaped up titles as a dung-beetle rolls together his ball of odorous treasure, Nehsi satisfied himself with the one. Hapuseneb stood higher than either of them, vizier of the Two Lands, chief minister and high priest of Amon, hereditary prince and count, Treasurer of the King of Lower Egypt, Overseer of All Works of the King—but those were only the tithe of Senenmut's titles, and none, in Nehsi's mind, meant as much as Nehsi's proud and lonely one.

Nehsi, so lightly titled, could move more freely than they, and with more ease through the intricacies of government in Egypt. He was pleased with it, content to watch others bury themselves beneath the weight of princely offices. Most of them in any case were obliged by rank or necessity to bow to him, to seek his counsel, to petition him for audience with the king.

He was a great prince. He had never thought to be such a thing; had expected to be content with a captaincy in the queen's guard, or if he was particularly fortunate, to become commander of the royal bodyguard. But Hatshepsut had insisted on raising him above the rank of simple guardsman, setting him in the rank and office of a prince, making him the steward of her affairs.

He had a house now, a prince's mansion, and the flock of servants that was required to keep it in order; estates and incomes scattered hither and yon; and a treasure-house that would not have shamed a king in Nubia. All through his king's bestowing, in recompense for his service.

There was always a woman in his bed, but never a wife. Somehow he had never seemed to come round to it. It was not for lack of interested women—ladies, too, and some of quite high rank, noble daughters or widows who sighed after his body and coveted his wealth. That he was reckoned beautiful he knew, though he was no longer quite as young as he had been. He had no lack of willing bed-companions, nor slept alone save as he chose.

But he had never taken a wife. He was beginning to think that he never would. If it was sons he wanted, he had a half-dozen, and daughters too, running wild in his house in the city. There was never any doubt as to who their father was: they were all larger than children in Egypt, blunter-featured, and richly dark of skin and hair and eye. One baffled and dimwitted Egyptian husband might have been hard put to explain his wife's night-colored baby, but she had feigned an illness and smuggled the infant into Nehsi's house when it was born. That was his daughter Tama, the image of him even at the tender age of three, and wilder than all the rest together.

She had committed some infraction that had her nurse in hysterics, something to do with one of the dogs and the kitchen cat and a vat of beer. Nehsi had been called to serve as judge and executioner. Just as he was about to administer the rod, the porter brought word that a king's messenger waited without.

Nehsi was not unduly put out to be diverted from the task of whipping his obstreperous offspring. He tucked her under his arm, ignored her yowling, which in any event had muted to a half-hearted whimper, and went to see who it was.

■ A messenger, indeed. He would flog the porter later for being a purblind idiot. The king herself sat in his reception room, with Senenmut

standing like a guardsman behind her. Nehsi suppressed a raise of the
brow at that. The scribe had grown no prettier with age; his thin and
weedy body had grown soft about the middle, even with the time he
reputedly spent among the horses that he loved.

At least the house-servants had had the intelligence to set the king
in the best chair and offer her refreshment. It was not the first time she
had come to his house, nor the first time, either, that she had played
her own messenger. It was an eccentricity she cultivated. No one ever
knew when the king might appear herself with this message or that. It
kept her courtiers nicely off balance, and won her more than a few battles thereby.

Nehsi was wise to her, though his servants were distressingly slow
to understand what she was doing. He greeted her with composure, up-
ended his now silent and big-eyed offspring, and sat with her in his lap.

Hatshepsut smiled at them both. "She looks more like you every
day," she said.

Tama wriggled in her father's grip. He considered for a moment,
then let her go. As he had expected, she went straight to the king and
clambered into the royal lap, curled up with her finger in her mouth,
and proceeded to go peacefully to sleep.

Hatshepsut regarded Nehsi over that small round head with its
tightly curling sidelock. He regarded her in turn, refusing to be flattered, though he knew that she, like every other woman in Egypt,
found him very good to look at.

Her lips twitched. "No wonder the palace servants and most of the
court walk in terror of you. You have the most appalling stone-hard
stare. Do you study it in front of a mirror?"

He held the stare for a while longer. Then he grinned at her. "Of
course I do. What brings you here, my lady? Anything interesting?"

She tilted her head. "That may be," she said. "I've had in mind a
thing or two, as always. Myrrh, for example. Do you remember the
myrrh-trees that that protégé of Lord Ranefer's brought him?"

"Indeed," said Nehsi. "As I recall, you have half a dozen in your
spice garden."

"Then you must remember what he said of them, that they came from the land of Punt."

Nehsi nodded. And waited.

She was accustomed to his silences. She went on easily, with a glance at her scribe, and such warmth in it that Nehsi wondered if either of them still believed that their liaison was a secret. No one ever spoke of it, but everyone knew. It was not permitted to be a scandal. She was king, after all. Kings could choose whom they favored, even in their beds. "I had been thinking," she said, almost as if to Senenmut, "that I might send an expedition to this fabled country. Everyone seems to have heard of it, and its spices are famous, but few have ever been there."

Senenmut was frowning. He looked angry. Nehsi suspected why; and in a moment knew surely. "Would you lead such an expedition?" the king asked.

"In a moment," Nehsi answered promptly. And so he would. Living in Thebes, ranging the Two Lands in the course of his duties, nonetheless he never quite lost the desire to see another country. His own Nubia he knew, having been there more than once. But to go farther, even as far as Punt—"In less than a moment, lady. When would you like me to leave?"

She laughed. Her scribe did not. He had wanted this, then. Was he weary of her? Bored with his myriad of titles? Greedy for yet another? Ambassador to Punt would be a new one, and unusual.

Nehsi did not see great profit in asking. The king, who seemed oblivious to her lover's sulkiness, said to Nehsi, "You may want to delay a little, if only to gather together your expedition. It's a long road, and little known, except among the spice-merchants. You'll need ships to sail there, and weapons for defense against raiders at sea and on the shore, and—"

"—gifts for the rulers of that country, and bribes for those lords and robbers whom we meet along the way, and a courtier or two, and guides, and—"

"—servants, soldiers, scribes." Hatshepsut loved to play the game of finishing one another's thought. She also loved to win it, to end with a flourish. This once, he let her. "And interpreters, of course. We mustn't forget those." She paused, sighed. "Oh, I wish I could go with you!"

"You could, you know," he said.

She shook her head. "No. If the king comes, however small the army she brings with her, it's no longer an embassy; it's an invasion. I don't want to conquer Punt. I want to trade with it. Exchange gifts and courtesies. Grow rich exchanging Egyptian gold for boatloads of myrrh."

"But if you conquer it," he said, "it's all yours for the taking."

"Conquest is expensive," said Hatshepsut. "Trade is much simpler. Then if the people who trade with us are intrigued enough by what we offer, they'll ask to see more of us. They'll study us. Imitate us. And in the end, perhaps, become us—ask to be made a part of our greater kingdom."

"That is . . . interesting," Nehsi said.

"Ridiculous, you mean," said Senenmut, more waspish even than usual. "It's not a thought most people could have. Gods think like this, you know. It's men who have to ramp about with weapons, conquering people who then devote their lives to begging for gold and grain and guards against their enemies."

"I meant," said Nehsi, "that it's a most unusual and intriguing way to think. Slower, too, than war; but as her majesty says, much less expensive."

"Do you accuse her majesty of stinginess?"

"Certainly not," Nehsi said calmly. "I find her a very practical and exemplary image of a king."

Senenmut regarded him narrow-eyed, but he had a face that none could read unless he wished it. Which, at the moment, he did not.

The king's scribe, that man of innumerable titles, gave way with poor enough grace. He would not forgive anyone who won this prize. Nehsi could not have said that he cared overmuch. He was going adventuring—he, who had dreamed of such things when he was young, and yearned for them through all his years of being the king's good and faithful servant.

38

HE EXPEDITION INTO PUNT WAS a mighty undertaking. Nehsi saw it begun in time so brief that those who were not mute with the shock of it were screaming in protest. He heeded neither faction. It would be done in the time he had allotted. Therefore it was done.

He had learned that from the king: to expect the impossible, to consider no alternative but that it be done, and thus to see it accomplished. Anything less encouraged people—courtiers and servants in particular—to grow slack.

They called him a hard man and worse, but on the day that he had set for the departure, the whole of the embassy was ready and waiting when he came out to his ship. It was a sea-expedition, this, north down the river of Egypt and across through the channel that had been dug by one of the old kings, that was most passable when the river ran at the flood. It ended in the eastward sea, on which his ships would sail southward into the land of myrrh, where the incense-trees grew.

The king and her ministers bade farewell to him at the quay of Thebes. Where another king might have put on his full panoply, so much gold that he could barely move, she chose the starkness of simplicity: white gown, pectoral like gilded vulture-wings embracing the disk of the sun, the Two Crowns. He in kilt and cloth headdress and heavy golden collar looked well beside her, and he knew it as well as she.

Amid all the people who had come crowding to see the ships sail into the incense-country, they two could be alone if they chose. No one could hear them through the roar of the throng, but they heard one another clearly enough, her voice pitched clear and his drum-deep. They did not say much, at that. There was nothing that needed saying; not between them who had been friends from childhood.

Still they dallied, while Nehsi's mariners readied the ship, and the last of the embassy straggled aboard, and the people of Thebes shouted and cheered. Then there were only the two of them, and her flock of ministers growing perceptibly bored. Nehsi was aware of his captain behind him, standing quietly but being conspicuous about it.

"The wind is freshening," Nehsi said, "and blowing for once from the south. Best we go."

"Yes," said the king. But she did not move, and neither did he.

He swallowed. His throat was tight. He had not been apart from her for any great while since they were children. He had lived as close to her as her shadow. Even when in late years he had traveled about the Two Kingdoms, acting in her name, he was never truly parted from her: she was Egypt, and while he was in Egypt his soul was never far from her.

Now he was leaving Egypt. He would not see her for months, seasons—a year, perhaps, or more.

He should have thought of that when he accepted this embassy. It would not have stopped him, but he would have had time to prepare. He might not have needed to stand here, as purely lost as he had not been since he was weaned, and with the same preposterous desire to open his mouth and howl.

Which of them moved first, he did not know. The embrace was swift, breathless, bruising-tight. Anyone who still believed that they were lovers would be gratified, surely.

Her scribes and historians no doubt would write lengthy speeches for both of them, full of beautiful words and elaborate phrases. In the plain and living world, she said simply, "Stay safe. Come back to me. May the gods keep you."

"May the gods watch over you," he said. He bowed low, for the edification of those who watched, and rose, and turned on his heel. He did not look back. He felt her eyes on him, distinct as the touch of her hand, but he kept his own fixed on his ship. The moment his feet were firm on the deck, the captain sang out to the oarsmen.

They backed swiftly from the quay, came about, turned prow to the north. The rest of the ships followed, precise and orderly before the king's face, catching the wind in their sails, riding the river toward the land of Punt.

■ Nehsi could retreat to his cabin and snivel because he had left his beloved king behind; or he could stand on the deck in the shade of the canopy, with the wind blowing back the lappets of his headdress, and let the people of Thebes see what a bold brave explorer he was. The morning was splendid, cool and clear, and the ship ran well, making good speed down the river. He dared not look back to see if the king still waited by the shore, gazing after him; if he did that, he would lose his famous composure. He kept his face turned to the north, and let it bathe in wind and sun.

Once they were underway, the crew settled into a kind of ease. They were good men; had been together on this ship for seasons now, sailing the trade-routes in the king's service. They were proud that she had chosen them for this voyage. He saw no sullen faces, no men slacking their work or refusing to move at their captain's command.

He nodded, approving. They would do well.

Of the embassy he was less certain. The scribes were of his own choosing, with Senenmut's help—the king's scribe had never been one to let jealousy interfere with his competence. Nehsi did not think that they would fail him. One of them, the youngest, earnest and shakily brave, was sitting in a corner of the deck, papyrus on knees, scribbling busily: recording the departure, Nehsi supposed, and embellishing it for posterity.

The servants, too, he trusted: they were his own. The guards were men of his old company in the palace, under a captain he had trained himself. The nobler members of the embassy had firm instructions to obey Nehsi in all things; they might even do it, in fear of the king and, more to the point, of the king's large and formidable ambassador.

Well, then, he thought as he surveyed his domain. It all seemed in excellent order, every man in his place. He had nothing to fret over.

Unless he chose to trouble himself with the one member of the embassy who was not of his choosing, the one whom the king had given him on the advice of the House of Life. It was a strange choice for those firm followers of tradition, but it was, they declared, the best in the circumstances.

The interpreter on whom he must rely in the land of Punt was of that blood and nation, perhaps even kin to its king, though Nehsi had no certain knowledge of that. It was a woman, which did not dismay him who served the king's majesty of Egypt. Her father had been an Egyptian of the minor nobility, her mother a woman of Punt whom that lordling had met on an expedition there, become enamored of, and brought home to be his wife. She looked Egyptian enough aside from the deeper reddish duskiness of her skin. The people of Punt were not like Nubians; they were closer to Egyptians, and most probably were kin.

She was not displeasing to look at. In fact she was a beauty. Nor did her youth dismay him: she was a woman grown, if a very young one, and learned, could read and write the language of Egypt. She was altogether an admirable creature.

With one singular exception. She had, from the moment she met him, said not one word to him. To others she spoke easily enough, if never volubly. She had proved to the satisfaction of the scribes, one or two of whom had a smattering of the language of Punt, that she spoke that tongue well and fluently; and the ship's captain, whose name was Sinuhe, agreed. But to Nehsi she said nothing.

When she was brought to him only the day before, and presented as the interpreter whom he had been awaiting, she had looked him hard and steadily in the face, then bowed to the exact degree that was proper for a woman of lesser rank before a prince of Egypt. The scribe from the House of Life who brought her there, who happened to be her uncle, did all the talking. Her name was Bastet, which was not terribly common in this age of the world: fathers were usually more careful of naming their daughters after goddesses.

Whether she had grown to fit the name or the name had grown to fit her, it was apt. She had a cat's smooth grace and watchful silence, and, he suspected, not a little of its ferocity.

While her uncle chattered on about her father and her mother and her upbringing and her erudition, all of which he proclaimed to be of the most excellent, she knelt in front of Nehsi with her little cat-face lowered and her hands resting on her knees, saying not one word. Nor did she speak thereafter, even when he spoke to her, calling her by name.

Her uncle, who though an incessant babbler did not seem to be a fool, said, "Don't mind her, I beg you, great prince. She's shy, but she gets over it. She'll be as voluble as you could ask for, once she stands in front of the King of Punt."

"One would hope so," Nehsi said. He tried again to startle a word out of her. "You! Girl. Did a lizard run away with your tongue?"

She kept her head bowed, her body quiet. She said nothing.

"She does this sometimes," her uncle said. "You mustn't mind her, my lord. She's been a little spoiled. Not sheltered, mind you, lord— she's been raised as free almost as a boy, though with the delicacy proper to a girl. She does know proper manners; she just chooses, sometimes, not to show them."

Indeed. Once her uncle had been escorted out and the girl—Bastet; of all names to give a child—turned over to the servants to feed and look after until the ships should sail, she proved herself friendly enough to her fellows. All but Nehsi.

Maybe she simply did not like Nubians. Or maybe she was afraid of him—though she looked a bold brash creature, from all that he could see. He frightened children sometimes, as big as he was, and dark, and not inclined to smile unless he had good reason.

Whatever caused her to do it, Bastet the interpreter sailed on his ship but had as little as possible to do with him. That would have to change. When they came to Punt, she would be interpreting for the people of that land to the commander of this expedition. It would be embarrassing if she declined to speak out of fear or dislike.

He could hope that she would warm to him, or at least bring herself to speak a word or two. To that end, the first night of the voyage, when they had moored in good harborage a gratifying distance down-river from Thebes, Nehsi summoned her to take the evening meal with him in his cabin high up on the ship's deck.

He was rather surprised that she obeyed the summons. It would have been like what he had observed, for her to refuse. When she came, she was dressed handsomely but not elaborately, with good sense for what a woman should bring to wear on a long voyage: good plain linen, a collar of faience beads, a gleam of gold rings in her ears, and a wig of good quality, well made. She had scented herself with oil of roses: a rare choice, and appealing.

She brought with her a companion, one who shocked Nehsi into speechlessness.

"Papa," said his daughter Tama, whom he had left safe, he thought, in the strong arms of her nurse. "Bastet said I had to stop hiding in the linen-chest. She said you'd whip me till I bleed. You won't do that, will you, Papa? I'll scream."

"What in the name of Set and Sobek—" Nehsi drew a breath that was sharp enough to cut. "What were you doing in the linen-chest?"

"Coming with you," Tama answered. "Nurse said I had to take a good look at you, so I could remember. You aren't going to come back, she said. You're going to die. I don't want you to die."

"I am not going to die," Nehsi said through gritted teeth. That idiot of a nurse, however, when he got his hands on her . . .

Tama shook her head at him. "Nurse said you are. You're going to Punt. Punt is far away. It's not even Egypt."

"I am not going to fall off the edge of the world," Nehsi said. "I promise you. Have I ever broken a promise?"

"No," said Tama.

"Well then," Nehsi said.

She thought about that. To do it, she climbed into his lap and wrapped arms about him, as far as she could reach, and rested warm and faintly milk-scented against his breast. He looked down at the top of her head in heart-deep love and profound exasperation.

"Gods," he said. "I have to find a boat to send her back. A servant whom I can trust, to make sure that she doesn't slip away and follow. A guard or six to keep her safe."

"I wouldn't bother," said Bastet. At last: words from her, and perfectly matter-of-fact, too. "I'll look after her. How much trouble can she be?"

Nehsi startled himself, and probably the girl as well, with a snort of laughter. "You see her here, and you can ask that? She had to have planned this for days, and like a general of armies, too, to know just which chest was going in my ship, and just when to hide in it and not be detected. How did you find her?"

"I was hungry," Tama said in his lap. "I came out to get something to eat. Bastet was watching. She knew I was in there, she said."

Nehsi turned his hard stare on Bastet. "And how did you know that?"

He was sure that she was going to go silent on him again, but for a miracle she answered. "I knew where I would be if you were my father and I were determined to keep you from dying in a foreign country."

"But how did you—"

"I knew," said Bastet in a tone as flat as it was final.

Nehsi opened his mouth to press her further, but desisted. Those whom the gods spoke to, who knew things that others did not know, were not always inclined to explain themselves to common mortals.

Of course she might have seen the imp climbing into the chest, and omitted to mention it.

He would not pursue that, he decided. Not for the moment. The servants were waiting for them, shifting from foot to foot in the way they had when dinner was growing cold. His cook was already beside himself; and when Merenptah was upset, all the servants suffered.

Nehsi allowed the meal to be served on the deck of his ship, each dish brought steaming from the kitchen-boat moored alongside, passed over the sides by servants with deft hands and an unwavering eye. Tama partook as the others did, with exemplary manners. Under any other circumstances she would have made her father proud.

After a fine roast duck, fresh-caught on the way, and one of Merenptah's famous cakes, Nehsi should have been free to rest as he pleased. Instead he contemplated his scapegrace daughter and this oddity of an interpreter, and sighed.

"To be sure," Bastet said, echoing his thought with uncanny accuracy, "it would be a great inconvenience to send the child home. If I agree to look after her—since I have little else to do before we come to Punt—surely she can stay."

Nehsi did not like the shape or the taste of that at all. And yet it was tempting. It was easy; it was simple. It put him out very little.

Still. A child so young on a voyage so long, into countries little known, but known to be dangerous . . .

"I'll guard her," said Bastet. "I'll look after her, protect her. I can shoot; I'm good at it. You just ate the duck I shot this morning."

Nehsi's eyes widened slightly. He had not seen the shot, having been engrossed in something or other—probably a nap—at the time; only heard the cry as the bird came down, and the scramble to fish it out of the water before a crocodile found it.

Bastet must have taken his expression for incredulity. "Yes, that was I," she said with a flicker of temper. "I was trying to make myself useful."

"Clearly you need to be useful," Nehsi said. "Very well, then. Play the nurse if you will, but have a care. If she escapes again and is hurt, I may remember that a traveler can find guides and interpreters in any country he comes to. Punt is by no means unknown to Egypt—there may be Egyptians there even now."

"But none who speaks the language as one born there," Bastet said with a remarkable recovery of calm. "I won't let your lion-cub escape. Even," she said, "if she bites me."

"I won't bite you," Tama said. "I don't do that."

"Good," said Bastet.

39

BASTET GOT ON VERY WELL WITH Tama, kept her in order to an impressive degree, and even kept her quiet when there was need of it. A long voyage was difficult for a child so young. Even a ship as large as this one was still a small thing under the vault of heaven, with nowhere to run that was not full of men or oars or baggage. She could not swim in the river: quite apart from the fact that it was swollen with the flood, it was full of crocodiles. Any one of them would have been delighted to dine on such a morsel as Tama was.

They sailed through Egypt as swiftly as they might go, pausing only to take on water or provisions. It was a long way into Punt, and the flood would not last forever; while it ran high, they must cross the channel into the sea.

That was north of Memphis and then east on a narrow arm of the river, wider now with flood. They had passed out of the humid marshes of the Delta and into the Red Land again, across the bleak outer reach of Egypt. The Bitter Lakes stretched in a chain with river between, harsh with salt, curving south toward the arm of the eastern sea.

Here was the edge of Egypt. On the right hand as they worked their way east and south was the outlier of the Red Land. On the left lay the broad desert of Sinai, where servants of the king mined turquoise and malachite and copper. There was danger here if they were delayed, if the passage was broken or blocked, if they ran aground before they reached the sea.

Wild tribesmen lived in this desert, children of the sand, who made their living leading caravans across the desert. They would raid ships in the bitter lake and in the channel that the kings had dug, for anger at the profit they were losing; for sailors paid them no tribute for crossing their country, nor hired them to guard their passage.

Nor did Nehsi doubt that every tribe in Sinai knew what this fleet of ships was, laden with gifts for the lords of Punt. He alone, as a prince of Egypt, would fetch a splendid price, whether they offered him unharmed to his king in the Two Lands or sold him gelded in the markets of Asia.

He forbore to trouble his sleep with such terrors. His fleet was superbly armed and guarded, and his sailors were fighting men, men who knew well the art of defending their ship. As they passed under oar and sail through the land of the tribes, they mounted strong guard by day and kept watch at night. Tama he removed, much against her will, from her bed beside Bastet, and took into his own, safe in the cabin within a circle of armed men.

Perhaps their show of armed force prevented attack; or maybe the gods protected them. They passed the Bitter Lakes and came unmolested to the kings' channel. The flood, that had reached its height while they were in the Delta, had begun to subside. But there was water enough, Nehsi hoped, to carry them through to the sea.

Here was the worst danger of ambush. The channel was clear—he had sent men ahead to be sure of it, men with strong backs and light boats, who made certain that neither sand nor reeds encroached upon the passage of a fleet of ships. They had built upon the labors that the king had decreed in this past year and more, opening the passage and making it as wide as they might, so that not only this fleet but many after it should make the passage. Her ambitions were as noble as she herself was: she meant this to be but the first of many such voyages, her greeting and welcome to the lords of Punt, who thereafter would be her friends and allies.

All that shrank in his mind to simple fact: the sky overhead, blue vault of heaven; the channel in its deep-dug banks; the beds of reeds and the stretches of sand and stone, and the watch kept by day and night against raids from the desert. His scribes kept count of the days, recorded the length of each journey from sunrise to sunset. Nehsi let his own reckoning slide into the long stream of days, each much like the one before: sailing ever and ever on to the Great Green, as people in Egypt called the sea.

The scent of it grew stronger with every day. It seeped into his bones: salt and seawrack, fish and weed and a sharpness that had no name but sea-scent. And then at last, still early of a morning, the channel that had been all his world for so long opened endlessly wide.

Then he heard the surge and sigh of the sea, the waves washing the shore. It was narrow here as seas went, though broader than any river; one could see both shores, and laugh at the small figures running on the left hand, brandishing tiny sticks of weapons, even letting fly a shaft or two over the water.

The tribes had come at last to raid his ships; but they had come too late. "Surely," Nehsi said to the wind that freshened, catching the sail and lifting his boat till it leaped upon the waves, "the gods have held us in their hands."

■ They worked their way down the shores of the world. It was wider than Nehsi had ever known, even knowing the length and breadth of Egypt. This was vaster by far, full twice and thrice, four times, even five times the length of his country that he had thought so great.

The crew of his ship were amused, though they tried to be polite about it, since after all he was a great prince. They called themselves men who had seen both earth and sky, who were wise to every wind that blew. It was not an empty boast. Their hearts were wider than he had known before, their eyes accustomed to horizons that made the edges of Egypt seem narrow and circumscribed.

"And yet it is a great country," he said to Bastet as they sailed past a stretch of mountains that seemed to hold up the sky. "The greatest in the world."

"But the world is larger by far," she said. She seemed more at ease than he was. She had been born in Egypt, but she had grown up hearing tales of Punt and all the lands between, speaking their languages, remembering them as a child could whose mother told tales both vivid and richly wrought. She told them to Nehsi on the long days of voyaging, when the wind bore them without need of oars, and much of the crew could take its ease.

Her uncle had told the truth after all. Her crippling shyness at the beginning, which she never either excused or explained, had warmed and opened into a wonderful ease. Tama had wrought that. It was impossible to maintain a polite distance with that child finding more mischief to get into than one could possibly imagine, considering how small a ship was.

They had taken to dining together in the evenings. Nehsi was careful to see that everyone knew the privilege of his table, inviting as many as could fit in the cabin, and varying it every day; but Bastet was always there. And sometimes, if he was so inclined, it was only the two of them and Tama, and maybe the captain Sinuhe.

They ate what they could shoot or trade for, drank beer brewed from their store of barley, and kept the wine for great occasions, since some of it at least must come intact to the King of Punt. It was enough for comfort: surprising, a little, as far from home as they were.

Comfort was rare enough else. The farther south they sailed, the stranger land and water seemed. And they began to run into weather.

Nehsi had heard outlanders complaining that Egypt had no weather. It could be hot or less hot or even almost cold. Clouds came, went. Once in a rare while it rained. In certain seasons storms of sand roared out of the Red Land, or a fierce wind that maddened men and beasts, and often brought swarms of locusts, or stinging flies.

But honest weather as it was reckoned on the rest of the world—which seemed mostly to be storms of rain—Egypt seldom had.

Not so here on the eastern sea. Calm they could contend with: the oarsmen broke out oars and rowed. Storms of wind were frightening, and in one the sail rent in two; they had to pull ashore for a day or two, on guard against attack, and mend it. But when the clouds rolled in, so deep a grey they seemed almost black, and the water roiled, laced with foam, and rain began to lash their cheeks, the strong men of Egypt shivered and cursed.

The sailors laughed at them. "Call this a storm?" they said. "Now when we sail the Great Green, the northern sea, when it's winter and the wind blows as keen as knives—*that* is a storm. This is a sea-goddess' kiss."

It was bitter enough for Nehsi's taste, which no doubt proved that he was soft. He lent a hand as he could, which was not much in a ship as well manned as his. Mostly he huddled in the dim close air of the cabin with Tama and her self-named nurse, and struggled to keep the child entertained. She would have been out dancing in the rain, easy prey for the waves that lashed up over the prow. He had to keep a solid grip on her and tell her stories till his voice was hoarse; and then Bastet took up the task. Thereafter they did turn and turn about, amusing Tama while the rain hammered down and the boat heaved and rocked in the swell.

The storm lasted three days. Nehsi lost count early, but the scribes kept the reckoning, and Sinuhe the captain appeared well able to tell day from night, even such black and filthy days as these were.

They could not put in to shore while the storm ran. It drove them ahead of it—a storm out of the north, so that they hastened into the south at impossible speed. The sailors labored day and night to keep the ships afloat, and to keep them together as they could. It seemed that the gods favored the voyage, wished them all to come to Punt as soon as might be; but cared little how they suffered in the doing of it.

Even the passengers did their turns at bailing-bucket and steering oar. Nehsi, the strongest of them, left his daughter to her nurse and took the longest watches. He had to be ordered to sleep by a shadow-eyed and perpetually dripping captain: driven into his cabin, and knocked flat on the bed there. It was already full of Tama and her nurse, a fact of which he did not become aware until he woke with a double armful of warm and breathing sleepers.

Tama curled in the middle, finger in mouth. Bastet had folded her body about the child's. The two of them fitted smoothly into his side.

He loathed to move, but the sheer unwontedness of quiet after the roar of the storm made him twitch. And light: it shone through the ports, dazzling his dark-accustomed eyes.

He crept out as softly as he could, taking great care to disturb neither of the sleepers. Sun half-blinded him. It was just risen, riding low over the hills of Sinai. The sea surged and rolled under it, agitated still but never as it had been.

The storm had passed. The sky was a clear and cloudless blue. The waves were no higher than they might have been on a day of brisk wind, as this was. Warm wind, soft wind, with a scent in it that made him think of spices.

The ship's timbers steamed with wet. He had forgotten what dryness was; his whole body was sodden, heavy with water. He stripped off the leaden weight of his kilt and left it lying, and went to lend a hand with the last of the bailing.

Most of his sailors were naked, too, letting the sun bake them dry. They rid the ship of its burden of rainwater, all but the brimful barrels that would see them, the captain said, nigh as far as Punt. He was pleased. They had water enough, their ship was undamaged, and the rest of the fleet made its way back to them as the day wore on, all but one ship; and that came in sight just at sundown. In the morning it would catch them.

Merenptah the master of cooks had somehow kept a fire going through the storm. At evening he laid out a feast: fish of the sea, bread fresh-baked, a cheese that had been aging in a secret barrel. He even produced a prize, a jar of dates preserved in honey, such sweetness as Nehsi had not tasted since he left Egypt.

Nehsi, exhausted with daylong labor, ate swiftly and in silence, hardly aware of who ate with him. Tama was there, he knew that; but she let him be. So did Bastet. He ate till his hunger was sated, and sought a bed that was—for a miracle—dry.

■ This time when he woke it was still night, though late. The moon rode high. The stars shone beyond the ports of his cabin, that lay open to the breezes. They were cool but not cold, and he was warm under a blanket he did not remember wrapping himself in, with the same double warmth beside him that he remembered, dimly, from the morning before.

Tama again, and Bastet beyond her. Tama's face was a shadow in the moonlight. Bastet's he saw clearly, its lines carved clean, limned in silver. The hair that he had never seen, hidden as it was under head-scarf or wig, was uncovered. She wore it cut shoulder-long, a riot of midnight curls. Pity, he thought, to conceal it. Plaited and weighed down with beads, it would make an admirable imitation of a wig.

He rubbed his own close-cropped skull and grimaced. Ah, well; but what he grew was as thick as a fleece, and beastly hard to keep in order. Egyptian fashion suited him well enough.

He folded his hands under his head and gazed up at the moon, the blind eye of Horus as Egyptians called it. What it was called in Nubia he did not remember. He was a Nubian by blood but never by upbringing. In that he was all Egyptian.

He deliberately did not think of the woman lying so close beside him. He had brought no woman with him. It was a singular omission, but one that he had not thought to remedy. A lord who dragged his women behind him wherever he went had always struck Nehsi as a bit of a fool. Had he no self-discipline? Could he not find ample consolation wherever he was?

Besides, none of his maidservants had been eager to go. All of those who had been willing were men. There were women on one or two of the other ships, companions to his noble companions. Sailors did not bring their wives or their lovers. It was ill luck, they said.

And here was the lordling's daughter from Bubastis, named after that city's goddess, sound asleep and perfectly innocent, with his daughter in her arms. That she was beautiful he never forgot. That she was female was unmistakable.

A man could ease himself over the side. Sailors never minded, though they might grin and offer commentary. Nehsi was too proud to resort to that. He remained where he was, while the moon sank from its zenith and the boat rocked gently on the breast of the sea. He was amused, rather. Wry. A little embarrassed.

None of which he would ever admit to Bastet. She was young enough to be his daughter. Clearly she had no interest in him, except that he was Tama's father. To her he would be an old man. He had six-and-thirty years by his closest reckoning: well into middle age. She must have had fifteen, if she had so many. An infant; a child.

Not that that had ever stopped or even slowed him with a maid-servant, but she was well born. Her father had trusted him to keep her safe on this journey.

So he would do, then, though his manly parts ached with restraint. They had seldom been denied before.

It would do them good, he thought, even as he slipped out to cool them, and the rest of him, in seawater.

40

RATHER FORTUNATELY FOR NEHSI'S peace of mind and body, the storm had brought the fleet almost to the borders of Punt. They had yet a narrow mouth of the sea to pass through, dangerous with reefs; and the storm had shifted them. They picked their way through, gauging depth with line and oar, and more than once levering a boat off a reef that had not been there when its captain sailed these waters before. But they passed through, if slowly.

Then Nehsi saw that, as wide as the sea had seemed, it was but a narrow thing beside this vast and sighing expanse of water. Here was the Great Green itself—and yet, the mariners told him, it was nothing to the ocean beyond. There the land dropped out of sight altogether, and any who sailed there must travel by sun and stars.

No one of Egypt ever had, that anyone knew of. This was as far as sane men went, along this sandy shore with its fringes of reef.

It was hot here, even compared with Egypt in summer; and damp, a heat as heavy as the worst of the Delta. The breezes that wafted from the land were pungent with spices.

"This whole country smells like a temple," Nehsi observed as they sailed in close to the land. When he drew a breath, he grew dizzy.

"Wait till you're actually in it," the captain said. "You'll think there must be a priest under every bush and stone, waiting to chant this rite or that."

Nehsi grinned, leaning on the rail of the lookout's post. Spray bathed him as the ship breasted the sea. He licked the salt from his lips and peered under his hand at the sandy anonymity of the shore. Far inland, he thought he could see the rise of hills or mountains, though perhaps they were only clouds.

"Oh, no, that's mountains," Sinuhe said when he asked. "It's desert in there, and mountains rearing over it. Makes our Black Land look soft and lush, it does, though our Red Land gives it a fair contest for horrors."

"So where do they live?" Nehsi asked. "What do they live on?"

Sinuhe's glance hinted that he should know that, and to be sure he did, but he wanted to hear it now, in sight of this country. It made it real somehow; turned dry and wordy knowledge into living substance.

In any case he received the answer he wanted. "There's rivers enough," Sinuhe said, "which gives them water to drink and to feed their crops and herds, and fine defense against invaders. And they trade. Incense, of course. Ivory. Ebony, gold, unguents. Terebinth, kohl. Monkeys. Hounds. Panthers and slaves."

Nehsi whistled between his teeth. "They're rich."

Sinuhe nodded. "Gloriously rich. And eager to trade for our bits of linen and mirrors, and a sword or two or a spear, and a few barrels of our blue glass beads."

"Foreigners," said Nehsi the Nubian, not meaning to dismiss them; trying to explain them.

Bastet heard him. She did not, as he had half expected, upbraid him for false judgment. She went silent, that was all.

Silence seemed to be her way of letting a man know when he had displeased her. She was taciturn at dinner that night, speaking, if she spoke at all, in monosyllables.

Nehsi refused to humble himself with an apology. She had not told him that he had offended her, or explained why. Until she did, she could sulk in solitude.

That night when he went to his bed on the deck, she was nowhere near it. She had taken Tama to her old place in the corner by the water-barrels, spread her pallet there and gone to sleep.

■ They came to Punt on a hot and breathless morning, when the sea was like grey-green glass, rolling softly as it neared the shore. The sailors sweated at the oars, rowing to the beat of the drum, and chanting what from its tune should have been a hymn of praise to the Egyptian river-god, but its words extolled the charms of a certain famous lady who lived and loved in Memphis. It heartened them immeasurably, though Nehsi would have preferred that Tama not take up the words and the tune. She perched on one of the huge hawsers, as thick as a man's waist, that ran the length of the ship on either side, and made her own ditty of the sailors' song.

As she celebrated the breasts of Neferneferure, which swelled like pomegranates, Bastet swooped on her and carried her off. Nehsi laughed to himself and turned back to the lookout's post. They were coming in to the land now, rocking hard on the swell. The shore curved deeply there into harbor with a narrow mouth.

High above the harbor stood a rocky promontory. Something moved up there, a figure shrunken with distance but moving and call-ing out like a man: a high, wailing cry that echoed inland.

That, Nehsi had been told to expect: the watchman of Punt, set there to look for ships that came to trade in his country. As they rowed into the harbor's mouth, they saw him running down along the rim, into the sandy bowl. There in the quiet water stood the strangest city Nehsi had ever seen.

In Egypt people built in mudbrick, or in reeds along the river's bank. Here they built in reeds, or something like them, but not on the undefended shore. They built in the harbor itself, on pilings above the water. Skiffs ran from house to house, or ramps that stretched to the land, with people running along them, calling to one another.

They were handsome enough people, like dark Egyptians. The men were as tall, which made them small in Nubia, broad in the shoulder, well-muscled and strong. Their beards were striking in their familiarity: grown long and wound into a thick plait suspended from the chin. Just so was the king's beard in Egypt, but that was never grown on the king's chin, even when the king was not a woman; he wore it for state occasions, and took it off to be at ease.

As strangely familiar as the men were, the women were truly odd. Some were slender enough, but many were gone exuberantly to fat: great-breasted, huge-bellied, wobblingly vast in the rump. Such rumps as these, Nehsi had never imagined among the slender women of Egypt or the strong tall women of Nubia. He did not know whether to be fascinated or appalled.

The children were as children everywhere, lissome and quick, tugging at the hands of mother or father, begging them to hurry. Some broke free and ran down to the water, hopping from foot to foot, calling out in their language. It sounded like the crying of birds.

"They say," said Bastet, appearing suddenly beside Nehsi, " 'Welcome! Welcome to the Sun-god's land! Who are you? Where do you come from? Are you gods out of heaven? Have you brought gifts for us? Come and talk to us!' "

"Tell them," said Nehsi, "that we come in the name of Amon-Re, who is god over all gods, and in the name of his daughter, the king, who rules in Egypt."

She seemed to think little of wasting such courtly words on children, but she spoke in the same language they were speaking—he hoped in the words that he had told her to speak.

He had to leave the prow and consider the duties of an ambassador. His bodyservant was waiting in the cabin, looking more than slightly impatient, with his bath all drawn and the razors ready, and everything prepared to make him fit to stand in front of a foreign king. He sub-

mitted to it without protest. He did like to look well. It honored his
king, whose voice he was in this country.

■ From the expressions of the sailors as he emerged again into the sun,
and from the evidence of his own mirror, he looked well indeed. He
happened to catch a glimpse of Bastet's face: she looked whitely
shocked, as if the sun had grown too much for her. He spared a moment's worry, and not only because he needed her to speak for him.
Illness in this remote and barbarous country could be a deadly thing.

She seemed well enough when she came to his side, standing on
the deck while the ship finished mooring just offshore. She had taken
care for her appearance, too: put on her best gown and her wig, and
painted her face becomingly, and donned a collar he had not known
she had: beads of lapis and ivory and gold, and a broad disk of beaten
gold, such as, he took note, some of the men wore who waited on the
shore. Others of them wore disks of ivory or black ebony or what
seemed to be shell, gleaming softly in the sun.

She had had her own disk worked into a pectoral in the Egyptian
fashion, and splendid it was, too. She looked, he thought, like a princess,
erect and proud, and—he could not help thanking the gods for that—
slender as Egyptian women were. No billows of flesh; no huge shelf of
rump, only a sweet womanly curve that begged a man's hand to stroke
it.

He whipped his thoughts back to their proper course. The crowd
on the shore flurried briefly, then parted, opening a path in the sand.

These were the chieftains, the lords and princes. They rode on donkeys, with an air that proclaimed their pride in the privilege. Last of
them all came a handsome man of early middle years, with a beard
longer and more richly plaited than any of the rest, and a disk of gold
on his breast, so broad and so resplendent that it rivaled the sun.

But he paled beside the woman who rode with him. Her donkey
was of surpassing smallness and delicacy, a beautiful silvery creature
with ears like the the fronds of a palm-tree. She sat on its back like a
mountain atop an obelisk.

She was the pattern from which the rest of the women were cut, the sun to the moon of their strangeness. Her flesh swelled in rolls and folds on arms and belly, thighs and knees. Her breasts hung vast and pendulous, their huge nipples clear to see under the garment that she wore: white Egyptian linen of the finest quality, girdled beneath the swell of her middle, sewn to circle the vastness of each thigh, cut to the knee below. Round her vast neck lay a collar of golden disks bound together with rods of gold. On her head, tied with fastidious neatness, was a golden ribbon, a diadem, for she was a queen, the queen of this country, which her people called the God's Land.

Nehsi took great care to determine that no one laughed. No one even grinned, though he saw lips tightened and jaws clenched. Nothing like it had ever shown itself to Egyptian eyes: this vast grotesquerie of a woman on her tiny donkey. The young scribe who never stopped scribbling had dropped to his favored corner of the deck and begun to draw furiously, eyes fixed on the procession that approached across the sand.

Nehsi was forgetting his duty in the fascination of so much strangeness. He recalled himself abruptly, and descended into the boat that waited, where Bastet and a pair of scribes were already sitting, and rowed in princely state to the shore of Punt.

■ The people of this country, diligent in their courtesies, had pitched a pavilion some distance from the water. It had an Egyptian look to it, but with oddities: poles tipped with ivory, and golden embroidery along its edges, depicting in a strange style, half Egyptian, half foreign, a procession of beasts and birds. There in the cool shade were people who must be servants, offering jars of water, beer, and something fierce that was, Bastet said, a kind of barley spirit. A sip or two of that was enough to convince Nehsi that he should smile and pretend to drink the rest, but refrain from draining the cup.

Here the queen and the king of Punt received him sitting on chairs made of the tusks of elephants. He was given another, which he took after he had made obeisance: bowing as a prince to a prince who stands slightly higher, but certainly not as to a king in Egypt.

The queen, seen close in the shade of the pavilion, was no less grotesque than she had seemed on the strand. Her face was as odd as her body, long-boned, heavy-jawed. But her eyes were those of a lovely woman, dark and almost distressingly beautiful in that oddity of a face. Her voice was deep and sweet, like dark honey. It was she who spoke; the king her husband was content to sit listening.

It was a strange, hesitant colloquy. Each of them spoke in his or her own tongue, with Bastet between, rendering it into words that the other could understand. Her light voice faded after a while to a kind of echo. Nehsi, accustomed to embassies in Egypt, acknowledged the strangeness and then forgot it, focusing his mind and body on the exchange of greetings and courtesies. It was a dance; like all dances it had its steps and its cadences.

The heart of it was buried deep, and took long to arrive at. First these majesties of the land that they called Tomery, Beloved, must bow low and low again to the god of the sun, who, they declared, was none other than Amon-Re of Thebes. They were most particular in this regard.

"But in your country, it is said," the queen observed, "he rules remote and distant, except when he comes to love one of your queens. Here is where he lives. This is the country that he loves. He is our king, our near and present lord. We live by the breath of his mouth."

"Our king is Amon's own child," Nehsi said. "She rules from the throne of the Two Lands. She speaks with his voice; she sees with his eyes. She is the living image of Amon."

The queen inclined her head. "He has blessed your country greatly; and indeed he loves it." She paused. "So it is no rumor or falsehood. Your king, the one whom you have raised to rule above you, is a woman."

"Yes, majesty," said Nehsi. "Maatkare, she is named: the Truth of Re."

"Re is truth," the queen said, nodding, "and life and strength. Is she beautiful, your king?"

"More beautiful than anything," Nehsi said; and no matter if he offended this most ugly of women.

She did not appear angry, nor even perturbed. "It is good," she said, "that a king be beautiful. See, my king, how beautiful he is."

Her king neither blushed nor looked down. He had been chosen for his beauty, perhaps. He was younger than his wife. He had the look of a man who took great care for the comeliness of his body, oiled and plucked it to show it to best advantage, and exercised it to harden the smooth gleaming muscles.

The queen stroked his arm and smiled, but her eyes were on Nehsi, weighing him with clear intent. "You are beautiful," she said, "and wonderfully so. Do you have a wife, O beautiful one?"

Bastet spoke the words levelly, but her voice had roughened. Not much, not enough for most to notice, but Nehsi was attuned to its cadences. He glanced at her sharply. But she was being nothing and no one, wearing no expression, simply saying what she was told to say.

Nehsi answered, since he had been asked. "No, O queen. I have no wife."

"Shame," said the queen of Punt, "that a man so beautiful should have no wife to keep him virtuous. Are you a great lion of the bed-chamber, then, O prince?"

"Lions," said Nehsi, "are lazy beasts, drowsing the day away. It's the lionesses who hunt and fight and rear their young."

"Just so," the queen said. "But the lions will fight when they must, when the lionesses are occupied or overmatched. Then he comes, their great-maned king, and conquers all their enemies, and sires sons upon the bodies of his queens."

Nehsi flushed under the blessed darkness of his skin. "I have been a warrior, lady, and a guardsman of the one who was then my queen. My sons are at home in Egypt, learning to fight and hunt and rule a domain. My daughters—"

"Such as this one?" the queen inquired.

Nehsi caught himself before he whirled roaring on the one she smiled at. He turned with dignity.

There was Tama, whom he had thought safe under armed guard in his ship, peering from behind a guardsman's kilt. The man—boy, if truth be told—looked as startled as Nehsi.

"Papa," said Tama in the ringing silence. "You forgot to bring me."

"I did not—" Nehsi caught himself again. He jabbed with his chin. The guard, blushing furiously, reached to catch her. But she was gone, darting across the tent, coming to a halt in front of the queen of Punt.

Nehsi suppressed a groan. Before he could swoop down on her and clap a hand over her mouth, she said in her clear uncompromising voice, "I've never seen anything like you before."

Bastet, damn her, rendered the words in the language of Punt— at least, she must have done, because the queen laughed. It was wonderful laughter, richer even than her voice in speech, like deep music. "Come here," she said, and beckoned.

Bastet did not need to interpret that. Tama, who could be perfectly obedient when she had a mind to be, did as she was told. She climbed into the lap amid those billows of flesh, and she let herself be embraced, and did not either shriek or object.

The queen held her at arm's length, looking her over with evident approval. "You do your father justice," she said. "You'll be a beauty when you're grown."

"No one is as handsome as Papa," Tama said. She frowned. "Why does Bastet have to talk for you? Can't you talk like a normal person?"

"I know a little Egyptian," the queen said, "but not enough. Would you like to teach me?"

Tama nodded.

"Well then," said the queen. "Ask your father if I may borrow you while he tarries here. He might say no, mind you. A father is well advised to keep his daughter close."

"With that child," Nehsi said, "such a feat is near impossible."

"I'll come and teach you," said Tama, "but I have to be with Papa, too. He needs looking after."

"So do all men," the queen said, "and beautiful men in particular."

"Papa is the most beautiful man in the world," said Tama. "I'll teach you. First you must learn to say my name. It is Tama. Sometimes people say Tamit, which means 'she-cat,' but my proper name is Tama."

"Tama," said the queen of Punt obediently.

Tama nodded. "You learn well," she said, sounding so exactly like the tutor Nehsi had hired to teach his sons their letters, that he resolved to interrogate the man when at last he came home again, and discover how often his imp of a daughter had intruded on her brothers' lessons.

The queen of Punt was pleased: she looked almost comely as she smiled. "I shall be a good pupil," she said to Tama. And to Tama's father: "Rest if you will; eat, drink, ask for whatever pleases you. I'll return your daughter before evening."

Nehsi opened his mouth, shut it again. When he spoke, it was hardly more than a sigh. "As you wish, O queen."

41

TAMA WAS AN ADMIRABLE AMBASSADOR to the Queen of Punt. Nehsi, resigned but watchful, sent a man with her who carried no weapon but who was strong enough and skilled enough to defend her.

It was not that Nehsi feared she might be attacked. But he did not know these people. They might reckon that he had given his daughter to their queen, and be dismayed when he wanted her back again.

He did not try to prevent her going to the queen. That was admirably done; worthy, if he dared think it, of his own king.

While Tama taught the queen to speak a few words of Egyptian, the rest of the embassy traded splendidly with the people of Punt. Their beads and gowns and mirrors were received as if they had been gold. In return they gained all the wonders that the captain had spoken of, and more.

Nehsi had made it clear that he would be most pleased to trade in the glory of this country, the incense-trees that made the air so richly pungent. They brought him boughs and bundles so strongly scented that the nose gave up in despair. They took him to the hills where the trees grew. He stood in the midst of them and looked about, and knew what he truly, honestly wished to do.

"Can these be taken back with us?" he asked through his interpreter.

His guides murmured among themselves, taking so long about it that he grew impatient and was about to speak. Then the leader of them said, "For that, we must ask the queen."

She was with Tama, as always. She greeted Nehsi in Egyptian, and not too terribly accented, either; though those few words clearly exhausted her store of knowledge. Thereafter she spoke through Bastet— or through Tama, who in teaching this queen her own tongue had become astonishingly fluent in the language of Punt.

Through the two of them Nehsi presented his petition. "My king loves myrrh beyond any other unguent," he said, "and cherishes the trees that grow in her garden. It would be a great gift to her, and great joy, if we were to bring back such of the trees as our ships can carry."

"That is a great thing you ask," the queen said. "The trees are our greatest treasure. If we give them to you, you'll not come back to trade with us again, or to make us rich."

"On the contrary, O queen," Nehsi said. "My king would promise, I'm sure, not to plant the trees save in her own garden, nor to trade in their fruits or their seed. These would be for her own pleasure, and for her delight."

"Well," said the queen. "And you would promise to come back often, and trade with us?"

"For myself I may not promise such a thing," Nehsi said, "but for my country I can do it. You have known Egypt for time out of mind. It will be pleased to trade with you, and not only for your incense-trees. Your riches are immense and beautiful, and much to be desired."

"Your words are sweet," the queen said, "and your daughter is delightful. I'll not trade for my trees, O prince. I'll give them to your king as a gift. This is the sun-god's country; she is his daughter. I'll send her this remembrance of him, and of us who also are his children."

■ When the queen of Punt gave a gift, she did not give it by halves. A handful of days after she had announced the giving of the gift, as Nehsi went down to his ships from the camp that they had made on the strand near the town, he found them in uproar. On the shore stood a very fleet of carts, each drawn by a team of donkeys; and in each cart, wrapped with as great care as the mummy of a king, lay a shape of root and bole and branch, redolent of temples.

Thirty-one myrrh-trees. Thirty for the king's pleasure, and one because, as its tender declared, it would pine for its grovemate else. They were wrapped in spells and in the goodwill of the people of Punt, sustained by their own earth packed carefully about the roots. Nehsi himself saw them laden in his ships, a few for each, and each with its attendant, to look after it and cherish it until it came to Egypt.

He had lingered because there was so much to do, and because the queen had grown so fond of Tama. But the season advanced, and he yearned for his own country again; and even more than that, the face of his king.

Once the yearning began, it sharpened to pain. A poor explorer, he; he traveled so long and so far, and in the end he fell ill of homesickness.

He thought he concealed it well. He even spun out his departure in proper and courtly fashion. The most difficult part of it, the return of Tama from the queen's house, he left till nearly last. But time ran on, and he had to go. His ships were ready, their cargo laden and stowed, even to the trees that stood up like strange masts. All that was left was to gather his people, and to bid the people of Punt farewell.

There was a feast, the night before they would depart. The king and the queen of Punt spread tables in the Egyptian fashion, but as always, in their own way: under the same pavilion in which they had first received Nehsi's embassy, its walls rolled up so that it lay open to the breezes. The tables were strewn with flowers, the serving-maids clad in them and in precious little else. There was a whole ox roasted for their pleasure, and a whole sheep, and a procession of other and stranger beasts and birds, fruits, greens and roots that grew in the earth.

Nehsi sat beside the queen of Punt. Tama was in the queen's enormous lap, being fed dainties and spoiled horribly. There had been no discussion as yet of her departure. Cowardice on Nehsi's part, perhaps. If there must be a battle, he preferred that it be brief.

It was a grand feast. His people had got on well with the people of Punt; there were friendships made, alliances confirmed, and not a few women who would weep when the ships set sail. One or two sailors had come to him begging for leave to bring a wife on the voyage home. Nehsi, who had not been born a fool, sent them to their captain. As he had expected, they slunk away, heads hanging. Sailors loved and left women wherever they went. A woman of Punt, abandoned in Memphis or Thebes, might well have cause to curse the man whose love ran cold as soon as he set eyes again on the women of Egypt.

Not that the ships would be empty of people from Punt. The trees had their attendants; and the king had asked that one of his sons be permitted to join the voyage with his wives and his servants and a prince or six, to come as envoy before the king of Egypt. That, Nehsi could hardly refuse. His ships would be laden to the limit, and would sail the slower for it, but it would be a triumphant return, gods willing, to the quays of the Two Lands.

Tonight, his last night in the God's Land, he knew the stabbing of regret. He would not be sorry to leave the heavy heat, the perpetual strangeness, the people whose language he had never properly learned to speak. And yet he had grown fond of this strange country. It was like a living temple of Amon.

"Truly," he said to its queen over the feast, "the sun-god blesses this land with his presence."

She raised her brows. "Ah; so he's spoken to you, then."

"I'm not worthy of a god's notice," Nehsi said, "but I feel him here. It's the incense-trees, I'm certain. He loves their scent above all others. It's meat and drink to him."

"Indeed," said the queen of Punt, indulgent as a mother whose child, albeit slow-witted, comes round in time to a proper understanding. She embraced Tama, who was still in her lap, and kissed her. "This child could be raised under the god's eye."

There; at last. Nehsi let his breath out slowly. "So she shall be," he said with care to betray none of his tension, "in the courts of Egypt, where the god's child is king."

"Egypt is mighty," the queen said, "and beautiful, and blessed by the god. But here is his heart and his home."

"She has been greatly blessed, to sojourn for a while in the god's own country."

"She might be blessed beyond measure, were she to be fostered here, under the god's eye."

"That is a great honor," Nehsi said, "and a generous offer. But she is Egyptian. She will grow to womanhood in Egypt where she was born."

The queen ran a finger down Tama's dusk-dark cheek. "Egyptian, O man whose name means simply 'Nubian'?"

"Her mother is a lady of Egypt," Nehsi said levelly, "and I was born in Thebes. My blood and face are of Nubia. My heart is wholly Egyptian."

"Tell me, little one," the queen said, looking into Tama's wide-eyed face. "Are you Egyptian?"

Tama nodded.

"Would you like to stay with me?"

Nehsi held his breath. Every instinct of outraged fatherhood cried to him to snatch his daughter away. But he was his king's voice in Punt, and this was the queen of that country. If he offended her, he destroyed everything that he had wrought.

But he could not give up his daughter. She was the one of all his children who looked and, gods help her, acted and thought like her father. He loved her. He could not give her away.

Tama looked from the queen to her father. She did not seem perturbed, nor in any way confused. She said clearly and without evidence of doubt, "I like you very much. You learn Egyptian very well. But I can't stay if my papa goes. He's my papa."

The queen regarded her with an expression that Nehsi, who had always prided himself in his ability to read faces, could not comprehend at all. "Fathers send their daughters to fosterage often, even in Egypt. It's useful. It helps them to win alliances and to become rich."

"Papa is already rich," Tama said. "I do like you, lady dear. I want to come back and teach you again. But I have to go home. Nurse will be upset if I don't, and Papa will miss me."

"I could make you stay," the queen said.

"I'd run away," said Tama. She slipped from the queen's lap, neatly eluding the hands that reached to catch her, and climbed into Nehsi's arms. From there she looked gravely at the queen of Punt. "I'm going wherever Papa goes."

Nehsi braced himself. If there was to be a rising of armed men, his people were unarmed. Even the king's soldiers had left their weapons on the ships, all but the small knives they used for cutting meat.

They would fight as they could, and escape in such order as they might. The ships were ready. It was ill luck to sail at night, but if they must, they must.

The queen did not rise, did not denounce him, did not command her men to fall on his and destroy them. She remained where she was. Her broad unlovely face with its beautiful eyes was empty of expression. It was unlikely that she had ever been denied anything that she wanted: such was not the common lot of queens.

At last she spoke, heavily, wearily, with sadness that might have tugged at Nehsi's heart, had he had any choice but to be the cause of it. "It is clear to see whom she loves best. That's well, I suppose. A daughter should love her father. The god blesses her for it."

"You are generous," Nehsi said, "and wise."

She shook her head. "I am practical. I know that I could have you seized and killed, but she would only hate me for it. And you would never suffer me to take her and keep her."

"That is wisdom," Nehsi said, "as befits a queen."

The queen shrugged. "One does what one must. Promise me at least, that if she can, she will come back."

"If she can," said Nehsi, "she will."

It was not much of a promise, but it was all she asked for. He would be sorry to see the last of her. Her body was grotesque, even hideous, but her heart weighed heavy as gold on the scales of justice.

42

THEY LEFT THE LAND OF PUNT IN the heavy warmth of the morning, riding a fair wind northward on the breast of the sea. Tama, clinging to the lookout post on the stern of Nehsi's ship, wept to leave her friend.

The queen of Punt sat long on the strand, mounted on her absurdly pretty little donkey. Her figure shrank slowly behind them, nor ever moved, even to raise a hand in farewell.

■ It was a long voyage home, heavy as their ships were, laden with splendors. They sailed as far from land as they might, on guard against raiders; when they had to put in to shore for water or provisions, the king's soldiers at last earned their bread and beer. Word had flown northward that the king of Egypt's ships returned from the incense-country, and that they were rich beyond the dreams of a simple tribesman.

Strong arms and keen bronze and Amon's blessing protected them. They lost a man to an arrow on the stony shores not far north of Punt, wrapped him tight in linen and perfumed him with myrrh and brought him home with the king's trees, but no one else took harm. Nor did any storm vex them, though the wind blew strong enough to fret Nehsi for the welfare of the trees he carried so carefully.

Day by day they sailed closer to Egypt. When they came at last to the mouth of the king's channel and found it open still and running strong with the flood, Nehsi stood on the deck of his ship and cried thanks to Amon and to the river-god. He flooded high yet again in the king's honor and for the passage of her heavily laden ships into the Bitter Lakes, and past them to the river of Egypt.

In their own country they eased at last. Even the sailors, heavily taxed by the labor of rowing and sailing against the current with the river at flood, sang for joy. Red Land and Black Land opened arms to embrace them. The river spread broad before them.

A full year they had been away from Egypt, and yet it might have been but a moment. It was all the same. Cities of mudbrick and brilliantly painted and gilded temples, white blaze of light from the pyramids on the western shores of Memphis, rich black fields growing green as the river receded from its flood.

They sailed the length of Egypt, all the way down to Thebes. There at last Nehsi saw the change that a year had wrought. On the western bank, where had been a stretch of barren desert and sudden crag looming above the temple of an old king, something new and splendid had taken shape.

The king was building her temple at last, the one that she had dreamed of while she was the queen regent. It would honor her while she lived and remember her when she was dead, and sing the praises of the gods in stone.

When Nehsi left it had been a stretch of newly leveled earth and little else. Now it spread wide against the loom of the cliff, opening its arms about a great ramp that led upward to a broad colonnade. Already pillars rose against the fierce blue of the sky, only a few now, but a promise of the many that would come.

He with his one-and-thirty myrrh-trees, his gold and ivory and ebony, monkeys, hunting-dogs, lionskins and panther-skins, shrank small indeed beside that great work of the king's mind. Her mind, and the hand of her beloved, her man of many titles, the brilliant and gods-gifted Senenmut.

They were waiting for him on the quay of Thebes, the king and all her ministers in their finest array, with music and dancing and songs of welcome that were almost audible over the roar of the crowd. Of all of them, Nehsi saw only the one: the small straight figure beneath the Two Crowns. She was more beautiful than he remembered, and more splendid; he had forgotten the light of her eyes.

He bowed down at her feet. She raised him up, great honor and hardly unexpected, but the touch of her hand made him tremble. Her smile was kingly restrained, and yet his heart knew that, had she been even a little less royal, it would have been a broad and joyous grin. "Nehsi," she said. Only his name; but he needed no more than that.

■ His gifts delighted her to no end. The myrrh-trees in particular: she welcomed them as if they had been princes, addressed them one by one, promised that she would set them in the garden of her temple, as the god her father willed. "You will worship him in joy and gladness," she said to them, "and send your savor up to heaven."

She feasted him, of course: three days it lasted, and his companions were made as rich as princes. The prince of Punt with his three wives and his lords and attendants were made most welcome, given a house to live in while it pleased them, and made free of the Two Lands of Egypt.

It was all grand and glorious. But when it was ended, when Nehsi looked again at becoming the queen's chancellor and her servant, the ships and their captains and crews went back to their roving and trading, the scribes to their places in the House of Life, and the lesser ambassadors to the daily round of the court.

And Bastet the interpreter, Tama's erstwhile nurse and companion, prepared to return to her father's house near Bubastis. She had grown silent again as they sailed deeper into Egypt. He had not seen her at the feast. She was living somewhere, surely, but he did not know where. He would have thought that she had gone home to her father, but a niggle at his heart told him that she was still in Thebes.

He did not know why he should trust such a thing. He was not the kind of man to whom gods spoke, nor did he have the gift of knowing things, as Bastet did. But this he knew. She was still in Thebes.

It need not have mattered. She had done her duty, and done it well. The king had rewarded her richly. She could go home, share the wealth of the king's gift with her father, and still have dowry enough to entice a prince. He was pleased for her. She was his friend, after all.

Not that they had ever admitted to friendship. Dinners shared, and adventures with his imp of a daughter, and long hours of trading and treating with the people and princes of Punt, all made the word itself unnecessary. It simply and purely was.

A friend would not leave Thebes without bidding farewell to her friend. Her silence troubled him, her absence from the celebrations, her retreat into nothing so much as sullenness. He understood it, or thought he did. Her year of glory was over. Now she must be plain unembellished Bastet again, daughter of a minor lord in Bubastis.

If he felt bound in chains, albeit chains that he had chosen, how tightly constricted she must feel, who was a woman, and young, and nobly if not royally born. It had been an ill thing, maybe, to set her free for so long. No person of rank in Egypt was free: of duty, of obligation, of service to the king.

Thinking on all these things, rising from his bed in the morning after the third day of feasting, Nehsi soothed his pounding head with good plain Egyptian beer, and called for his bodyservant. He would bathe, he thought, and dress plainly, and go hunting for Bastet.

■ It was not so very long a hunt. He found her in his own house, sitting in the garden, watching Tama play with the monkey that she had brought back from Punt. Her expression was oddly fierce. When she turned her eyes on Nehsi, they were furious.

He refused to recoil from anger that he had done nothing to earn. He sat on a bench near her under an arbor of roses from Asia, and took time to breathe the sweet intoxicating scent. Tama was teaching the monkey to set pebbles in orderly rows, for what purpose Nehsi could not discern; but it seemed high and serious.

Bastet, having seared him with her glance, went back to glaring at the child and the monkey. Nehsi allowed the silence to stretch. It was peaceful, in its way. His own house about him, Egypt's sky overhead, Egypt's earth underfoot: he was happy, even in Bastet's manifest unhappiness.

When she spoke she startled him. Her voice was sharp, as angry as the rest of her. "I have to leave tomorrow. I don't want to."

"Then why do you leave?"

"What else can I do?"

"Marry me."

Nehsi had not meant to say that at all. He had never even thought of it. But there was his tongue, running on ahead of him, and she staring at him as if he had turned into the Queen of Punt.

He refused to swallow the words. He let them hang in the air till she must answer or go.

She did not answer, precisely. She said, "That is an interesting notion."

"Preposterous, I'm sure," he said.

"Rather." She frowned at her feet in their gilded sandals. New, he noticed. She must have been enjoying the fruits of her new wealth. "I don't suppose it's my dowry you're after."

"I am not," he said, "the sort of man who can never have enough of riches."

"I hadn't thought so."

She was not angry, either. He had half expected her to be furious; to rail at him; to call him every kind of fool. Instead she sat quietly, not too far from him, watching Tama play with the monkey.

"Is it," she asked after a while, "because you need someone to rein in your daughter?"

"I honestly never thought of it," he said.

"I'm good at it," said Bastet. "Except when I'm busy being your voice-in-the-air with foreign queens."

"That is so," Nehsi agreed with careful blandness. Careful because for all her studied calm, she thrummed with tension. He could not tell whether it was because she wanted him, or because she loathed the idea and could not bring herself to say so.

Though it was unlike Bastet not to say exactly what she thought. She asked him, "Do you remember when I first met you, how I was then?"

"Vividly," Nehsi said. And he did. Her silence; her refusal to utter a word. Tama had coaxed her into speech, just by being Tama.

"I was thinking," Bastet said. "It takes me a while to think, sometimes. What I was thinking was that, sooner or later, I was going to marry you."

Now it was Nehsi's turn to stare at her in flat astonishment. She seemed unaware of it. She was watching Tama and the monkey, both of whom seemed perfectly oblivious to the conversation that went on above their heads.

"You were so beautiful," she said. "The most beautiful man I'd ever seen. I couldn't speak. What could I say, that wouldn't make me sound like a fool?"

"You never sounded like a fool to me," Nehsi said.

She seemed not to hear him. "And I was remembering who I was, what rank I had to claim. And you a great prince, the king's most faithful servant. You'd never look at me. I wouldn't, if I were as beautiful as you, and as noble, and as great in respect. And of course I'm so young. An infant, really. Nothing worth your attention."

"So," he said. "Was that why you took on Tama? To get my attention?"

Her eyes flashed on him, caught all off guard, as furious as he could ever have wished. "Of course not! That was a thing that needed doing—and patently no one else was going to do it."

He grinned, startling her straight out of her temper. "Of course not indeed. I've thought many of the same things. You are beautiful, you know; and will be breathtaking when you're older. Were you a homely child?"

"Horrible," she said. "Gawky and gangly. Bones everywhere."

"So was I," Nehsi said.

She glowered at him. "You're indulging me. You think I'm just a child."

"I think you may find me old and tedious, once you've opened your eyes to other and younger men."

"Never," said Bastet with perfect certainty. "Yes, I'll marry you. On one condition."

Nehsi raised his brows.

"No other wives. Only me."

His brows rose higher. "What, are you so jealous as that?"

"More," said Bastet. "I know how many women you have here, how many you've had—and how many mothers have borne you children. There'll be no more of that while I'm your wife. If you're to have a new crop of children, it's I who'll bear them for you."

"Now it is very odd," he said, musing half to himself, "but I was in Punt for a year, and never lay with a woman. I don't believe I've gone so long without since I was a boy."

"Maybe," she said, "you've lost the art."

He growled. She showed him her teeth. "Witch!" he said. "You laid a spell on me."

"Not a one," said Bastet.

"Your face is spell enough." He took it in his hands. Such big hands, such a little face, big-eyed and pointed-chinned like a cat's. He meant the kiss to be the lightest touch, a brush of lips on lips; but she was of another mind altogether. She was fierce, and hungry enough to startle him.

Yet they did not embrace, did not fling one another down right in front of Tama and the monkey, and eat one another alive. It was a simple kiss, if such passion was simplicity.

He had hunted waterfowl as they said in Egypt, with many a courtesan, and many a lady who put the courtesans to shame. This was a child clearly, a maiden, artless and untaught. Yet she was not shy at all, nor afraid, nor in awe of him for his size or his age or his rank. She had known him for a year, with no more between them than friendship, and never less.

Somewhere between kiss and kiss, she said, "Do you remember the storm on the sea, that raged for three days, and we were all certain that we would drown?"

He nodded. "Who could forget?"

"That's not what I remember," she said. "I remember when it was over, you went out of your cabin and went to help the sailors. Your kilt was wet—everything was wet. You let it drop and went naked. The way you dropped it, the way you walked away, the pure and simple splendor of you . . . I thought that I would die."

"I thought," Nehsi said after a pause, "that you were asleep."

"No," she said.

"And I thought," he said, "that you never saw me at all, except as someone who was pleasant to talk to."

"I made sure you thought that," said Bastet.

"Clever," he said. "Wise, I suppose."

"I did try to be wise," she said. "Maybe I shouldn't have."

"I like a woman who is wise," said Nehsi. "I've always wanted one for my wife."

"Yes, but do I have to be wise always? May I be silly now and then? For variety?"

"Certainly," said Nehsi.

"Good," said Bastet, and kissed him again, almost chastely, but such fire that he gasped. He, the prince, the great lover of women. "But you still haven't promised," she said when it was done. "No other wives or women or lovers. Only me."

"You drive a hard bargain," he said.

"I have to," said Bastet. "I'm very jealous. If you had another woman, I think that I would kill her."

He could believe that. Cats were small and delicate and sleekly graceful, but they were hunters. They killed; and what they killed, they ate.

Well. He had been called lion and panther, and both of those were no more than outsize cats. "Very well," he said. "Only you."

"Then I'll marry you," said Bastet.

<hr />

43

THE WEDDING OF NEHSI THE NUBIAN was a splendid affair, and a mighty shock to the women of the Two Lands. The men were mildly startled, too, but less so than their wives and daughters. Anyone who had seen the young woman from Bubastis could well understand how she had captured the Lion of Nubia. And after a year in Punt, too, with her on his very ship—they nodded wisely, and looked at their own wives, some of them, and sighed. Of course a man who looked like that would marry a beauty.

They married in a festival that put to shame the king's welcome of the travelers, and settled down to producing sons and daughters as handsome as themselves. Those, with Nehsi's elder offspring, made a noble tribe, an army born and bred to serve the King Maatkare.

Senenmut, childless by his own choice and the gods' will, and wifeless, too, looked on them and sighed. He had been ferociously jealous of Nehsi for winning the prize of the expedition to Punt, but while Nehsi was gone, Senenmut had bent himself to a great and glorious labor. He built the temple that the king had dreamed of, Djeser-Djeseru the beautiful, at the gate of the Red Land, with its face to the rising sun.

He chose the beauty of simplicity, but simplicity transmuted into art. There was a temple already in the place that the king had chosen, tomb of a king who had died half a thousand years ago. Senenmut set his own king's temple beside it, in harmony with it, because the land desired it. He built a causeway, a long ramp rising up to the height on which he built the temple.

There on that height he raised up a forest of pillars, each a simple fluted column, plain to starkness in itself, but beautiful as it marched in ranks with all the rest. He built his temple of light and shadow, and within it, in the two great courts, he set yet more colonnades, and avenues of sphinxes, each of them bearing Hatshepsut's face.

The temple was full of her. She was everywhere, carved in kingly majesty among the marching pillars, painted and limned upon the walls, circled within the beauty of her names and her royal titles. If she must be king, then she would be king and king again, for as long as her temple endured.

The Horus, powerful of souls, the Two Ladies, rejuvenated of years, Horus of gold, divine of appearances, King of Upper and Lower Egypt, Maatkare, son of Re, Hatshepsut who joins with Amon.

In the shrine of Hathor beyond the courts of the sun, the goddess' image wore her face, her peculiar beauty that to Senenmut was the only beauty there need ever be. In the shrine of Anubis the guide of the dead, she was remembered over and over. Even in the storerooms, the priests' houses, the secret corners and crannies, he carved her name.

And he carved his own, and his likeness with it, even in the shrine of Amon, in the niches where the priests would keep the sacred vessels; everywhere that a name or a face could be carved. It was beyond presumption. Yet he had to do it, for her sake. She must not be forgotten. In forgetfulness was death, death of the spirit.

He knew what Egypt did to kings who defied tradition. It let their bodies die in the natural order of things. Then it killed them in memory: effaced their names, rendered them as nothing, forgot them utterly. So it had done with the foreign kings who had ruled not so long ago, but whose names were all forgotten—banished, destroyed by the vengeance of those who came after.

Egypt would not kill Hatshepsut. She would live while her name lived, and while her temple stood—and he would live with her. If there was a word for a commoner who believed himself worthy of remembrance even as was a king, then it was not written or spoken in Egyptian; but it must exist in some language, somewhere.

He explained to the gods why he did it, lest they be angry. Amon in particular, her father to whom she prayed every hour of every day, heard him out, or at least did not strike him dead where he stood. "I love her, you see," he said. "I want to live as she lives, and protect her, even beyond the gates of death. She will never look after herself as I can, in carving our names everywhere, and our faces, so that we never die."

It was not an explanation that any priest would accept. Senenmut, Steward of Amon in the Two Lands, knew that very well. A god, however, might be more supple of mind.

Certainly Senenmut was not prevented, even when he built his secret place, the tomb of his body with its passage that ran beneath the very temple of his king. He had another in the valley where princes were laid to rest, and that one tenanted already by his father and his old nurse—and, great grief in this time that should be triumphant, both of his brothers.

Amonhotep, the young, the beautiful, died of a fever that he had caught while boating on the river. He stayed out too late; night-demons caught him and carried him off in a great wailing of women. He had been going to marry a wellborn girl. She wept over his coffin, and had to be carried from the tomb by maids with fans and fainting-potions. Not half a season later she was married to a princeling from the south, and happy in it as far as Senenmut ever heard.

So much for fidelity, he paused to think.

That was grief. But when Ahotep died, Senenmut came near to dying with him.

It was even less fair and just than Amonhotep's fever. Ahotep went with a company of the king's soldiers to preserve order in Asia. He should have remained in Thebes, but the wife whom he had married in such joy had soured into a termagant. A child might have softened her, but the gods were never so kind. She screeched in his ear till she deafened it; and then he had won himself a captaincy and gone to Canaan.

He died there, not even in battle. He was drilling troops under the sun that was never so strong as that of Egypt, and he fell down dead, as if struck by the arrow of a god. He had done nothing to offend any divinity; his general had taken great care that Senenmut should know that. He was simply and irrevocably gone, laid in the tomb that Senenmut had built for himself. Senenmut laid him there with his own hands, opened the senses of his body, limned his name with stark simplicity: Ahotep, whom he loved.

Tall, strong, handsome Ahotep who was all that Senenmut was not. Senenmut remembered him so, in the pride of his manhood; but in youth, too, gawky and exuberant, and in noisy, uproarious childhood. All that he kept in memory, in his house that echoed empty, with his mother Hat-Nufer wandering grey and lost and old, and Ahotep's wife gone silent. His death had done what his living self had never sufficed to do: it had quelled her.

Senenmut had meant to cast her out, but in sight of her wan quenched face he could not bring himself to say the words. Thus she stayed; and when she faded, as she did with grievous swiftness, she too was laid in the tomb by her husband's side.

It was full, that tomb, overburdened with grief. But the one where he meant to rest, his great tomb, great enough for a king or for a king's beloved, was his deepest secret. The men whom he hired to build it were sworn with great oaths to betray the truth to no one. He bound them in the name and the power of Amon himself, secured by the names of Anubis and the judges of the dead. Warded in terror, oathbound to silence, they made him a tomb worthy of a king. In its deep chamber he painted with his own hand a sky full of stars, so that he might remember even in death the march of the seasons and the wheel of the sky over the land of the living.

He did it for her. He told himself that, and the gods, too. He would be her guardian spirit. Had he not sworn that he would die and go before her?

He did not tell her everything that he did. She would understand, he did not doubt it, but what she did not know, she could not be guilty of. Nor did he confess his fears for her. Those she would scoff at, and not gently. "Amon defends me," she would say as she often had before. "He will see that I live forever."

Senenmut would see that Amon kept that promise. That power was given him by the queen's will and the god's gift.

■ She was grown great in her kingship; but she was still Hatshepsut. Senenmut had heard someone whisper that she took her vitality from the king whose regent she had been.

He still lived, and grew from boy to youth to man in silence that might have passed for meekness. Hatshepsut endeavored not to repeat the mistake that she had made with her daughter Neferure. She gave him somewhat to do. She left him his weapons and his soldiers. And she made him a priest of Amon, one of those who offered incense before the god—incense from her own trees that her embassy had brought from Punt. It was a minor office, but necessary; for it was the scent of myrrh that nourished the god and sustained his presence.

Thutmose endured. Senenmut could find no other word for it. When it was required by tradition or by policy that both kings show themselves before the people, he put on the crowns and lifted crook and flail and sat enthroned beside the elder king. Otherwise he went quietly about his ways, interfering in nothing, saying nothing. Being a cipher like his father, Hatshepsut observed in scorn that had abated not at all since he was a child and she his regent. Biding his time, Senenmut was inclined to think.

"Then why does he do it?" Hatshepsut demanded when Senenmut was unwise enough to voice his thought.

They were in her temple then, inspecting the completion of Hathor's shrine with its many images of the king. Hatshepsut, the living Hathor, as she was Horus and Isis and own daughter of Amon, stood before the goddess, but her thoughts were on her lesser king. "Why does he bow his head and suffer me, if he is not the mooncalf he seems?"

Senenmut noted with part of his mind that her voice echoed oddly in the newly completed space. He would need to alter it a little, soften the echo, transform it into a whisper of sacred mystery.

The rest of him focused on what she had said. "Maybe," he said, "he can see as clearly as any other man in Egypt. He recognizes the light of Amon in you."

"A light in which he is singularly lacking." She paced the paving of the floor, stroking her foot along it, taking note of its smoothness.

"We should do the shrine of Anubis in black granite, don't you think? It would be striking."

"Indeed," said Senenmut, who had other intentions for the chapel of the jackal-headed god.

She knew what that particular blandness of tone meant: her glance was swift and rather wry. "You will of course do as you think best," she said, "for glory and for remembrance."

"Indeed," Senenmut said again, but warmly this time; a warmth that made her smile before she turned away, intrigued by the carving about the base of the goddess' statue.

44

WITH THE DEATHS OF HER TWO younger sons, each so close upon the other, Hat-Nufer began to fade perceptibly. When her husband died she had kept her strength. He had always been so vague, so gentle a presence; his absence diminished her but little. But her sons had been the world to her.

She who had seemed indomitably ageless grew gaunt and grey. Her voice was seldom lifted in its old strong outcry against shiftless servants. She kept more and more to her chamber, too weary, her maids said, to get up or dress, though she would be bathed and clean even in extremity.

Senenmut, eldest and last alive of her sons, gave her what joy he could. It was difficult. He was busy; caught up in the queen's temple, her tomb, her recent and powerful conviction that she must be buried with her earthly father, which meant opening old Thutmose's tomb and shifting his grave-goods and seeing a new coffin made for him, inscribed with his daughter's name and her reverence. Senenmut was as full of Hatshepsut as her temple was, and there was little left of him for his house or his servants or even his mother.

He tried to visit Hat-Nufer every day, usually in the evening after the day's work was done. She was always dressed for him, a wig on her head, her face painted and a golden collar about her neck. He could not fail to see how thin she was, or how transparent the skin of the arms that reached to embrace him.

He told himself that she would rally. She was Hat-Nufer, the lady of the house. His brothers' deaths came nigh to breaking them all, but Senenmut had recovered. She was older, that was all. He, so much younger and with so much to engross his mind, had to come out of grief or fail in his queen's service. She had no such escape. But time would heal her, and exasperation with the servants' slackness.

He did what he could. He visited her each evening; he saw to it that the servants came to her for their orders; he tempted her with this dainty or that from the king's table, with the king's complicity. Hat-Nufer was never gracious; that weakness was not in her. But she ate what he brought, or tried, and she dealt with the servants. His house continued in reasonable order.

Nevertheless she was fading. Part of her had gone into the tomb with each of her men who died. There was not enough left to keep her strong.

One evening she was not in her chair in her wig and her gown, waiting for him to come and pay his respects. Her maid tried to tell Senenmut that the lady was resting; he could come back tomorrow. He set her aside still chattering, and strode into his mother's bed-chamber.

Almost he could not see her, she was so small and shrunken. Without her wig and her paint and her kohl she was a tiny, withered thing, her hair all grey, the skin of her face drawn close to the skull.

She was not dead, not yet, but he knew the scent of it, heard the flutter of wings in the shadows. Her voice was hardly louder than those, if no gentler than it had ever been. "I told that silly girl to keep you out. What do you want?"

"To see you, Mother," Senenmut said. He was master of voice and face at least, calm, matter-of-fact, betraying none of his shock.

She saw it regardless. "Yes, I look hideous. What do you expect? I'm dying. I'd hoped you wouldn't notice for yet a while."

"Until you were dead? Until then, Mother?"

"If possible," she said, "yes." She paused to breathe, and perhaps to compose herself. Not for grief or compassion; for anger. This weakness must vex her sorely. "I don't want you dripping tears in my face. Or hating me, either. I'm tired. I'll be glad enough to go."

"But," he said. "Mother, you aren't old enough to die."

"How old is old enough? I've buried a husband and two grown sons and a daughter-in-law. All that's left is you, and you have her." She did not need to say the name. They both knew whom she meant. "You'll miss me, I suppose. You'll need to get in someone who can keep the servants in line. Make sure it's someone sensible, who doesn't think you'll marry her just because you've put her in charge of the house."

Senenmut opened his mouth to protest that no one would look after his house unless it was Hat-Nufer, but that was foolish and he knew it. He said instead, "I'll see if there's a man who'll do it. Apuhotep, who's been managing the horses—he has a pack of sons. One of them might be looking to raise himself in the world."

"Apuhotep's not too incompetent," Hat-Nufer conceded. "His wife is a sensible woman. If there's not a son who can do it, see if he has a daughter. A woman is always better for managing a household. She's tougher. She sees more and tolerates less."

"But," said Senenmut, "she might think she has hopes of better things."

"Not if she has any sense," Hat-Nufer said.

"I'll send to Apuhotep in the morning," Senenmut said, "and ask if he has a suitable prospect."

She nodded. Once it would have been brisk. Now it was weary, and her face was paler than it had been when he came in. "Good. You're not trying to tell me I can do it all. Have you come late to sense, or are you just in a hurry?"

Senenmut realized that he had been standing, looming over her. He drew a stool to the side of her bed and sat on it. "I have all the time you need."

"Well," she said, hardly more than a sigh. "That's not much. Don't let the king work you too hard. She trusts you, which is good, and makes good use of you, but she forgets to allow for the little luxuries: food, sleep, time to yourself."

"I don't forget," Senenmut said.

Hat-Nufer snorted. "You have the worst memory in the world for such things. Left to yourself, you'd starve to death. Maybe you do need to find yourself a wife, if only to keep you fed and make sure you sleep."

"I think not," Senenmut said gently.

"I didn't think so, either," Hat-Nufer said. She sighed and closed her eyes.

As simply as that, as easily and as quietly, she slipped out of the body. He felt her let go, as if she had been holding her souls bound until she said all that she had to say; and having said it, without pause or farewell, she left him.

He looked down at the husk of her as it lay in her bed. It was empty. No life burned in it. No breath stirred.

"I expected you to linger," he said. "I should have known."

Her body returned no answer. Nor did her spirit upbraid him from the shadows. He set a kiss on her brow that was already growing cold, and went to summon the embalmers.

■ He would not feel empty; could not indulge himself in grief. He had too much to do. All his kin were dead. Only he was left. He, and his king.

He did not close up his house in Thebes. His rank and his titles required that he keep it. But he was in it seldom, except for appearance's sake. It was too empty of living presence; too full of memories. His days he spent in building tomb or temple. His nights he slept in the palace, in his lady's arms.

She grieved for Hat-Nufer as he could not seem to do: wept at the news of her death, and mourned at her funeral. Senenmut did not know that there had been liking between them, but respect there certainly had been. Hat-Nufer would have been pleased to be seen to her tomb by a king, though she would never have admitted it.

And when she was truly gone, Senenmut shut and sealed the door of his tomb. He would not lie there. His place was elsewhere, within reach of the queen's temple.

It grew in beauty, shining under heaven. Its walls and its colonnades were all complete. Only the smaller things were left: the carving of an inner chamber, the painting of a wall or two, the planting of the king's myrrh-trees in their sunlit garden. The scent of them as they were set at last in their places, their roots uncovered gently and then covered over again, their branches spread in homage to the sun, was so strong that it perfumed the whole of the temple. The priests hardly needed to burn incense; the living fragrance wrapped them all about.

So it was in the whole land of Punt, if the embassy's tales were true. Senenmut had had that journey carved in the temple, drawn from the young scribe's scribblings on the backs of the ship's accounts. There was the city in the water; the men with their plaited and kingly beards; the women with their great rumps; the king in his beauty and the queen in her monumental ugliness, marching in procession before the strangers from Egypt. Senenmut was not a jealous man, nor enduringly petty. He could make Nehsi's expedition immortal by carving it in stone, for the glory of their king and the remembrance of those who had traveled so far to bring back such riches.

■ The completion of Djeser-Djeseru, the beautiful temple, sacred to Hathor and to Hatshepsut the king, was a festival to rival the return of the voyagers from Punt. The king herself dedicated the temple to Amon and to Hathor and to Anubis the guide, jackal-god, guardian of the dead. Her face stared back from every wall and every image therein. Her name was carved everywhere that a name could be carved. Let Egypt try to forget her: this temple would remember, from outermost colonnade to innermost shrine, and even to the tomb that lay hidden and secret beneath, with its sky of stars and its images of Senenmut who loved the king, the golden one, the Horus, Maatkare Hatshepsut.

45

A T AN AGE WHEN MOST WOMEN BEGAN to grow old, Hatshepsut seemed to have entered her prime. She had reached her fortieth year. She was King of Upper and Lower Egypt, secure on her throne, blessed by the gods, beloved of Amon.

On a morning not long after she celebrated her natal day, she held audience as always. It was a propitious day according to the calendar, excellent for those who came seeking justice. She had decided a contention between the lords of two nomes. She listened now to a woman and the man who was her husband.

"But I left him," the woman said, "because he took the daughter that I bore him and sold her."

"I told you," the man broke in, "that if the next one was a son, you could keep him."

"And the next one was a daughter," the woman said, "and you fed her to the crocodiles."

"I did not!" the husband said. "While you napped instead of looking after her, she wandered down to the river."

"And you pushed her in."

"She fell in. I tried to catch her."

"You didn't try very hard."

"*You* were asleep and snoring!"

"Your pardon," the king said mildly. Her voice was light and not particularly loud, but it penetrated the wall of their quarrel. They seemed to remember where they were, and who she was: smallish slender woman sitting above them, wearing the tall crowns. They fell on their faces.

"Oh, please," she said, "do get up. Madam, you wish what? To be divorced from this man?"

"No," the woman said; and hastily, as an afterthought, "majesty. I want him to let me keep the next baby, no matter if it's another daughter."

"You want to remain married to this man?" Hatshepsut asked.

The woman shrugged. "He's all right. He doesn't beat me often. When he does, I usually deserve it. He just won't let me keep my babies."

"Do you beat him?" the king asked.

"Sometimes," the woman said, "when he deserves it."

"So then," said the king. She turned the force of her gaze on the husband. "Why did you take her children away from her?"

"It was only the first one," he said. "We had a good harvest, but locusts came and ate it. We had no stores: we sold them to buy a team of oxen, and the oxen took sick and died. The baby was pretty. The headman from the next village down the river, his wife was barren and pining for want of a child. They paid us a whole year's worth of barley, grain and seed both, for the baby. She grows up a headman's daughter, maybe gets lucky, marries a scribe. Her daughter maybe marries a lord. And our blood goes up in the world. Instead of staying on a no-ox farm that barely gets flooded except in a good year."

"Did you have such foresight when you did it," Hatshepsut asked, "or did it come to you after?"

He flushed under the sun-darkened skin. He was not as old a man as he seemed, Senenmut realized, watching from behind the throne. Sun and famine and hard labor had toughened him to leather. He was probably no more than twenty years old. In his sudden shyness, his stammer as he spoke to her, for a moment he looked like the youth he was. "I—great lady, great king, I did what I had to do. We had to eat; and there was another baby coming."

"Your daughter? Does she prosper?"

"I hear she does," he said.

"You haven't seen her?"

"Lady," he said, "I work a no-ox farm. She's a headman's daughter. Her like doesn't look at the likes of me."

"I saw her," the wife said. "She was as plump as a little river-horse.

She has a nurse, as if she were a princess, and a whole box of toys to play with."

"Then you concede that she is well served by what your husband did to her?"

The woman nodded. But she said, "I want to keep my children. They're mine."

"So they are," Hatshepsut said. She beckoned to Senenmut. "Here, see it written. Two oxen for this man who speaks so honestly, and a farm's worth of barley seed, and the blessing of Min on his fields. For this woman, all children that she can bear and raise, as long as she and her husband can feed them."

"And if they cannot?"

"They do what they must," said Hatshepsut. She took up crook and flail and crossed them over her breast. "The Great House has spoken. So let it be done."

■ "Your name is blessed in the hovels of the poor tonight," Senenmut said as they lay together. There had been no passion tonight; simply the warmth of shared presence, and the comfort of conversation.

She shifted in his arms, sat up and clasped her knees, looking as young as she had been when they first were lovers. Her body was softer, but only a little, and only a little less slender; the breasts were high still, her face unlined. The years had been kind to her. She had not hardened as a woman could who ruled over men. She was as beautiful as ever, and fully as beloved.

She frowned, pensive. "They may curse me," she said, "when famine takes them again, and the oxen get sick and die, and he has to sell another baby to keep the family fed."

"You expect that?" he asked.

"No," she said. "But it will probably happen. Ill luck likes a familiar face. Meanwhile they praise me and bless me and worship at my feet."

"That's as it should be," said Senenmut.

Her eyes flashed on him. "Don't you start flattering me! I get enough of that from my courtiers."

"Of whom I am one," he reminded her.

"Yes, and you carve my name everywhere, and call me king and goddess, more beautiful than anything in the world. That's policy, my love. A king has to do it in order to continue as king."

"People believe what they're told to believe," Senenmut granted her. "But you are king. You are goddess. You have done well by your people. Egypt is prospering. Neither flood nor harvest has failed since you took the throne—that poor man and his bad luck notwithstanding."

"Sometimes I wonder," she said, "how long it will go on. Seven years of prosperity, we've had. Won't there be seven years of want thereafter, to preserve the balance of the world?"

"Only if you fail to please the gods," said Senenmut. "And that, I don't foresee. They'd have struck you down seven years since, if they disapproved of what you've done."

"Gods' time is not as ours," she said. "It may have taken them this long to notice."

A shiver ran down his spine. It was only a breath of air through the room, chilling him in his nakedness. "The gods have noticed," he said with as much confidence as he could muster. "They've blessed you with riches. They've smiled on your judgments."

"I hope so," she said. Her frown did not lighten. "In the sunlight I know that it is so. In the dark, when the shadows crowd upon me, I wonder. My father, the man who loved my mother, who raised me—what would he say if he saw me as I was this morning? How angry would he be?"

"He called you his little king," said Senenmut. "I think he knew."

"I do try to propitiate his shade. I give him offerings. I built a new tomb and set him in it, to lie beside me when my time comes. He'll roar at me, Senenmut. He always roared when he was angry."

"Has he been roaring at you in dreams?"

"Sometimes," she said. "I'll be my small self then, committing some infraction or other—eluding my nurse to play with the horses; hiding behind a pillar in the hall where he holds council. And he'll roar, and call me scapegrace and worse. And then," she said, "he'll sweep me up and hug me tight, and say I should have been a boy; I've got gall."

"There, you see," said Senenmut. "He approves. He finds it outrageous, as what dead king would not, but he's no more able to deny you than any living man."

"That's how I do it, you know," she said. "I don't let myself think that I'll be denied. And I'm not. But every time I do it, every time I push the limits—I wonder. Will it end now? Have I gone, at last, too far?"

He slid closer to her, wrapped arms about her. She was cold and much too still. Her back was rigid. "Then why do you push?" he asked. "Why do you do it?"

"Because I can't do otherwise. You used to tell me I was mad. I am, you know. The god makes me so. He's a fire in me. He wants so much of me, dreams so much through me . . . sometimes I think there must be nothing left, that I've burned to ash."

"There is everything left of you," Senenmut said; meaning it, too. "You're stronger now than you ever were. Stronger, wiser, more beautiful."

"More flattery," she said, but she was warming, softening to his embrace. "I shall have to invoke him again, remember him in the Two Lands, bind my name with his so tightly that no one can divide us. He shores up my strength. In him, as in Amon who begot me, I find my kingship's heart."

■ She slept after that, which surprised Senenmut somewhat. He lay awake. Was it that after all she grew old? Or was her fire growing cold? It had never been like her to worry that she was not strong enough.

Maybe she always had; but she had never had the courage to say so. It took strength to confess one's weakness. She loved him, trusted him, but she told no one everything that was in her heart. She must always be king, always goddess; the mortal woman was allowed the pleasures of the flesh, but doubts and fears . . . those she had never admitted.

Not until now. She was strong, and she was king. If there was any whisper of rebellion, Senenmut had not heard it. Those few who had protested her crowning, who defended the young king against the one they called usurper, were long gone. Mutterers in corners had fallen silent, or had succumbed to her will.

She must be on watch constantly. He was part of that, he and the people who served him. But every king lived so, on guard against ill-wishers and worse. They were disposed of. The king was protected. So the world went, whether the king was safely male or most unsafely a woman.

He mounted guard over her sleeping body. If he could have guarded her dreams, he would have done that. He loved her beyond measure, lived for her, even endured this kingship, because she believed that it was Amon's will. The tale of her mortal father was built on air and half-formed remembrance, but that she was Amon's daughter, she believed implicitly.

It was not his place to doubt it. Such light and fire as were in her did not come from any earthly source. Amon had begotten it; or close enough.

"Father Amon," Senenmut said softly, lest she wake and be troubled. "Watch over her. Defend her. Protect her from harm."

46

"MY FATHER AMON," SAID THE KING, "has set in me a longing; a yearning to do a great thing."

Her counsellors regarded her in varying degrees of wonderment. They knew her too well to be astonished, but when she spoke as she did now, they had learned to expect the unexpected.

As always, she gave it to them. "I shall embellish his temple," she said: "his great house that you, my lord Ineni, have made. Look you, how a king raises a shaft up to heaven, inscribed with his names and the names of the god and the king's reverence and his deeds for the god's glory. I shall do just such a thing—but since I am I, and there is no one like me, I shall raise the highest that has ever been.

"An obelisk that reaches clear up to heaven," she said. "A pillar of the sky. I shall cast it in electrum, in gold and silver mingled, as precious together as either alone."

Her treasurer, Thuty the endlessly precise, made a strangled sound. She arched her brows at him. A lesser man might have quailed before the utter blandness of her expression, but he said without hesitation, "No."

"No?" She had reared like the cobra in her headdress, golden hood flared, deadly and beautiful. "No? Am I not the richest king in the world?"

"You are not rich enough," said Thuty, "to cast an obelisk in electrum. You might have enough gold for it, mind you, if you make it smaller than the ordinary; but you'll have nothing left to pay the workers, and as for keeping the kingdoms in funds . . ."

"You are a petty-minded counter of barley-grains," she informed him. "For my father's glory, should I not do what no one else has done before?"

"You could," said Senenmut, evolving the thought as he uttered it, "build it of stone and sheathe it in electrum."

She pondered that, eyes narrowed, painted brows knit. "Stone, you say? From where?"

"Aswan, I think," he answered. "The good red granite, that can be cut whole from the living rock, and carried on barges into Thebes."

"Yes," she said, still musing on it. Her eyes brightened. "Yes. Yes, that could be done. And more than that. *Two* of them. Two pillars of heaven. Since gold is so scarce, says my treasurer, and stone so plentiful."

"If you do two," Thuty said, "there's not enough gold and silver to sheathe them both. Tips only. Twelve baskets' worth. That's all."

It was great vexation to a king to be so constrained by the niggling of her treasurer; but Hatshepsut could not have forgotten that it was she who had objected to the trouble and expense of her husband's wars. She bowed, if not with grace, then with resignation. "Very well. We'll do what we can. We'll do it quickly. A year, no more, for the honor of my father's name."

"Why?" Ineni the builder demanded in Thuty's ringing silence. "Why so brief a time?"

"Because," she answered promptly, "if it were too easy or too slow, it would never be as great a sacrifice."

"A year," said Hapuseneb, shaking his head. "And two of the things. I don't envy the man who has to do it for you."

"I won't," Ineni said. "I'm not a madman. I won't work myself to death, either."

"I will," Senenmut said—heard himself say it, as if he had nothing to do with it. He was not thinking at all. He was seeing in his mind's eye the temple of Amon at Karnak, that vast and arrogant place, terrible in its beauty. And she would add to it; would proclaim her kingship in the most virile way of all, with a twofold monument.

As if her temple, her Djeser-Djeseru, were not enough. This was pure vaunt, bravado bare.

"I'll do it," he said. "A year? I'll give it to you in half of that. Only give me men, and time to prepare. A month—I'll have it all ready and set to begin."

"You are as great a fool as she is," said Ineni with a curl of the lip.

"Probably," Senenmut agreed, amiable as he always was with Ineni, because it drove that prince of builders to distraction. "Djeser-Djeseru is finished. I need something else to engage my mind."

Ineni sniffed loudly. He had not been asked to build the king's temple. That was her dream, and Senenmut's. He had dug her tomb instead, and set her father's body in it. He grew old; he was not often now in Thebes, but in his mansion near Abydos, resting, fishing, hunting waterfowl. "A man needs rest," he said. "You'll get none if you carry out your boast."

"Oh, I'll rest," said Senenmut. "When I'm done, when the king's obelisks stand in the temple, I'll rest as I never have, not even when I was young."

■ "Don't kill yourself," the king said to Senenmut. He had spent the day and half the night drawing the plans for the undertaking, and spread a blanket in a corner of his workroom, and roused at dawn to begin again. By the time she found him, someone—he never remembered who—had persuaded him to bathe and shave and change his kilt. He was presentable, if hollow-eyed.

At first when she came in he did not know her. She was a stranger, a lady of the court in wig and golden headdress; her face in its mask of paint could have been anyone's.

But her voice he knew, and her hands tugging him away from his worktable, pushing him into a chair, holding a cup to his lips till he drank. Braced for wine or beer, he nearly spat out the cool clean water that was in the cup.

"I've never seen you like this," she said. "Your assistants are saying that you're possessed."

"By what?" he asked, honestly curious.

"They aren't specific," she said. She sighed a little, and though the room was open and anyone passing by could look in, kissed him softly on the lips. There was no passion in it. It was simply love, and worry that surprised him.

"Oh, come," he said. "You've shown me a task that's worthy of me. I'm delighted with it."

"Djeser-Djeseru wasn't worthy of you?"

"But that's done," he said. "It rises in beauty; it gladdens my heart. I could fiddle with it, I suppose, and work on the tombs, and pass the time in small things. This, now—this is a great work, a grand challenge. To quarry the stone, carve it, sheathe it in bright metal, raise it in your father's temple, and all within a year, is a feat that men will remember for a thousand years."

"You have a year to quarry the stone," she said. "That was my boast."

"And mine was half a year," he said.

She shook her head at him. "You'll have all that you need," she said. "Whatever it is, ask, and it shall be given you. My treasurers have their orders, and my masters of works. What I wish to inscribe on the stones—"

"I know," he said. "It will all be done. Do stop fretting over me. I'm happy. I'm always like this when I'm happy."

"Are you glad," she asked, "that you will be gone from Thebes for half a year, and away from me? Do I bind you too tightly? Do you need to be free?"

He stared at her. His mind, which had been running on through the reckoning of men, wages, and materials, stumbled unwillingly to a halt. "What ever makes you think that?"

"When I sent Nehsi to Punt," she said, "you sulked for months. You wanted to go. I wondered then if it was the glory you longed for, or the respite from me. Now you leap into this undertaking with grand glee. What else am I to think but that you need to be apart from me?"

He suppressed a sigh. "Oh, lady. Oh, beloved. You understand what it is to want glory, to want it so badly that you'll sacrifice any-thing for it—even tradition so hallowed with years that no one dreamed it could be broken. This I do for you, for the splendor of your name; but for myself, too. I want it. I need it."

"So," she said, a little wearily, a little wryly. "You are a man after all, and I am a woman. You yearn for great things. I yearn for you, and dread the parting."

"I'll come to Thebes as I can," he said, "if I can. And when it's over I'll come back to you. That I promise you."

She nodded slowly. "I surprise myself," she said. "I don't want you to go."

"You could," he said, "send someone else. Ineni, Hapuseneb—"

"No," she said. "You'd hate me for it."

Since that was true, he did not answer.

She embraced him with sudden fierceness. "Look after yourself. Re-member to eat and sleep. Don't wear yourself away. A year is more than soon enough."

"Half a year," he said, set on it, determined to do it.

■ With the full power of the king's name and a free hand in her trea-sury, Senenmut gathered a force of laborers several thousand strong, with all that they needed for the work ahead of them. The king sent great logs of cedar and sycamore; boats and barges for the men and their tools and provisions; smaller luxuries: tents, blankets, even a lovely young thing with a lute and a smile, who said that his name was Har-mose. He had a sweet voice, and he seemed to know every song that had ever been sung in Egypt. Senenmut called him guard and nurse-maid, dog and servant, spy for the king. Harmose only smiled and tuned his lute, and sang a song of a dog and a monkey and a tree of fruit.

Harmose was not the only king's man who followed Senenmut to Aswan. Thuty the treasurer came too, to keep the accounts. Amon-hotep, an older man than Senenmut's brother of that name who had died, who had been Senenmut's right hand in much that he did since Hatshepsut took the Two Crowns, was Senenmut's second yet again, and capably so.

And Nehsi came, the king's chancellor, bringing his wife but leaving all but one of his tribe of offspring behind, the dark beauty who was his daughter Tama. They were escaping, and rather gleefully, too. Senenmut was ready to begrudge the Nubian's presence—*he* had not been allowed to sit in Nehsi's shadow when Nehsi went to Punt—save that Nehsi came to him not long before they left Thebes.

It was not uncommon for the king's chancellor to visit the king's master of works on this errand or that. But Nehsi had not come to Senenmut's house except on the king's errands, nor had Senenmut invited him. They served the king together as they might; they respected one another. They were not, however, friends.

On this morning Nehsi came not as the king's man but as himself. Senenmut received him over breakfast, which, because he was courteous, he offered to share with Nehsi. The Nubian declined to eat, but did accept a cup of beer, which he drank with evident enjoyment. "It's good," he said.

"Yes," said Senenmut. "It's made on my estate. The brewery's nearly as illustrious as the horses."

"I had heard of it," Nehsi granted him. "Its reputation is deserved."

Senenmut nodded. He spread a round of bread with softened cheese, and ate it not because he was hungry but because the king would ask her Nubian if Senenmut had eaten, and Senenmut did not want to vex her with yet more fretting for his welfare.

Nehsi drained his cup of beer, declined a second. Senenmut ate his bread and cheese. When the silence had grown almost intolerable, Nehsi said, "I don't suppose you're delighted that I'm coming to Aswan."

"I can't say I am," Senenmut said.

"You know she worries," said Nehsi. "She was going to send Hapuseneb, but he told her to send me—and ordered me to bring Bastet.

She's an excellent lady of the household. She's offered to oversee your house, and to take over such duties as you may find tedious, with as much as you have to do."

"That is generous of her," Senenmut said.

"She is fond of you," said Nehsi.

"One wonders why," said Senenmut.

Nehsi shrugged. "Who can fathom the mind of a woman? I'll tell you true, it wasn't my doing that I was given this duty. They conspired between them, my wife and the king. They think you'll be well served if I do whatever needs doing, under your command of course, and completely at your disposal."

"And you? Does that gall you?"

"No," Nehsi said. "I think you may be mad to think you can do this as quickly as you promise—but I'll do my best to help you."

"Why?"

"Because," said Nehsi, "the king loves you. She's afraid for you. She thinks this will be too much for you."

"Everyone does," Senenmut said with an edge of irritation. "Do believe me: it isn't."

"She believes you," Nehsi said, "or she would never have let you do it."

"And she sends you with me, to make sure my nose is wiped and my kilts are clean."

"That's Bastet," said Nehsi with the glimmer of a smile. "I'm to keep the workers in order, and oversee the overseers."

"Leaving what for me to do? Sit on a hill and watch?"

"I've never been a builder," Nehsi said, "nor a carver of stone. Men I know. Stone, wood, the shaping and building of monuments—no. That I leave to you."

"That's fair enough, I suppose," Senenmut conceded after a while. "She frets too much, and gods know why; but I confess, I could use you. We'll need every good man we can get, to do what we have to do in the time we're given for it."

Nehsi inclined his head. "I thank you. You are generous."

"Don't cherish any illusions. I'm practical. Tell your wife that I thank her for her offer, and I'll take it; provided that she promises not to fuss over me. I hate to be fussed over."

"So do I," said Nehsi. "I'll make her promise."

"You do that," said Senenmut.

When Nehsi had gone and Senenmut should be going himself, he lingered for a while. That was not a friend, he thought; but neither was it an enemy. Fellow servant, that was it; and the king trusted him. So did Senenmut. Liking was no part of it, nor needed to be. Nehsi would do well by his king, and therefore by Senenmut. Senenmut was not sorry, after all, to have him.

47

THE SUN BEAT DOWN LIKE A HAMMER on bronze. The air shimmered with heat. Men shouted; hammers rang. The shapes of the two obelisks were drawn in the red stone of the quarry; the lines of men followed them, entering the mountain as they called it, hewing the great shafts out of the living rock.

Senenmut, seated on a hill under a canopy with the scribe Tetemre and the singer whom the king had sent to nursemaid him, watched with tight-drawn intensity the hewing of the nearer obelisk. Harmose plucked soft notes on the lute, each one like a drop of water falling in a pool. The sound of them was somehow comforting, a remembrance of coolness in that bleak and burning place. Nothing green grew here. There was only the red stone and the blue vastness of the sky, and the river beyond, the roar of its cataract almost drowned out by the clamor of the quarry.

There was a town just north of this place, a city as it was reckoned in these parts, hard upon the borders of Nubia. Its people mostly had Nubian faces; Nehsi for once looked almost ordinary, though no one that Senenmut had seen was as beautiful as that. Here most of the workmen were from farther north, but some had been brought in by the good offices of the governor of Aswan, who looked to share a little of the glory.

It was a sweaty undertaking, daylong, nightlong by torchlight. Senenmut had lost the memory of sleep. The men labored by turn and turn, day and night. The night laborers had nothing to fear from ill spirits: Senenmut had seen to it that a company of priests walked the quarries each night at sunset and midnight and in the dark before dawn, blessing them in the gods' name and casting out any demons that might be lurking.

They had begun one obelisk before the other, tracing the shape of it in the stone and setting two long lines of men to hewing it out. It was the tallest that had ever been, two dozen manlengths and somewhat more from base to tip. The raising of it would be an awesome thing. It would tower up to heaven, taller than the cedars of the Lebanon, taller than any other work of men's hands.

Senenmut confessed them to no one, but he had his doubts of this thing. It was too tall; it would break of its own weight. He should shorten it by a manlength, two, four, perhaps one more than that.

But he had begun it, and it was taking shape in the quarry below him. It was nearly freed of its surrounding stone. The men who had hewn it out had gone to begin the second shaft. Stonemasons were in the trench now, carving out the four sides. When it was lifted up and carried out to the river and thence into Thebes, it would be smoothed and polished, its sides carved with words as the king directed, its tip sheathed in electrum.

The crews were waiting with the rollers, the huge logs that the king had given, the sledges on which the shaft would ride down to the river. The barge that would carry it was tethered there, enormous beyond the belief of the boatmen who had flocked about it all the way up the river from Thebes. It dwarfed them. Its length was thrice the height of the obelisk; it rose towering from hull to upper deck. Nothing like it had ever sailed the river of Egypt; nor, Senenmut suspected, ever would again. It was built of precious sycamore, great beams gathered from the whole of the Two Lands of Egypt, sent here by the king to build the ship that would bear her obelisks to her city.

It was vast, enormous, huge beyond believing. It was purely Egyptian, and absolutely royal.

Down in the quarry, the chief of overseers, none other than Nehsi the Nubian in a kilt that shone in the sun, stark against the gleaming darkness of his skin, raised an arm in the signal that they had agreed on. The shaft was ready to raise from its bed. Senenmut sprang to his feet and leaped down from his eminence, with the scribe and the singer trailing behind.

Nehsi seemed in his element. He grinned wide and white as Senenmut halted panting at his side. It was hideously hot down here, like the breath of a furnace. He passed Senenmut a jar that proved to be half-full of beer—excellent beer, too. Bastet had lured Senenmut's brewer away from the villa, and brought him to this desert place to practice his art among the workers and their overseers. He was content, Senenmut gathered. Men who worked hard and long under the burning sun were marvelously appreciative of good beer.

Senenmut drank deep and passed the jar to Harmose who happened to be behind him—in his shadow as usual. It rather amazed him that he had stopped minding that perpetual presence. The sweet voice and the fine touch upon the lute had a great deal to do with it; and the boy's temper was as sweet as his voice. There was no guile in him that Senenmut could discern. He was simply and completely as he seemed: the queen's servant, given to Senenmut to keep him well and in comfort in this terrible place.

Harmose left a few swallows for the scribe, handed him the jar and wandered a little way down along the rim of the cutting. The carvers had drawn back. Strong men labored now to lift the shaft. The overseers' whips cracked. Men shouted, fierce, rhythmic: *"Heave and roll! Heave and ho!"*

Up out of the earth. Up, oiled by the sweat of a myriad men, lifted on ropes, balanced, hanging in the air, sinking down with awesome slowness onto the sledge that waited for it.

In the moment of its pausing, the cry of the workers paused likewise. And Senenmut heard it. A soft sound, hardly louder than the hiss of breath through his teeth. The cracking of stone.

He shut his eyes, but his ears could not stop listening. He heard the groan, the long exhalation of breath as the workmen saw what he had seen.

The obelisk had cracked. Its base was flawed. It sank back down into its bed, lowered by no command but by one common will.

Someone, somewhere amid the lines of men, uttered a brief and thoroughly heartfelt curse. He spoke for them all. So long a labor, so grueling in the sun—and all for nothing.

Senenmut sprang to the edge of the cutting. He had not known he had so much voice in him until it roared through the burning air. "Up! Up, go on, to work! We've two more to cut, and time's flying!"

■ "You're obsessed," Bastet observed. It had taken Nehsi and Harmose and Thuty and both scribes, Minmose as well as Tetemre, to drag Senenmut back to the house that had been given him in Aswan. He would never have left the working, but for them.

It was cool in the house, sweet with the scent of blossoms from the garden. Harmose played his lute while the high ones dined. There was wine, sweetened with honey and chilled in the river. All the men had bathed and dressed in clean garments, put on their ornaments, made a festival, though there was nothing to celebrate but the failure of their effort.

"We'll do it," Senenmut said to them, ignoring Bastet. "We'll have to double up shifts, that's all, and be more careful in raising the shafts from their beds. Though it could have been a flaw in the stone. We'll have to look, to see. If there's time."

"If you please," Bastet said, clearly and distinctly and in such a tone that even Senenmut could not shut his ears to her. "Tonight we are not digging stone in the quarry. We are enjoying a civilized dinner in a half-civilized place. Let us babble of trivialities. Let us sing; let us play on the lute. Let us be, for this brief hour, something other than workmen for the king."

"But—" said Senenmut.

"Be quiet," Nehsi said amiably but with inflexible will. "We'll be frivolous till the night is old. Then we will sleep. And in the morning we'll rise rested and go back to our labors."

Senenmut did not want to do that, but he was sorely outnumbered. He had to eat, drink, watch them be merry. Then he suffered their putting him to bed, all but sitting on him to be sure that he stayed there.

They left Harmose to watch over him. Poor Harmose: his eyes were black-circled even without the kohl that made them beautiful. More than once Senenmut saw him swallow a yawn. But he stayed grimly awake. Senenmut would sleep, his manner said, or Harmose would die making sure of it.

"Oh, do go to bed," Senenmut growled at last. "I won't get up before dawn. I promise."

"I don't believe you," Harmose said.

"What, do you take me for a liar?"

"No," said the singer. "I take you for a man who doesn't know when to stop. You're making yourself ill, trying to do it all at once."

"I am not ill," Senenmut said.

"Aren't you? You're skin and bone. I hear you coughing when you think no one notices. You coughed up blood yesterday. I saw it."

Senenmut shut his eyes. "Gods. Am I safe from nothing and no one?"

"Not if you kill yourself," said Harmose.

Senenmut covered his face with his hands. It was true. He had been coughing a great deal since he came to the quarry. It was the stone dust. It got into everything, especially a man's lungs. "That was dust," he said, "not blood. The stone is red here. So is its dust."

"I know the color of blood," said Harmose, innocent and obstinate. "You have the lung-sickness. I know all the faces of it. It killed my mother and my father and both of my sisters. Go to sleep now. In the morning I'm calling in a physician."

"You are not," Senenmut said firmly. "I am not ill. I've breathed too much dust, that's all. I'll wear my mantle over my face after this. Will that content you?"

"No," said Harmose. He spoke the word as eloquently as Hatshepsut herself did, and with as little yielding in it.

Senenmut sighed deeply. It caught on the bottom of his lungs. That was much higher than it should have been, and paved with knives.

He tried to swallow the fit of coughing, but it was mightier than he. It rose up. It conquered him wholly.

Harmose held him while he tried to cough up his lungs. Those arms were slender but they were strong. They were nothing like a woman's. He did not know why he should trouble to think that, except that the part of him that was thinking was very far away from the part of him that was coughing.

Mostly he was angry. Of all times to fall sick. He had months of work left to do, and the first of his obelisks had failed of its promise. He had no time to rest or to indulge infirmity.

"Don't," he struggled to say. "Don't tell her. She'll fret even worse."

The king, he meant. Harmose understood. "I have to," he said. "She made me promise."

"Then wait." That came easier. The fit was passing. It always did; he told himself it always would. Stone dust and a little catarrh. That was all it was. "Wait," he said. "Hover if you will, make me eat and sleep. But don't tell the king I'm sick. She'll half die of worry."

"The king needs to know," Harmose said stubbornly.

"When we come to Thebes is soon enough. She'll see for herself then, if there's anything to see. Now let me be. I'll sleep, I give you my word."

Harmose did not want to do as Senenmut commanded, but Senenmut set his jaw and his will and closed his eyes. After rather too long a while, Harmose left him. The footsteps went only as far as the door. He would sleep across the threshold, the fool. Senenmut let him do it. It was more effort than it was worth, to begin the argument all over again.

48

THE SECOND OBELISK ROSE CLEANLY from its bed, borne up by the will and the effort of the men who had carved it out. No crack marred it; it was perfect, though rough still, a raw shape of stone that would find shape and beauty when it was brought to Thebes. Its mate, the third that they had carved in this place, proved likewise unflawed. The one of them that had failed they left where it lay, a monument to their labor and a testimony to the magnitude of it.

Those that would go to Thebes, the gods willing, rode on sledges and rollers from their bed in the quarry to the river's side. That was much closer than it had been when they began the labor, almost half a year before. It was flood time, swelling time; necessary for the huge barge that would carry the stones down the river.

As long as it had taken them to carve the stones out of the earth, it was still more than a day or two or three before they were dragged and rolled to the barge. Then they must be lifted up the vast sides into the places prepared for them—without snapping of ropes or crushing of men or collapse of the ship beneath that massive and doubled weight.

The first was a breathless undertaking. The second nigh killed them all with apprehension. No one such stone had ever been cut or carried; and here were two, on a ship of such size that the mariners muttered of unbalancing from its height or of sinking from its burdened weight. Senenmut himself climbed up on the lofty deck, far above the water, and from that dizzy height did what he could to direct the moving and placing of the stones.

They must be placed just so, balanced with utmost delicacy, end to end along that vast length of barge. A hand's breadth too far to ei-

ther side, and the barge overturned, and the river had a sacrifice of all
their labor, their sweat and blood.

He prayed as the stones rose each from its sledge, swaying in the
light wind, borne up by the strength of every man who could grasp a
rope. He begged every god he knew to uphold the stone, to strengthen
the lines, to sustain the ship as it rocked perilously under the massive
weight. The groan of tortured beams was clearly audible above the
chanting of his laborers and the droning of priests who prayed as devoutly as he. He felt the shift of the barge underfoot, the precarious
moment when it could, oh so easily, have tipped on its side and cast
them all into the water.

It held. The stone rose. It poised on its enormous supports, swung
ponderously, sank down into the barge. "Farther back!" Senenmut
cried. "Back, I say! *Back!*"

Guided by his shouts and the bellowing of the foremen, the crews
settled the stones one by one into their cradles on the barge. It rode
low beneath the weight of them, wallowing in the water. But—all the
gods be thanked—it did not sink to the bottom. It had no grace, no
lightness. But it was, it seemed, seaworthy.

■ There was festival in Aswan that night, round about the bank
and the barge, by torchlight on the strand and by lamplight in the
workmen's tents. Senenmut honored them for a while with his presence. They expected it; they would have been distressed if he had refused.

In the morning they would begin the journey to Thebes. The
house in which he had been living was stripped bare, everything packed
and laden on a lesser boat that would follow the great one. He would
travel with the stones, of course. They were bound up in his essence.
Sometimes he fancied that they were the measure of his life, nigh on
forty man lengths, a scant handful less than the count of his years.

One thing was left to do before he mounted the barge—before he
could even sleep. The stonecarver waited in the quarry by light of
torches. Senenmut had marked the place. With brush and paint he drew
on the stone what the carver should carve: himself as he wished best to
be, bowing low before his king. Under it he wrote in passion that

seemed somehow fitting in this of all places, under the cold stare of the stars. He named her, gave her her beautiful titles.

Then he named himself. It was pride beyond pride, perhaps; the same pride that had caused him to carve his face and his name everywhere in Djeser-Djeseru. *Her dear companion,* he wrote, *much beloved, steward of her daughter Neferure, pleasing to the heart of the Lady of the Two Lands. All that I did, I did for her glory.*

When he had written it all, the carver came in with his chisels and began, meticulously, to cut and carve and limn. Senenmut lingered as long as he might. But the night was speeding, and dawn was not far away. He must be on the barge when the sun rose.

He felt light, as if he had wings. Earlier, before he came to this place, he had coughed a great deal. But standing here, inscribing his feat and his love on the everlasting stone, he knew no infirmity, no frailty of the flesh. He was all whole, young and strong, and his great work ready now to be finished in Thebes.

■ They made the passage slowly, their fleet of boats circling round the ponderous weight of the barge. Two-and-thirty boats drew it, and in each three nines of oarsmen. Skilled mariners and engineers, with priests and workers of magic giving such aid as they could, saw it through the swollen waters, the reefs of stones, the beds of reeds that reached to choke its advance. Senenmut on his perch oversaw them all, though there was little for him to do but watch.

Runners went every morning in relays to Thebes. The king was eager, waiting in her city. She had built the pedestals on which the stones would stand, prepared the temple for their coming, set in train the festival of their arrival. She had made of it a grand celebration, a royal jubilee. The Myriad of Years, it was called: the great affirmation of the king's power, the feast of its renewal, a beginning made again before the whole of the Two Lands.

The barge could not be hurried. Too much haste, the engineers insisted, and it would sink. It was shipping water at a rate that did not unduly alarm them, though it looked horrendous from below. It would come to Thebes, they promised, and its cargo with it. But not if it was pressed harder than its fabric could bear.

He endeavored not to fret. They crawled down the river. People came to see the king's barge go by, to stare at the stones it carried and to exclaim over the size of them.

And then at last, with the suddenness of all things that seem too long awaited, they came in sight of Thebes. Its walls rose up out of the Black Land, beyond the river's flood. Senenmut's own beautiful temple, Djeser-Djeseru of the western shore, shone before him. He sat poised as it were between his two great works, filled with a gladness that was almost too much to bear.

She was waiting for him: she and all the rest of her city, her armies, her navies, every strong man in Egypt, brought here to aid his laborers in the moving of the obelisks from river to temple. Those gleaming creatures, those beautiful young men in their soldiers' kilts, were so alien to his eyes after his naked or loinclothed, sinewy and unlovely but indomitable workmen, that he almost forgot her for staring at the massed ranks of them.

But she stirred, glittering under her golden canopy, and he ceased to be aware of anything else. The barge wallowing toward the quay, the mariners in their boats, the engineers calling out commands, the priests raising their chants and their incense, all faded and vanished before the light of her face.

She was more beautiful than he remembered. Here she was king and goddess, and nothing of the woman in her. But the eyes in the stillness of her face—those were vividly alive, fixing on him, drinking him in.

He could not tell if she was shocked. He had lost flesh, he knew, gone all leathery and brown; and several of his teeth had chosen these months to bid him farewell. He could hardly be a sight to gladden the eyes of such beauty.

And yet it seemed that he did. She did not smile; that was not a kingly thing to do. But her eyes were splendid with joy.

■ The work of lifting the stones from the barge and conveying them to the temple was nigh as great as that of bringing them down from the quarry. But where Senenmut had had only his crews of workmen, here he had the whole army and the navy, the men of Thebes, princes and commoners, priests and courtiers and idlers of the street. They were all caught up in the glory of it, leaping to offer a hand, to draw the king's obelisks to Amon's temple.

So many hands, so much eagerness, almost defeated itself. Senenmut and Nehsi between them, and such of the engineers as could fight their way through the crowds, made order of the tumult, saw the new workers and the old arrayed in ranks, and set them to the labor. Commanders of the army and captains of the navy helped as they could. In short enough order it was a useful working-party that had been shaping for an unruly mob.

The king could not in propriety set hand to rope and pull with the rest, but she could lead them, and encourage the women and the children to dance and sing, escorting them with rejoicing to her father's temple.

Joy, it was all joy. Singing, shouting, throwing the full weight of body and souls against the massive resistance of the stones. So compelled, inevitably they yielded. They rode up from the river. They slid through the gates into the vast pillared hall, the greatest in the world, huge almost beyond comprehension; but they were not dwarfed by it.

There, for that time, they rested. The people departed in gladness: high ones to the palace, commons to the streets and market-squares of Thebes, where the king's bounty had laid a feast.

For Senenmut it was all splendid, all glorious; and never mind that there was a great deal of labor still to come, what with polishing and carving the roughness of the stones, and sheathing them in electrum made from Thuty the Treasurer's doled-out baskets of gold and silver, and raising them in the court of the temple. For this day he could let himself be glad, because he had come home again, and she was here, and happy as he had never seen her, even at the building of Djeser-Djeseru.

■ "Did I do well?" he asked her.

They were alone at last, if not in each other's arms. That would come later. Now they had snatched a moment between feast and feast, run away like children to the wall that happened to look toward the temple of Amon, and stood hand in hand, concealed by the parapet, and gazed on the loom of the temple. Nothing from here betrayed the marvels that lay within. Later, when the obelisks were gilded and raised, they would shine from far away, like towers of light.

"You did very well," Hatshepsut said to Senenmut. She laughed as freely as the girl she had never been allowed to be. "Oh, you were glorious, riding in atop that great monster of a barge, with my stones at your feet."

"And I did it in half a year, too," he said: "and well for us I did. Even with the flood, it was hard going through some of those channels. I never saw such a draught on a ship before, and neither has anyone else."

"No one has ever done what you did," she said.

"What you dreamed," he said. "I was only the hands. Yours were the mind and the will. I did it for you, my beloved. Always and only for you."

"And for your own glory," she said. She leaned against him. With her royal emblems laid aside, she could have been any noble lady come to keep her lover company on the palace wall. Her eyes were on the temple. "I can see them now. The sun will rise between them, and send rays of light up to heaven."

He nodded. "Every morning they will remember you. Every evening they will catch the last light of the setting sun. They will stand for a thousand years."

"And a thousand more," she said, "and yet a thousand."

She turned still clasping his hand, and looked into his face. A little of the light had left her. She saw him now, rather too clearly. "Have you been ill?" she asked, direct as the thrust of a spear.

He shrugged. He thought of denying it. He had never lied to her; he could not begin now. "A little," he said. "Stone dust is hard on the lungs. I'll recover, now I've come home."

"You had better," she said. "You have a great task to finish. Then when that's done, I'll see that you rest."

"I do intend to," he said.

49

HEY CARVED THE GREAT OBELISKS in the court of the temple, much vexed by wanderers-in and gogglers-at until the king detailed a company of her guards to keep the crowds of the curious away from the workers. They shaped and polished and made them beautiful, and set on them the names of four kings: all three of the Thutmoses, none of whom could be slighted, and at the summit, sealed in electrum, the name and titles of Maatkare Hatshepsut.

By his will I did it, she had them carve in the hard red stone. *He led me, my father Amon. Well I knew the desires of his heart.*

There was one who wandered in nearly every day, but he could not be kept out. He came in his guise of a minor priest of Amon, a burner of incense before the god; but all the guards knew him, and Nehsi, taking command of them as often as not, forbade them to bar his way.

Thutmose had grown up well. He had no height; his was a line of smallish men. But he was solidly built and strong, and he looked uncannily like his aunt the elder king. A life of exercise in the training fields had bronzed his skin and strengthened his body. Beauty, alas, he would never have: his face was too odd, full-cheeked and narrow-chinned, with a jutting prow of nose. But he was an attractive young man, graceful in his movements, well known among the soldiers for his skill with bow and spear and sword.

He was nearly twenty now. By rights he should have emerged from the regency some years since. But Hatshepsut was king, and a king in the full pride of her youth and power did not step down for a younger king. He had sat through her feast of the Myriad of Years, watched her run the race that every king ran who would renew his strength and the strength of the Two Kingdoms. No one had read the expression on his face. It was pure and hieratic stillness.

In the temple, watching the stoneworkers carve his name and that of his father and grandfather, and of his aunt, too, he seemed much more a human creature. He was curious as any young man would be, asking questions where he could do it without interrupting, waiting with laudable courtesy for the answers.

The workers were not in awe of him. If he had come crowned and in his majesty, they would have fallen at his feet. But a shaven priest in a plain kilt, perched on a stray block of stone, watching bright-eyed as a painter outlined in vivid colors the glyphs that shaped his own name, Menkheperre Thutmose, was nothing to be afraid of. He was a living god, but this was the great god's temple. His presence here seemed somehow fitting.

He never spoke to the elder king's ministers who came and went, overseeing the work of the carving and gilding, nor did he acknowledge them beyond a glance or an inclination of the head. Except Nehsi. They had always got on well together, considering that Nehsi was wholly Hatshepsut's man.

It might be that Thutmose knew the virtues of silence. Nehsi, who had never been a chatterer, found it restful. They stood often side by side, Nehsi at ease but on guard, Thutmose watching the carving. Nehsi could not be there every hour of every day; he had duties that crowded close and filled his days from dawn till long after sunset. But he was there often enough, and perhaps it was the young king who brought him.

When they finished carving the third Thutmose's names and titles and set to work on Hatshepsut's, Thutmose happened to be present. He watched them limn the glyphs one by one, cutting carefully so that each stood forth from the stone. They had already carved the words of her royal vaunt, that she was more beautiful than anything in the world. He read that aloud, with the ease of one who reads well and quickly. When Nehsi glanced at him he said, "Do you believe that?"

"I believe that she is beautiful," Nehsi said.

"Oh, yes," said Thutmose. "But more beautiful than anything? Is she?"

"What do you reckon beautiful?"

Thutmose thought about it. It was this slowness, this deliberation of mind, that led people to think that he was slow-witted. But that, he most certainly was not. He could judge swiftly when he must: on the training field, at the reins of a chariot, on the hunt. It was only in speech that he came close to being hesitant.

After a while he said, "To me a horse is beautiful, running in the yoke of a chariot. The flight of Horus' falcon in the morning. A woman seated by a lotus pool, combing her hair."

"Why, you are a poet," said Nehsi.

The dark eyes narrowed, contemplating temper. But Nehsi was not mocking him. "I do not believe," Thutmose said, "that nothing in the world is more beautiful than that one." He paused. "Do you?"

Nehsi did not answer.

"Yes," Thutmose said, as if he had. "I shall never make such a boast."

"A king should boast of something," Nehsi said.

"Then I'll be the greatest king and conqueror the world has ever seen."

Thutmose looked as unmartial as it was possible to be, dressed as a priest and sitting on a block of stone left over from the carving. Still Nehsi was not moved to laugh. "That's a worthy vaunt," he said.

"She," said Thutmose, "speaks continually of peace. See, they carve it on her stones: how she raises them in peace, and proclaims her power through gentler means than war. What is wrong with war, that she sets herself against it?"

"She says that it is costly and wasteful of blood and spirit," Nehsi said.

Thutmose curled his lip. "That is woman's thinking. A man knows better. *You* know better. I've seen you in the practice-yards. You're a fighting man. And yet you bow at her feet."

"She is my king," Nehsi said.

The younger king regarded him sidelong. "And she always will be. Yes? That too I'll never understand. How men love her; how they fall down before her."

"Do you envy her?"

"No!" But then Thutmose said, more slowly, "Yes. Yes, I do. I watch how she wins men's souls. She does it so easily. A lift of the brow, a tilt of the chin, and every man's heart is in her hand. I have no such art, and no grace. If I try, men forbear to laugh—after all I am the king—but I see how their eyes mock me."

"No one laughs at you," Nehsi said, "even in his heart."

"Don't lie to me," said Thutmose. "I know what men say behind my back. That here am I, a man grown, and I suffer a woman to set her foot on my neck. I'm afraid of her, they whisper. I'm so much less than she; I can't move for fear of offending her."

"You would do well," said Nehsi, and his voice was cold, "to learn to be reasonable about her. She could have deposed you or had you killed. She did neither. She means you to be her heir."

"She despises me."

Nehsi could not deny that. He said, "So do you despise yourself. Be a man, my lord. Be as strong as your lineage allows you to be. You are not the least of the men of your line."

"I am still less than that one woman."

"She is older than you," Nehsi said, "and has ruled since before you were born. She learned the arts of kingship at your grandfather's knee. Your father, however noble his memory, was not greatly gifted in kingship. She ruled for him, and with his consent."

"She ruled well." The words seemed dragged out of him. Nehsi admired him for suffering himself to speak them. It was hard to tell the truth. "She . . . does . . . rule well. Better now than I."

"If you would test that," said Nehsi, "you might contemplate taking on your share of the kingship."

"My share?" Thutmose was sneering again, and not to his advantage. "My share is here, ladling incense into the burners for some greater priest to light. She'll never give me more. She dares not. For if she does, Egypt might remember: it has a second king. A king who is a man."

"You wait for her to give," Nehsi said, "when you could take."

"She would never let me take anything," said Thutmose with bitter certainty.

"Have you ever tried?"

Thutmose fixed him with a long and burning stare; then turned abruptly and strode—it could not be said that he fled—down that vast and pillared hall.

Nehsi watched him go with some regret. It had not been wise, perhaps, to provoke this of all discontented young men. A lesser man, a soldier perhaps, vexed to immobility by his women—yes. But the woman who wielded such power over Thutmose was Hatshepsut the king. Nehsi's lady. The one whom he would serve until he died.

Nonetheless it ate at him to see a spirit so stunted and embittered, and no need for it to be so. They had done ill who raised that child—and Nehsi counted himself among their number. On his own ground Thutmose was capable, even brilliant. But before Hatshepsut he could show none of it.

It was a curse, perhaps. A jest of the gods. Hatshepsut had worshipped her father, despised her brother-husband. That brother's son, she could not love or even respect. And he—perhaps in his heart he was desperate to win her admiration, even to love and be loved by her who after all was his blood kin; but nothing that he did sufficed. He would always be inept and stumbling, hopelessly awkward before her.

Yet, thought Nehsi, in himself this Thutmose was nothing like his father, and very much indeed like the great king his grandfather. No one chose to remember how that Thutmose too had been slow of speech except at need, deliberate unless necessity demanded that he act with blinding swiftness; and he too had seemed hesitant, even simple, to those who did not know him well. It was as if their minds worked so swiftly that their bodies could not keep pace.

Hatshepsut remembered none of that. With his daughter the first Thutmose had been at his best always, moved to match her quickness with quickness of his own. When she saw him in council, saying no word perhaps from beginning to end, she called it wisdom, and an art of ruling that let his counsellors talk themselves out. Then when they had reduced themselves to silence, he uttered a few firm words that settled everything; and they yielded to his kingly judgment.

She never waited for this younger Thutmose to do the same. Nor had time softened her contempt for him or his fear of her. Nehsi knew little of despair, but when he pondered the two of them, he knew something remarkably like it.

"What I fear most," he said to Bastet, "is not that it will go on for years as it is now, as ill a thing as that will be. No; I'm afraid it will change, and not for the better. He's a deep one, is Thutmose; and when he takes a thing into his head, he never lets it go."

"And he hates Hatshepsut." Bastet nodded. "I see it, too. I think everyone does. It scares me, how he sits so quiet and never says a word. Men like that—when they break, they shatter everything around them."

"She won't listen," Nehsi said. "I've tried to tell her; nor am I the only one. She won't hear us. Her husband was a weak-spined fool. She's sure his son must be the same."

"Well then," said Bastet. "If she won't do anything about it, then someone else must."

He stared at her. "No man can kill a king. The gods will destroy him."

"That was not what I meant," Bastet said, exasperated. "And you should know it. He needs to be kept occupied—the more, the better."

"A war would be just the thing," Nehsi mused.

"You know Hatshepsut will never agree to that," Bastet said.

"Pity," said Nehsi. "Asia has been restless of late. It's thinking of breaking itself free of us, I think."

"But she won't do anything about it."

"She is not incapable," Nehsi said, pricked almost to sharpness. "She simply does not see where war can be of any use."

"Even," said Bastet, "where it is. She's spent far more on these great rearing vaunts of hers, and on that temple she is so proud of, than her husband ever did on his campaigns. Sometimes I think Thutmose should get up his courage and tell her so."

"You know what she would tell him," Nehsi said. "She makes and builds; she rules in peace. The Two Lands are the better for what she does, and the gods are pleased, and bless her with prosperity."

"Maybe she should let him build a temple. Or lead an embassy."

"She won't give him that much power," said Nehsi. "She can't afford to."

"No," said Bastet. "But in the end she'll have to do something. He won't sit still forever, or keep bowing his head."

"Which is what I said to begin with," said Nehsi. He dug fingers into his aching temples. "Ah, gods. I don't know what to do."

She laid cool hands over his. "We watch him, and we do what we can to stop him if he shatters. That's all we can do."

He looked up at her as she stood over him. Sometimes, he thought, she seemed much older than he, who was still young enough that strangers mistook her for one of his daughters. "Are we presumptuous?" he asked her. "He's a living god. We're all too mortal."

"If the gods give us the gift to see, they expect us to use it."

It might be youth that made her so certain. Or wisdom. Or perhaps, thought Nehsi, both. He sighed and bowed his head. She worked fingers into the knots in his neck and back, rousing them to sharper pain, and then to a blissful ease.

If only this trouble of kings might be resolved as swiftly. There might be no help for it at all; no hope but to watch them play it out, even to extremity.

50

THE DAWN WIND WAS ILL, AND might be dying. Senenmut had left his mare, his beloved, his king's gift, at home while he labored in Aswan. She had been bred then and had come in foal. While he oversaw the sheathing of the king's obelisks in gleaming golden metal, she delivered herself of a handsome filly. The young one had done well, and the birth had gone as it should. The mare was up, nursing her foal, seeming well; but then, with deadly swiftness, she took sick.

When he was brought to her by a white and trembling stablehand, his master of horse was with her, and the man who looked after the mares and the foals. She was down, thrashing in the straw.

Someone, Senenmut noted with distant precision, had had the wits to remove the foal. An old mare who had lost her colt, but who had remained heavily in milk, had been persuaded to nurse the filly.

The Dawn Wind was beyond caring for the loss of her child. Senenmut was cursed with clear sight. He could not see hope where there was none. She had the foal-fever, and it was killing her.

She was only an animal—a horse, a creature who had never spoken a word, nor uttered a prayer to any god. And yet he grieved no less to watch her die than he had at the deaths of his kin. She had been born in his hands. He had raised her, trained her, cherished her companionship. She had been used to paw with her foreleg, demanding tribute, as imperious as any queen. Now she lay still, except when she struggled, senseless with pain.

She died with her head in his lap, too worn by then with pain to struggle against it. He smoothed her forelock, worked a tangle from her mane. The people who stood about had blurred in his sight. He had forgotten who they were. "Call the embalmers," he said.

One of them ventured to remonstrate. "Sir! They won't come for a horse."

"Call them," he said, and kept saying it until one of them obeyed him.

While he waited for the embalmers, he remained where he was. All the life was gone out of her, and yet her neck kept its silken softness. He rubbed it where it was stiff with sweat, grooming her with his fingers as she had loved to have him do.

Only a horse, he thought. Indeed. Only the companion of his heart, the joy of his days, a delight in memory when he was away from her. She had never grieved him, never caused him pain; had only loved him as a good beast can, with all her great heart. She was not even very old, still in the prime of her life, dead because he, the arrogant one, had insisted that she give him a foal to enrich his herd.

"She will guard the gate of my tomb," he told the embalmers when they came. "Wrap her well and surround her with words of power. When I come to the Field of Reeds, I would see her waiting there in her harness, with the chariot behind her."

The embalmers bowed to him. That was more than their usual reverence, but he had paid them extraordinarily well. They took up the mare, with no little muttering at the weight and the mass of her, and carried her away. He resolved to visit them on the morrow, to be certain that she lay in her own vat of natron, and for the full seventy days, so that she was well fit to travel into the Field of Reeds.

When they were gone and the Dawn Wind with them, Senenmut was seized by a fit of coughing. There were knives at the bottom of it, as was not unusual; but these felt as long as swords. He could not stop once he had begun. Blind, doubled up, spitting blood, he was still aware of hands on him, lifting him, carrying him away from that place.

■ Senenmut was infuriatingly weak, but not so much that he could not finish his labor with the obelisks. "I'm wearing myself out even more, fighting with you, than I would if I just went out and got to work," he snapped to Hapuseneb.

The First Prophet of Amon, who should have been far too lofty a personage to sit in Senenmut's bedchamber and bar his way to the door, fixed him with a disconcertingly level stare. "So stop fighting with me. Do you want another dose of the wine?"

Senenmut hissed in exasperation; or tried to. Everything he did seemed to set off another spasm of coughing. Hapuseneb held him up until the fit had passed, and wiped away the issue of it. He said nothing, only held the cloth so that Senenmut could see.

Blood. Of course there was blood. His lungs were full of knives.

"Just don't tell her," he managed to gasp.

"She already knows," Hapuseneb said.

"She doesn't, either. Or she'd be here."

"Well," said Hapuseneb. "We didn't tell her everything."

"Good," said Senenmut. Cursing, but silently, as he began to cough again.

He was dying. He could not seem to stop it. He called in healer-priests, who should have been able to do something useful; but all they did was raise a reek of ordure and put the steward of his household, the heretofore endlessly amiable Harmose, out of temper. Senenmut had to raise himself up as much as he might and dismiss them; and that prostrated him for hours after, while Harmose alternately sang to him and upbraided him for a fool.

One thing in particular he wanted, and would be outraged if he

could not have it. He wanted to see his obelisks raised in the temple of
Amon, set gleaming on their bases and towering up to heaven. Hapuseneb could not hover over him through every moment of every day,
and Harmose had to sleep, if only in snatches.

In one such respite, Senenmut prevailed on his servants to set him
in a litter and carry him to Amon's temple. He had always hated to
travel so, hot and stifling behind curtains, but in this extremity it was
a useful thing. No one could see him or move to prevent him.

The obelisks were nearly finished. One was tipped already with
gleaming electrum. They were sheathing the other as he came, doling
out the precious alloy with scrupulous care, covering the tip and no
more. All below it was beautiful with carving, with the names of the
kings, their titles, and Hatshepsut's own words wrought forever in
stone.

He laid his hand on the base of the first, completed obelisk. It was
enormous, seen so close: its thickness half again his height, its length a
dozen times that. It seemed impossible that a thing so massive would
be raised to pierce the sky.

They were already preparing it, readying the ropes and the scaf-
folding. The pillar was ready on which it would rest. They must take
great care: even as wide as that hall was and open to the sky, it was
forested with pillars. A false move, the slip of a line, and the great shaft
could come crashing down, taking with it half the hall.

Men of genius though his engineers were, they fretted appallingly
over his presence there. Everyone seemed to think that if he took to his
bed and forgot everything that he had ever been or done, he would
somehow, miraculously, be well again. No use to tell them that they
were fools. They could not help but know it; and yet they persisted.

As did he. Weak though he was, he was more stubborn than they,
with excellent authority over his servants. Each day they brought him
to the temple. He lay in his litter in a shaded corner and watched the
king's obelisks grow beautiful. Then with much shouting and straining, echoing in the holy place, they raised first one and then the other,
and set them upright where they had been meant to go.

It was as the king had envisioned. The sun rose between them. The light of them shone brilliant far up and down the river, marking the site of Thebes with doubled splendor.

She herself came to see them raised, stood motionless and exalted as they reared up within the roofless hall. She did not see Senenmut then, which was entirely as he wished it. This moment should be unmarred by fretting over mortal things.

But when her obelisks were raised, when she had celebrated the feast, the culmination of her Myriad of Years, and when the Two Lands were quiet again, returned to their round of days, she came to Senenmut.

He had not attended any of the celebrations. He would have wished to appear, to give her honor, but his body would not allow it. He could not rise or walk; could only lie in his bed, which he had his servants carry out of his dim and stuffy chamber by day and lay in the garden in which he had planted a myrrh tree, scion of those that grew in the garden of Djeser-Djeseru. He had never greatly loved that scent, finding it too cloying for his taste, but now it seemed to lessen his sickness. He could breathe easier for it. When he coughed, the pain seemed a fraction less.

When she came into the garden, he was lying in the shade in the half-drowse that was all the sleep he could have now. He did not mind greatly. Soon enough he would sleep and never wake. He was propped in cushions so that he could breathe, and draped in a linen coverlet. Like Hat-Nufer before she died, he insisted that he be clean, bathed and shaved and made presentable, so that he did not shame his servants.

He was glad of that insistence now, though it taxed him sorely. The horror in his king's eyes was for his thinness, his terrible weakness, and not for that he was squalid and stinking of sickness.

She swept toward him in a waft of perfume, so beautiful that he nearly wept. Her gown was embroidered with gold, her wig crowned with the Two Ladies, Wadjit and Nekhbet, serpent-goddess, vulture-goddess, protectors of Egypt. She must have come from some kingly duty: she had never visited him so before, in the daylight, as king and goddess.

She knelt beside him, heedless of her gown on the raked sand of the path. For a moment he thought that she would lift him and shake him. "I heard," she said, soft and furious. "At much too long last, someone had the courage to tell me why you slighted my festival. I had thought you merely obsessed, unwilling to leave your labors."

"I was," he said. His voice was barely there, but she heard him clearly enough.

"They kept me away from you," she said. "When I would have summoned you, they distracted me with sudden duties, or pretended that you could not be found. They lied to me. I'll flay them for it. I'll feed them to the crocodiles."

"Don't," said Senenmut. "I made them do it."

"Even Hapuseneb? Even that prince who is greater than you?"

"Hapuseneb is a sensible man. He knows when it's best to do as I ask."

She tossed her head like an angry mare. "You conspired against me. I could put you to death for that."

He laughed helplessly, though it racked him with coughing. He had to stop: she was terrified, and when the blood came she gasped. She did not shriek or burst into tears as a lesser woman would have done. She found the cloth where it always was, near his hand, and did what was necessary.

After the spasm had passed, he lay unmoving. His eyes had gone dark. His body had no power to stir itself. His souls struggled within it, the bird-winged *ba* and the shadowy *ka,* held captive still by the struggling breath; but the bonds had grown feeble.

Not long now, he thought dimly, unvexed by fear. His only dread was for her, that she must watch him die. He would have spared them both that if he could; had known it was futile, even in the trying.

He heard the wail rise up in her. She thought him dead already. He gathered all of his strength that was left, reached for her hand, held it for a moment before his fingers went slack and fell away. "Listen," he said to her. "Listen to me."

"Don't!" she cried. "Don't talk. You need to rest."

"No," he said. "Listen. Tomb—I built tomb. Two of them. One for kin. One for me. Secret place, near your temple. Not secret enough. There is another place. Another— Listen!" for she was trying to stop

him again, and she must not. He saw the Guide, the dark one standing there, a shadow more distinct by far than the living shape of her
face. Jackal's head, sulfur-eyes, broad man-shoulders, hand outstretched, beckoning, bidding him be quick.

"Listen," said Senenmut with a resurgence of strength: Anubis' gift,
and he was grateful for it. "I had a third tomb made, a truly secret place.
The men who made it, I bound to silence; several with blood. See me
buried there. Hapuseneb, your Nubian—I trust them. Let them do it.
Pretend that my body goes in the second tomb, make a mummy of
reeds, wrap it and strew it with amulets and perform over it all the rites.
But let my body itself lie where none but you three know. There I shall
guard you, your name and your living essence, for all the thousands of
years." He was nearly done. He mustered the last few words. "In the
casket in my chamber, under the collar of gold. It's written there,
where I must lie."

"Nehsi?" she asked, the fool, taking refuge in distraction. "You want
him to do this? You never liked him."

"Trusted," he said, "always. Liking never mattered. Tell him. And
Hapuseneb."

"You won't die," she said. "You can't. I won't let you."

He sighed, though it caught, tearing him with coughing. He thrust
the words through it. "Beloved. King and goddess. Even you are not
more powerful than death."

"But what will I do? How will I live in the world, knowing that
you are not in it?"

It was not a great pleasure to take this memory into the dark: his
king, his beloved, gone weak at last, clutching at him like any common
woman.

She read this thoughts in his eyes. He saw how she drew herself together, how her chin set, her eyes went hard, even through the tears.
His heart, poor staggering thing, swelled till it must surely burst. Ah,
gods, how he loved her. How glorious she was, how strong; how splendid a king.

"I will live," she said, and her voice barely broke. "I give you my
word. I will live without you. But never—never shall I forget you."

He smiled. The Guide was waiting, growing faintly impatient.

The hand was still outstretched, strong beautiful deep-tanned man's hand.

But there was one more thing that he must do, one more thing that he had to say. It was simple but utterly necessary. In a voice as clear as if he had never been ill—the god's gift again, doubly and trebly blessed—he spoke her name. "Maatkare," he said. "Hatshepsut."

51

NEHSI THE NUBIAN AND HAPUSENEB the priest of Amon met in a dark place in the deeps of the night. Neither had any great fears, nor did Nehsi's sons; but it was an eerie place nonetheless, the house of the embalmers in the city of the dead. Jackals prowled in the dark; nightbirds hooted; spirits of the dead fluttered and whispered.

They were not to go into that dark house. The embalmer whom the king's gold had persuaded would bring the body out, wrapped tightly and sealed, redolent of natron and spices. They had a coffin for it, borne in a litter on the shoulders of Nehsi's six strong sons.

No one offered commentary on this thing that they did. The king commanded it. It had been the dead man's last wish, she had told Nehsi. He would not have done it for that, but for her, so quiet as she had been, so still and so quenched, he would happily have died himself.

He had the map, drawn in Senenmut's hand, tucked into his belt but limned in his memory. Hapuseneb had seen it, too, and the king. They had all taken note of the place, and gasped at the audacity of it; but Hapuseneb, laughing suddenly, had spoken for them all. "Clever, clever man! Yes, that will do; it will do indeed."

Nehsi, remembering, smiling to himself, scratched at the postern gate to the house of the embalmers. For a long while nothing stirred.

Just as he moved to scratch again, the door creaked open. A shaft of light pierced the darkness: a lamp, quickly shielded. Nehsi recognized the face that he had been told to look for. Something dark lay on the floor behind it, wrapped like a bundle of sticks, and weighing no more than that, either. The jars of its vitals stood beside it, each crowned by its attendant divinity.

Nehsi's son Seti, eldest and boldest, advanced to take the body in his arms. Nothing was left in it of quick-tongued, quick-witted, heedlessly arrogant Senenmut. It was a husk, a dry dead thing. But the king had loved it.

While Hapuseneb doled out the gold that the king had promised, Nehsi saw the body settled in the litter and the jars laid beside it. It hardly needed the strength of all six strapping boys, but for passing through the city in the guise of a lord and his attendants, it had been a useful ruse.

Hapuseneb counted out the last of the the gold into the waiting hands. It vanished into a purse. The embalmer vanished with it, taking the light with him. The door snicked shut. Nehsi heard the slide of a bar.

They were alone in the dark again with the jackals and the nightwalkers, the dead souls and the mummy in its wrappings, laid in a litter like a lord too prostrate with drink to walk. Senenmut would have appreciated the jest, Nehsi thought as they picked their way through the city of the dead.

They had a long way to go, out of the necropolis and down along the river to the moonlit gleam of Djeser-Djeseru. It was deserted, its priests long since gone to their beds. The great courts were empty, the chapels silent, dark but for the flicker of the nightlamps. Nehsi, whose nerves in most things were as steady as a man's could be, was as twitchy as a cat. If anyone found them here or discovered what they carried, all the king's care would be for naught.

In the morning the temple would be full of people. The time of embalming was over. The thing of reeds and deception that bore the name of Senenmut for the world to know, would be brought past this place to the tomb that he had built, and laid to rest in the lesser of his secret places—the one that he had feared was not secret enough. The king would perform the rites over the false body and sanctify it with her presence.

Tonight he went truly to his tomb, to the most secret of secret places, the shaft dug deep beneath an innocent storeroom. Nehsi found the king there, attended only by his daughter Tama. They looked as strange as he felt, the king pale and still, Tama unwontedly quiet.

After everything that Hatshepsut had done, even to taking the name and the titles of king, one would have thought that this would be as nothing. And yet it was no light thing to tamper with the dead—even if the dead had commanded it.

Nehsi was shamefully grateful to surrender command of the enterprise to his king. She took it as her right, set foot on the stone that seemed no different than any other in that smoothly fitted paving, and stood back as that portion of the floor slid away. A shaft opened, and a stair descending in it.

They could not carry the litter down this narrow passage. The body in its coffin was unwieldy enough. The boys were quiet, gods be thanked; even sullen Minhotep refrained from cursing the dark and the steepness and the difficulty of the passage. They were all overawed by it, however unwillingly.

It was like many another shaft running down to a tomb. No time or effort had been spent in adorning it. Its walls were hewn from the stone of the cliff, smoothed but unpainted.

The chamber at the end of it was mildly startling. One expected it in a tomb, but in this place so secret that no one living knew of it save those who stood in it now, it might have been more likely to find nothing but the hewn stone.

Senenmut must have done the painting himself. As in the tomb in which his false body would lie, the ceiling was a sky full of stars, ordered and named in their mystical ranks, but enfolded here within the body of Nut, sky-goddess, night-goddess, whose arching form stretched from floor to ceiling to floor again. Across the walls that were empty of her marched a procession of judges of the dead, led on each side by jackal-headed Anubis, and bowing before Osiris in judgment.

The god of the dead had Hatshepsut's face. And Nut also; she was the king, subtle yet unmistakable.

Nehsi glanced at Hatshepsut, to see how she responded. Her face was expressionless. She was staring at the sarcophagus in the chamber's center, a huge block of black granite, carved over and over with Senenmut's name and hers, her face and his, and at intervals the lost and lovely face of the princess Neferure.

The sarcophagus was open, waiting. Inside it lay a rolled papyrus. Nehsi recognized the glyphs upon its case. It was as he had expected, the Book of Coming Forth by Day, the ancient gathering of spells and magics and simple wisdom that guided a soul through the land of the dead.

There was nothing else in this chamber. No wealth of grave-goods. No food or drink, no carved and painted servants, no promise of life and prosperity in death. Only the book, the stone, the painted walls. Senenmut had looked for no life beyond life, no joy and no repose, only this ceaseless guardianship in the temple of his king.

Nehsi could not call him a fool, or condemn him for sacrificing his life after life. No man could ever have loved a woman as this man loved Hatshepsut. And yet no singer sang of it; no story hallowed it. They had loved in secret, nor betrayed themselves save to those who knew them both well, and could see how the air sang between them when they were together.

Hatshepsut, left alone, gone silent in her solitude, saw Senenmut laid in the sarcophagus and the jars arrayed to north and east, west and south. There could be no formal rite of the dead here. All that would be done in the morning with his false body. But she opened the gates of his senses for him, spoke the ancient words and chanted the blessings, with Hapuseneb echoing her, strengthening her with his strong sweet voice.

Nehsi sensed no change in the air, no greater awareness once the prayers and the magic had sunk into silence. The dead remained dead. The lid of the sarcophagus ground into place over the body, drawn by the sweat and the labor of Nehsi's sons. When Senenmut was sealed within but his souls set free, one hoped, to do as they and the gods willed, the king paused over the sarcophagus.

Now, Nehsi thought, at last she would break. But she did not. She stood erect and still. Her hand rested on the stone where his heart should have been, had it not been in the jar that lay at her feet. She had not wept since he died, that Nehsi knew of. Her grief was too deep, too strong for tears.

She turned abruptly, nearly oversetting Tama who stood behind her. She never saw or took heed. She walked blindly out, back through the passage, up the stair, into the temple that her mind had conceived and Senenmut had built.

■ That was Senenmut's true funeral. The false one, the one that the world knew of, went on in royal splendor, with wailing and keening of women, processions of princes, an astonishing number of commoners come to pay their respects to the commoner who had become a great lord of Egypt. No word was spoken, then as ever, of his long sojourn in the king's bed. It was as if the cruelty of crowds was suspended and their rumormongering quenched, gone quiet before the king.

And when it was over, when the tomb that was known to workmen and certain princes was sealed, and the one that held his kin and, now, his little red mare, was likewise shut up for everlasting, then the world went on without him. He had been a great presence in Egypt, a lord of many titles, loved or hated as his merits deserved. There were empty places now where he had been. His house was shut up, his servants sent away or sold, his villa closed and his horses dispersed.

Hatshepsut would not give either house or estate to another man. They were allowed to fall into dust and silence. She never spoke of them, or of the man who had dwelt in them.

It was not forgetfulness. Far from it. It was grief so complete and so perfect that it could accept no other in his place, nor conceive of a world without him in it.

Yet she went on. She gave up nothing that was hers as king. If anything she took on more: more powers, more offices, more duties and obligations. She buried herself in the cares of kingship, made herself so purely and completely king that nothing of the woman remained.

Nehsi grieved for that more than he could ever have grieved for Senenmut. That arrogant, irritable man with his caustic wit and his irresistible brilliance had taught her to preserve her humanity. Now there was no one to do it.

Nehsi might have once; but time and duty had taken him apart from her, given him a wife and children, separated his life from hers. When he looked to bring them together again, the gulf was too wide. He was on one side of it, lord and prince, servant of his king; she on the other, king and goddess, loving him, he never doubted that, but as a king loves her most loyal servant. Not as a woman loves a man.

They could not have that. The gods had not willed it. He could only try to strengthen her with his presence, invite her to speak to him when they were granted a few moments alone together, reach as he could across the barrier of time and rank and sorrow. She was never there for the touch of his hand. She had shut herself away.

He had done everything that he could do, short of picking her up and shaking her as if she had been one of his children. He contemplated that, knowing what it would cost him if he roused her anger, but almost beyond caring. Almost. His wife's face, the thought of his children, the youngest still nursing at his mother's breast, restrained him.

Time and the gods must heal her. Nehsi would do what he could, but if that was not enough, then it was in the gods' hands.

52

THUTMOSE THE KING HAD GROWN from silent and subdued youth into a warlike manhood. He was as much among the soldiers as ever, training with them, marching when they passed in review, sitting in the councils of the generals.

And yet he had never been to war, never raised sword or spear on the field of battle. Maatkare Hatshepsut did not wage war. She waged peace. She ruled through embassies, through trading ventures, through the force of her name in any land that offered fealty to Egypt.

"And it is not enough," he said to the gathering of generals, on the day that happened to be his birthday. He was four-and-twenty, a man grown by any reckoning, but something about him was still young and oddly unformed. He had been late to grow into everything else; why not the solidity of manhood?

Nehsi happened to be among the generals that day. He had heard rumors that dismayed him, tales of unrest in Asia. The king would send another embassy, he supposed, or demand a greater levy of tribute, thereby occupying the restive peoples and quelling their impulse toward rebellion. The generals, as one might expect, proposed another solution altogether. And Thutmose was foremost among them.

"The center of the unrest," he said, "is Kadesh. Its king, it's said, musters three hundred princes under his banner. He has ambitions, and those are lofty. To conquer Asia; to drive Egypt back within its borders. Perhaps he would even rule us as the foreign kings did."

A growl ran round the circle. No one had ever forgotten or forgiven the invasion of Egypt by kings from Asia, who ruled for a hundred years, until King Ahmose rose up and destroyed them.

Thutmose, Nehsi took note, suffered no hesitation of speech in front of these men, nor any lack of either quickness or intensity. He paced the room in which they kept council, a room appropriately warlike, painted with scenes of the first Thutmose's battles. He reminded Nehsi of a panther crouched to spring or a cobra coiled to strike: pure power tightly leashed, held just at the point of bursting free.

This was a dangerous man, Nehsi thought. The swift brilliance that Nehsi saw in him here was never uncovered before the elder king; nor had Egypt seen it. Only these men, these lords and generals, who lived for war.

They were his. There could be no doubt of it. Whatever they might have said to one another, in Thutmose's presence they were silent, waiting upon his pleasure.

He halted just before he struck the far wall, and spun on his heel. The figure of his grandfather reared up behind him, lofty in his chariot, smiting his enemies. "It has been thirty years," he said, "since a king of Egypt waged war in Asia. My father ventured a campaign or two, a skirmish, but nothing of moment. Not since my grandfather's day has a king made his presence felt outside of the Two Lands."

They nodded, some gravely, some with passion that came close to anger. Nehsi held still. Thutmose fixed eyes on him, eyes that glittered as if with fever. "You'll go back to her, won't you? You'll tell her I spoke sedition here."

"That depends," Nehsi said, "majesty. Is this sedition?"

"How can it be? I am king." Thutmose lifted his head at that, arrogance that verged on self-mockery. "She will never agree to a campaign."

"Have you asked her?" Nehsi inquired.

Thutmose stiffened. "What use is that?"

"Much," said Nehsi, "if she agrees with you."

"But she never will."

"Do you know that? Do you know it for certain?"

Thutmose drew breath as if to prolong the argument, but shook his head instead and said, "I'll ask her, then. I'll wager you a good bronze blade that she forbids us to lay hand to weapon."

"I'll take that wager," Nehsi said.

■ Hatshepsut laughed in her nephew's face. "What, a war? Do you know nothing else to do or say or think? Listen to you! Armies this, soldiers that. Asia is quiet, has been quiet for thirty years. If it shows any sign of restlessness, I'll send my messengers, and all its rebellious princes will fall groveling at my feet."

Thutmose, quenched and stammering as always in front of her, nevertheless discovered in the depths of anger a new and unlooked-for courage. It stripped the mask from his face, showed her the vivid and hating creature within. "They mock at us. They laugh, and call us fools, weaklings, cowards and slaves. Send men, strong men, to show them what Egypt is. Prove to them that our strength has not failed because we bow to a king who is a woman."

She could have seen then what in truth he was; but temper blinded her, and decades of contempt. "Are you asking me if you can lead an army into Asia? Do you think I'd let you go so far away or wield so great a power? I'll not have you drain the Two Kingdoms of their young men and empty their treasuries, simply so that you can play at soldiers."

"It is not play!" His voice had risen. It was light, without great depth or force; so raised, it was distressingly shrill. "Can you not understand? Peace succeeds only against enemies who also want peace. These enemies want war. And they will get it, regardless of the cost to themselves or to Egypt."

"I see nothing of the sort," Hatshepsut said, flat and final. "Don't you have duties in the temple? Go, perform them. Leave the tedium of kingship to those better suited to endure it."

Nehsi, watching, bit his tongue. Thutmose raised his clenched fists as if he would strike her. She looked him levelly in the face. He spun on his heel, mute with fury, and fled.

In the ringing silence after his departure, Hatshepsut said mildly, "I shall have to find something else for that boy to do. But not, as Amon be my witness, a war."

"It might not be an ill thing," Nehsi ventured, "to let him lead an army somewhere reasonably harmless. Give him strong generals, unshakably loyal to you; surround him with guards who will protect him from himself as from his enemies; and if he takes the bit in his teeth even then, you well might consider allowing him to take the forefront of a battle. The gods willing, an enemy's arrow may find him."

"No," she said in revulsion so strong that he flinched. "Never say such a thing. Never, ever. Child and fool and simpleton he may be, but he is king of Egypt. No mortal man may slay a king."

"Are you a mortal man?"

In that instant, Nehsi saw hatred in her eyes. It was brief; it passed; but its memory lingered like a scar in his soul. "Even I," she said with terrible softness, "will not kill a king, or arrange to have him killed."

Nehsi bowed low and low, even to the pavement at her feet. "Lady," he said. "Great king."

Once she would have raised him and told him to stop his nonsense. Now she said above his head, cold and remote, "Leave me."

He raised himself to his knees. Her face above him was as cold as her voice, and as unyielding. There was nothing in it of the woman who had been his friend, his dear lady, his king whom he loved.

Still he tried once more to break through the wall of her obstinacy. "Lady, please. Listen to me. That was a backward child, but he has grown into a man; and he hates you."

"He is afraid of me," she said, "and with good reason. Did I not dismiss you?"

"Lady," Nehsi said, bowing low again. He had no choice then. He backed away from her as her servants did, making a sacrifice of his pride.

And she said no word, offered no forgiveness. She was his king; he was her minister, and he had presumed too far at last. He was no longer welcome in her presence.

Hatshepsut had, perhaps, erred. She had sent Thutmose back to the temple in which he was a minor priest, one of many who offered incense before the god. In so doing she had set him in mind of a thing, a dangerous thing, and one that should not have been possible.

Nor would it have been if Hapuseneb had not fallen ill. It was a convenient illness but not, Nehsi ventured to believe, caused by anything other than age and weariness and the gods' will. One forgot that the priest was not a young man; he was so lively by nature, so quick with his wit. But he was old, and age had caught him at last.

"Do you know," he said to Nehsi from his sickbed, "Senenmut has been dead half a dozen years; and I was years older than he to begin with. I miss him, old friend. I miss him sorely."

"So do I," said Nehsi. "He might have been able to make our king see sense."

"If he could see it himself," Hapuseneb said with a snort. His sickness was of the lingering kind, a blueness to the lips, an inability to stand up without falling over; it neither clouded his mind nor greatly interfered with his capacity for conversation. He was short of breath, to be sure, and needed to rest between bouts of chatter; but he pressed on regardless. If his servant-priests ventured to remonstrate, he drove them off.

He paused for breath, his lips so blue that Nehsi was alarmed; but he would not let anyone hasten to his aid. "Yes, Senenmut might have been some good in this affair—though he was never able to make her see the truth about that boy, either. Do you see in him what I see? He's locked in a cage now, but when he's set free, he'll fly as high and fast and far as Horus' falcon."

"She's never seen it," Nehsi said. "I doubt she ever will."

"She may have to," said Hapuseneb. "I need to rest now, and you have things to do, I'm sure. Come back tonight. There's a place I'll have my lads show you, and a thing that you should hear."

"What—" Nehsi began.

Hapuseneb waved him into silence. "Tonight. Come back; come quietly, and come alone. I'll have a man meet you at the postern. He'll show you what you need to see."

Nehsi sighed irritably, but he assented to the priest's game. For game it was, and too much like Hapuseneb, whose predilection for levity was well and widely known.

One should indulge a dying man. If that too was not a jest.

No; Hapuseneb had a look Nehsi knew too well. Men who had it did not live long.

■ Nehsi returned to the temple near sunset, when the shadows had grown long and the lamps were being lit in the houses of Thebes. His own house would be lively at this hour, with the tribe of his sons returning from their various duties and offices, and his wife and his daughters coming out to welcome them, and the servants running back and forth, fetching this and that.

He would have given much to be there and not here, dressed plainly, unattended except for a lone quiet guard who happened to be his son Seti. He had not been advised to avoid notice, but he knew Hapuseneb. If it had been wise for him to come in state as a prince of Egypt, the priest would have said so.

Therefore Nehsi came as a simple man, a petitioner to the temple, or perhaps a priest coming in late for his season before the god. The one who let him in was familiar from Hapuseneb's sickroom, a plump young man with a bright eye. He might be a cousin or nephew of Hapuseneb: there was a resemblance.

He did not chatter, which was in his favor. He led Nehsi quietly and competently through the maze of the temple, avoiding traveled ways, keeping to the shadows as much as he might. If he thought it peculiar to be creeping about like a thief in his own place, he did not mention it.

At length he brought Nehsi to a room of no particular distinction, except in one respect. Hidden in a niche behind the statue of some half-forgotten king was a door that opened silently, and beyond it a passage full of whisperings and murmurings. The reason for it came clear when the priest beckoned Nehsi down and round a corner, and then touched his arm, bidding him halt.

Nehsi suppressed the hiss of surprise. He had heard of such places but never seen one. He should have expected to find one here, in the most powerful temple in Egypt. This was a spyhole, a listening-post that looked out through cleverly cut and concealed openings into a privy chamber.

He doubted very much that the choice of the chamber was happenstance. Plots within plots had been the way of Amon's priesthood for time out of mind. And there in the chamber sat a gathering of priests, brown shaven heads, white kilts and mantles. The one who spoke to them was a priest also, clad as they were, but he carried himself as the king he was.

Thutmose had let the elder king show him the way through his difficulty. He had gathered what looked to be a fair selection of the more influential priests. But not Hapuseneb. Not the First Prophet, the high priest. Even if he could have risen from his bed, Nehsi doubted that he would have been welcome in this gathering.

"He'll be dead soon," Thutmose said, "and a new First Prophet set up in his place. Then whom will you look to, sirs? A king who for all her strength has begun to grow old, or a king who is in the full flower of his youth?"

"That other king may be no longer as young as she was," one of the priests observed, "but she is as powerful as she has ever been. What can you do to oppose her?"

"Ask rather," Thutmose said swiftly, "what you will do when she dies as she inevitably must, and you find yourselves in the service of a younger king."

"She's not as old as that," said another of the priests. "She could live another thirty years. What if she decides to dispose of you before she dies—or to make another man her heir? Or even," he added with the suggestion of a shudder, "a woman."

"There is no one," Thutmose said. "And she will not harm me.

She's both too arrogant and too afraid of the gods' wrath."

"As you are, who have suffered her regency these past one-and-twenty years?"

Thutmose did not rise up in rage, which rather surprised Nehsi. "Perhaps," he said with studied calm. "And perhaps I needed so long to gather my strength."

"What have you, then? A few generals; a pack of soldiers. All the rest is hers."

"Not necessarily," Thutmose said. "Those generals and that rabble of fighting men, reckoned together, make a mighty number."

"Well then," said a man who had not spoken before, a soft and deceptively lazy voice, a face that Nehsi, from this angle, could not see. "Are we to understand that you'll stage a rising of the army in Egypt?"

Thutmose shook his head impatiently. "Of course not! I want a pair of solid realms to rule once her so gracious majesty is dead. I can't have that if I'm fighting a civil war."

"So?" said the lazy one, and Nehsi imagined a lift of brow. "You'll sit quietly, then, and wait for the gods to take her."

"The gods will do as they will," Thutmose said. "I'll rule alone in the end, king and god as she is king and goddess now."

"Certainly," said the languid voice. "Are you threatening us with terrors that may be decades distant? Or is there something that you want of us?"

"Something that I want, yes," Thutmose said, "and something that I can promise you." He paused. They waited, trained to patience as courtiers were. He said, "I want alliance. Your aid and your support of my cause and my kingship. Your First Prophet is dying and will soon be dead. The king will tell you whom you may choose to follow him, but the right of decision is given to you. Choose one who is pleasing to her, but who will serve me when and as I ask."

"And if we do that? What do you promise us in return?"

He hesitated for the space of a breath. Nehsi did not think that it was fear. Caution, rather, and care in choosing his words. "When I am king," he said, "I have no intention of sitting at home mourning a dead scribe, dwelling on the glories of a single expedition sent to Punt, a temple built, a pair of obelisks raised. These are the least of the things that I shall do.

"I shall go forth," he said, "I, Menkheperre Thutmose; I shall gather the greatest army that ever was, and lead it into Asia. My grandfather conquered Nubia and Syria. Since his time they have both slid away from us. Their people mock at ours when we walk in the streets of their cities. Their kings speak of setting themselves free of us, of casting us back into the deserts from which we came."

"Is that all you will do?" the languid one asked. "Ramp about with bow and sword, and spend the treasuries on empty bloodshed?"

Thutmose's eyes glittered with passion that Nehsi had never seen in them, not even in mock battles among the soldiers. "You echo her words as if they were inviolable truth. And yet I tell you, priest; I tell you all. What is it that war brings into the Two Lands?"

"Death," said one of the priests.

"Death for some, but that is the price the gods exact. For many more, it brings wealth: gold, jewels, captives, all the booty of a conquered nation. When a nation pays tribute it pays as little as it can—and less of late, since our elder king has been so indulgent with the whinings of its embassies. The spoils of war are greater than anything that a nation might offer of its own accord."

"You can strip a country bare," the languid one said, "and leave nothing for the next year's tribute."

"That's not wise warfare," Thutmose said, "or good husbandry. Neither is it wise to leave a nation alone, to let it grow strong until it casts off the yoke. Do you let the ox run wild in the field, or do you keep it hitched to the plow, tilling the land for the harvest of Egypt?"

"What are you saying?" the languid one asked; not so languid any longer, beginning to grow interested.

"Amon has great estates in Asia," Thutmose said, "and wealth unimaginable in every part of the world. That wealth can hardly be safe if Asia succeeds in revolt. If Amon stands behind me while I go to war, Amon will not only defend its interests; it will share in the spoil."

"How great a share?"

"That," said Thutmose, "is a matter for discussion."

Glances flickered round the circle. The one who had been speaking shifted until Nehsi could see his face. It was vaguely familiar, as belonging to someone whom he had seen among Hapuseneb's attendants.

For all Nehsi knew, this was the one who had betrayed the gathering to Hapuseneb, and caused the elder king's Nubian to be brought where he could hear and see it. If so, the man played the game extraordinarily well. "All of this is purely speculative," he said, "in the absence of any real power on your part."

"With Amon behind me," Thutmose said, "I have all the power in the world."

The priest reflected on that. His brows went up. "Indeed," he said. "If Amon's daughter finds herself at odds with Amon's priesthood . . . what a difficulty that will be."

"I too am descended from the god," Thutmose reminded him.

"But she is his own daughter," the priest said. "That would weigh heavily with the more devout among us."

"She will not always be the living Horus," Thutmose said. "When she becomes Osiris, will you stand with me?"

"When she becomes Osiris," said the priest, "Amon's temple will bow before Amon's son as it has done from the beginning of the Two Lands."

"That will suffice," Thutmose said.

53

"NONE OF THAT PROVES ANYTHING," Nehsi said to Hapuseneb, "except that the younger king makes sure of his position once the elder king is gone."

"Did it occur to you to wonder," Hapuseneb asked, "why he should be doing it now of all times, with Asia on the edge of revolt? He knows he'll never get his way while he remains subservient to the King Maatkare."

"You think," Nehsi said, "that he may not be intending such subservience for much longer. But he'll never break free unless she dies."

"Yes," said Hapuseneb.

Nehsi frowned. "You think he'll try something."

"I think," said Hapuseneb, "that once I'm safely dead, he'll reckon himself strong enough in his alliance with Amon that he can do whatever he judges necessary."

"Even that?"

"Do you doubt that he's capable of it?"

Nehsi shook his head. "I've seen the way he walks. Stallions walk so when they're bitted too strongly, just before they break free and bolt."

"Trampling whoever held them, and killing that one if they can." Hapuseneb drew a breath that rattled, and closed his eyes. He looked dead then, a grey-faced corpse. "Watch her carefully, old friend. It won't be something obvious—don't expect that of him, warrior though he may be. He's a dark and secret creature. He'll do it in such a way that no one can ever charge him with it, or be certain that she died of anything but the gods' will and her own mortality."

"All kings die and become Osiris," Nehsi said, reciting the ancient words as if their meaning had only now come clear. "And she, as he said, is no longer young." He flexed his hands. They ached sometimes of late: he was not a young man, either—in fact he was older than she. The stubble that grew on his shaven skull glinted more silver than black, these days.

He was still strong, and so was she—in the body at least. "Gods," he said. "When did we begin to grow old?"

"Yesterday," said Hapuseneb. "Youth will always conquer, unless it's disposed of by wary age."

"And that, she will never do. I could curse her honor, and her reverence for the sanctity of the king. I fear very much that he has no such scruples."

"He doesn't need them," Hapuseneb said. "He can call her usurper and dispose of her as Ahmose did with the foreign kings."

"You think he will," said Nehsi.

"I think," said Hapuseneb, "that a man with a strong stomach and no dread of the gods' wrath might well choose to remove this threat to our lady."

"I am not that man," Nehsi said with deep regret. "I can't do it, no more than she can. Even to protect her. I've failed her, Hapuseneb. At the last, when she needs me most, I can't act as I know I should act."

"I don't know about that," Hapuseneb said. "You can't kill him, no more than I could: I'm godbound too, and constrained by the sanctity of kingship. But you can guard her, protect her against him, see that she lives as long as the gods have willed for her."

"And then?" Nehsi asked. "What then?"

"Then, my friend," said Hapuseneb, "the gods must provide."

■ Nehsi pondered long on what he had heard and seen. He increased the guard on the elder king, not so much as to be obvious, but she was watched always. She gave him no thanks for it. She had withdrawn into herself, become a cold husk of kingship. Even the affection with which she had regarded her people was gone. Friends she had none. Her allies and her ministers loved her as they always had, as they always would; but she had shut them away. She received their worship as if she had been the image of a goddess wrought in ivory and gems and gold: upright and still, with beautiful blind eyes, and no living warmth.

There was nothing that Nehsi could do to make her human again. The one who could have done it was years dead. When he tried regardless, she ignored him or sent him away.

He came to her at last in a passion of frustration, faced her of an evening as she prepared to sleep. Her gowns and her jewels were laid aside, and she was clothed in a linen shift. Her maids had just finished cleansing the paint from her face and were anointing it for the night with sweet oils.

Nehsi was admitted because he had command of the guard. She saw him: her eyes flickered as he passed the door. She did not greet him, but neither, he noticed, did she dismiss him. He took heart from that.

It came to him with a small shock that he had never seen her beauty bare. Always since she was a child she had presented herself to him with her face painted, her eyes drawn long with kohl and malachite. Tonight the mask was taken away. Beneath it he saw the aging woman, tired and faintly haggard, the corners of her mouth drawn down by the weight of years and cares and kingship. The cap of curls that she had allowed to grow beneath wig and crowns was shot with grey.

And yet she was still beautiful. The face that in Thutmose was too odd for handsomeness, in her was drawn fine, its royal arch of nose imperious rather than overwhelming.

Her maids finished the last of her toilet, bowed, glanced uncertainly at the man who stood by the door. He must have bulked huge, shadowed and silent. Perhaps his anger showed on his face.

"Go," she said to them.

They wavered, hesitating, but in the end they went.

And Nehsi had what he wanted, what he had not dared to hope for. He was alone with his king.

He had been going to shout at her if he must, shake her, dare her wrath and even the shame of the lash if he could only catch and hold her attention. Instead he stood mute, as Thutmose so often did, unable to explain why he was in such awe of this lone small woman with her tired eyes.

Then she lifted those eyes, and he knew. Because she was Hatshepsut.

That, strangely, strengthened him. He said without pause or preliminary, "Thutmose will kill you if he can."

She raised her brows. Stripped of paint, they were strong still, plucked into a perfect arch. "Have you proof of this?" she asked, remote as she always was now; distant and cool.

"I have seen him in Amon's temple," Nehsi said, "driving bargains with the priests who will rule when Hapuseneb is dead. He offers them the spoils of Asia in return for alliance, and for a blind eye turned upon him if you die untimely."

"Indeed?" She seemed neither surprised nor alarmed. "What would you have me do about it? Put him to death for sedition?"

"That," said Nehsi, "you would never do. Nor could I; and believe me, majesty, I thought of it. An arrow in the dark, a poison in the cup, and you would be safe forever."

"Safe, and without an heir."

"And condemned by the gods for allowing a king to be destroyed." He shook his head. "Lady, you know me better than that; or you did once. I would ask you to ponder the danger, and to consider what to do about this young king who begins at last to strain the bonds you set on him."

"Bonds that he never resisted, nor saw fit to question." In that he heard her old, almost welcome exasperation. "If he had ever proved that he was worthy to take up the burdens of a king, I would have laid them upon him."

"Would you?" Nehsi asked her. "Truly, lady: would you? How do you reconcile this contempt for him with the truth, that when you die he will rule in your stead? Do you care so little for the welfare of Egypt?"

In her eyes he saw no love for him, not any longer; but she had not driven him out. In that he took what comfort he could. "Every breath I draw is drawn for Egypt," she said. "It troubles me, yes, that I leave no better heir. I shall see him married, I think: find him a woman who is strong enough to rule as I ruled when his father was king—and who can bear him the heir that he requires. Would that content you, O great lord?"

She mocked him, addressing him as if he had been as royal as she. He refused to bristle at it. "That would be useful," he conceded. "It has also come to my mind that while you find and train the lady, he might be well distracted if he were given what he yearns for. A command in the army, lady. Nothing of great moment—not the command of Asia, lest he make himself strong there, then come back and destroy you; but something sufficient, a garrison in Nubia perhaps, or one of the outposts of Libya."

"If he is indeed as clever as you insist, he'll know he's been sent into a kind of exile, given a sop to his pride while he's kept out of the way. He might even," she said, "begin to suspect that his plotting is known, and be driven to do something desperate."

"If you are on guard," Nehsi said, "anything that he does, you can counter. And you'll be safe from his machinations in Thebes."

"That is if he is as clever as you think," she said. He heard her in a kind of despair. She who saw so clearly in all things, could not see Thutmose at all. She never had; she never would.

"I shall ponder what you have said," she said, coldly formal again, though she had been warming a little. "It would be well to find a wife for him—even as backward as he has been, he is long past the age when a man should marry and beget sons. Look you to the young women of Egypt; and look well to the children of Nefertari, for one who may rule as queen while her husband plays at soldiers on the borders of Libya."

Nehsi sighed, but he bowed and let himself be dismissed. It was a poor concession that he had gained from her, but it was better than nothing. She would think on his words; she would consider what to do with Thutmose. She might even act swiftly enough to prevent him from moving against her. His deliberation, his long habit of waiting upon the moment, might serve her now as it had served her since he was a child.

Or it might not. There was no telling. He could only wait and pray, and stand such guard as he could, and hope that it would be enough.

54

*H*APUSENEB THE PRIEST DIED AT the end of a poor flood, as poor as those before it had been rich. The rising of the river had ceased early. The king had been forced to hasten to Memphis for the festival, nearly coming too late. In so doing, she was not in Thebes when the Prophet of Amon slipped into the long sleep.

He died without pain, which was a blessing. His heart simply stopped, his breast ceased to rise and fall. She came home from Memphis to officiate at his funeral. She did not weep. Her wailing was as formal as the chanting of a priest, her beating of thighs all ritual, no passion in it; no great outpouring of grief. All of that she had spent when she buried Senenmut.

Nehsi began to think thoughts that would once have been unthinkable. Not of her death; not that. But of her fading from the splendor of her youth. She was not the ruler that she had been. Her judgments, once tempered with mercy, grew harsh and cold. People no longer cried out for love of her. They feared her; wondered at her; worshipped at her feet. But the warmth that they had had for her was gone.

It well might be time for a younger king—or a queen, a Great Royal Wife. The difficulty of finding a lady of the proper lineage, age, and fertility, who would be as acceptable to Thutmose as to Hatshepsut, was enormous and perhaps insurmountable.

Nehsi did what he could. Though it galled him to leave her, he did so: abandoned her for this brief time in order to protect her more completely thereafter. He traveled the length of Egypt, guesting with this lord or that, making himself amiable to princes, searching in the temples for a singer or a dancer of the line of Nefertari. The rumor of his venture ran ahead of him. Men began to fling their daughters and sisters and even lesser wives at him—or to conceal them where they hoped he could not find them.

All the while he did that, he made certain that Hatshepsut was guarded. His son Seti, in command of her bodyguard, was under orders to guard her with his life, or answer for it to Nehsi himself. It was not enough for Nehsi's peace of mind, but it was the best that he could do.

Of Thutmose he heard nothing. The younger king might, it was said, be given a command at last; but no one knew where or when. The strongest rumor had it that he would amass a great army, the largest that had ever been seen in Egypt, to put down the rebellion in Asia. Not only Kadesh had risen, Nehsi heard, but Syria and the coast of Palestine. Even Mitanni, that great empire to the north and east, was said to look with interest on the rising against Egypt.

But Hatshepsut made no move against it. She ruled in Thebes as she had since she was young, received embassies, sent out trading ventures, saw to the affairs of the Two Lands. At the festival of the harvest, such as that was, she thrust aside those who muttered that the failure of the flood and the smallness of its fruits was an omen. She proclaimed as always her names and her titles, her power in the Two Lands; and she said, as Nehsi heard it proclaimed in the city of Asyut where he was determining that the nomarch had no marriageable daughters: "I rule in peace; with peace the gods have blessed me. Under my hand the Two Lands have grown strong."

"Peace," people muttered in Nehsi's hearing, not knowing or perhaps not caring who he was. "We'll all have peace when we're dead. What's the use in it now? We haven't had a good war since the first Thutmose was king."

"Do us good," someone said in the marketplace of Bubastis. "Give the young bloods something to do. Get the army off its backside and into something useful. Bring in loot to make us all rich."

It might be, Nehsi thought, that people's thinking had changed; that the poor flood and the thin harvest turned their hearts away from the king whom they had loved for so long. And it well might be that Thutmose had played a part in it. Those were his words spoken among the market-stalls and bandied in the taverns; his eagerness for bloodshed in the mouths of those who had never, any more than he, faced an enemy in battle.

"She's a woman, after all," they said. "What do women know of fighting? Of course she wants to keep the boys at home. Women never want us to go out and have a nice hot battle. No wonder we're going hungry this year, and the beer's piss-thin and the king away in Kadesh is calling us a pack of pretty boys. We've got a woman for a king."

Time was when that was a great boast: that they were the servants of Maatkare Hatshepsut. Now they turned their backs on her, and remembered that there had been another king before her, whose place and titles she had taken.

At that, although he had found no woman of suitable rank or lineage, Nehsi abandoned his journey, cursing its futility, its waste of his time and substance, and turned back toward Thebes. He traveled so swiftly that he outran the king's couriers. But not the murmur of discontent that was in Egypt. It grew greater toward the Delta, lessened as he drew near to Thebes, but everywhere he heard the sound of it.

His daughter Tama met him at the quay of his own city, standing with the air of one who has been waiting since the world was young. Such conspicuous patience was as characteristic of her as the wild tumble of her hair under the wig that she discarded more often than not; but there was an edge to it that brought Nehsi leaping from his boat even as it slid toward the shore.

He might be growing old, but he could still spring like a panther. He landed lightly enough beside his daughter. Her belly was swelling, he noticed. She had married before he left, having made a surprising choice of husband: a tall, quiet, scholarly person from the House of Life, who happened to be notably older than she. He was also a lord of a house of princes, not too distant kin to the king, and as wealthy as any father could wish. He placed no obstacle in the way of his wife's freedom, which had the peculiar effect of keeping her for once at home.

That, Nehsi thought, might have something to do with his own fears for the king. She embraced him, fierce and brief, and said the thing that he had dreaded most to hear. "The king is ill. She's asking for you."

■ Hatshepsut who had never been ill a day in her life, who had bypassed the fevers and rheums that laid others low, who was blessed by the god her father with health and strength beyond the lot of most women in this age of the world, was ill indeed. No one dared whisper it, but she might be dying.

It had struck fast and hard, her physician said to Nehsi: a fierce cramping in the belly, a great resistance to aught that was fed her, and a flux that went on and on, and would not yield to any physic.

"Poison," Nehsi said.

The man pursed his thin lips. "Possibly. But there are other indications, suggestions that it might be something in her own body. Such can befall a woman in particular as she ages; and her majesty has been much vexed with the ending of her womanly courses."

Nehsi regarded him narrow-eyed. He had been a loyal man from his youth, but who was to tell now who was loyal and who was not? When a king grew old and took sick, and a young king waited with taut-strung eagerness to take the throne, a wise man shifted his allegiances as quickly as he might.

Nehsi could not be wise. He was Hatshepsut's man. So he would remain until he died.

He left the physician standing there, and went in to the king.

As young as he had been when the first Thutmose died, he remembered the air of that sickroom. Vividly: for now it was the same. The crowding courtiers, priests and healer-priests, physicians, servants and hangers-on. The shifting of glances, the slow stirring of bodies now toward one another and now away. Even in the king's own chamber, allegiances were changing, minds turning toward the world that would go on after the king was dead.

She could recover. She had been strong, and might be still. But her age, the nature of her sickness, the young king whose face Nehsi did not see among those here, turned this waiting into a deathwatch.

She lay in the midst of them, a small and shrunken figure under the coverlet of purple from Tyre, with her head propped on a headrest of chalcedony. She wore no wig, but her face was painted. It seemed all enormous black-rimmed eyes, a living amulet, a doubled Eye of Horus set in the deathmask of a king.

There were amulets in truth on her breast, a clattering mass of them, and the workings of spells scattered all about her. Nehsi caught the unmistakable scent of the dung that was reckoned essential in healing magic. It might, he thought, be meant to mask the loosing of the bowels in death.

She was not dead yet. She saw him coming through the crowding faces. The light in her eyes nearly broke him. He had not seen it in months—years. She was glad to see him, as she had used to be; smiling as he bowed over her, catching his hand in both of hers. They were bone-thin, and cold; as cold as her eyes were warm. "Nehsi," she said. Her voice was a husk of itself.

He knelt beside the bed, in part for homage, in part for ease of speaking to her. People craned. He noted distantly how suddenly they were gone, driven back to the room's edges. The one who had driven them, no less than Tama herself, mounted guard over the king and her father, and held off even the most indignant courtier with a hard and implacable stare.

Nehsi, safe in what was almost solitude, said softly in her ear, "Tell me what you ate, that did this to you. Did he bribe your taster? Corrupt the wine?"

She shook her head, still smiling, though with an edge of pain. "Not poison after all. Women's trouble, the doctors say."

"The doctors have to stay alive after you're gone," Nehsi said.

"He wouldn't do it," she said, as stubborn as ever. "He's not brave enough. It's the gods, Nehsi. The god my father. Two sevens of years he gave me under the Two Crowns: more than woman has ever had. Now the rest of the gods demand their own back. They want a man again over Egypt. The flood is their sign. Fourteen years it rose high and splendid. This year it hardly rose at all. There would be famine in the Two Kingdoms, if we had not been wise and gathered the excess of the harvests."

"You don't honestly believe that," Nehsi said. "It's much too convenient."

"The gods like convenience," she said. "Sometimes. They find it amusing."

She was not going to listen to him or believe him, no matter how obvious it was that if a god had killed her, it was the living Horus who so feared and hated her. She could not have done such a thing. No more could she conceive of another who would do it.

"You were always the wisest of women," Nehsi said to her, "but when it comes to that one, you are a perfect fool."

"Someone said that to me once," she said, "about my husband. It's a curse, I suppose. Every king should have a curse. I'm fortunate that this has done so little harm."

"It has done great harm. It has killed you."

"Hush," she said, though he had not raised his voice. "Hush, dear friend. It's grief that makes you wild. I know. I was . . . so . . . wild after he died: my beloved whom we buried in the place that you know. He was at me constantly, too, over that stumbling boy."

"He was a wise man," Nehsi said, "and foresighted."

"He's waiting for me," she said. She sounded lighthearted, untainted by fear. "Hapuseneb, too. And my father. They'll all roar at me, I'm sure. I'm going to laugh and tell them to be sensible. Everyone dies. How many women can say that they died and became Osiris—king over the dead as Horus is king over the living?"

"One or two," Nehsi said, "long ago." And when she frowned: "But none as glorious as you."

"I should hope not," she said with some asperity. She raised a hand that trembled with weakness, and patted his cheek. "Go away now. Greet your wife, bellow at your pack of children. Come back to me when the sun sinks low. Yonder jackals slink off then to their lairs. We'll have a little peace."

Nehsi did not think that the jackals would retreat tonight. The translucence of her face, the light in her eyes, told him that he had done well to arrive so quickly. She might not see another morning.

He said none of that. He bowed low and kissed her hand, and left her to the scavengers. "Until evening," he said, "my lady and king."

55

NEHSI WENT HOME AS HATSHEPSUT bade him, to Bastet's strong embrace and the uproar of his offspring. But having seen that all was in order there, he took Tama with him, and a pair of his sons whom he found idling about the stables, and went hunting.

He was not hunting the young king. He returned to the palace, to that wing of the old queens' house which had remained occupied through the reign of a woman who was a king. There dwelt Thutmose's concubines, such of them as he had, and his mother Isis.

Isis, like her son, had yielded with apparent submission to the rule of Maatkare Hatshepsut. But like Thutmose, she had kept her counsels, and bided her time.

She was still beautiful. Like the goddess for whom she was named, who also had been born a mortal woman, or so some of the priests said, she seemed blessed with ageless youth. Nehsi reflected unkindly that she owed much of it to the artistry of her maids, and the rest to a certain emptiness of mind that kept her face smooth, unmarred by lines of care and character.

Nonetheless she was marvelous to look at, as beautiful as any woman in Egypt, wigged and painted and adorned in her solitude as if she had been still the cherished concubine of a king. He remembered her perfume from long ago, the oil of roses that spoke of innocence and of childlike simplicity. Nothing could be less like the unguents that the king favored, complex as they were, and rich with myrrh.

Nehsi had his doubts of her intelligence, but of her shrewdness he was perfectly certain. She had lived as quietly as a woman might who knows better than to provoke a king. She might, and on this Nehsi gambled, have persuaded her son to wait as she waited, until the King Maatkare had begun to fail of her power.

It was difficult to believe that, looking into her sweet and baffled face. She had always been afraid of Nehsi, as a child is, because he was so large and so visibly strong. That fear had not altered with the years' passing. It made her shrink a little as he bowed to her, hand to cheek as if she feared that he would strike.

He would not allow her to sway him so, to soften him into dealing gently with her. Having done proper obeisance of a prince to a king's mother who had not been a queen, he remained standing over her. She lacked the will to bid him sit, although it would have removed his looming shadow.

He would not take it away unless she commanded him. He looked down at her, at her flower-sweet terror, and indulged himself in a moment of pure contempt. It was worthy of Hatshepsut, that contempt. It hardened him for what he must do.

"My king is dying," he said.

She blinked up at him, seeming witless; but he knew better. "I heard that," she said in her sweet voice. "I am sorry for it."

"Are you? Or are you sorry for how it came about?"

"She is grown old, they say," Isis said. "She was queen for so long, since she was a child; and then she made herself king. She has grown weary. The life trickles out of her."

"She is no longer young," said Nehsi, "but she should have lived for yet a while. As she will not. Because your son made sure of it."

"My son?" She was all innocence, all wide eyes and astonishment. "Does she blame him because she had to be king? Nothing ever compelled her to wear the crowns. She could have given it all up when he came of age, and left him to bear the burden."

"That is not what I am saying," Nehsi said, lowering his voice to a growl. "Don't play the child with me; and don't pretend to innocence. Your son decided at last that he had had enough of being younger king to an elder king whom he both fears and hates."

"What, poison a king? How could he do such a thing?"

"Easily," said Nehsi, "if he told himself that the king was a usurper, and that the gods had turned their faces from her."

"My son is innocent of any wrongdoing," Isis said.

Nehsi fixed her with his hardest stare. "Yes? Then was it you who did it? Poison is a woman's weapon. From a man and a warrior I would expect a knife in the dark, or an arrow in the back."

"I have done nothing," Isis said.

"I don't believe you," said Nehsi. "I think you found someone to procure the poison, and someone else to administer it. Did she drink it in her wine? Eat it at the feast? Was it given more than once? Tell me."

"I have done nothing," she repeated. He watched her consider tears, but discard them. That was well. Weeping would have made him angry. Then he might have done something even less wise than this that he was doing.

"Listen," he said, "and listen well. You may deny what you have done until the gods themselves cast you down. But I know. I remember. I will never forget."

"I could have you killed," she said.

He showed her his teeth. "Oh, do that! I'll haunt you from beyond the dead. My spirit will flutter about you, bird-winged in the day, man-tall in the night. Everywhere you look, you will see me. Every word you speak, you will hear the echo of my voice. I will stand forever as close as your shadow, supping your breath, eating away your name. And when you die, I will be waiting for you."

She had gone pale. "You can't do that!"

"I can," he said, "and I will. Unless you do a thing for me."

Even in her terror, she was a canny creature. Her eyes narrowed. Her mouth went small and tight. She was not so beautiful now, or so sweetly childlike. "What are you asking of me?"

"In truth," he answered, "little. Only keep a rein on your son. I know what he means to do once my king is dead. He will destroy her if he can: efface her name, pull down her monuments. Promise me that you will prevent him."

Her eyes went wide again, but the innocence was gone from them. "But, sir, how am I to do that?"

"As you always have," Nehsi said. "By coaxing, wheedling, even threatening. He will not touch the name or the memory of my king."

"If he is truly determined, no force of man or gods will prevent him."

"No force but yours," said Nehsi. "You taught him to hate her. Now teach him to stand well away from her memory. Or I haunt you. I walk in your every dream. I take you with me on the paths of ordeal, and when my heart is weighed on the scales of Justice, yours too shall be set there, and shall inevitably fail. How will it be for you, my lady, to have been judged among the dead while yet you live, and found wanting?"

He paused. She had drawn together, shivering as if with cold. Her pallor would have alarmed him if he had allowed himself to care. "I will hold you to this," he said. "Your son will not kill my king's name and memory as he has killed her body. You will make sure of it."

She looked up at him. For all her terror, her eyes were narrow, sly. "But I shall die before him. Then he will do as he pleases."

"You would do well to see that he pleases to let my king's memory be."

"I won't promise you that," she said.

He hissed, which made her start. "You will try."

"You should go to him," said Isis, "and not torment me. I'm only his mother. He is the one who will do whatever he will do."

"I am only half a fool," Nehsi said. "He who would not hesitate to slay a king would hardly pause at a king's minister."

"He is afraid of you," she said.

"Oh, I'm sure. But he is a man. He will cast down his fear and set his foot on it, and brandish his sword in its face."

"You aren't going to go away until I promise. Are you?" Her voice was faint and small.

"I am not," Nehsi said.

"Then I promise." She lowered her head till he could see only the crown of her wig. "I will do what I can. I will not even have you killed. It will hurt you a great deal to be nobody after having been a great prince for so long—and to be without her. That will be anguish, won't it? It's little enough to keep my son from killing her memory, for a while. In the end he'll win. You won't haunt me on the other side of death; the gods won't let you."

"But on this side of it," Nehsi said, "I can make your life a perpetual misery."

"I don't want that," said Isis. "Go away now. You have what you wanted."

"I shall make very sure of that," Nehsi said.

■ It was all bluster and empty threats, but it was all he had. He left her sitting there, terrified and crafty at once, and all her beauty vanished, wiped away by the words that they had spoken together.

There was one more thing that he must do before he returned to his king. His son Seti had taken a few hours' rest in the barracks. Nehsi found him in his bed with a plump maid beside him; hauled him up, great hulking young man that he was, and flung him headlong on the floor. He sprawled there, gasping with shock.

Nehsi set a foot on his neck. "You failed me," he said, his voice so low it was no more than a rumble in his chest. "You've let her die."

"She is not dead yet," Seti said from the floor, with a fair degree of snap in his voice for a man who lay prostrate under another man's foot. "All the physicians are saying that it's women's trouble. Was I to tell the gods to keep that from her till you came home?"

Nehsi kicked him onto his back. He glared up at his father, little cowed, though he knew better than to resist. Nehsi could not suppress a small crowing of pride in this son that he had sired. "The physicians are in the younger king's pay," Nehsi said almost calmly. "As you should have known. She's been poisoned. It's so obvious, I wonder at you. Are you securing yourself with Thutmose, too? Has it occurred to you that your father is old and will die soon enough, but you have to live with this king for years thereafter?"

"I had hoped," Seti said through clenched teeth, "that you would think better of me than that."

"I might," said Nehsi, "if she had not fallen ill under your guardianship."

"It happened in a moment," Seti said. "She had entertained a few lords and their ladies in her private dining chamber—something to do with a change in the taxes of the Tenth Nome, and the wedding of one of the nomarchs' daughters. The wine was a new vintage, and strong. Most drank it as it was. She had hers watered—heavily, I noticed. The waterjar was the same that is always there. We gave a bowl of it to one of the barracks dogs later, after she fell ill. It's still romping about, chewing shieldstraps to shreds. We never found any evidence of poison."

"Then someone came in and changed the water while you were fretting over her illness. That's the simplest thing in the world to do."

"I know that," Seti said. "But we found nothing, therefore we can prove nothing."

"The water should have been tasted before it was given her," Nehsi said, "as every other drop she drank and morsel she ate was tasted. But no one thought of the water, did he? So simple a thing. So easy to detect if she had drunk it plain, but she drowned it in wine, and with it the taste of the poison."

"Are you going to put a few servants to death? You can start with the steward of her dining chamber. He was near the waterjar rather often."

"I well may do that," Nehsi said with a growl in his throat. "Now tell me what should prevent me from beginning with you."

"Nothing," said Seti.

Nehsi lifted his foot abruptly and pulled Seti to his feet. He struck his son in the face, a hard, backhanded blow. Seti withstood it without expression. "That is for your failure. This," he said, pulling the young man into a tight embrace, "is for your courage in telling me the truth."

Seti stood back when his father would let him, hands on Nehsi's shoulders, not smiling, not quite, but his eyes were warm. And relieved, Nehsi noticed. That was well. A son should walk in proper fear of his father.

"Father," Seti said. "Do you want me to go hunting a king?"

"I would dearly love," said Nehsi, "to bury that young man deep and set a mountain on his grave. But my king will not kill a king. No more will I. He lives; there's no help for it. I've done what I can to make certain that he takes no more vengeance on her than he has already."

Seti bowed his head. "I still have to live under him," he said. "Have you given any thought to how all of us will do that?"

"As we can," said Nehsi. "If we live in quiet for a while, show ourselves no threat, in the end I think he'll have the sense to use us as we may best be used. If not—if he has in mind to destroy all who were loyal to her—then we'll do what we can do. I have kin in Nubia, and your mother has kin in Punt. We've no lack of places to go, if Egypt closes itself to us."

"I don't want to leave Egypt," Seti said.

"Nor I," said Nehsi through tightening throat. "Pray the gods we never have need of it."

"But you," Seti said, "may not want to live in Egypt without her."

"Oh, no," said Nehsi. "This land is full of the memory of her. I'll guard it while I live; and after I am dead, if I must, I'll continue."

"But she may not die," Seti said. "The gods may preserve her." Nehsi said nothing to that; and Seti looked away, ashamed as well he should have been, of his fit of happy folly.

56

SLOWLY AT FIRST, THEN WITH TERRIBLE swiftness, the sun rose to its zenith over Thebes of the kings, and sank toward the western cliffs. Its light spread long over them, red as blood. The sky filled with fire.

Beyond that fire, on the other side of the horizon, lay the land of the dead: the land to which the king was going, and swiftly now, without either fear or regret.

Nehsi returned to her then as she had commanded. Her pack of jackals lingered, but Nehsi had taken thought for that. Eager though they might be to be present at the moment of her death, their bodies knew both hunger and thirst. He saw to it that a banquet was spread for them in one of the greater halls. They fell upon it with greedy delight. He left them so, and sought his lady's chamber.

Only a few of the physicians lingered, and a handful of priests, and her maids still huddled in a corner, too stark with grief and fear to join the others in the feast. They were as nothing and no one.

Hatshepsut was awake. She fought off sleep, he suspected, lest she miss any moment of the life that was left to her. When he knelt beside her, she took his hand in her two thin cold ones. "You look so grim," she said. "Don't grieve for me. I go to be Osiris."

"I grieve that you leave untimely," he said.

"It is not untimely," she said, "when the gods allow it to be."

He stared at her. "Where did you learn such resignation? The lady I know would have been raging against her murderer, seeing to it that he was punished."

"He has been punished," she said serenely. "He stood aside while I ruled for years as king. Usurper he may think me, terrible creature, a female who dared to wear the crowns and bear the titles that only a male should claim; but not even he can deny that I ruled well. I brought peace to Egypt, and prosperity beyond any that it has known before. No one can say that these two kingdoms fared ill because their king was a woman."

"Ah, lady," said Nehsi. "You were always wiser than I."

"Of course," she said. "I am your king."

He wept then, without warning, unable to slow or stop it. She held him till he was done. It should have felt like presumption, and yet it did not.

When he lifted his head, she smiled at him. "Better?" she asked, sounding for all the world like Bastet when one of the children had taken a tumble.

"Better," he said roughly. His throat was sore. "Oh, gods. Everything is so dark, with your light gone out of it."

Her smile warmed and deepened. "I'll be with you as I can. Listen for my wings. Look for my eyes in the dimness. Bless my name then, and remember me."

"Do you think that I could ever forget?"

She shrugged, the barest lifting of a shoulder. "The living go on living. The dead fade and are forgotten."

"Never," he said fiercely. "Never!"

"I do hope not," she said. Her voice was hardly more than a whisper, a murmur in shadow. "I meant to be remembered forever and ever. All that I did, I did for that. And for Egypt. Always for Egypt. Remember my name. Remember me."

He named her as he must always do, so that he might strengthen her memory. "Maatkare," he said. "Hatshepsut."

She smiled. "Remember," she said again. "Remember me."

He saw the life slip out of her: the dimming of light in her eyes, the passing of breath, even—or so he imagined—the shape of the *ka* that was the shadowy image of her. It paused in its going, and met his stare with eyes that shone lambent in the gloom. He bowed low and low. "Fare you well and forever," he said, "my lady and king."

Epilogue

〰〰〰〰

(*Thutmose III, 42*)

~~~~~~~~~

ENKHEPERRE THUTMOSE STOOD in the great pillared court of Djeser-Djeseru. Men labored feverishly about him, yet he stood quiet, smiling a faint, almost languid smile. He smiled so when one of his ladies had pleased him well, or when he saw the heads and hands and private members of his enemies heaped at his feet; for he was a great warrior, the greatest that the Two Lands had ever seen.

They called him Thutmose the Great, the mighty one, the scourge of Asia. He was not as young as he had been, but he was strong. He intended to live for many years yet, and to spend much of that life on the battlefield where he was most vividly alive. The rest of it he would spend ruling in Egypt, being the king that for a score of years he had been forbidden to be.

Her face was all about him, her name carved on every wall and pillar and statue. In this place of all places in Egypt, there was no escaping the name or the memory of that one whom he had both hated and—yes—guiltily, tremblingly adored, Maatkare Hatshepsut.

His mother had held him back for long years. But Isis was dead. They were all dead, all those loyal ministers, Thuty the Treasurer, Ineni the builder, Nehsi the Nubian whose presence had loomed huge and shadow-dark; for whom even in death Thutmose knew a shiver of apprehension.

He thrust it down and set his foot on it. Nehsi was dead. So too was Isis, that shy and gentle creature with her surprising core of stubbornness. Only the day before he had laid her lovingly in her tomb, opened her senses to the life beyond living, and sealed her against the depredations of thieves. Now he made certain that her soul would be as safe beyond the horizon as her body was in the valley of the dead.

His smile widened as the workman nearest him, wielding hammer and chisel, put out the eyes of a sphinx that wore Hatshepsut's face. Her name was gone already from its plinth. Men beyond toppled statues with a splendid roaring and crashing. Others advanced through the temple like an army across a field of battle, cutting out her name and the name of her cursed arrogant fool of a lover wherever they might find it.

A runner halted panting in front of him and flung himself down. "Great king! Foreman bids you, if it pleases you, come with me."

Thutmose wasted no words on him, but followed where he led. Through the temple first, but out of it thereafter, up toward the loom of the cliff. As they went they passed throngs of laborers, ringing of hammers, shattering of stone.

It was scarcely less quiet under the sky, but as they went on, the clamor muted. When it was almost gone, Thutmose heard it raised anew, just ahead of him. They clambered up a last steep slope and came to a halt.

There stood the foreman of a division of his workmen, trembling with either fear or eagerness. There was no mistaking what he pointed to: the shaft of a tomb.

Men had hacked open the door already, but waited for Thutmose before they ventured within. They had the look that men of the daylight always had when they came face to face with the dead: white, shocked, afraid. Thutmose shook his head at their frailty. "Open it," he said.

They flung themselves flat in obeisance, then did as he bade.

It was a splendid tomb, as one might expect; laden with golden treasure that Thutmose could well and properly use. Great queens had been buried in less opulence than this commoner who had shared the bed of a king. He who should at most have been buried among princes on the other side of the cliff, had presumed so far as to set himself within sight of Djeser-Djeseru. From the angle and length of the shaft, his body might well rest beneath it. Thutmose could feel the bulk of the temple overhead; fancied that he heard a distant and muffled crash as yet another statue fell in shards.

He turned his mind from that, and even from the gold that gleamed in the light of the foreman's torch. A sarcophagus stood in the center of the tomb-chamber, sealed as was proper, overlaid with words of guard and protection.

Thutmose, living Horus, king and god, had no care for the feeble magic of the dead. At his command, his men set lever to the massive lid, and thrust it up and away. The wooden coffin lay bared within.

One enterprising fellow with an axe hacked away at it. Splinters flew, rich with gilding. Then at last the wrapped body lay before them, sheathed and heaped in amulets, with a crown of withered flowers laid upon its breast.

A kind of madness flared up in Thutmose. He took up the dead thing in his own arms, lifted it high, and flung it down.

It broke like a bundle of reeds. He caught his breath; someone cried out, curse or mere astonishment, he never knew.

It had weighed as light as dried reeds, and shattered as reeds shatter. For reeds it was, bound and shaped into the image of a man. No dry dead bones crumbled inside of it. In the jars of the vitals were mockeries: dates preserved in honey, a handful of stones, the mummified body of a cat, a bag of barley flour.

Thutmose stared at them. The rage that had possessed him heretofore had been cold, clear, and very practical. He would preserve his mother's safety among the dead by destroying her enemy; and he would destroy that memory among the living, so that he and he alone would be remembered as king and god. It had been, and would still be, a beautiful revenge.

That had been cold anger, cherished for forty years, until at last he could let it loose. This was a white heat. Senenmut the arrogant, Senenmut the accursed, had dared even beyond death to mock a king.

And yet Thutmose laughed. "Oh, you reckoned yourself clever," he said to the face that was painted on the wall beyond the sarcophagus: deep-lined hook-nosed unlovely face with its long wry mouth. "But I have won the war. I have slain her among the living and among the dead. She shall be utterly forgotten. None hereafter shall remember her."

The painted face went on smiling, mocking him, even as a workman scoured it from the wall. *You may try,* it said. *You may even think you succeed. But you will never find my body where it is buried; and you will never destroy her utterly. I have seen to that: I, Senenmut, who was born a tradesman's son in Thebes.*

"Air," Thutmose said, "and empty wind. You are dead. So too is she. Dead for everlasting."

Even through the clamor of workmen, the hacking, the chipping, the shattering of stone, he heard a flutter as of wings, a flicker of laughter. *So you dream,* it said, *O king of vaunts and battles. So you well may dream.* And all about that dry dead voice, the murmur of her name, the name that Thutmose would have caused to vanish from the earth. *Maatkare,* it whispered. *Hatshepsut.*

~~~~~~
Author's Note

MAATKARE HATSHEPSUT WAS NOT THE FIRST or the only female king of Egypt, but she is the most famous, and certainly the most notorious. Her story, its events and characters, needs little embellishment in order to "work" in modern narrative terms. I have had to invent almost nothing, nor was it necessary to enliven the story with invented protagonists. Senenmut and his family, Nehsi the Nubian, Hapuseneb the priest, the two Thutmoses, Isis the concubine, all are historical figures. Even Senenmut's little red mare was a real horse; her mummy was found in the "public" tomb of her master, along with the mummies of his parents and his brothers and his brother's wife. Of all the characters in this novel, only Nehsi's wife and children, and the occasional spear-carrier, are fictitious.

I did choose to invent the third tomb of Senenmut, in addition to the two that are known, and the deception of his "official" burial. Likewise there is no evidence that the concubine Isis, mother of Thutmose III, was ever a servant of Hatshepsut or had anything to do with the then-queen; and the princess Neferure is in no way known to have died in childbirth. Nor is it known for certain that Thutmose had anything to do with the death of Hatshepsut, although this has been proposed by more than one scholar.

No one knows, either, why it took Thutmose twenty years after Hatshepsut's death to wreak his terrible vengeance on her memory. He was a master of biding his time, but that seems rather excessive. Two decades seem time enough for certain powerful and perhaps intimidating friends of the female king to have grown old and died; perhaps Thutmose did swear an oath or make a promise, which he could not break until after the death of the one to whom it was sworn. Whatever the reason, it is one of the great oddities of history that a man of such genius, perhaps the greatest of all the warrior Pharaohs of Egypt, lived the first twenty-odd years of his life in near-total obscurity, completely overshadowed by the power and personality of the woman who dared to be king—then, a full twenty years and more after her death, turned suddenly and viciously against her.

■ In spite of Hatshepsut's fame, few books have actually been devoted to her life and history. General histories of Egypt, of course, never fail to mention her. Accounts of the great trading voyage to Punt are frequent and detailed, as are descriptions of her mortuary temple at Deir al-Bahri: the temple which she herself called Djeser-Djeseru. There is a very good if rather opinionated summary in Barbara Mertz, *Temples, Tombs and Hieroglyphs* (New York, 1978)—readers may know this popular Egyptologist more readily under her pseudonyms of Elizabeth Peters and Barbara Michaels. Mertz is one of those who postulates that Thutmose III had a hand in Hatshepsut's demise.

As for the peculiar beauty of this great queen and Pharaoh, the dedicated museumgoer need only visit the Metropolitan Museum in New York City, a whole room of which is dedicated to the works and images of Hatshepsut. Her face once seen is difficult to forget. The resemblance to portraits of her co-king, her nephew and stepson, is striking. There can be no doubt that they were of the same family. They seem to have shared a similar personality as well, though hers turned conspicuously to the arts of peace, and his, perhaps in rebellion, to those of war. Her achievements alone would have rendered her remarkable, but even more striking is the degree of dominance she exercised for so long over her brilliant and bellicose fellow king.

A novelist, like a scholar, can only guess the reasons why. Unlike the scholar, however, the novelist is privileged to choose among the possibilities and to elect the one that seems most suited to the requirements of her narrative. In the case of Hatshepsut, that process of selection proved in the end quite simple, and needed almost no invention. The history itself is almost pure story.